FOR THE LOVE OF BEASTS

FOR THE LOVE OF BEASTS

BY: LUCILLE ANSER

To the dreamers who wander through worlds unseen

THE DUCHIES OF
PHYRRA
GALADAR
COBURY
ARONDIR
KENCE
OQIRA
ESADON
BEOR
DRAM
ACANTIA
BITON
HOLITH
FRALTA
RATHIAN
PETRA
ILLEROSS
VRIG
N
THE EPOTTUM SEA
GUILD OUTPOST
CAPITAL CITY

PRONUNCIATION GUIDE

Iowyn Morgnah (EYE-oh-win MOR-guh-nah)

Ulric Ornthalas (ULL-rick ORN-thall-us)

Loyla Cento (LOY-lah SEN-tow)

Ellis Albilot (ELL-iss AL-bih-low)

Odea (Oh-DEE-ah)

Mortem (MORE-tem)

Ikris (ICK-riss)

Temphon (TEM-fon)

Viona (VEE-oh-nah)

Ydall (EE-doll)

Phyrra / Phyrran (FEAR-ah / FEAR - an)

Galadar / Galadari (GAL-uh-dar / GAL-uh-dar-ee)

Arondir / Arondiran (uh-RON-deer / uh-RON-deer-an)

Rathian (RATH-ee-an)

Vrig / Vrigan (VR-ig / VR-ig-an)

Acantia / Acantian (uh-CAN-tee-uh / uh-CAN-tee-an)

Beor / Beorish (BAY-or / BAY-or-ish)

Oqira / Oqirese (oh-KEY-rah / oh-KIH-rese)

Holith / Holithan (HAUL-ith / HAUL-ith-an)

Deupin (DYOO-pin or DOO-pin)

Batterfly (BAT-er-fly)

Gargantula (gar-GAN-chuh-la

Cerline (SIR-line)

THE DUCHIES OF PHYRRA

RATHIAN

Capital City: Petra

Duke of Rathian: Archidamus Rebeck

Guild Master: Ewan Cento

Outposts: Northern, Eastern, Southern, Western, and Central

VRIG

Capital City: Illeross

Duke of Vrig: Aldric Corvinus

Guild Master: Violetta Imbrex

Outposts: Northern, Eastern, Southern, Western, and Central

ACANTIA

Capital City: Biton

Duke of Acantia: Renaud Metellus

Guild Master: Ketteline Rosemund

Outposts: Northern, Southern, and Central

BEOR

Capital City: Dram

Duke of Beor: Casimir Thibodeaux

Guild Master: Erich Robion

Outposts: Northern and Southern

OQIRA

Capital City: Esadon

Duke of Oqira: Zheng Hu

Guild Master: Takara Misa

Outposts: Northern and Southern

ARONDIR:

Capital City: Kence

Duke of Arondir: Dominik Dunleavy

Guild Master: Peadar Foxe

Outposts: Northern, Southern, and Central

HOLITH:

Capital City: Fralta

Duke of Holith: Mauricio Manzanedo

Guild Master: Carmelo Crezin

Outposts: Northern, Eastern, and Western

GALADAR:

Capital City: Cobury

Duke of Galadar: Philip Glendower

Guild Master: Desdemona Mairil

Outposts: Northern, Eastern, Southern, and Western

CHAPTER

1

"Stay down!" Ulric grunted, his sword being fended off by the gray werewolf in front of him.

Iowyn – hunkered down behind a fallen tree and out of sight – rolled her eyes. "No shit?"

She had zero field experience. Not to mention that she was a monstralogist, not a hunter. Of course, she would stay behind the tree where it was safer. The fact that Ulric thought her so idiotic stung a little.

A swift kick to the wolf's abdomen sent it hurtling backwards, giving Ulric enough time to grab for the crossbow at his back, loaded with a single silver-tipped bolt. The werewolf regained its footing and lunged at Ulric, swiping at him with an open paw.

Iowyn winced, hoping that she wasn't witnessing Ulric's death, but the large paw swiped just short of Ulric's body, and instead only hit his arm, knocking the crossbow out of his hands. With a thud, the crossbow landed just a few feet shy of where Iowyn crouched.

Ulric's green eyes locked with Iowyn's from across the clearing.

"Don't!" he yelled, as if he knew exactly what was coursing through her mind. The werewolf crouched to lunge at him again from behind.

Iowyn's eyes widened as she pointed to the werewolf. "Watch out!"

Ulric spun back around, just in time to brace himself for impact as the wolf took him to the ground. He braced his arms against the

1

body of the creature. The werewolf gnashed its teeth only inches away from Ulric's face.

Iowyn held her breath as Ulric held back the werewolf's jaws and claws from anything vital. A frenzied swipe left a scarlet gash on his tanned cheek. How this man had lasted years alone as a solitary in the Guild was beyond Iowyn, because right now he looked like he was in the deepest shit possible with this werewolf. And this was the man that was supposed to keep her safe?

Ulric struggled in vain to get the werewolf off of him. Each time the wolf's teeth gnashed closer to his face, Iowyn felt her stomach drop. Sure, she'd only known this guy for about a week, and he'd been nothing but an asshole to her, but that didn't mean she wanted to watch him get killed.

Iowyn glanced towards the crossbow, only a few feet away from her position, and made her decision. "Fuck this," she muttered, launching over the fallen tree trunk and running for the weapon on the ground.

Unlucky for her, the movement was enough to catch the werewolf's attention. It pushed off Ulric's chest, inciting a deep grunt from the hunter, and started stalking towards Iowyn. She reached the crossbow, and picked it up, noting that it was much heavier than Ulric had ever made it look. As she turned towards Ulric, the werewolf stood only a few feet away from her, and she knew that there simply wasn't enough time to bring the crossbow up to her shoulder and fire the bolt.

Shit.

The werewolf lunged, and Iowyn instinctively shut her eyes, bracing for the pain of whatever horrible death the werewolf would give her. Her best bet was on evisceration. Maybe being eaten alive. But it never came.

The werewolf let out a yowl, and Iowyn opened her eyes to see Ulric on its back. Black blood oozed from where his knife was plunged into the space between its neck and clavicle. "Shoot it!" he yelled.

The werewolf began reaching backwards to try and grab Ulric or knock him off its back. Iowyn raised the crossbow to her shoulder, but with the wolf writhing and shaking, she hesitated on pulling the trigger. What if she hit Ulric instead? Sure, she wasn't crazy about the guy, but one silver bolt was all they had. She wouldn't stand a chance alone if she missed.

"For fuck's sake! Shoot it!" Ulric yelled again, much more of a stern plea than an order.

"Shit!" Iowyn swore to herself, shutting her eyes and pulling the trigger. The butt of the crossbow slammed back into her shoulder, the force hard enough to leave a bruise, and the release of the string flung the bolt forward. The werewolf wailed, then Iowyn heard a large thud hit the ground in front of her.

Iowyn opened her eyes one at a time. The werewolf laid crumpled on the ground, still as death. Ulric stood behind it, bloodied knife in hand. He looked at Iowyn and then to the crossbow in her hands.

"Did you..." he began to ask, and she could see the wheels in his head spinning as he took her in. "Did you fire that with your eyes closed?" Ulric gritted his teeth.

Heat rose in Iowyn's pale cheeks, and she gave him the grimacing smile of someone who had been caught red-handed and gulped. "Maybe?"

Ulric stepped over the wolf's body and yanked his crossbow from her hands. He slung it over his back and moved past her to continue walking through the trees.

Great, now he was even more ticked off.

Although, part of Iowyn felt more slighted by the fact that she didn't even get a thank you. But then she noticed that he was leaving her behind. Alone. In the dark woods, where gods only knew what was lurking in the shadows.

"Hey!" she shouted after him. "You can't leave me here!" Iowyn raced to catch up to Ulric. Damn those long legs of his. She had to walk twice as fast to keep up with him at all times.

Ulric gave an agitated sigh. "Don't remind me."

Iowyn scoffed, batting away low tree branches before they could hit her in the face or snag at her clothes or raven hair. "I just killed that thing. You could at least say thank you or give me some credit, you know."

Ulric turned on her so fast that she had to keep herself from slamming into him with her forward momentum. "Credit? You want credit?" He huffed a laugh at the idea. "My report to the Guild is going to outline every single time you undermined my command on this assignment."

Iowyn had to keep herself from scoffing as heat rose to her cheeks again, but not from embarrassment. After an entire week of dealing with this jackass, she was over it. She reset her features before lowering her voice. "And my report is going to reflect all the times you needed me to help your sorry ass!"

She wasn't backing down to him. Not this time. Not after all the shit she'd gone through to get to this point. She was finally out in the field – finally living her dream. There had been countless times she had proved him wrong during this assignment. She didn't care if she had no experience as a hunter. He'd been nothing but an asshole since the moment they met.

Ulric raked a hand through his chocolate brown curls. "You're a gods-damned pain in my ass, you know that?" He took a step closer. His emerald eyes were piercing her very soul. Iowyn had no doubt in her mind that he wanted her to shrink away, to flinch, but she wasn't going to give him the satisfaction.

She stood up taller and gave him a fake smile. "If you have a problem with me, I suggest you write the problem on a piece of paper, fold it up, and shove it up your ass, Ornthalas. You're stuck with me until the Guild deems you worthy of being let off probation."

Iowyn had known since she was assigned to Ulric Ornthalas a week prior that he was on probation with the Guild, but for what exactly, she still had no idea. Hunters could be put on probation for a variety of reasons, none of them good. It was usually the punishment for first offenders, when the charges brought against them couldn't be ultimately proven. Most hunters found guilty of any of their crimes were just sent off to Smokheim, the island far across the Epottum Sea, where creatures worse than the ones in Phyrra dwelled, and no hunter had ever returned.

She guessed that Ulric getting a partner after being a solitary in the Guild for so long was part of his punishment. After an entire career of working solo, getting put with a monstralogist with zero field experience to boot was just for good measure. Most partnerships between two members of the Guild were duos, a pairing of two hunters. Very few hunters chose to be a part of a dyad – the partnership between a hunter and a monstralogist.

Ulric's jaw clenched at the mention of his probation, and Iowyn internally braced herself for whatever he decided to do next. Was he angry enough to hit her? Nothing so far would indicate to her that he was that kind of man, but Iowyn knew all too well that men were unpredictable when angry, and she had done nothing but her best to vex Ulric at every opportunity.

She hadn't brought up his probation. Hadn't even mentioned it since meeting. Part of her thought he would address it himself, but she found out rather quickly that that wouldn't be the case. She had a right to know, after all. What had her new partner – the person who was meant to protect her – do that could have been so bad as to warrant probation?

Ulric stared at her, his eyes flicking between hers. He let out a long breath through his nose, and turned back around, continuing on his path through the forest.

Iowyn blinked, dumbfounded.

Nothing? After a week full of snide comments and jabs, he had nothing more to say?

She followed after him, albeit at a distance. The full moon illuminated the ground through the trees, letting her see more of her surroundings in the dense forest through the dappled moonlight. A batterfly fluttered across their path, its iridescent wings shimmering in shades of white and grey, casting an enchanting glow as it danced among the flowers. The small flying rodent was completely unbothered, oblivious to the death of a much larger creature that had just transpired. As quickly as it had come into view, the small creature was gone, most likely on its way to drink its fill of nectar from the new blooms of spring.

Iowyn brought her attention back to Ulric. Mud was smeared across the back of his brown quilted vest, and his tan skin peaked through a few tears in the long sleeves of his dark green shirt. He would either need to buy a new one, or mend the tears himself, if he even knew how.

Ulric slowed his steps, enough to allow her to catch up to him. He kept his eyes forward and hand on the hilt of his sword. He scanned the forest around them, as if another werewolf might jump out and attack.

"You never answered my question before," he said finally to break the silence.

Iowyn looked at him.

Odd subject change. Even odder was the implication that he had actually wanted to hear her answer. She had been talkative for

most of the assignment to fill the awkward silences made from
Ulric's lack of conversational skills. She told him about herself, but
she had figured from his blank and distant expression whenever
she spoke that he had found some way to tune her out.

"Actually, I've answered every question that you've asked me.
Unlike you," she countered.

Since meeting nearly a week ago, she had tried to get to know
the man that was to be her partner, and asked him all the usual
questions in order to do so. Where was he from? Did he go to
University? Did he have a family? All met with silence. She had
figured that it was because he was unsure of her, so whenever he
asked her a question, she made sure to answer it. She might have
even answered his questions a little too thoroughly, but she wanted
more than anything to stay in the field, and being Ulric's partner
assured that.

Still, he had yet to answer any questions about his own personal
life.

"You must mean the question you asked me right before the
werewolf came out of nowhere and nearly killed you?"

The corner of Ulric's mouth lifted into a slight smirk for a
fraction of a second. It was the first time that Iowyn had seen him
do anything other than frown. So far, he had been nothing but
scowls or looks of complete indifference. But as soon as it had
appeared, Ulric reset his features and wiped it from existence. "I'm
not used to having to babysit while fighting something like that,"
Ulric supplied.

Iowyn rolled her eyes. She didn't need to be babysat. She was a
full-grown woman. Iowyn thought about shooting back some quip
at him, but instead she racked her brain.

What had he asked her? She remembered that it had been a
rather personal question, as if he had wanted to get to know her
better. Which had caught Iowyn off guard considering how closed

off he had been for the majority of this assignment together. "Remind me what you asked again?"

He turned his head towards her. "What? That big brain of yours can't remember?"

Iowyn scowled at him then looked away. "Fine then, I guess you don't get your answer." From her peripheral, she could see Ulric roll his eyes.

"How can you stand to be a part of the Guild?"

Her brow furrowed. "And why exactly do you want to know that?"

Ulric shrugged. "We're partners until further notice. I need to know you better to be able to trust you."

"And I don't need to trust you?" she replied.

He looked down at her, confusion palpable on his face. "What do you mean?"

Iowyn gritted her teeth. "*What do I mean?* Are you serious? Trust works both ways, Ornthalas."

Ulric stared at her. He was either waiting for her to go on, or didn't understand what she was saying.

Iowyn let out a breath in exasperation. "I have done nothing but try to get to know you this entire week. But have you even let me know a single thing about you?"

Ulric stayed silent.

"The answer to that, is no. You haven't."

"The questions you ask are unimportant."

Iowyn rolled her eyes and groaned in frustration. "You are un-fucking-believable." She stopped in her tracks, her hands balled into fists at her sides.

Ulric took a few steps before realizing that Iowyn was no longer walking beside him and turned around. "We don't have time for this."

"Odea, spare me. *We*," she gestured to the space between them, "are nothing."

"*We* are partners," he countered.

"Then start acting like it!" she screamed back.

Ulric stared her down, as if he thought that it would scare her into action. When she didn't move, he repeated, "We don't have time for this."

Iowyn let out a flustered scream and stormed past Ulric, smacking her shoulder into his side as she did. This man was unbelievable. Expecting her to continue to answer his questions while never answering any of hers, then talking about trust? How could he expect her to give and give and not ever get anything in return?

She broke through the trees into the meadow where they had stashed their mounts before going on foot to track the werewolf. Before Iowyn could take another step, something grabbed her forearm, and she was whipped around to face Ulric.

His eyes bore into hers, and Iowyn's heart leapt in her chest. Ulric's eyes were unsettling to her at times. Their emerald color looked almost otherworldly, and there were times she swore they grew deeper in color. With the addition of the bleeding gash on his cheek, he looked more wolfish than normal.

"You should really do something about your cheek," she commented.

He ignored her. "Are you going to answer my question?" His voice was low, his tone almost a growl.

"Why is it so important that I do?" she challenged. A good question. Would he even answer it?

Ulric didn't falter. "I'm a hunter in the Guild. You're a monstralogist. I hunt creatures down and kill them. *Kill* the creatures that you love so much."

Iowyn pulled her arm from his grasp. "That's different."

"How?"

"You're a hunter, not a poacher. You don't hunt creatures for sport or for fun. You hunt them for the Guild. Because they're endangering people."

Ulric kept her gaze, and she could see in his eyes a kind of dissonance, like he heard what she was saying but couldn't quite understand.

Iowyn sighed before explaining further. "Yes, I love creatures, and that love for them is a big reason why I went to University to study and become a monstralogist in the first place. But I also know that there are certain creatures that are dangerous and end up killing people if given the chance. Killing creatures is horrible, true. But if those creatures are killing people, then I understand that the world would be a bit better if perhaps they were dealt with."

Ulric was silent, like he was mulling over what she said in his head. She continued, "It's not like the Guild gives orders to hunt down a herd of unicorns just minding their business. I'm here to help people like you keep the bad creatures from wreaking havoc on the defenseless people of Phyrra. That's the Guild's purpose. That's my job."

Ulric stared at her. His eyes searched hers, like he was trying to discern if she was telling the truth. He gave her a short nod and then made his way to his large black mare, Shadowfoot. The horse was quite possibly the only creature on this earth that Ulric was personable towards. Just like that, he was closed off again, and she was left standing there, confounded by their interaction.

Iowyn shook herself as she made her way into the middle of the meadow. To say that Ulric confused her, was an understatement. He could be completely indifferent one moment, then talk to her like a real person in another. Or be yelling and fighting with her at one moment, and then act like it never happened the next. It made no sense to her, like he always needed to revert back to feeling nothing and show zero emotion.

Iowyn lifted her thumb and forefinger to her mouth and whistled for Dren, her deupin.

She heard him first. His large splayed paws thumped rhythmically against the ground as he raced towards her. He breached the treeline, and she was met with the large brown eyes that were set in a slim bovine face. He had all the facial qualities of a deer, but the large upright ears and teeth of a canine, not entirely dissimilar to the wolf they had just killed. Black fur with a dappling of gray covered his entire body, save for a single spot the size of a large gold coin near the middle of his back of orange. His large black nose caressed her outstretched hand as he stopped inches in front of her, his ivory antlers glistening in the moonlight. She reached up to stroke the thick maned fur of his neck, and he bellowed in delight at her touch as she scratched.

"Aw, did someone miss me?" she cooed.

Dren brayed back at her.

Dren was much more of a pet than a mount. Not unlike a domesticated dog, Dren obeyed simple commands, but also followed Iowyn around like a lost puppy whenever she let him.

Ulric cleared his throat behind her. "We need to get going."

Iowyn rolled her eyes, but quickly retrieved Dren's saddle and bridle from the branch of a nearby tree and put them on him before leading him back into the forest towards the body of the werewolf.

They would need to bring the remains back to town with them to prove to the townspeople that the werewolf was indeed dead, and that the Guild had kept their promise to supply aid. Support from the public was important when it came to Guild operations. While the Guild were their own independent agency in Phyrra, they were funded through tithes and donations from the citizens of the duchies and the eight dukes. Keeping the people happy, kept the dukes happy, and allowed the Guild to work across Phyrra, providing the service of exterminating the more malevolent creatures.

After stopping in town, they would take the corpse to the nearest Guild outpost, so the scrivens could conduct their research and add to the immense store of knowledge of the Guild's archives.

Iowyn dropped Dren's reins once they had returned to the cover of the trees. She didn't need to lead him like a horse. Dren would follow Iowyn anywhere she wanted.

"He's an obedient beast, I'll give you that," Ulric commented.

Iowyn shrugged. "What can I say, he loves me."

"How long have you had him?"

She paused, wondering if she should even answer. Why should she be the only one opening up? But she counted on her fingers to figure out the answer. "A little over seven years. We're pretty sure he escaped from a traveling circus or something because deupins don't live anywhere near Calluna. Or even Arondir. He was a lot smaller then, but he just showed up one day eating everything possible in my dad's vegetable garden. He's been mine ever since."

She waited for him to ask her something else, but he didn't. Perhaps this was a good chance to ask him a question herself?

"What about you? How long have you had Shadowfoot?" she asked.

Silence drifted between them, and any hope that Iowyn had that he would answer vanished. She was ready to forgo her entire endeavor of trying to get to know Ulric altogether and resigning herself to never ask him another question so long as she lived.

"Eight years," he answered. "I got her the day I left home for University."

An answer and supplemental information? Had the underworld frozen over? Maybe what she had said about her needing to trust him too had finally sunk in.

While he was being receptive, Iowyn decided to try and ask him something else. She couldn't help herself. "You went to University?"

The corner of his mouth upturned slightly, and stayed that way this time. "You sound surprised."

"Well, no offense, but if that's the case then you seem to have some gaps in your education. I mean, you didn't even know that werewolves aren't humans cursed to turn into wolves every full moon."

The myth of werewolves being humans was widespread throughout Phyrra. So much so, that it was nearly impossible to get people to believe the truth. A huge reason for bringing the remains of the wolf to the town was to explain this to the townspeople, so they could stop pointing fingers at people they believed could be the werewolf. Werewolves were simply the offspring of a direwolf and common wolf, but researchers still weren't sure why the mixture of animal and creature genes contributed to the anomalous characteristics of the werewolves, like being bipedal, and becoming frenzied under a full moon. Many hypothesized that having the mixture of magical and inert bloodlines caused some kind of imbalance in nature, resulting in the horrific offspring.

"They don't really give us that much background on creatures in the venatology department. They just teach us the most effective ways to kill them," he explained.

Venatology, or the study of the hunt, was the course of study that most hunters took before joining the Guild. Even though it wasn't required, those who graduated from University in venatology were automatically accepted into the Guild.

Iowyn cocked a brow, somewhat dubious. "And yet I had to be the one to tell you about silver for werewolves?" she teased.

Ulric grunted, but she could still see the hint of a grin and a slight redness in his tan complexion. Perhaps she was beginning to chip away at some of that hardened exterior after all.

CHAPTER

2

Ulric would only admit to himself that Iowyn wasn't completely useless like he had originally thought. While her upbeat personality and smart-assery coupled with her know-it-all attitude had been grating at first, he was beginning to not only get used to it, but now with the assignment over, he may have been starting to enjoy the levity a little.

Maybe his probation and the stress of the assignment had turned him into more of a jerk than usual. But he was stuck with Iowyn as his partner for the foreseeable future, so he needed to at least try to get used to her.

And maybe he knew that she was right when she had said that trust worked both ways. Maybe he could let her know some things about him without crossing any of the lines he wanted to stay far behind.

To say that Iowyn perplexed him was a bit of an understatement. Why anyone like her would willingly want to go out into the field was beyond him. Sure, he had willingly signed up for the Guild as well, but he was an experienced hunter, not a scholar. Whatever had possessed her — or any other monstralogist for that matter — to risk their life in order to study beasts more closely, it had to be something close to madness.

Throwing monstralogists into the field was still highly contested in the Guild itself. Of course, the Masters saw no harm in it, but they weren't the ones out in the field. Not any more at least. They at least had the decency to give hunters the choice of whether they wanted to participate in a dyad. Ulric, like many other hunters, would have certainly refused had he had any choice in the matter. But the success of the trial partnership between Blake Ophedian and Ird Smildenn had proven to be quite fruitful for the Guild. The good press from Ophedian's books hadn't hurt the first Guild approved field monstralogist's case either.

Iowyn was surprisingly quiet on the way back to the werewolf's body, and Ulric found himself studying her from the corner of his eye. She was surprisingly calm, considering the fact that she had just stared down a beast that could have easily killed her in one blow. Her white linen blouse was still immaculate, tucked into her leather pants. A small brass hilted dagger was strapped to her thick belt. He'd found it comical, for it to be her only true form of defense, but then again, most monstralogists stayed in the dank archives of a Guild outpost as scrivens.

They came back upon the body of the werewolf. It was close to seven feet tall and probably close to six hundred pounds. How they would even attempt to get it back to town or the outpost was beyond him. Ulric had barely been able to hold off the thing once it had pounced on top of him. His cheek was still throbbing as blood rushed to clot where the wolf had clawed him. He probably would have lost his eye if the beast had swiped just a few inches higher.

Ulric looked at Iowyn and the beast she rode. "You think he could take it?" he asked, gesturing to Dren.

He had been dubious of Dren when he first met Iowyn. The deupin was a creature that seemed to be an amalgamation of wolf and deer that Ulric had only ever seen from afar. It wasn't uncommon for people in the mountains to have tamed deupins at their disposal for traversing across the ranges, but it seemed a formidable kind of beast for a newly promoted field monstralogist to have. Seeing Iowyn treating one like a pet was a shock to him to say the least.

Dren was much larger than his mare and had much more musculature than even the stockiest of horses. Hopefully it wouldn't be too much trouble for him to carry the wolf across his back.

Iowyn blew out a breath, looking at her beast then to the large corpse on the ground. "I don't see why not."

Ulric circled the body, trying to figure out the best way to go about getting the damned thing up high enough to sling it over the deupin's back. But Iowyn must have already made up a plan in her head as soon as Ulric had suggested it. She led Dren around to stand in front of the body, then pulled a radish from the inside of her jacket, using it to coax the creature to lie down before giving it to him. He happily devoured the small vegetable with his sharp teeth, and she patted his head between his antlers. "Stay down," Iowyn ordered lightly. She held her hand out and backed away slowly, and then went to one side of the corpse locking her arms around one of the wolf's upper limbs.

Iowyn looked up at Ulric and blew a piece of her raven hair that had fallen from her braid out of her face. "Well?" she asked. "You gonna help me or just stand there?"

Ulric went to the other side of the dead creature, grabbing it in a similar way.

She was smart, he'd give her that. Most of the plans that had rushed through his head were more complicated and would have required rope and a tall tree to try and hoist the body up. At least, that's what he would have had to do if he were still working alone. But Iowyn had simplified that kind of plan and figured out a way without equipment in almost no time at all.

He counted to three, and they heaved the werewolf's body forward together with all their might. Ulric's side moved considerably more than hers. The creature was now diagonal across the deupin's back. He would give her credit for trying. Iowyn was tall for a woman, but she definitely had the body of a scriven and not a hunter. Apparently lifting all those heavy books and tomes in the archives didn't equate to muscle mass.

He walked over to her side. "Switch with me," he said, more of an order than a suggestion.

Iowyn ignored it. "I've got it." She strained again as she tried to lift the body.

Ulric pursed his lips. "Steady the other side. I'll get it."

Iowyn sighed and let go of the arm. Ulric took her place. He counted down once more – for her more than himself – and heaved the werewolf the rest of the way onto Dren's back.

Iowyn went back to Dren's face, taking his reins in her hand. "Okay, bud, now get up."

The beast tucked his paws underneath his body, and slowly stood up. He groaned and faltered for a brief second, adjusting to the immense weight of the body, but was soon standing upright.

Iowyn scratched under Dren's chin. "Good boy, Dren."

The beast brayed at the praise.

She turned around, giving a sigh of content. "Let's get going then."

Ulric grabbed Shadowfoot's reins and began leading the way out of the forest and into town. "That was some quick thinking," he commented. It was the closest thing to praise that he'd said to her all week.

Iowyn raised her brows in surprise. "Answering questions and now giving compliments?" She put her hand over her heart. "I'm touched."

Ulric shook his head. "Forget it." He should have known better. This girl did almost nothing but give sarcastic remarks to everything.

"No, no. You just complimented me. That's a huge step for you." Iowyn lightly punched his shoulder.

He rolled his eyes. "Whatever, Beastie."

She laughed. "Beastie? Is that what you think of me?"

Ulric winced, he hadn't meant to say it out loud, at least not loud enough for her to hear. He had been calling her Beastie internally since first meeting her. They had clashed immediately with him calling her a worm, which was the term that most hunters liked to use for scrivens and monstralogists. They were just like the little worms that chewed through stacks of books, eating up knowledge ad nauseam, and quite useless when it came to *literally* anything else – at least anything practical and needed to survive out in the field. Most were just content to stay holed up underground in the Guild's archives conducting their research on the carcasses of creatures that hunters brought in.

Iowyn had made it very clear that she was no worm. At the mere mention of the term, she had thrown her drink – hot tea, mind you – in Ulric's face and put her brass dagger to his throat. It was quite possibly the least worm-like thing she could have done, and although he was impressed, the action had hurt his ego a bit more than he would like to acknowledge and proved to him that she was much more beast than worm.

"It's my only explanation for your affinity with creatures," he lied. "You must be one of them to make them like you so much."

She pursed her lips in a thin line as she thought it over. "I'm sure you meant that as a dig, but I'll just be the bigger person and take it as flattery, Ornthalas."

The sleepy town of Leeside awaited them on the edge of the forest. Street lamps were lit, their globes flickering with soft yellow light. There were less than five hundred people who lived in the small town. All the roads were red dirt that had been tread over and compacted over the years by travelers and its own citizens. When they finally stepped foot in the center square, Ulric and Iowyn were swarmed by townspeople almost immediately. They all wanted to get a look at the creature that had been killing their livestock and threatening the lives of their loved ones.

The questions came in a frenzy all at once:

Who was it?

Look around, who's missing?

If it's dead, then why's it still a wolf?

Are they sure they killed the right thing?

Ulric held up his hands and asked for the crowd to quiet down as they came closer, but the request fell on deaf ears. They were just as frenzied as ever, yelling and asking for answers.

Ulric turned to where Iowyn *should* have been for some help, but she wasn't by his side like she had been just a few seconds before. Ulric scanned the crowd. "Fuck," he muttered under his breath.

Where did she go? She had *just* been here.

Ulric continued to look in the crowd, but her pale face and raven hair eluded him. Where the fuck would she go?

An ear-splitting whistle from the opposite side of the crowd garnered everyone's attention, and Ulric's eyes widened as he saw Iowyn. She stood atop a well, elevating herself above the crowd.

"Fuck," he groaned. This was either going to be completely fine or go horribly wrong. It was the only two options when it came to her.

Since meeting Iowyn, Ulric realized that she had a knack for two things: finding trouble, and somehow miraculously getting out of it. It was as if Ydall, the goddess of luck and fortune, had both blessed and cursed the poor girl simultaneously at birth.

All heads in the crowd had now swiveled in her direction. Iowyn made eye contact with Ulric only briefly before she started, and he hoped for Odea's sake that his glare was enough to make her rethink doing anything completely idiotic.

"Listen up all of you! For the last *fucking* time, werewolves are not cursed humans! If I have to say that one more time to get it through your thick skulls, I'm really gonna lose it! *That*," she paused, pointing at the creature on Dren's back, "is a werewolf. Which we know through *extensive* research is the failed offspring between a regular wolf, and a direwolf. Anybody got a fucking problem with that?"

Ulric pinched the brow of his nose as hushed whispers flowed through the crowd and dissolved into silence. Cursing out an entire town was not usually the best way to deal with this kind of situation. But did Iowyn care? No.

Iowyn smiled and let out a huff of air. She looked proud of herself. "Good. Now that you know that your wolf problem is taken care of, we hope that you continue to support the Guild and our efforts."

She gave a smile and a short bow before climbing down from her perch on top of the well and walking around the crowd and back to Dren's side.

Ulric surveyed the crowd. Everyone seemed too stunned from Iowyn's outburst to speak, like they couldn't believe that she just cursed them all out. Even Ulric couldn't believe that she'd been so brash to do it himself.

"We'll be leaving now," he announced while also doing his best to size up anyone who might become a problem for them. The crowd parted as they walked through. Ulric's eyes never stopped sweeping their surroundings until they were on their way out of Leeside.

"I don't think any of them expected you to speak to them like that," Ulric said.

Iowyn sighed, like she was annoyed. "What can I say? I was sick of them not listening to us." She crossed her arms. "I mean, how many fights did you have to break up between all of them this week? How many times did I explain to them that the werewolf wasn't somebody in town? It isn't my fault they were so up their own asses that they didn't want to listen."

Ulric shook his head. "You can't curse up a storm to a crowd because you're fed up. In a different duchy – a different town, even – you could be drawn and quartered for that."

It was true, and she knew it. He knew that she knew it. She was too smart – read too much – *not* to know it. Which meant that she also knew that she could get away with it in Galadar, one of the more progressive of the eight duchies.

Iowyn tilted her head and gave Ulric a wry smile. Her amber eyes sparkled with what Ulric could only guess was mischief. "Aw, are you trying to protect me from angry mobs?"

Ulric rolled his eyes at her flippancy. "Whatever, forget it. Get murdered for running your mouth. See if I care."

But he did care. Not because he *cared* about her. Gods no.

Because he had to keep her alive as part of his probation. If she died, then he would lose everything and be sent on a ship to Smokheim, basically a death sentence. Of course, if all else failed, he could find a way to get back home and seek asylum with his family, but that was certainly not an option that he wanted to take.

Keeping his head on a swivel for her was going to be the death of him. Ulric just knew it.

CHAPTER

3

Ulric kept his eyes on Iowyn as they made their way to the closest Guild outpost. She was more or less forced to walk beside Dren since the werewolf's body covered his entire back, leaving no place for her to ride. She had been steadfast for the first few miles, but as the sun rose in the east, Ulric could see her endurance was waning. They had been up all night, tracking the wolf that was now no more than a husk. Even Ulric was fatigued, and he had been riding since Leeside became a speck on the horizon.

He still couldn't believe the nerve of her to get up and curse at an entire town. He could have a temper himself at times, but he was never so reckless about it. It was as if she had no internal voice telling her that it was a terrible idea and could quite possibly put her in danger. How she was ever cleared for fieldwork, he couldn't tell, at least not from what he'd already seen of her.

She constantly undermined his authority, disregarded orders, and pointed out the flaws in his logic. Logic that had kept him alive for years now. She also seemed to have an uncanny knack for getting into trouble. Luckily, Iowyn had yet to get herself into a bind that truly warranted Ulric's intervention.

Ulric and Shadowfoot had been riding behind Dren, keeping the steady pace along the red dirt road with large trees that flanked them on either side. If Iowyn was content to walk, he would let her. She had yet to complain. He would give her credit for that at least. He was honestly more surprised that she hadn't filled the time with her constant prattling.

In the silence, Ulric had been transfixed, watching the swing of her long black braid between her shoulders as she walked. The only thing that had broken his concentration was seeing the side of her face contort in pain.

Without thinking, Ulric spurred Shadowfoot forward, bringing them to Iowyn's side, and scooped her up and into the saddle in front of him. She shrieked at being plucked up from the ground, and whipped around in the seat. "What are you doing?"

He kept his face neutral. "You shouldn't walk anymore. You'll hurt yourself."

She scoffed, and made to move out of the saddle, but Ulric wrapped his arm firmly around her middle and held her down in the seat. Iowyn struggled against him. "Let me down. I'm fine!"

Ulric didn't budge and did his best not to think about the way her backside rubbed against him as she struggled. "There's at least five miles left. It'll go faster this way."

"Ulric," she ground out. "Let. Me. Go."

He blinked. Iowyn had never called him by his first name. Since their first meeting when he pissed her off, she had only ever called him Ornthalas. Never Ulric. It was enough to catch him off guard for just a fraction of a second, let his grip slip just the tiniest amount. Iowyn made a break for it, bailing from the saddle. But he snapped himself out of whatever had taken hold of him and plucked her from the air before her feet could hit the ground.

He placed her back in front of him and squeezed her middle, enough to cause her to let out her breath and breathe back in shallowly. Ulric lowered his head to her ear, and tried not to think of the scent of vanilla, coupled with something else he couldn't quite place, invading his senses as he whispered, "Sit still, and shut up. You aren't going anywhere."

Iowyn stilled in his grasp, and he released the pressure he was exerting on her ribs. As soon as she could take a full breath, she was talking. "I'll sit still, but I'll be *damned* if I listen to you tell me to shut up. If I—"

She gasped as Ulric applied slight pressure again. He had a pretty triumphant smirk on his face as she whipped her head around to glare at him. "Stop doing that!"

"I wouldn't have to if you would just do as you're told."

Iowyn grumbled something under her breath as she turned back around. He waited for her to continue on some kind of tirade, cursing him up and down and imploring Odea or even Mortem to end her suffering. Gods knew she had quite the mouth on her. But instead, she sat in front of him, tense but quiet, playing with Dren's reins in her hands. With Iowyn off the ground, Shadowfoot and Dren began ambling on a bit faster without threat of the carcass falling off Dren's back. They would hopefully be arriving at the outpost in the next hour, be able to get rooms, and sleep until the sun rose again the next morning.

Within five minutes of being in the saddle, Iowyn's body relaxed, and Ulric felt her back press into his front. Her head rested back on his shoulder, lolling slightly with each step Shadowfoot took. He looked down, and for the first time saw her face free of all expression and without her amber eyes burning into him. Her lips parted slightly and soft but deep breaths rose and fell in her chest.

At least now he knew the rest of the ride would be silent and free of fighting.

Iowyn hadn't realized that she had dozed off. They had been in the middle of the forest one second, and the next she was waking up from the creaking of the large wooden doors of the outpost shutting behind them.

Waking up in Ulric's arms.

Iowyn sat up straight, removing herself from the warmth of Ulric's body. Shadowfoot was stopped, so she lifted up Ulric's arm and ducked below it to dismount, swinging her leg over Shadowfoot's head. Her feet hit the ground, and shocks of pain shot up from her sore soles up into her calves. She winced at the impact, but did her best to walk it off.

"Have a nice nap, Beastie?" Ulric's voice came from the saddle, amusement lilting in his tone.

Iowyn didn't turn around, but shot over her back, "Stop calling me that!"

She went to Dren and gave him a once over. He brayed at her. The sound was hoarser than usual. He was for sure tired from hauling the werewolf's dead body overnight. She grabbed his reins and went into the front gate towards the scriven quarter of the outpost. The sooner she could drop off the corpse, the sooner her and Dren could have a well-deserved rest.

Guild outposts were most commonly located in the north, east, south, west, and central regions of a duchy depending on how large it was, and almost all were built the same. Walled stone forts that housed their own kind of miniature city inside of their perimeter. The largest building in the center was the garrison. It served as the base of operation for the outpost and was where officials offices could be found.

The Guardsmen's post was its own building next door. The Guardsmen acted as the Guild's own law enforcement officers. Hunters with exemplary records and recommendations were invited to join their ranks and don the scarlet capelet. They were in charge of keeping the peace within the outpost walls, but also were tasked with keeping troublesome hunters in line. Hunters on probation – like Ulric – were meant to check-in with the Guardsmen whenever they came to a new outpost.

The barracks and stable were the next largest buildings. Any traveling Guild member could get a free room for the night, complete with their own private bathroom. It was a small luxury, to always have a place to sleep, so long as you were close enough to an outpost.

The scriven quarter, only denoted by a small mound and grassy earth with large carved double doors, was the place where almost any and all research on creatures happened. The entrance itself looked like doors that led to nowhere, as there was no structure to see, at least, not one above ground. It also doubled as the entrance to the outpost archive, a library that held all the outposts' knowledge, and what was shared by other outposts, inside the subterranean vault.

Smaller buildings like the falconry, armory, blacksmith, mess hall, and infirmary could be found throughout the walled-in outpost.

Iowyn walked up to the scriven quarter and knocked on the large front double doors, right below the carving of the gryphon head that stared down anyone who passed. The gryphon was a symbol for the scrivens, as it was the symbol of Temphon, the god of knowledge and scholars, among other things. Libraries across Phyrra were adorned with statues of the creature, in the hopes of pleasing Temphon. It was also superstition that the statues would help protect the knowledge held within a library or archives walls, and the lives of those inside.

Iowyn waited a few moments before knocking on the doors again. It was early enough in the morning from what Iowyn could tell by the sun's position in the sky, so there had to be several scrivens inside already performing their morning duties. The door cracked open, and Iowyn was met with the face of a timid young man with short red hair. The silver scriven pin of a gryphon head glinted against the dark shirt he wore.

"Yes?" he asked softly. "Can I help you?"

His skin was pale, much like her own. He squinted against the bright light of the sun outside. Most scriven spent their time in the darkness of the archive, accustomed more to the dimness of candlelight than the full brunt of the sun.

Iowyn gestured over her shoulder to Dren. "I've got a fresh werewolf carcass for you."

The man's eyes widened, and Iowyn could hear excited but hushed murmurs behind him. A much older man with a long white beard, most likely the curator of the archive, pushed past the young man and held the door ajar. "How long has it been dead?" the old man asked.

"A few hours."

More excited murmurs came from inside. A team of four scrivens with a cloth stretcher came out from the dark bowels of the archive to retrieve the corpse, like they had been waiting for her to arrive.

They worked together as a team to gently unload the body from Dren's back, and haul it back inside. The old man walked up to Iowyn, taking her hand in both of his and shaking it energetically. "Thank you so much. We hardly ever get fresh specimens like this. It is truly a gift." His eyes went distant as he whispered, "They'll be so pleased."

Iowyn smiled softly at him. "You're more than welcome. It's the least we can do."

The old man grinned from ear to ear as he followed the rest of his cohorts back inside, a youthful pep added to his step. He was already prattling off orders as he shut the door.

At one time, Iowyn would have been welcomed inside, even helped with the dissection and research of the creature. But she wasn't one of them, not anymore. She worked in the field, denoted by the shiny new golden pin on her jacket of a sword plunging through the head of a dragon. Her heart twinged with something she couldn't quite place as she stared at the now closed doors.

Dren's wet nose nudged her arm, snapping Iowyn out of her thoughts. "Come on, let's get you cleaned up," she cooed, leading Dren towards the stables. The werewolf had barely been dead for a few hours, but that hadn't stopped Dren's coat from smelling like decomposing flesh. Flies were landing and taking off all around his back, and even though she was exhausted, Iowyn wasn't about to let Dren be devoured by flies while she slept snugly in a bed.

She found a water pump outside the stable and took off Dren's bridle and saddle. She went into the tack room, finding various grooming tools, including a bucket, some brushes, and towels. She filled the bucket full of water, pouring it over his back and neck. From one of his saddle bags, she fished out a bar of soap and lightly swiped it over his dappled coat until small suds began to form. When she could no longer smell death on her beautiful boy, she refilled the bucket and rinsed him off, then set to drying him off as best as she could with the towels.

Iowyn reached down to grab a brush on the ground, but a larger hand grabbed her forearm. "Let the stable boy do that."

She should have known that the tanned hand belonged to Ulric.

She wrenched her arm from his grasp and picked up the brush. "I'm perfectly capable of doing it myself."

Ulric was quicker than her and snatched the brush from her hand. "I didn't say that you weren't. But you're basically a zombie right now. Get some rest before you end up hurting yourself."

Iowyn wanted to fight him but he was right. She was exhausted and had barely kept her eyes open to wash Dren. "Fine," she grumbled.

Ulric whistled, and out came a stable boy to take Dren away. Ulric gave him some instructions as well as a few silver coins, and

Iowyn gave Dren a few reassuring pats on his shoulder. "Go with him. He'll take care of you," she ordered her beast. Dren gave a small grunt and followed the young boy into the stables.

With Dren out of sight, Iowyn felt whatever energy she had been holding onto leave her body. Ulric grabbed her hand gently. Another thing that she had no fire left to fight. It was the last thing she remembered before waking up in a dark and private room in the barracks.

CHAPTER

4

The seeking falcon peered at Ulric from outside the window as he opened his eyes. He'd left it open, enjoying the chilled breeze as he slept. He could see the sun was just barely peeking over the horizon past the massive bird. At least he had slept for the whole day and night.

The falcon's sapphire blue and phthalo green plumage shimmered like polished metal in the early morning light. It simply stared at Ulric and cocked its head each way, waiting for him to take the parchment scroll in the leather tube tied to its leg.

He got out of bed and padded over to the window. Ulric held out his hand for the falcon to scent. Its eyes glowed bright yellow like the sun, and it stood on one foot, extending the leg which held the message towards Ulric. He worked carefully to undo the leather straps that held the tube shut and retrieved the scroll inside. Seeing that the message had now been delivered, the falcon outstretched its large wings and took off into the morning air.

Ulric didn't bother opening the scroll right away. He still needed to write and send his report on the werewolf assignment. Writing reports was always the worst part of the job.

It had been difficult for Ulric to keep everything straight at first, especially when an assignment could end up lasting multiple weeks, even months. He had gotten the bright idea to start keeping notes after he was reprimanded for sending a light, two-page report on a months-long assignment in Holith. They were enough to jog his memory of events, but sitting down and actually writing the full report was like pulling his own teeth out. Getting a new venture scroll with a new assignment, however, was enough motivation to get him going this morning. Although he would have liked another day or two to rest.

Ulric showered and dressed. In the mirror, he tugged away the bandage on his cheek and inspected the three-inch-long gash. It had stung like a bitch when he finally got around to cleaning it. The parting gift from the werewolf had thankfully scabbed over and showed no real signs of infection. When it healed, it would leave a fresh pink scar on his otherwise tan skin.

The scene was etched vividly in his mind as he stared at his reflection in the dimly lit room. The gnashing teeth in his face. The large paws with black claws swiping wildly at him. The red slash across his cheek was a painful reminder of how close things had gotten to going terribly wrong. Would he have survived if Iowyn hadn't been there?

Of course he would have. He would've been alone and not distracted by trying to keep someone else safe while fighting a fucking werewolf. His sole focus would've been on the wolf, not split like it had been last night.

As he touched his fingers to the wound on his cheek, he remembered the moment when the enormous wolf lunged at him. Instead of running or freezing in fear, as many might have done, Iowyn had defied his commands to stay put. With a fierce determination in her eyes, she had sprinted towards the crossbow, grabbing it just in time to divert the wolf's attention away from him. It had been enough to give him the crucial seconds he needed to regain his composure.

Iowyn's reckless act of bravery had likely saved his life, but it had also put her in grave danger. Deep down, he was thankful, but it wasn't an option for her to put herself in danger like that again. Not with Smokheim hanging over his head.

With a sigh, he turned away from the mirror and sat down at
the little desk in the corner of the room, and started writing his
report.

Clink! Clink! Clink!

Iowyn opened her eyes to the darkness of her room. The
curtains were pulled shut against the window, blocking out the
morning light that threatened to spill into the space.

Clink! Clink! Clink!

The sound came again from behind the curtains, and Iowyn
groaned. She was perfectly comfortable under the warmth of the
covers, but she knew it would be best to just get up and get it over
with. She flung the covers off her body and went over to the
window. She shut her eyes tight as she opened the curtains, and
kept them shut for a few seconds to let her eyes adjust to the bright
light outside.

Clink! Clink! Clink!

The seeking falcon didn't care to wait. It held a letter in its
beak, its eyes glowing yellow when it finally saw Iowyn.

She braced herself for the brisk midspring air as she opened the
window. The falcon stepped off the sill and hovered in the air,
flapping its large wings to stay aloft. Iowyn held out a hand and the
falcon dropped the envelope into it before flying away.

Iowyn quickly shut the window, a shiver running through her
body. She looked down at the letter, the familiar feminine
handwriting causing a smile to creep onto her face. Iowyn padded
back to the bed, diving under the covers, trying to savor the
remaining warmth they held. She tore open the envelope.

IOWYN YRSA MORGNAH!

Just WHEN exactly were you going to tell me that you were going to be starting fieldwork?!

I sent a letter to the Western Galadari outpost, where you were SUPPOSED to be, only to get a note sent back to me that further correspondence be sent by seeking falcon?!

Don't get me wrong, I'm happy for you. You just think that you could give a girl some warning? Or, you know, mention it in literally ANY OF YOUR OTHER LETTERS?! Did you think I wouldn't support you? I know better than anyone that this is what you've wanted since you were a kid.

I would appreciate it if you sent me a letter as soon as possible to let me know that you aren't dead. Who's your partner? Are they nice? If they aren't, just say the word and I'll set them straight. You know I will.

As for me, I've finally gotten my new partner since Ollie retired. If I could go back and fix it so that we ended up as partners, I would. (And you know I definitely could have, but no, you had to go and start fieldwork without me knowing!)

This man is barely three years older than me, but has a superiority complex like no other. From what I do know, he didn't even go to University, but somehow he knows more than me? I don't think so.

To make things worse, this man spends literally every second he can talking me up. My only bit of reprieve is the fact that Dad put us on night patrol, which means he has to shut his mouth for hours at a time and leave me in some semblance of peace. (Another reason why I need you to write me letters. I have nothing to fucking do on night patrol.)

I hope you're okay, Wyn. I hate not knowing where you are or what you're doing, or that you're even okay. All I do know for sure is that your partner better take care of you, or I'll be going on a little manhunt. (I only assume he's a man, but it can be a womanhunt too if need be). I don't know what you're facing now with your assignments, but I don't need to tell you to be careful!

And please write back to me! I want to hear EVERYTHING!

Love,

Loyla

Iowyn set down the letter and grabbed her pack from the bedroom floor. She rustled around to find an ink pen and her pad of lined paper. It would be best to send off a letter back to Loyla as soon as possible, or else she knew her friend would be sending a falcon a day.

They had met in University, when Iowyn had been so enamored by the campus that she hadn't been looking where she was walking, and ran right into Loyla. Iowyn had apologized profusely, even though she had been the one knocked to the ground and the six foot tall venatology and monstralogy double major had barely budged. Loyla helped her up and showed her to the dormitory, only to find out that they were in fact each other's roommates.

When they graduated, Loyla entered the Guild as a hunter and had been assigned to Rathian, mostly due to her father. Guild Master Ewan Cento had wanted to keep an eye on his daughter, which meant Loyla barely ever got any assignments outside of Rathian. Iowyn had been assigned to the Central Acantian outpost's archives as a scriven. Even with her degree in monstralogy, she needed a few years under her belt as a scriven before the Guild would even think of promoting her to fieldwork.

The last time she had seen Loyla was a little over a year ago, when she had single handedly gotten Iowyn from the Central Acantian outpost to Western Galadari at Iowyn's request. She hadn't told her friend why exactly in the letter, just that she needed out and fast. Loyla was there within a few days, and had basically used all of her skills and connections to get Iowyn a transfer off the books.

Being friends with the daughter of a Guild Master had its perks at times.

Dear Loyla,

I'm sorry that I didn't let you know about requesting fieldwork. To be honest, I wasn't even sure if it would be approved. It all happened so fast, and I was approved almost as soon as I requested it.

As for my partner, he's okay, I guess.

He doesn't talk much, and only answers my questions when they are related to the assignment. I wish I had your problem of him talking too much. I feel like I'm talking to a brick wall most of the time.

He also called me a worm, but I think I've proven him wrong about that on multiple occasions now. I actually killed the werewolf we were tasked with taking down. He might have helped a bit, but I was the one that shot it. Don't worry! I'm fine!

We're currently at the Eastern Galadari outpost, but we will probably get new orders any day now, so who knows where I'll be when I write you next,

Stay safe.

Love,

Iowyn

She tore the piece of paper from the pad. It wasn't a long letter, but it would do for now. She would do her best to write Loyla more as things happened. Words seemed to evade her when it came to writing everything at once. She folded up the piece of paper and walked over to the desk, finding a supply of envelopes in the drawer. She would send off her letter on the way to the mess hall, and work on her report for the Guild at breakfast.

Ulric found Iowyn an hour later in the mess hall, writing her own report, pen in one hand, and toast in the other. Her raven hair was braided into a crown around her head, and she looked well-rested compared to the last time he had seen her, basically sleepwalking through the barracks as he held her by the hand and doing his best to keep her from running into anything.

He grabbed a plate and waited in line to get food, then made his way over to the small round table Iowyn was sitting at alone. Three Guardsmen sat at the table next to her, their scarlet capelets draped over their left shoulders. Ulric didn't miss the way they eyed him, like he was some threat they might have to take down. He'd done what was expected of him and had checked in at the Guardsmen's post last night, right before finding Iowyn outside of the stables. Now every Guardsman in the outpost knew he was there.

Ulric ignored the Guardsmen as he sat down with his tray next to Iowyn and began eating. Iowyn's attention didn't leave the parchment in front of her. Her amber eyes transfixed on the words she wrote down. She didn't even look away to take a bite of toast or eggs, almost like her left hand had no idea what her right hand was doing, and vice versa. They moved completely independently of each other, one writing, the other feeding.

He sat silently watching her until she came to the end of her last sheet of paper, and signed her name underneath, letting out a breath.

"You usually do a lot of writing while eating?" Ulric asked, taking a bite of his own breakfast.

Iowyn looked up at him like he had just appeared out of thin air to her. "Huh? *Oh,* that." She shook her head as if to clear it from whatever she had been writing. "Old habit from University, I guess. Sometimes I'd just have to eat while writing my essays or I wouldn't have time to eat at all."

How different their experiences at University had been. In venatology, the study of the hunt, there were no essays or exams, at least, none of the paper variety. Aspiring hunters were trained in various forms of combat, weaponry, and the best places to strike to kill. Whereas Iowyn had probably never had to take a self-defense course during her time at University, and most likely had spent the majority of her time in the library.

Ulric pulled his own folded report from his back pocket and put it on the table. Iowyn's eyes flitted from his report back to her own. The spark of curiosity that lit in her eyes amused him. "You want to read it?" he asked.

She knitted her brows. "You'd let me?"

He shrugged. "Why not?"

Iowyn crossed her arms. "Because it's supposed to outline *every single* time I undermined your command on our assignment."

"It doesn't." Ulric went back to eating his breakfast. "Does yours reflect all the times I needed you to help my sorry ass?"

She looked back down at the report she had just finished. "Not as badly as it probably could have."

He gestured to his report with his fork before stabbing a few small sausages. "Go ahead. Read it."

She gave him a suspicious sideways glance before picking up the report and unfolding the few pages. Her eyes raked over the paper as she read, her eyebrows slightly furrowed in concentration. She flipped through each page, and when she finished, looked warily at Ulric. "Why were you so nice?"

"What do you mean?"

Iowyn held up the report. "You just talked about the assignment. Were strictly professional. Not one mention of my smartass remarks or being a pain in your ass?"

Nice wasn't exactly how Ulric would categorize his report. He had simply just omitted the things that he knew the higher ups at the Guild wouldn't care about, his opinion of her being first on the list. Had he perhaps gone easier on her than he had intended after she saved him from the werewolf? Maybe.

Ulric shook his head. "What I think about you isn't what they want to hear. They want to know about the assignment."

Iowyn was silent as her eyes went once again to her report. She bit her bottom lip, as if mulling something over.

"But your report is supposed to be about me, isn't it?" he asked.

Iowyn sighed before nodding. "They asked me to write about the assignment, yes. But they were more or less wanting reports on you and how you do your job." She picked up her own report and held it out to Ulric. "It's only fair. I read yours, you read mine."

Ulric swallowed the last of his breakfast and took the papers from her hand. But instead of reading he simply set them down on the table with his own and neatly folded them. He picked them up and stood up from the table. "I'll hand these in now. Don't forget to pick up your payment, and – uh – other stuff."

Ulric had always found it a little archaic for the Guild to make all the women take Viona's root. Named after the goddess of fertility, the root kept whoever took it infertile so long as they ingested it regularly. There was no rule for the men to take it. Iowyn would get a bag of it with her payment for completing the assignment.

Iowyn blinked up at him, puzzled. "Wait, you aren't going to read mine?"

He paused, looking at the reports in his hand, then back to her. He could know exactly what she thought of him. But what fun would that be? Ulric smirked, "No, I don't think I will."

Ulric was either playing games with her or fucking crazy, and Iowyn wasn't so sure as to which one she preferred.

Of course, it was entirely possible that as soon as he walked out of the mess hall and out of her sight, he would read her report. But something in Iowyn told her that he wasn't going to – that he meant it when he said that he wouldn't. Had she failed some kind of test by reading his? Did the fact that she read it reflect badly on her? What did it matter? Why did she even care? Ulric had shown one shred of decency, and all of a sudden she felt as though *she* was the jerk. If he was playing some kind of game, then he was definitely winning, and Iowyn didn't like that one bit.

Or perhaps, he truly didn't care. No mind games involved at all. He certainly hadn't shown any expertise in the complicated thought department. Playing mind games required you to think steps ahead of your opponent, and Ulric just hadn't seemed like that kind of combatant. At least not on purpose.

She groaned thinking about all the possibilities as she stuffed her leather pack with her things. Ulric had slipped a piece of paper under her door while she was in the shower to be out and ready to leave by noon. They had gotten a new venture scroll, which meant they would be heading off for their next assignment. So much for some extra rest and relaxation, but that was life in the field. If Iowyn had wanted a cushy day off, she should have stayed a scriven in the archives.

When she felt like she had everything packed after rechecking her bag for the third time, Iowyn slung her pack onto her back and left the barracks for the stables. Dren's antlers gave away which stall he was being kept in. The bony white prongs floated above the stall doors.

Iowyn unlatched the door to Dren's stall, and greeted him with a sweet potato she had swiped from the mess hall. Dren happily padded in place at the sight of the large orange tuber. Iowyn held it out to him, and his large canine teeth made short work of the treat. She inspected his fur, since she hadn't been the one to finish grooming him, and was pleasantly surprised to see that his coat had been brushed and even clipped a bit shorter for the coming summer months. "Somebody got a haircut, huh?"

Dren stood taller and let out a low bellow. She took it as his way of showing pride in his appearance. As Iowyn started to outfit Dren with his saddle and bridle, she felt a presence behind her at the stall door, and turning only confirmed her thought as to who it might be.

Ulric leaned against the doorpost with his arms crossed, and Shadowfoot was already saddled and ready to ride behind him. She noted the venture scroll in his hand, but finished making sure Dren's saddle and bridle were comfortably fastened.

Without a word, Ulric walked inside of the stall to her side, and held out the scroll to her. Iowyn looked down at the rolled parchment dubiously, and wondered what could be so important inside that he wanted her to read it for herself. "What? Don't tell me you can't read," she joked, as she took the scroll.

Ulric said nothing as she unfurled it and read:

Assignment #43895
Location: Calluna, Duchy of Arondir
Guild Members: Ulric Ornthalas & Iowyn Morgnah
Report:
Children reportedly going missing. Investigate. If a creature or creatures are deemed responsible, dispatch with utmost haste. Return bodies of said creature(s) to Central Arondiran outpost. Give written and oral reports to Guild Master Foxe upon completion of assignment.

She reread the scroll several times to be sure.
Calluna.
Ulric simply gave her the hint of a smirk. "Looks like someone's going home."

CHAPTER

5

Home.

It seemed impossible. But included inside the venture scroll was a small map of Phyrra outlining the route they were to take to get to her hometown in Arondir.

How long had it been since she had even set foot in Calluna? She'd just celebrated her eighteenth birthday when she left, and now was nearing her twenty-fourth. Had it really been six years since she saw her parents?

Iowyn shook her head free of her thoughts with a sudden realization. "Wait… You remembered that?"

Iowyn had told Ulric only once where she was from – on the first day they met when she had formally introduced herself to him. Right before he called her a worm.

Ulric shrugged her disbelief away. "Contrary to what you might believe, Beastie, I have a pretty good memory." He walked out of the stall to Shadowfoot and mounted.

Iowyn looked back down at the scroll, just to make sure it really did say Calluna. For some reason, she just couldn't bring herself to believe it.

Ulric spurred his horse forward to walk out of the stables. "Come on, we have a boat to catch."

Ulric had expected a much different reaction from Iowyn when he gave her the scroll. Excitement, elation, even maybe some happy tears, but instead, she just looked uneasy. It wasn't what he had anticipated from the woman he had been with for the past week. Iowyn had been a pain in his ass, sure, but she had also had a somewhat sunny and optimistic disposition about her that whole time.

She was oddly quiet on the ride to the port. Hadn't asked him a single question like he had expected, not that he would probably answer. Getting to know each other was a complicated thing. He felt like he knew enough that he could trust her if things got hairy. She'd more than proven that when she went and put her own life at risk to grab his crossbow to shoot the werewolf. He figured that she felt the same, but she just kept asking questions, prying. She too often asked personal questions, and while they seemed innocent, Ulric wasn't about to tell her anything that he didn't want her to know. Besides, for all they knew, they could receive a new missive and cease being partners at a moment's notice. Ulric wasn't looking to get attached. It would be easier if they simply kept each other at a distance.

They arrived at the port with plenty of time to find their ship, The Druid. From what Ulric knew, it was one of the many ships under contract with the Guild to give passage for members to the various duchies. Going by ship across the gulf would cut down travel to Arondir by almost a month, and time was always of the essence when it came to Guild work.

Ulric and Iowyn dropped off their mounts with the loadmaster of the ship for boarding. Iowyn gave him directions on what to do with Dren, as the loadmaster had practically spluttered at the sight of the deupin. Ulric was beginning to find people's reactions to Iowyn's beast rather amusing. Even some of the most experienced horsemasters would have no idea what to do with such a creature. Once she assured them that Dren would eat the same things as the horses, they were usually a bit more accepting of having him in their stables.

Iowyn started for the gangplank when Ulric's hand grabbed her wrist. "There are some rules I have if we're going to be traveling together."

Iowyn looked down at his hand on her arm and cocked a brow. "Okay?"

"First, don't use your real name," he stated. "Or mine."

"Why does that matter?"

"It's easier if you make up aliases on the road. That way, if one of us gets into trouble, there's less of a chance of someone finding you through your name later on," he explained.

"Do you get into trouble on the road often?" she joked. But Ulric's eyes hardened to give the impression that he wasn't kidding. Did he get into trouble? No. But *she* certainly had a penchant for it. Her smile fell and she pulled her wrist away from his grip. "Okay, make aliases. Got it."

Iowyn strode for the gangplank again, but Ulric grabbed her wrist once more.

"Oh no you don't. There's more."

Iowyn sighed. "Seriously?"

"Second thing, like not giving out your name, don't tell people the real reason you're passing through." He stepped forward and raised his hands to her chest. She barely had time to react before he grabbed her hand and placed her golden Hunter's Guild pin in it. "And take that off if you don't need it. Not everyone is friendly to hunters."

"But I'm not a hunter. *You are,*" she pointed out.

Ulric shrugged. "Guilty by association."

Iowyn sighed and stuffed the pin into her pants pocket. "Any other rules, Ornthalas?" She gave him a placating smile.

"Yes, one more." Ulric paused, and pursed his lips. He wasn't quite sure what were the best words to use for his final rule. "We don't sleep together."

Iowyn stepped back in shock, and then a moment later, burst out laughing from the sheer absurdity of the thought. The look of confusion on Ulric's face only made her laugh even harder. She tried to stop herself before tears started gleaming in her eyes. "Oh, now *that's* funny."

Ulric crossed his arms. "I don't see why."

He really didn't. They were both young and attractive people. Things happened between partners in the Guild all the time, and most of the time, it never ended well. While still on probation, Ulric didn't want things to get messy.

Iowyn snorted. "No offense, Ornthalas. I'm sure you kill it with the ladies all the time. But after this past week, you have done zero favors for yourself in that department as far as I'm concerned."

Ulric gritted his teeth. "Whatever."

The exchange left an awkward tension hanging in the air as Ulric and Iowyn stood on the gangplank, and Ulric found himself wishing he hadn't even brought it up. The hustle and bustle of the port around them was the only reprieve from what would have otherwise been silence.

Iowyn looked off towards the merchant booths near the harbor. Perhaps it would do them some good to separate for a while. "We have some time before the ship leaves. Why don't you explore the market for a bit?" he offered.

Iowyn gave him a dubious look and crossed her arms. "Is this some kind of test?"

Ulric rolled his eyes, "For Genova's sake, I'm trying to be nice here."

"Really? You're going to let me go off by myself?"

He waved off towards the market. "If you keep your dagger close, you should be fine." Ulric had been in this harbor a time or two. It never seemed too dangerous to him. Besides, he found he needed time alone and away from her and her constant prattling. "Just be back here in thirty minutes."

She took out a silver pocket watch from her pocket. "Thirty minutes. Got it." She looked back toward the merchant booths and smiled before leaving Ulric on the gangplank.

Iowyn had been perusing the merchant booths, looking at all the fine things the eight duchies had to offer. She found herself getting lost among the stalls that had fine jewelry from across Phyrra. The countless boxes of silver and gold rings, bracelets, and necklaces shimmered in the sun. She only wished she had anywhere near the amount of money to buy something so nice for herself.

As she browsed, Iowyn thought about Ulric's rules. She must have hurt some manly pride of his by laughing at him, but she just couldn't help it. She found herself laughing quietly to herself even now each time her mind brought up Ulric's third rule.

Sure, he was attractive in a rugged kind of way, but Iowyn wasn't just going to sleep with him because he looked good. They were partners, assigned to do a job together. She wasn't about to go and blur the lines for a roll in the hay. Although Iowyn was hoping to maybe break down a wall or two and at least become some semblance of friends. Who knew exactly how long they would be assigned together?

She made her way through the street stopping at each stall as she went before she felt like checking her watch. Iowyn had five minutes before she needed to be back at the ship.

"Nice watch you have there."

Iowyn jumped as she turned her head to find someone standing next to her. The man was dressed in what she would consider rags, and smelled terrible. She stuffed her watch back in her pants, and he watched her hand leave her pocket as she stashed it.

"Thank you," Iowyn tried to sound polite and not frightened. "My father gave it to me."

He gave her a close-lipped smile. "Now what's a pretty thing like you doing in a place like this?" He crept closer. His breath was vile, and she could see why. His teeth were yellow and brown, practically decaying as he spoke.

"I'm meeting someone," Iowyn lied. She tried not to breathe in. Gods, did the man ever bathe? Or even own a toothbrush? She looked across the street bustling with people. "Actually, I think I just saw him over there, so I should get going." Iowyn didn't know if she was any good at acting, but she pointed in the general direction of the ship and was about to walk past the man when he grabbed her arm.

He clicked his tongue. "Not so fast. I didn't even get your name."

She gave him an appeasing smile. "Really, I should go find my friend. He's waiting for me." Iowyn tried pulling away but his grip tightened on her arm.

"Come on, what's your name?" His free hand began playing with a loose piece of her hair. There was dirt under his fingernails and grime caked on his hand.

"Let me go," she said, trying her best to sound stern. She hoped that it would somehow convince him to do so.

He gave a sinister smile. "I'll let you go," he whispered, "if you give me that watch."

The watch? That was what this was all about? Why was this man troubling her for an old watch when there were booths full of silver and gold jewelry throughout this market for him to swipe?

"Let me go," Iowyn repeated, her eyes searching her surroundings. Did no one really see what was going on here? If they did, no one seemed to care or want to get involved.

"Give me the watch." He gritted his rotting teeth and gripped her arm even tighter.

She grimaced at the pain. "You're hurting me."

"Good," the man replied smiling, as if he enjoyed inflicting the pain. He held out his open hand. "The watch."

Iowyn slowly reached for the pocket that her watch was in, and at the last second, brought her knee up so she could easily slide her hand inside of her boot and grab the brass hilted knife she had stashed there this morning. Iowyn barely had time to think before she stabbed downward, her knife going through the man's palm and pinning it to the table in the stall.

He screamed in agony and shock, letting her arm go. As heads around the street whirled to see what the sudden commotion was about, Iowyn pulled her knife out from the table. Blood squirted from the open wound. Iowyn dashed into the crowd, and looked behind her to make sure no one was chasing after her. She made it less than five strides away before slamming into a wall.

Except the wall caught her before she could fall, and Iowyn looked up to find the puzzled face of Ulric Ornthalas.

CHAPTER

6

A clamor arose from inside the stall, and Iowyn had no time to explain to Ulric just then what exactly she was running from. She regained her footing and grabbed Ulric by the arm, dragging him into a nearby back alley, surprisingly with little resistance. Iowyn pulled him down to a crouch behind a few trash bins and waited.

"What ha—" He barely started asking his question before Iowyn clapped her hand over his mouth. A mixture of fury and amusement danced in his emerald eyes as she released her hand from his mouth and put a finger to her lips.

The man that Iowyn had stabbed through the hand ran through the street with a few friends in tow, his other hand clutching his injured palm. "Where'd she go?" he yelled. "Where'd that bitch go?" He stormed up to a woman close by on the street. "A bitch with pitch black hair just came out here. Where the fuck did she go?"

The woman, no doubt terrified, shook her head and stammered, "I-I-I don't know who you're talking about."

He pushed the woman to the ground, yelling in frustration, then turned to the three men that had followed him. "Find that bitch, and find her *now!*"

The three men nodded and went off in different directions. One headed straight for the alley that Ulric and Iowyn were hiding in.

"Come on," Ulric whispered. He swung her around and pulled her up. He put his hand on the back of Iowyn's neck and began walking with her in front of him. With his hand on her neck, he

49

could steer her around, and Iowyn realized that with his dark, sapphire blue cloak and their height difference, she wasn't visible to the oaf clambering around in the alley. As soon as they were able, he turned them into a new street and then traveled a bit farther before ducking into another side alley.

Ulric turned Iowyn around so her back was against the stone wall, and he leaned over her, his hands on either side of her head. He brought his face close to hers, his cloak making her almost imperceptible to outsiders.

"What are you doing?" Iowyn whispered, her heart racing. She couldn't tell if it was from the adrenaline of stabbing a man and running away, or Ulric's sudden closeness.

"Pretending we're a couple that doesn't want to be disturbed," he murmured back. Iowyn hoped she wasn't blushing from his comment. "Now, do you want to tell me what that was all about?"

Iowyn pursed her lips. "What do you think happened?"

He gave her a stern look that told her that explanation wasn't good enough. "If we're going to be partners, we're going to have to trust each other. So tell me everything."

Iowyn couldn't help herself. "Well, my first kiss was with this guy named Maddox when I was sixteen, and—"

It was Ulric's turn to slap a hand over her mouth.

"You know what I meant, *smartass*," he warned. "What. Happened."

Iowyn rolled her eyes, and pried his hand from her mouth. "That *asshole* back there wanted my watch. I wouldn't give it to him, so he grabbed me and demanded it. So I stabbed him straight through his hand to make him let me go and made a run for it."

Ulric smirked, and something about the small upturn of his lips made Iowyn's heart skitter. "Guess you aren't going to be as helpless as I thought."

She cocked a brow. "You think I'm helpless?"

He looked down the alley. "I think you have the uncanny talent of getting into trouble."

Iowyn crossed her arms. "What? You think I *asked* for that creep to try and mug me?"

"I didn't say that."

"Then what?"

Ulric pursed his lips and let out a long breath through his nose. "You really want to know?"

Iowyn tilted her head. "Yes."

Ulric looked over her face, as if trying to see if she was serious. "Fine. I think you're naive and inexperienced."

She opened her mouth to argue with him, but he slapped his hand back over her mouth. "No, no. *I'm* talking now."

Iowyn wished her eyes could set him on fire or cut him – just hurt him in general. He took a step closer, their bodies less than an inch from touching. "I think that without me around, you'd be dead in less than a week. And I definitely think that you're some kind of cruel and unusual punishment for me from the Guild because I can't for the life of me understand why else they would put someone like *you* in the field."

The rage from his words enveloped her like a lit matchstick. Logic flew out the window of her mind as she opened her mouth and bit down on Ulric's finger. He pulled his hand away from her face like she had burned him. "What the *fuck* is wrong with you?" He shook his hand to dissipate the pain.

"I am *not* helpless," Iowyn spat, pushing him away from her. "And I worked my ass off to get here." She pointed a finger in his face. "You have no *idea* what I've been through to get here!"

"Oh really?" Ulric closed the distance between them again. "Please, do tell."

Iowyn gritted her teeth. The gall of this man. He expected her to just spill everything to him? And for what? Just to prove a point? "No," she lifted her chin. "You don't deserve to know."

He didn't. He done nothing so far as to earn the right to that story. *Her* story.

Iowyn expected some kind of reaction to her words, but Ulric's face gave away nothing. Maybe he really didn't give a shit about her.

She looked down the alley, checking their surroundings for any danger, and then backed away from him. She didn't look him in the eyes as she crossed her arms and muttered, "We're going to miss our ship."

Ulric stood there for a few seconds, staring at her. She waited for him to say something. Why else would he just be staring at her? But he said nothing. He just turned and took the first steps through the back alleys towards the ship.

They said nothing to each other the whole way back to the port.

Ulric knew deep down that he shouldn't have said any of those things back in the alley. But she had baited him into it. There was just something about her that irked him. Like she knew just what to say and do to push his buttons, to make everything more difficult for him.

Whatever he'd done to offend the gods and bring Iowyn into his life, he hoped he would atone for it soon so he could forget all about her and rid her from his life.

They boarded the ship with their bags in tow. Ulric had to show their transport papers before they could even step foot on the top deck. His eyes constantly surveyed their surroundings. Even though they were on a Guild-contracted ship, Ulric didn't know how well the Guild vetted their constituents. Just because they were supposed to be safe, didn't mean that there wasn't danger to be found around the corner. Iowyn had already proven that.

Her presence on the boat, for example, was garnering lots of attention from the crew of the ship. They had no doubt just finished a long voyage before coming to port, and were just about to start another. Ladies were few and far between for men on ships like this, and while Iowyn wasn't Ulric's favorite person in the world, keeping her safe was part of his probation deal and kept him from being shipped off to Smokheim.

One of the men near the top deck was already pointing out Iowyn to another crew member while wiggling his eyebrows. Another let out a high then low whistle at her, and Iowyn seemed completely oblivious to any of it. It was like leading a lamb into a den of wolves.

The man at the top of the ramp pointed out the direction of passenger cabins, saying that any open one that they could find was theirs to take. Ulric was quick to grab Iowyn's arm and drag her below deck before any of the crewmen topside could get any ideas.

He more or less threw her into the first open cabin he found with two bunks, much to her dismay. "What the fuck is it now, Ornthalas?" she yelled at him.

Apparently, she hadn't cooled down from their fight in the alley.

Ulric shut the door and latched the lock. He knew as soon as he made up his mind about this plan that she would meet him with resistance. "Listen to me, until we make it to the next port, you're staying with me."

Iowyn let out a huff of frustration. "You told me not even an hour ago, we don't sleep together, you *jackass*. I can get my own cabin." She made to walk past Ulric and unlatch the door, but he stood in front of her as an immovable wall.

She wasn't going anywhere alone on this ship. Not with predators afoot and nowhere for her to run. Not on his watch. And he had no doubt in his mind that he would castrate any one of them that tried.

"It's not safe for you here, Beastie."

Iowyn rolled her eyes and crossed her arms. "First off, stop calling me that. Secondly, what? One guy tries to mug me, and now I'm some fucking damsel in distress?"

Ulric's jaw clenched at her ambivalence. He would have to teach her to be more aware of her surroundings it seemed. "They were looking at you like they've been stranded in the desert and you're a four-course meal."

"They who?"

He gestured to the door. "The crew."

Iowyn scoffed, rolling her eyes again. "You're crazy if you think I'd ever let any of them touch me."

"They don't *care* what you want, Beastie. That's the problem."

Iowyn tried her best to get around him. "I'm fine, Ornthalas. I'll just get my own cabin and—"

Ulric slammed his fist against the door. "You don't get it, do you?" he yelled. "They want to *hurt* you. Do gods only know what to you. This isn't something that's up for debate. You're staying in this cabin with me, and you most certainly aren't going anywhere on this ship without me. Do you understand?"

Iowyn froze like a deer in a clearing that had just heard a twig snap. Her amber eyes went wide and fixated on the spot where Ulric's fist had collided with the door. She swallowed, meeting his gaze. "Alright," she breathed.

The fight in her was gone. Her combativeness had shrunk down inside of her until it was nothing. Ulric took a step towards her, opening his mouth to apologize – for what exactly he wasn't sure. He hadn't expected her to react in such a way to his explosion. It wasn't the first time he'd yelled at her, so he hadn't thought it would have such an effect on her. But she took two steps back from him, watching every movement he made with those wide amber eyes.

"Beastie," he started, "I didn't mean–"

"It's fine. I'll stay." she interrupted; her voice still soft. Iowyn retreated to the bed on the far side of the room and set down her bag. She wouldn't look him in the eye.

She was scared of him, and Ulric knew he had fucked up.

CHAPTER

7

Ulric had no real need to worry about Iowyn during their voyage across the gulf. The first night on the water had proven too much for the monstralogist. She became so nauseous that she could barely stray from her bunk. For the whole of their two-day journey, she could barely keep anything solid down. Ulric had been considerate enough to bring her a pail to puke in.

Her only reprieve from feeling absolutely awful was when she fell asleep. In between her fits of slumber, Iowyn could have sworn she saw Ulric laying in his own bunk, reading a small book. Her eyes had been too bleary to read what the title of the book was, and the more she thought about it, the more she thought perhaps her mind had made it up. While she lay in bed, Iowyn only hoped that Dren was faring better than her. As a creature from the mountains, she could only imagine what he thought of the turbulent conditions.

She knew they had made it to port when the ship finally stopped its fitful rocking. The light alleviation of movement allowed her stomach to stop swirling. She sat up from bed and heaved the last contents of her stomach into the pail before Ulric came back to the cabin to fetch her.

"We're here," he said.

"No shit?" Iowyn sneered. She didn't care about being rude. Not when she'd had an awful time on this godsforsaken ship, all the while Ulric had been able to come and go as he pleased from their cabin. And she had yet to forget his explosion once they had boarded the ship.

Ulric went to open his mouth, but Iowyn gave him a glare that she wished could cut him. "I swear to the gods above, if you rush me into leaving right now," her eyes darted to Ulric's pants, specifically his crotch, "I'm going to make sure there are no little Ornthalas's in your future."

The apple of Ulric's throat bobbed. "I'll wait above deck," he replied.

Iowyn gave him a mocking smile. "Good choice."

He left and shut the cabin door behind him.

Slowly but surely, Iowyn changed into a clean set of clothes. She mostly just wanted to wear something that didn't smell like bile. Luckily, she didn't need to do much packing considering she had barely even touched her large leather pack since getting onto the boat. Still, Iowyn checked and rechecked that all her belongings were where they were supposed to be.

The cabin door creaked as it opened behind her, and Iowyn let out an angry huff. "Ornthalas, I told you—"

She turned, but Iowyn didn't see Ulric's tall figure in the doorway. Iowyn froze when she saw the man from the market, wearing the same dirty shirt and slops he'd been in two days ago. A dirty bandage was wrapped around his hand from where her knife gored him. A yellow grin spread across his face. "So, this is where you've been hiding."

The skin on Iowyn's scalp prickled.

Bad. This was very bad.

Iowyn backed up until the back of her legs hit her bunk. There was nowhere for her to run in the small cabin.

"You know, when I heard my mates talking about some black-haired beauty on board, I thought to myself – there's no way it could be the same girl from the market." He entered the cabin, shutting the door. "I mean, what are the odds?" he asked. "Of all in the ships in the port, you just so happened to be traveling on the Druid?"

Iowyn reached a hand behind her and found her pack set on the bunk. She slowly fished in her bag for her dagger and cursed herself for not putting it on her belt when she'd dressed. From this moment on, she promised herself that her dagger would *always* go on her belt.

She swallowed the lump in her throat that grew as the dirty sailor came closer. "You still want my watch?" she asked.

He shook his head, chuckling to himself. "Oh no, I'm over that." All amusement left his face as he reached behind himself with his other hand and pulled out a knife of his own. "But I do think that I will be taking something from you."

As he neared her, Iowyn could smell his rank breath and sweat stained clothes. Had this man ever learned basic hygiene? She probably would have thrown up again if there had been anything left in her stomach.

Her fingers desperately rifled through her bag. With how often and meticulously she packed it, she would have thought she could find her dagger easily, but alas, her fingers came up empty.

The tip of the man's knife came to her chin, and he used it to tilt up her chin and make her look into his eyes. "Lucky for you, I'm a lonely man, so I'll be taking the only thing that women like you are good for."

The tip of her pinky came into contact with cold metal.

The sailor's bandaged hand went to her hip.

Her fingers swam through the content of her bag towards where she had felt the metallic object. It had to be the dagger. She couldn't think of anything else it could be, but at this point, she'd take anything she could use as a weapon. Her hand was just about to enclose on the hilt when the sailor's free hand shot from her waist and back behind her to grab her wrist.

He wrenched her hand out of her bag and twisted it into an uncomfortable position. "Tsk, tsk. You're being naughty, aren't you?"

The sailor removed the knife from her chin to grab the bag from behind her. He threw it across the room before pushing her back on the bed.

Iowyn had only one option left. In all honesty, it should have been the first thing she did. Her chest heaved as she inhaled slowly and let out the start of a scream. Her cry was cut off by a fist hitting her cheekbone and another hitting her ribs.

The knife flew back up to her neck. "Another sound, and it will be the last one you make."

Ulric stood on the deck of the ship as the wind whipped his chocolate brown curls across his forehead. The port city of Arkra was busy and bustling in the early afternoon. Merchants tried their best to sell their wares at their makeshift booths along the docks, and travelers from all parts of Phyrra gathered round.

Dren and Shadowfoot waited at a hitching post near the loading ramp. Ulric had paid the loadmaster handsomely to unload them first when the ship docked in the harbor. He leaned against the ship rail as a man came up to his large black mare. But Dren growled and snapped his teeth at the man before he could lay a hand on her. The stranger ran off as fast as his feet could carry him.

Ulric smiled to himself. "Useful beast."

But Dren only made Ulric's thoughts go to Iowyn. They'd more or less coexisted in silence for the whole trip across the gulf, mostly because she had either been throwing up whenever she was conscious, or sleeping. He'd felt sorry for her, and even emptied her pail for her while she slept, not that she'd probably noticed.

He ran his hands through his hair. Why did she have to be so stubborn? Why was it that every little thing between them had to explode into some kind of fight? Why did she vex him so? Why – out of every other person in Phyrra – did he have to get stuck with *her*?

He only had himself to blame for being put on probation. But what had happened in Beor… It had simply been a case of the wrong person being in the wrong place at the wrong time, and now he was paying for it. Now, there were people asking for Ulric's life on a silver platter.

There was a good reason that Ulric enjoyed being a solitary in the Guild. Ulric liked working alone. He only needed to worry about himself and could focus on just doing the job rather than caring about someone else's wellbeing. There had been a few times when he had been called on for extra help for more strenuous assignments, but that had always been his choice. He'd been high up in the ranks as a solitary, and had even been asked to join a few Guild parties full time, but he had always refused. It was better if he worked alone.

Now, he was as good as chained to someone else, losing the freedom that he enjoyed so much on his assignments. Working alone allowed him to take control and receive the due credit from his exploits. It also meant he could take the necessary risks without worrying about someone else trying to stop him. Most of all, it meant that he was only responsible for his own life, and not someone else's.

The words of the Guild Masters echoed in his head, *"You must keep your partner alive. Failure to do so will warrant immediate transfer to Smokheim."*

Transfer was the Guild's choice word for hunters being shipped off to Smokheim, as if it were the same as being assigned outpost work in any other duchy. But it wasn't. Smokheim was the

Guild's favorite way to get rid of problematic hunters. An island over three months journey by boat away, filled to the brim with beasts and creatures worse than anything that could be found on Phyrra. Sentence to Smokheim was a veritable death sentence. One that no hunter had ever come back from. The Guild's support from the dukes was the only thing that gave them the power to sentence a Phyrran citizen to such a terrible fate.

Ulric had enlisted with the Guild out of University, and he, like any other hunter, was free to tender his resignation whenever he so pleased. But the second that Ulric had been put on probation, that privilege had been voided.

It had been his choice to join the Guild after leaving home. He wanted to make a difference – the delusional dream of an optimistic eighteen-year-old who didn't know any better. Now he was stuck on probation with no end in sight. His one goal was clear: to not be sent to Smokheim. If keeping Iowyn alive kept him from being shipped across the Epottum, then he would do it.

A shrill scream from below his feet made Ulric go rigid.

"Iowyn," he breathed.

Ulric bolted to the steps that led below deck to the cabins, pushing a few crewmembers out of his way. He practically knocked the door off its hinges as he barreled into the cabin.

Iowyn lay on her bunk, while a dirty crewman worked to get her pants unbuttoned with one injured hand as the other held a knife to her throat.

Ulric didn't need to think about what to do next as he took three large steps to come up behind the man, wrapped his arm around his neck, and pulled him off Iowyn and the ground.

Iowyn blinked, not fully understanding what she was seeing. Ulric had an arm wrapped around her attacker's throat. His other hand fisted in the man's greasy hair. Choked gasps sounded from the sailor's mouth as he clawed at Ulric's muscled arm and kicked his feet wildly, his slops still pooled around his ankles. Ulric's green eyes shone with a fury she had never seen from him before. As he flexed, the man's choking became more fervent before ceasing entirely.

Ulric released his grip on the man and let him drop to the floor like a ragdoll. He stepped over the body and knelt on the floor by the bunk. His eyes raked over her, assessing her for damage. "Are you alright?"

Iowyn's mind raced at the question and how to possibly go about answering it. She was definitely hurt and weak from having little to no sustenance the past few days. Even though she hadn't made any sound after the scream, the sailor had hit her each time she'd made a movement that he didn't like.

A sharp stabbing pain shot through her side every time she took a deep breath. Her cheek stung below her left eye. She looked down at herself. Her belt had been unbuckled, but her leather pants hadn't been undone.

For some reason, she was less concerned with herself than she was about whether or not Ulric had just killed someone. "Is he?" she asked, unable to finish the question.

Ulric's jaw clenched. "No, but that can be arranged if you'd like."

She thought about it. The man had attacked her. Gone after her twice. But did that mean he deserved to die? Was she even the one to pass that kind of judgment?

Iowyn shook her head, refastening her belt. She stood up and sucked a breath through her teeth at the pain shooting through her side. Ulric grabbed her stuff from across the room and looped an arm around her middle without hesitation. She slung her arm over his shoulders. Iowyn shut her eyes tight, fighting off tears from the pain.

Ulric started walking them out of the room. But Iowyn stopped him before they got to the door. "Wait," she said.

Iowyn made Ulric let her go, and she walked over to the unconscious body in the middle of the room. An unbridled rage that Iowyn had only let herself feel a few times before coursed through her body, and for a few brief moments, the pain in her aching body subsided. It was like lightning striking her body and engulfing her in flames. She let out a guttural scream as she brutally kicked the body on the ground in front of her over and over again, until her foot went numb and she couldn't breathe.

She fell to the ground beside the body, and Ulric was quick to scoop her up again. She wrapped her arms around his neck and inhaled his scent of leather and oud. She let out a ragged breath as she stared into those deep green eyes of his. "Now we can go."

CHAPTER

8

Ulric did his best to get him and Iowyn out of the port town of Arkra as fast as possible, all things considered. He knew that her ribs were bruised if not cracked or broken, and had found the closest doctor in the next town that he could find.

The doctor wrapped her torso, all while eyeing Ulric suspiciously. They'd explained to him what had happened when they arrived, but the truth must not have been so convincing. If he thought Ulric had done this to her, the doctor wasn't saying, but his wary stare gave it all away. Iowyn must have noticed it too, because she kept telling him, "He didn't do it." The doctor's gaze didn't lessen. He checked Iowyn's head, then excused himself to go get some medicine from his supply room.

Ulric should have killed the sailor for what he did, and even more so for what he tried to do. Men who did that to women weren't men at all, and didn't deserve to live. In Ulric's book, men like that were no better than the creatures he hunted and killed.

What was worse was the guilt that he felt looking at her now. He shouldn't have left her unattended. They had made it to the harbor and that had given Ulric a false sense of security, which allowed for that sailor to find Iowyn all alone and unguarded.

"It's not your fault," she told him, as if she could read what he was thinking at that very moment. "I told you to go."

Ulric didn't know what to say to that, especially without telling her that she was wrong and starting a fight. She had told him to go, yes. But he didn't have to leave her. He could have been the stubborn jerk that he had been from the start and stayed with her.

But he figured that she would want to change into some clothes that didn't smell like her own vomit, and so he left and went above deck to enjoy some fresh air. He could have stayed at the door, but he hadn't. *He* left her alone. No matter what she might have thought, to Ulric, it *was* his fault.

The sight of Iowyn kicking the shit out of the man on the floor replayed again and again in his head. He hadn't expected it in the slightest when she had asked him to let her go. He had only ever seen a few people let out that kind of rage before. Iowyn hadn't struck him as the type to harbor such emotions, and Ulric was starting to believe that he had just seen a glimpse of something else. Something that Iowyn did her best to hide.

"Can you get something for me?" Iowyn asked, still sitting on the examination table.

"Whatever you need," Ulric replied, hating how desperate he sounded.

She touched her cheekbone and winced. "I need you to find some makeup for me."

"Makeup?"

"Just, find a store, ask for the lightest shade of powder they have. I'll pay you back."

"No need," Ulric was already halfway out the door.

The doctor came back into the room, running a hand through his salt and pepper hair. His dark eyes shot back towards the door, as if he expected Ulric to return at any moment. He looked kind, and by the look of his examination room, he was a doctor that practiced because of his want to help people, and not for the money. The legs of the examination table Iowyn sat on were beginning to rust. The tools in his bag looked old but functional. Even the paint on his front window that read "Doctor Jareth

Culpepper" was chipping away. Iowyn made a note to pay the doctor much more than whatever he would end up charging her for her bandage and the medicine he'd already given to Ulric.

Dr. Culpepper wrung his hands together before speaking. "I know that you don't know me Miss, but–"

Iowyn could guess his next words before he even said them. "Doctor, please. It wasn't him. It was a sailor."

He pursed his lips together. "I may be old, young lady, but I'm not a fool."

Iowyn blinked at the man, then shook her head "It wasn't him."

He crossed his arms. "This isn't your first time."

Iowyn's heart hardened into a heavy stone that sunk in her chest. She swallowed. "How–"

"Your partner came in all frazzled, absolutely beside himself, but you?" Dr. Culpepper shook his head solemnly. "You were rather put together for someone just beaten."

He came to Iowyn's side and leaned back against the rickety examination table with a sigh. "You orbital and zygomatic bones have broken before. I felt it when I examined the bruising under your eye. They never healed quite right because you never saw a doctor for them."

Iowyn looked down at her hands. No one had ever guessed it before, but she figured if anyone would, it would be a physician. She didn't quite know what to say. There was no denying the truth, and what good would it do? "I understand your concern. But the man that did that to me is gone. I left him a long time ago."

Culpepper's dark eyes studied her, stopping at the bruise right below her left eye. "Tell me that you feel safe with your partner, and I'll let you go."

Had she perhaps been asked that question a few days ago, she would have said no. But the look of fury in Ulric's eyes as he pulled her attacker off of her flashed in her mind.

"Yes," she said simply, meeting the doctor's gaze. "I do."

They had less than a day's ride to Calluna. Iowyn only hoped that she wouldn't look like she'd just been through the Pit when her parents saw her. Her pale skin always had an affinity for bruising easily. She looked into the compact that Ulric had bought for her and used the small sponge to apply the powder below her left eye.

Iowyn abhorred makeup. Not because of some twisted ideal for natural beauty, but because it reminded her of a worse time in her life. She'd turned the page on that darker chapter, and had vowed she would never have to cover up a bruised face again. She supposed she never thought about the fact that working in the field could lead to such injuries.

Ulric had been silent since leaving the doctor and heading out on the road. He rode ahead of her by about thirty feet, and she kept catching him looking back at her to make sure that she was okay. She could tell by the look in his eyes every time he looked at her that he felt responsible for what had happened in that cabin.

All she really knew was that whatever she had done to piss Ydall, the goddess of good luck, it must have been bad. Or maybe she had done something good for her? Considering she had gotten away from two attacks in the span of a few days.

Ulric looked back at her again, and part of her really just wanted them to go back to how things were before the ship. Being a pain in each other's asses. Iowyn spurred Dren forward until he was in step beside Shadowfoot.

Ulric looked her over, and Iowyn rolled her eyes at the worry on his face. "I'm fine, Ornthalas."

He didn't say anything. Just continued to look at her.

"Are you even going to ask me any questions?"

His brows knitted together. "Questions?"

"About Calluna? I'm a wealth of information about it, you know. One of the perks of growing up there."

Ulric frowned. "Beastie, I don't know if–"

"Ask me a fucking question, Ornthalas." she snapped. Iowyn wanted desperately to talk about anything that could get her mind off of what had just happened. Anything at all. "Please," she added quietly.

He sighed and ran a hand through his curls. "Fine. What's the terrain like?"

Iowyn snorted. Actually snorted. At any other time, she would have been embarrassed by the sound, but right now, she would take anything over silence and being alone in her head. "What's the terrain like? Seriously?"

Iowyn had yet to get a hand on how Ulric's mind worked. He could have asked her anything, and Ulric was worried about geography.

Ulric's lips set in a firm line. "It's good information to have."

"I guess, but it wasn't what I thought your first question would be. Though I do suppose I should have expected something like it. You're as serious as death sometimes." She pondered his question, thinking of her hometown and all the places she ran around growing up.

"The town itself is pretty flat. Dirt roads mostly, except the main road through town is cobblestone – but I guess maybe more of the roads could be paved by now. Small farms all around. There's a large lake to the north, and a river that flows southward from it. The farmers use it to fill their irrigation channels to water their crops. Once you get past the plain that everyone lives on, then you get into more forests and highlands. If you go farther west from town, there's a lot more meadows and rolling hills in the sparsest trees until you hit the coast."

Iowyn had spent hours out in the trees with her parents. They took her on picnics all the time when she was younger, and she had always tried to climb the tallest tree she could find. The kids in town would go out to the river to play after school, especially in the warmer months. They'd either find a shallow part to wade into up to their ankles and splash around, or toss sticks off the stone bridge and see whose stick would come out first on the other side. The meadows were the best place to find wildflowers and fresh wild berries to pick in the spring, and the hills were perfect for sledding in the winter.

Iowyn's heart panged at the childhood memories flooding in. Odd for her to feel so homesick when she was so close to being back.

Ulric asked another question. "Any history of specific creatures in the area?"

"No, actually," Iowyn replied. "Now that you mention it, I can't remember a time that we had any malevolent creatures in the area. Not when I was a kid at least. And no parents ever told us about any from recent memory either. All of our warnings were rather general. In fact, Dren caused quite a commotion when he showed up. No one knew what he was or what he'd do."

"Except you," Ulric guessed.

She smirked. "Being a *worm* is good for some things. There was a drawing of a deupin in some encyclopedia of creatures my dad got me for my birthday one year. I had to show it to the town magistrate to get him to let me keep him."

Ulric was quiet again, and he broke his stare on Iowyn to look ahead at the road. He seemed hesitant asking, "And you're happy to be going back?"

Her brow creased in confusion. "Why wouldn't I be?"

"You didn't seem too happy about the prospect of going back when you heard the news."

"How so?"

Ulric scoffed. "I told you that we would be traveling to Calluna, and you just stood there. A statue would have been more emotional."

Iowyn waved a hand dismissively. "I was in shock, that's all."

Ulric stared at her. Iowyn expected his emerald eyes to be hardened like they usually were, but when she turned to meet his gaze, she noted how soft they seemed. "It's alright if you don't want to go home."

"Why would you think I don't want to go home?"

"Because if you did, you would have started babbling my ear off about the place well before this."

Iowyn's eyes narrowed at Ulric. "Knowing me? You don't know shit about me, Ornthalas."

"Don't change the subject, Beastie. And don't lie to me either. We both know you weren't happy about getting this assignment." She hated how soft his voice was. Like he was afraid to be too harsh with her.

Iowyn sneered at him. "Maybe I just wasn't happy to be stuck on assignment with you again."

"Don't deflect."

Iowyn turned in her saddle and put a finger in Ulric's face. "Stop telling me what to do and how to feel! Gods, you're such a fucking asshole sometimes!"

Ulric tried to grab her wrist, but Iowyn flinched away from him before he could make contact. He pulled back. "You're the one making this into a problem, Beastie. Not me. If you'd just tell me why—"

"Why do I need to tell you anything?" She gripped Dren's reins tighter. "You certainly don't do the same for me."

Ulric muttered something, but it wasn't in the common tongue.

"What?"

Ulric shook his head. "Nothing."

Iowyn groaned. "See? *That* is exactly what I'm talking about. I can't fucking trust you to even tell me what the fuck you just mumbled under your breath!"

Ulric ran a hand over his face. "Fine! What will get you to trust me then?"

"How about answering harmless questions. Let me know more about you at least."

"Harmless questions?"

"Yes, like – I don't know – what's your middle name?"

Ulric arched his brow. "My middle name?"

"Yes! Me knowing that information is absolutely harmless, isn't it?"

Ulric paused for a moment. "And if I answer these harmless questions?"

Iowyn crossed her arms. "If you do, then I'll get off your back. For a while, at least."

He rolled his eyes and his head with it. "Fine, whatever gets you off my case. Now will you tell me why you're not happy to go home?"

Iowyn might have just gotten something that she wanted, but the fury that had been building inside of her finally exploded. "I feel guilty, okay? I haven't been home in six fucking years when I had more than enough chances to, and it's been so long since I've written my parents that they probably think I'm dead. Happy?"

Ulric sat silent in the saddle, his emerald eyes boring into her. But his face betrayed nothing. She waited for him to speak, but like so many times before, he said nothing.

Iowyn let out a growl of frustration. "Oh, and I guess now you have nothing to say? Fuck. You."

She didn't give him any chance to reply before galloping off and away from Ulric.

9

Once Iowyn had cooled off, Ulric had made sure that she took the rest of the medicine that the doctor had given him. Her face scrunched at the taste.

"Odea, spare me, that tastes like grass."

Ulric hid a smirk at her distaste.

Things were quiet between them, and he'd figured it would stay that way, but then Iowyn decidedly broke the silence.

"So? What is it?" Iowyn asked.

Ulric cocked a brow as he looked in her direction. "What is what?"

Iowyn rolled her eyes. "Your middle name, Ornthalas."

Ulric blinked at her. "That's really going to help you trust me?"

Iowyn scowled, and before she could even start to yell at him, he lifted his hands in defense.

"Okay, fine. If that's what you want to know."

"It is."

Ulric looked at her warily. He supposed that there was no harm in her knowing, and that had been the whole point, hadn't it? He would answer harmless questions, and she would be more reasonable, he supposed. Ulric paused for a moment, then answered. "Gedeon."

Iowyn waited a bit before continuing. "Ahem, now you're supposed to ask me mine."

"I am?" That hadn't been a part of their heated discussion.

Iowyn laughed and shook her head. "My gods, have you ever tried to get to know someone before?"

Ulric frowned, but asked, "What's your middle name?"

Iowyn smiled with a bit of triumphant air. "Yrsa."

"Yrsa? Like a bear?"

She shrugged. "Don't ask me, I didn't pick it."

The comment made him think of the people who probably did pick it for her, her family, which led him to ask another question without thinking. "How much family do you have in Calluna?"

Iowyn was quick to answer. "Just my dads and me."

Ulric's eyebrows raised. "Dads? As in, two fathers?"

Iowyn blanched. Her amber eyes widened, and she went rigid in her saddle. Her hand tightened on the reins. "Uh," she paused, as if she was wondering to herself whether to deny it or not, "yes." A slight blush tinged her pale cheeks with her admittance.

Ulric blinked at her. "Two dads?" he asked again. "And they're…" He trailed off, unable to figure out a way to ask his next question.

"Together? Yes," she affirmed.

"Interesting," Ulric mused.

Same gender couples weren't totally uncommon in Phyrra, but there were definitely some duchies that were much more tolerant of modern love than others. The traditionalists in places like Vrig, Holith, and Oqira were known to run such couples out of their borders. They held onto the old ways. Ulric had never seen a problem with people loving who they loved, regardless of gender. What really was unusual was them having and raising children.

"So, how do you play into it then?"

Iowyn looked puzzled by his question.

"I mean, how exactly did you come to be in their care?" he asked.

Iowyn rested a hand on her hip. "A stork dropped me on their doorstep."

Ulric scoffed, half-amused. "I'm sure it did."

She laughed at the displeasure in his tone. "Why do you care?"

He shrugged. "I don't. But not many people like your parents *are* in fact parents."

Iowyn bit her bottom lip and gave Ulric a sideways glance, looking him up and down cautiously.

Ulric half-frowned at her. "I've made sure you haven't died on multiple occasions now. I think you can trust me just a little bit, Beastie."

Iowyn sighed and went quiet. Minutes passed in silence. Ulric wouldn't press her about it. If she didn't want to say, then that was fine with him. He'd at least show her the same courtesy that he wished she would give him most times. Maybe this was a way of building some kind of mutual rapport with each other. He was content to sit in the silence, but then she answered.

"They found me on the road traveling alone. I was barely old enough to walk, let alone speak. They took me to the nearest town and waited for somebody – anybody – to come looking for me…" Her amber gaze went distant for a split second before snapping back to the present. "But nobody did. And they had always wanted to have a little family, so they took me in. Gave me a home. Gave me my name. Iowyn means *little wanderer*."

Ulric smirked. "Should have named you something that meant 'big mouth' or 'sarcastic pain.'"

She narrowed her eyes. "Ha, ha, very funny."

"I sure thought so." He was just about to give her a full smile when Dren let out a sharp howl and broke off into a run.

Wind whipped past Iowyn's face as she tried her best to wrangle Dren into submission and get him to slow down. The last thing she wanted was to hurt herself by falling from his saddle. He bounded over the hills and through the trees without any regard for the countless commands she yelled out at him. There was only one thing that made Dren go crazy and not listen to a thing Iowyn said.

Carrot cake.

He must have gotten a whiff as soon as they neared the top of the hill. The smell meant one thing. They were very close to home.

It was no use to try and get him to listen to her if she was right. So, she hunkered down in her seat and wrapped her arms around his neck. Dren was running like he was unburdened, like Iowyn wasn't sitting atop his back. Each stride was wild, unbalanced, and threatened to throw her off.

The beating of hooves thundered behind them, and soon enough, Ulric was riding next to them. "What's wrong with him?" he yelled across the gap between them.

"Carrot cake!" Iowyn yelled back.

Ulric looked at her like she was crazy. "What?"

Iowyn lifted her head to look at the horizon. "Look!" she pointed toward the far away shapes that made up the town that she knew all too well. She could make out the thatched roofs of the houses closest to the edge of town. The large stone steeple of the chapel rose above the other building, the brass bell glinting in the sunlight.

Ulric looked ahead, seeing the town himself. He held out an arm for her to grab.

Iowyn risked her balance on Dren's back to swat it away. "I'm fine!"

With Dren's every stride, Calluna grew closer. They would be there any minute. She could hold on until then. Part of her wanted to prove to Ulric that she didn't need to be coddled, and she really didn't want to give him the satisfaction of saving her, *again.*

Dren lifted his nose up and sniffed the air, as if to double check that his senses were leading him in the right direction. Iowyn wasn't sure she had ever experienced him running so fast in all the years she'd been riding with him. It was amazing and terrifying all at the same time. The deupin easily started to pull away from Ulric and Shadowfoot, and left them behind in his trail of dust. Iowyn held on tighter, fisting both the reins and the hair of Dren's mane in her hands, and she rested the side of her face against his neck. Dren veered off the road as soon as they passed over the stone bridge that stretched across the river, and Iowyn knew without a shadow of a doubt in her mind exactly where her crazed beast was taking her.

Dren slowed as they approached the back of a large building with red cedar siding on the edge of town. He finally stopped as they came to an old hitching post. Iowyn felt as though she was breathing just as hard as the deupin, although hers was definitely more from fear than exertion. She dismounted slowly, her legs shaking slightly, and tied his reins to the post.

Dren padded happily in place, and looked around expectantly.

She gave him a stern look. "I'm not sure you've been a good enough boy to even *deserve* carrot cake."

Dren tilted his head. He obviously didn't understand why she was cross with him.

Iowyn sighed, and gave him a light pat as she looked at the building that she and her parents called home. Now her own senses could smell the fragrant aroma of carrot cake that had driven Dren bonkers. She paused and closed her eyes, drinking in the smell of the spiced confection.

A steady stream of smoke rose from the chimney on the west side of the shingled roof. A tall oak tree – one that Iowyn had climbed since she was a little girl – stood proudly just a few feet from the back door of the bakery. Its tallest branches now soared well above roof. Iowyn came around to the front of the large building. The bakery window was empty, and the lights were off. A closed sign hung on the inside of the glass door. But next door, she could see the bookshop's front door was wide open to invite customers in. Muffled male voices filtered out from the door, the timbres of them all too familiar.

Iowyn took a deep breath and walked up the steps slowly. Would they be excited to see her? Or would they be angry with her? Would she even be welcomed in? She shook the questions away. She was here, and she would see them. Nothing would stop her.

Iowyn stopped in the doorway. No one was at the front counter to greet her. She looked down at her clothes and immediately thought that she should have worn something nicer than her normal blouse and leather pants.

The voices were moving through the bookshelves. They were close enough now that she could hear the conversation clearly.

The plummy voice sounded first. "I don't know why you insisted on making one if you aren't going to sell it, Bear. We certainly won't eat it all ourselves."

A much deeper, sonorous voice answered. "Fine then, if you don't want any, then I'll sell it."

"I didn't say that! I just don't want any to go to waste."

"Aha! So you do want some then!"

"Of course I want some! That cake is probably one of the best things you make."

"Aw, Burkey, that's very sweet of you."

A thin man wearing a white button-up shirt with a smart, satin paisley vest over top rounded the corner with a tall stack of books in his hands, followed by a much larger, imposing man in an off-white linen ensemble.

Burke froze at the sight of his daughter in the shop doorway, and dropped the pile of books he was carrying. His eyes went wide behind his rounded spectacles as he took in a shaky breath. "Wynnie?" he choked, and Bearen placed a hand on Burke's shoulder to steady him.

"Hi Dad," Iowyn replied sheepishly, still standing in the doorway.

This was it. The moment she would find out whether or not they hated her, and if she even had a home to come home to.

Bearen – it seemed – couldn't help himself. He walked towards her, his long strides eating up the distance. His large arms enveloped Iowyn and lifted her off the ground with ease. "Hi Pa," she said into his shoulder, hugging him back.

With having two fathers, it had always been easier to differentiate between the two by having two distinct titles for each of them. They had once discussed having her just call them by their names, but both found it silly. Bearen settled on being called Pa, due to the fact that he was older than Burke, and it seemed to fit his larger demeanor better. Iowyn did sometimes call them by their nicknames for each other though, Bear and Burkey. They would never be a traditional family in the slightest, so Bearen and Burke just went with whatever felt right when it had come to raising the little girl that had stumbled into their lives.

"Pa, I can't breathe." Iowyn giggled, even though her ribs were straining against the pressure, causing her the slightest bit of pain.

Bearen set her down immediately, clearing his throat. "Sorry, sorry!"

He was pushed to the side by Burke, who took his turn to hug his daughter, albeit much daintier than Bearen had. "We missed you so much," he said into her raven hair.

"I missed you too."

Burke pulled back, holding Iowyn's shoulders at arm's length. "Why didn't you tell us you were coming home?"

She gave a blushing grin. "To be fair, I didn't know until I was leaving. And I'm not really allowed to send falcons to people outside the Guild."

Burke shook his head in disbelief. "What are you doing here? Did you get kicked out of the Guild? You did, didn't you?" He turned to Bearen. "I knew something like this would happen, but you—"

"Dad!" Iowyn interrupted Burke's ramblings. "I didn't get kicked out. I'm here for an assignment."

"Assignment?" Bearen asked gruffly. He and Bruke shared a knowing sideways glance at each other.

Iowyn crossed her arms. In her best imitation of her fathers she said, *"Congrats, Iowyn. We're so proud! We always knew you'd do great things."*

Burke huffed, waving his hands dismissively. "Of course we're proud! You're our daughter after all." He turned to Bearen again. "She gets her smart-assery from *you,* you know."

A deep cough sounded from the front door of the bookshop, and both Burke and Bearen's heads snapped to whoever had made the sound behind her. Iowyn looked over her shoulder.

"Oh," Iowyn blinked at Ulric's sudden presence, taking in his windswept curls and the unamused look on his face – or maybe that was just how his face always looked? To be honest, he always looked somewhat cross to her. She guessed that it was only polite to introduce him to her fathers. "Um, Pa, Dad, this is Ulric Ornthalas," she paused, "my partner."

Bearen walked past his daughter and up to Ulric. He was used to towering over everyone – the man was close to seven feet tall on a good day – but Ulric was just about the same height as him, if not a tad shorter. He looked Ulric up and down, assessing the hunter in front of him. If Ulric was intimidated in the slightest, then he gave nothing away. He simply waited for Bearen to say something first.

Burke rolled his eyes at the show of male dominance. "My gods, it's like the battle of the stone walls."

Iowyn stifled a giggle. So this was what it was like when two strong silent types met face to face. She knew exactly what Bearen was doing. Sizing up the man that was traveling with his daughter, trying to figure him out.

She figured it would be best to cut this meeting a little short. She walked over to her father's side and wrapped her arms around his large forearm, like she'd done since she was a toddler. "Down, Pa. He's just a… colleague." It was the best thing she could offer up to summarize what she and Ulric were to each other, and it was all she could come up with in the moment to get Bearen to back down.

"Will your *colleague* be staying with us?" Bearen asked.

Iowyn almost laughed at the insinuation behind Bearen's words.

Ulric held up a hand. "There's no need for that, sir. I can stay at the inn in town. I was just making sure she made it to you safely."

Bearen gave a curt nod. It was most likely the only approval Ulric would get from him at this time. Bearen looked down at Iowyn, and she gave him a small smile. Bearen started to return it, but his smile dropped and his eyes widened.

"What–" Iowyn started, but her words were cut off by Bearen lightly grabbing her chin and angling her head into the light. His finger touched her cheekbone, and Iowyn winced.

Bearen's head whipped to Ulric, and one of his large hands fisted in the front of Ulric's tunic. Bearen's words came out low and deadly. "Did you fucking touch her?"

"Pa! No!" Iowyn shouted, ducking under his arm and placing herself in between the two men.

Bearen's brown eyes, now ablaze with dangerous intent, didn't leave Ulric's face. To Ulric's credit, he didn't balk.

"Pa! Look. At. Me," Iowyn ordered, her voice as stern as she could make it. She was one of the only people in Phyrra who could get away with talking to the bear of a man in front of her that way.

His brown eyes locked with hers. His chest heaved with every breath, like the anger inside of him was threatening to boil over to the surface.

"He didn't do it. He *stopped* it. Let. Him. Go."

Bearen did, but he also made sure to give Ulric the slightest push backward as he released him. Iowyn took her father's large arm again and walked him back and away from Ulric.

Ulric backed away towards the door. Not a terrible idea, Iowyn thought, considering that Bearen could very well pounce on him as soon as he turned his back. "I'll find you tomorrow," was all Ulric said before leaving.

Burke came up and slapped Bearen on the arm. "You menacing brute! You can't be like that to strangers!"

Bearen didn't even bat an eye at the slap, just crossed his arms. "Look at her face and tell me that I can't be like that."

Burke's hazel eyes studied his daughter's face for himself, pushing his glasses up the bridge of his hawk-like nose. He took her chin in his hand and angled her head into the light the same way that Bearen had. "Oh, Wynnie," he breathed. "What happened?"

Iowyn sighed. "It was nothing."

She really didn't want to tell them. It would just worry Burke to no end and turn him into a complete mother hen. And Bearen would go to Arkra himself to find the ship and kill the whole crew, gods-willing. Lying to her fathers was terrible, yes. But it was also sometimes necessary. She had promised them that she would be safe when she left.

"*Iowyn*," Bearen warned.

"Really!" Iowyn gave a small laugh. "You should see the other guy."

Especially after I kicked the living shit out of him, she thought.

Burke and Bearen exchanged a sidelong glance.

"It was just a tiny misunderstanding," she lied. She'd gotten quite good at telling a better version of the truth to her fathers as a teenager. She always admitted that something happened, but the details – well she would make things seem a lot better than reality had played out. The words came out effortlessly as the story manifested in her mind. "Ulric and I were finishing up some questioning in a tavern. The guy was drunk, and mad at his friend. He swung, his friend ducked, and I was the next closest person."

Another sidelong glance.

"Ulric took care of it, and I'm okay. Honestly," she looked at Bearen, "I think you'd be rather happy with how he left things. Can we go upstairs now?" she asked.

Burke looked to Bearen, who gave another short nod. Burke took Iowyn's arm and began leading her to the back of the shop, where a hidden hallway between the bakery and bookshop held the stairs that led up to their home above. Burke could hardly stop himself from changing the subject and babbling about all the things she missed while away.

"Since you've been gone, the blacksmith's son, young Henry, has taken up the hammer and forge. And remember old Dame Eleanor, the herbalist? She's passed on her wisdom to her granddaughter, Eliza. The old shop burned down after a stray ember got caught in the rafters, but they rebuilt a new one in its place …" He continued with recounting all the changes and local gossip, until they came to the green door at the top of the stairs.

Their home was just the same as the day she left. A large central room that was half kitchen and half sitting room with two doors that led to each bedroom on either side. It was small, but cozy, and to Iowyn, it was the best sight after a long journey on the road.

"We didn't touch your room," Bearen said.

"It's just how you left it," Burke added.

Iowyn turned to them, and all of a sudden, she was hit with immense guilt all over again. It was like a boulder sat on her chest when she looked at them, so happy to have her back home. Tears welled in her eyes.

"Oh dear," Burke spluttered. "What's wrong?"

"Dad, Pa," she sobbed. "I'm so sorry."

Bearen and Burke looked puzzled at their daughter's sudden apology. "Whatever for?" Burke asked.

"I didn't write. I didn't come home at all, for *years*." The tears spilled over her cheeks, and her nose went fuzzy. "I should have at least written to you. Let you know that I was okay. But I didn't. I *couldn't*. I felt like there was nothing to write about, and I didn't want to disappoint you. I-"

Her sobs were cut off by Bearen wrapping his arms around her again. She stopped apologizing, and just sunk deeper into Bearen's embrace. Six years' worth of missing them and missing home came out all at once.

"You could never disappoint us, Wynnie," Burked whispered softly, rubbing her back. "And while you writing to us would have been nice, you're also an adult, living your own life."

"The Guild never sent us a falcon saying that you were hurt or in trouble, so we never worried." Bearen said. "Well, *I* never worried."

Burke gave him a light slap on the arm.

Iowyn sniffled, the tears slowly waning.

Burke smiled, "We still love you, Wynnie, all the same."

Bearen let go of her, and went over to the oven in the kitchen. "On that note, how about some carrot cake?"

Iowyn smiled and wiped her nose with the back of her sleeve. "As long as Dren gets a piece."

"Oh my goodness!" Burke exclaimed. "Dren! I almost forgot about the furry beast! Where is he?"

"The hitching post," she replied, pointing to the window that overlooked behind the building.

"Oh, gods no," Burke breathed, rushing to the window.

Iowyn was quite confused by the look of horror on his face as she followed him to the window. The old hitching post must have rotted a bit since she had last been home because Dren had broken free, the post still tied to his reins, but dragged alongside him. He was in the middle of Burke's vegetable garden, eating anything and everything that was ripe enough.

Burke gasped and opened the window, shaking his fist at the deupin. "Bad, Dren! Get out of there!"

Dren looked up to the window, and brayed. Apparently, he had grown impatient waiting for his cake.

CHAPTER

11

After dinner and dessert, Iowyn retired to her room. Her
fathers had been telling the truth when they said that they hadn't
touched her room since she left. Clothes that she hadn't even
thought about for years still hung in the closet. Pieces of paper with
various notes on creatures were strewn about the top of her small
writing desk, like she had just written them yesterday.

Blake Ophedian's first book, *The Realm of Enchantment: A Guide
to Magical Creatures*, was open to a chapter all about chimera. The
entire volume was a firsthand account of all the creatures Ophedian
had faced in his first assignments with the Guild as a field
monstralogist over thirty years ago. He was the first scriven to ever
get out of the Guild archives and be allowed to work alongside a
hunter in the field. Together with the hunter Ird Smildenn, they
traversed the duchies and set right the wrongs made by magical
creatures. He had been Iowyn's hero and inspiration for becoming
a monstralogist in the first place.

Iowyn secretly wondered what her life would have been like
had Bearen not gotten her the book for her fifth birthday. She
supposed that she might have a job in town, and maybe even be
married. The thought sent a swift shiver up her spine. It seemed so
wrong – so incompatible with everything that she had ever wanted
for herself. Of course, she wanted to find love like everyone else in
the world. But there were times that she felt like she was too young
to settle down at the age of twenty-three.

Iowyn picked up the worn copy of Blake Ophedian's book and
thumbed through a few pages, remembering how Bearen would

read it to her at night, much to Burke's dismay. She could hear them arguing about it in her head like it was yesterday.

"She's a little girl!" Burke protested. "She should be reading about fairy tales and princesses in far off lands, not deadly adventures where people get torn apart by gods-only know what."

Bearen rolled his eyes as he handed the book to her. "The only parts she actually likes about those silly books are the unicorns and dragons." Iowyn began to flip through the pages, marveling at all the watercolor illustrations done by Blake Ophedian himself. "Besides," Bearen continued, "it won't hurt her to know what's out there."

"She's **five***, Bear. Five! She doesn't need to know any of this stuff yet."*

Iowyn stopped on a full spread illustration of a lake, a large snake-like head poked out from the water, and several humps with spiky scales jutted out from the water behind it. Her finger traced over the letters in the bottom corner. She sounded out the word, "S-ser-ser-pent." Iowyn looked up at Burke with a hopeful smile.

Burke let out a heavy sigh, but smiled back down at his daughter. "That's right, Wynnie. Serpent."

Iowyn smiled at the small memory.

Stacks of other books on creatures took up space on the floor, and more were tucked away on the haphazardly stacked shelves against the wall. Many of the books and volumes that she had accumulated over the years had been gifts from Bearen and Burke for her birthday or Yule. A good number had been bought through her own labor. Iowyn would find a book that she wanted, then negotiate with Burke as to how many days or hours she'd need to work to have earned it. "At this rate, you'll be able to open your own archive," Burke had joked.

Across the walls not burdened with bookshelves, Iowyn had covered up any blank space with her own depictions of creatures.

Doodles from when she could barely hold a pencil butted up against the sketches of her later years.

Her eyes settled on the small bed in the far corner of the room, and a knowing smile spread across her face. The day she left for University in Petra, Iowyn had been so focused on not forgetting anything, that she in turn had forgotten one of the most important things to her. By the time she had realized, Iowyn was already more than halfway to the capital of Rathian, and she couldn't bring herself to ask Bearen or Burke to send it in the mail for fear of it getting lost in the post.

She knelt beside the bed and lifted the mattress. In the center of the bed frame, there lie a thick leather-bound journal. Iowyn's fingers skimmed over the cool black leather of the cover as she picked it up and set the mattress back onto its frame. Sitting on the floor, she opened up the front cover. The untidy but familiar scrawl of her younger self greeted her on the first page.

Property of Iowyn Yrsa Morgnah
If lost, please return by seeking falcon.

She had been eight years old when Burke had gone off on a business trip and brought her back the monstrous journal. He thought it a fitting gift, considering that she had been using up almost every loose sheet of paper and parchment that she could find in the house and shops to take down notes or draw. Even back then, Iowyn had been confident that she would be a field monstralogist in the Guild.

She had wanted to become a monstralogist ever since she discovered the definition of the word when Bearen started reading her the tales of Blake Ophedian and Ird Smildenn slaying evil creatures and meeting benevolent ones along the way. Iowyn wasn't so much into the slaying of the creatures, as she was into the mysticality of them. The fact that dragons and unicorns were actually real, and that she could have the chance to see them? It was enough to make any child dream.

Iowyn flipped through the pages. A lifetime's worth of compiled notes and drawings of various creatures copied from other texts flickered past her eyes. A soft smile tugged at her mouth. She would have so much more to add now.

Ulric sat at the bar, twirling an empty glass across the wood. This was the first night he'd been rid of Iowyn since getting the werewolf assignment. He felt both relieved and utterly disquieted at the thought. She was home, and safe, he told himself. She'd be spending the night with her fathers, and hopefully not galavanting around town with a creature possibly on the loose. He had no reason to worry about her dying tonight.

The barkeep waltzed up to where Ulric was sitting, threw a towel on the bar, and placed a glass of an amber liquor in front of Ulric.

"On the house," he said. "You look like you could use it."

Ulric lifted the glass and downed it. The familiar burn of alcohol was a welcomed distraction. He knew he was going to have to simply trust Iowyn to not do anything stupid for one night while out of his sight. But what could he say? She seemed to have a knack for finding trouble.

Ulric let out a breath. "Thanks."

The barkeep started wiping down the top of the bar. "What are you in town for?"

Ulric looked the barkeep up and down with a furrowed brow and frown on his face. He was used to people questioning his presence when he came into town. He was always an outsider wherever he went.

The barkeep slightly rolled his eyes. "Look, in a small town like this, I know just about everyone. You're an unfamiliar face is all."

Ulric thought it over in his mind. This barkeep could be useful for information, better to make friends with him now so he'd be more likely to help out later.

"Work," Ulric replied. It wasn't a lie, but best to be vague until he knew just what he was dealing with in town.

The barkeep chuckled. "Fair enough. I'm Elmer, by the way." He brushed his dirty blond hair out of his eyes before holding out his hand for Ulric to shake. He was young. Probably no older than Iowyn was. Maybe they had grown up together.

He took the man's hand. "Ulric."

Elmer smiled. "Nice to meet you, Ulric. If you need anything, don't be afraid to ask."

The barkeep turned to walk away, but a question popped into Ulric's mind. "You said you know just about everyone in town?"

Elmer turned back to Ulric and shrugged. "Just about."

Ulric looked him up and down. "And what about those who've left town?"

The barkeep smiled and tapped a finger to his temple. "I've got a pretty good memory, if I do say so myself."

"What about an Iowyn Morgnah?" Ulric asked.

Elmer's eyes sparkled at the name. "Now that's a name I haven't heard in a while."

"You know her, then?"

Elmer shrugged. "About as well as you can know someone in a small town like this, I guess. But how do *you* know her?"

He thought about not answering for a second. "I'm working with her."

Another twinkle passed over Elmer's hazel eyes. "She's back in town?"

Ulric nodded, looking into his empty glass. "For the time being."

Elmer studied Ulric with a sly grin. "Is she why you're drinking so heavily this evening?"

Ulric blew out a breath. "She's just…" He struggled to find the right word because at the moment, there were a lot of words he would use to describe her.

Elmer smirked, grabbing a glass to wipe down, "A little spitfire? Yeah, pretty much."

"I was going to say something more along the lines of a pain in my ass. But I guess spitfire works."

Elmer chuckled to himself. "Oh, man. You don't know the half of it. One time in primary, Carter Cormick put her braid in his ink pot, and when she flung it over her shoulder, it splattered all over her homework and ruined the whole thing. He laughed and laughed, but she turned right around and punched him square in the nose for it. Nearly knocked him out, and gave him two black eyes that he had for almost a month. And that's just *one* instance where her temper got the better of her."

The corner of Ulric's mouth upturned slightly. "So, she's always been like this."

"Oh, yeah. Bearen made sure she could take care of herself if she needed to." Elmer poured Ulric another drink.

"Bearen. He's the bigger one of the two? The baker?"

Elmer nodded. "Not that you asked, but my advice? Let her do her own thing, she's much more agreeable that way."

Ulric almost laughed at the suggestion. Iowyn doing her own thing was part of the problem. But he would let Elmer think whatever he wanted. "I'll keep that in mind."

"So, what's it like?" Elmer asked, changing the subject. "Working for the Guild?"

"Who said I was in the Guild?" He'd barely been in town for a few hours, and hadn't even gone to the town magistrate to let him know that he was there from the Guild to help with their creature problem. How did this kid know?

Elmer looked Ulric up and down. "Well, no offense, but you look like a hunter. Not to mention, I know Iowyn left town to go to University in Petra, and it was always her dream to be like Blake Ophedian."

Ulric studied Elmer before answering. "You're pretty observant then." Not that Elmer really needed to be. From what Ulric knew, Calluna was a small town. He was sure there were times where a person couldn't take a shit without the whole town knowing about it the next day.

Elmer smiled. "So, what's it like?"

"It's," Ulric thought about it for a bit, "certainly never boring."

Working in the Guild meant he was constantly on the move, almost always in danger, and now with the addition of Iowyn as his partner, Ulric found that there was never really any time to fully relax.

"I bet you've been all around Phyrra," Elmer commented, a faint little twinkle returning to his eyes.

"Just about," Ulric answered. "But I don't get to do a whole lot of sightseeing."

Elmer looked down at the bar. "At least you've been somewhere though."

Ulric felt a twinge in his sternum at Elmer's words. He'd felt the same way once. Had left home for that exact reason, to see the rest of the continent and make some difference in the world. But whereas Ulric had made it out of Illeross, Elmer was still here in his hometown.

"I'm sure you'll get where you're going eventually," Ulric offered up. He downed his glass again and stood up from the bar.

"Thanks for the drink." He fished out a few coins from his pocket and placed them next to his empty glass.

"Anytime," Elmer replied, pasting on a smile.

Ulric paused before continuing. "I might be back to ask you some questions tomorrow, if that's alright with you?"

Elmer gave a friendly smile. "Sure thing. I'm here most times." He turned to continue wiping down the bar and tended to the other patrons.

Ulric went up the stairs to his room, the alcohol helping him find a peaceful slumber faster than normal.

Iowyn woke early to the familiar smell of bread and pastries wafting up from the bakery below. The scent was so nostalgic and wistful that she felt her eyes water.

Home. She was home.

Even if it was just for a little bit, until this assignment was over, she was back with her parents in the one place that she always felt she belonged.

As she stretched in bed to rid her body of any grogginess, her stomach growled. She got up and dressed for the day in her usual long sleeve blouse and pants, then made her way down the stairs into the bakery. Bearen was already at work, singing his working song, the words of which Iowyn knew by heart.

Iowyn skirted around the work table in the center of the bakery, which was primarily used for kneading and rolling out the various doughs for all the different recipes that Bearen kept stocked in the front shop. She knew both Bearen's bakery and Burke's bookshop like the back of her hand. She spent almost all of her time outside of school in one shop or the other helping out. It was never truly work to her since she enjoyed helping out her fathers in any way that she could. And it also didn't hurt that they paid Iowyn for her time, whether with books or with money. That money had been enough to support her while she was at University, and she hadn't forgotten that.

Bearen finally turned away from his work to notice his daughter. "Well good morning. Looking for a treat for breakfast, are we?"

Iowyn's stomach growled as if in reply.

Bearen chuckled. "I'll have some cinnamon rolls out of the oven in about ten minutes, or there's a batch of bagels and croissants in the front display you could snatch up."

"I'll wait for cinnamon rolls." She sat down on a nearby stool, watching Bearen work. It felt like a dream to be back in the bakery. The heat from the ovens warmed her to her bones, and the sweet scents of sugar and vanilla seemed to envelop her in a welcoming embrace. She could hardly believe that she had ever taken mornings like these for granted, and had denied herself the chance at one for years.

After eating a fresh out of the oven cinnamon roll, Iowyn went to the tiny shack that served as a stable for Dren and the family donkey Josephine. In her hands were two slices of carrot cake. Dren tried his best to take both pieces for himself, but Iowyn was able to distract him long enough with an extra radish to give the second piece to the old, graying donkey.

Dren padded in place, eager to get out and run, but Iowyn shook her head at the beast. "Not right now, Dren. I'll be back for a ride later. I promise." She gave both Dren and Josephine plenty of pats before departing to find Ulric.

The sleepy town was just waking up, and Iowyn passed several recognizable faces. They, however, didn't seem to recognize her. Had she really changed so much? She doubted it, but perhaps just not being around for so long had caused her to slip into obscurity in her own hometown.

"Iowyn?" a voice behind her asked.

The voice didn't sound all too familiar to her, so she turned slowly and ever aware of the dagger strapped to her belt. Her eyes met with deep blue ones from her past that she would have known anywhere.

He was older now, obviously, but somehow looked just the same as the day she left. His thick black hair was still in its short, quaffed style that he had always kept it in. The only thing that was different was the slight stubble on his chiseled jaw and the deepness of his voice.

"Maddox?"

He smiled, and the signature dimple on his right cheek made an appearance. It *was* him. That smile could only belong to Maddox Varkin. He was two years older than Iowyn, and she – along with every other girl with eyes in Calluna – had had the biggest crush on him growing up. His family was well off, his father the town's tailor. But none of that had ever mattered to Iowyn. Their connection had grown from a love of books.

The bookshop bell chimed as a new customer walked through the door. Iowyn crouched down below the front counter, looking for the pen she had dropped, stood up at the sound. At least, she would have, had her head cleared the countertop. Her head smacked into the wood, and she grabbed her head, simultaneously shouting, "Fuck!"

She stood to her full height, lightly massaging the back of her skull, when her eyes met those of Maddox Varkin.

Fan-fucking-tastic

She had just made a fool of herself in front of quite possibly the most attractive boy in town.

"You okay?" he asked, a slight grimace on his face, like he was almost embarrassed for her.

"I'm fine." Iowyn faked a smile. "What can I help you with?"

Maddox shifted on his feet, looking around the bookshop. "Is your dad around? He's usually the one that helps me."

Any levity in Iowyn's heart turned to lead. Did he not think that she was capable of helping him? Was it because she was a girl? Or because she was younger than him? Or did he simply just not want to talk to her?

Iowyn shook the thoughts away, continuing to plaster on her pleasant smile. "Dad's gone to Grusskarten for the week, it's just me here to help right now."

Maddox frowned. "Oh, alright."

"But I know just about everything about this place that he does, so maybe I can help you?" she offered.

Maddox looked Iowyn up and down. She could have sworn that she saw the faintest tinge of pink in his face, but there was simply no way it could be what she thought. Maddox Varkin had never given her the time of day. In fact, she couldn't even think of any time that he might have even spoken to her before today.

No, Maddox Varkin definitely wasn't blushing at her.

He stayed quiet and shifted his weight again. Iowyn drummed her fingers against the counter. "I can't help you if you don't tell me what it is you want, Maddox."

He shook his head. "Right, of course. Uh, your dad usually has some books picked out for me whenever I come around."

"Okay," Iowyn said, lengthening the two syllables. It was something to go off of, but not very helpful. "What kind of books?"

Maddox seemed scared to say it out loud. He shifted again on his feet, and cleared his throat. "Mysteries?"

Iowyn gave a slight smirk and came out from behind the counter. "Come with me."

Maddox followed her to the section of the bookshop where Burke kept the mystery novels. She pointed out a few books that she had loved reading herself. "Nathaniel Cipher has a couple series that are pretty good, and you can never go wrong with anything written by Octavia Thornfield."

Maddox's eyes roved the section. He looked unsure and a little overwhelmed at all the books to choose from. Iowyn pulled a book from the shelf. "Try this one, The Murders of the Midnight Phantom.*"*

He took the book from her, looking at it skeptically.

She rolled her eyes and turned the book around in his hand for him. "Read the back. If you don't like it, put it back." Iowyn left him among the shelves and made her way back to the front counter, a little miffed. She knew what she was talking about, but it seemed that Maddox hadn't thought that she was as knowledgeable as her dad. She was used to that, but it didn't mean that she wasn't growing tired of it. She wasn't a little girl anymore.

She was fourteen, and knew more than most people who came into the bookshop, thanks to her unlimited access to all the books inside its walls. Iowyn was almost to the point where she barely needed to even listen during class because she had already read books on the topics years ago. History was a breeze, and grammar was a no-brainer to her at this point. The only subject she ever struggled in was math, and that was simply because numbers made less sense to her than words on a page.

Iowyn found her pen next to the leg of her stool as soon as she came around to the backside of the counter. She picked it up, and was ready to get back to double-checking her figures in her father's ledger, when The Murders of the Midnight Phantom *was plopped onto the counter.*

"I'll take it," Maddox said.

Iowyn was a little surprised to say the least. "Ten copper," she said.

Maddox fished into his pocket and placed a silver on the counter. Iowyn picked it up and went to the coin drawer behind her. She counted out the fifteen copper in change and put it into one of the burlap bags that Burke kept for large amounts of change. She handed it over to him and almost dropped the bag when his hand touched hers.

He didn't miss a beat and put the small pouch into his pants pocket. She expected him to take his book and walk out the door, but he lingered for a bit.

Iowyn swallowed lightly. "Do you need something else?"

"You've read this, right?" he asked.

Her brow furrowed slightly. "Yeah?"

Maddox nodded to himself, grabbing the book off the counter. "Maybe, when I'm finished with it, we could talk about it?"

The question took her by surprise. Maddox Varkin wanted to discuss a book with her? She mentally slapped herself to pull herself together. She needed to be cool about this. "Uh, yeah. Sure, I don't see why not?"

Maddox smiled, a dimple appearing on his right cheek. "Cool. I'll see you around."

He left out the door, and Iowyn felt her heart explode.

Iowyn's heart skipped a beat as the flood of memories came rushing back all at once.

"You're back," Maddox said, his voice dreamy, almost like he didn't believe his own words.

She nodded and offered him a shy smile. "Got into town last night."

He took a step closer. "It's been what? Six years?"

Iowyn grimaced. Was he angry with her? She thought that they had left things on somewhat okay terms, but who knew after all this time what feelings he harbored for her. "Maddox, I—"

"I missed you," he interrupted.

Iowyn raised her brows, and her heart fluttered in her chest. She took in the rest of him. The navy uniform and the silver eight-pointed star pin on his collar jumped out at her. "Are you… are you the constable now?"

Maddox smirked, that dimple in his right cheek appeared, and his hand reached up to scratch the back of his neck. "Yeah, I – uh – have been for a while now."

Iowyn couldn't help but roll her eyes playfully. "Mystery novels weren't enough for you anymore?"

Maddox closed the gap between them, taking one of her hands. He looked around at the town around them, but they were the only ones around at that moment. "Look, there's so much I need to tell you. Can we go somewhere?"

Heat rose in Iowyn's cheeks at Maddox's closeness. She wanted nothing more than to go with him, but a nagging in her gut told her that she needed to do her job and find Ulric first.

"I can't right now," she said, and his face fell. "But I could tonight? You can come around to the bookshop. We can talk then?"

He lifted a hand and tucked a stray piece of her raven hair behind her ear. It was something so intimate for someone she hadn't seen for years to do, she thought.

"Okay, I'll come by tonight."

Iowyn waited for him to let go of her hand and walk away, but he lingered, staring into her eyes. Iowyn bit her lip and jutted a thumb over her shoulder. "I gotta go, Maddox."

He dropped her hand and took a step back. "Right, right. Of course, I… I'll see you?"

Iowyn let out the tiniest laugh. "Yeah, you'll see me."

Maddox backed away, still facing her – like he still didn't believe that she was truly real, and she would disappear entirely if he so much as blinked.

Iowyn laughed again and waved before turning around. "Bye, Maddox."

"Bye," was all that she heard back from him in a distant and wistful voice.

CHAPTER

13

The Itchy Badger was Calluna's only inn and tavern, and it was the largest building in town. For all intents and purposes, it was a hub of activity for the townspeople.

Iowyn knew the owners of the Itchy Badger. They were a large customer of Bearen's, always needing an extra surplus of bread and sweets when their own kitchens couldn't keep up. Abigail and Jackson Stoutsen were a lovely older couple who worked tirelessly to keep spirits high in town. They always found ways to be able to bring in entertainment to play on the Badger's stage, and constantly hosted themed nights at the tavern to give the townspeople a small reprieve from the drone of everyday life.

Iowyn entered through the front door of the large timber framed establishment. The large fireplace held a small fire, enough to warm the patrons of the tavern from the slight midspring chill of morning. She ambled past the multitude of chairs and tables to take a seat at the bar. Surprisingly, Jackson wasn't the one manning the bar, but a much younger fellow – probably her age – was.

"What can I get ya?" he asked, grinning widely.

"Just some tea would be fine," Iowyn replied.

"Tea?" he asked, like it was an absurd order.

"It's a little early for anything else, don't you think?"

The barkeep chuckled. "I guess you're right." He turned away and went to work preparing a cup of tea.

Jackson usually worked the bar from open to close. He said many times that working and seeing people all day kept him fresh and young. She could hardly believe he'd give it up so easily to a

102

young man like this one. "Since when isn't Jackson behind the bar?" Iowyn asked, genuinely curious.

"You know Jackson?" he asked.

"I grew up here, I used to know just about everyone," she admitted.

The man stole a glance at Iowyn from his shoulder. "Funny, you don't look familiar to me."

"Well, I've been gone for a while. Went to University."

The man stopped making the tea, and turned around with a quizzical look on his face. "Iowyn? Iowyn Morgnah?

For some reason, the man being able to guess her name was a little weird to her. She didn't recognize him, but then again, she was probably one of the only people in town to leave Calluna for University in recent years, so perhaps it wasn't too far-fetched that he'd know that. She still couldn't place him in her memory though, so she rested a hand next to her dagger on her belt, just in case. "Yes?"

He slapped a hand down on the bar, and Iowyn jumped at the sudden movement. "I heard you were back in town. I should have known from the dark hair and those eyes. These years have been good to you, haven't they?"

Iowyn looked the man over. He had dirty blond hair that fell into his hazel eyes. His tan skin was freckled under his eyes and across his nose. She hated when her mind knew that she should know something, but it was as if the information was on the other side of a tall brick wall with no door that she couldn't scale. She knew it was there, but she just couldn't see it.

"It's me! Elmer!" he exclaimed, still smiling and standing up a bit taller.

At the sound of his name, recognition clicked in her brain. "Elmer?" she questioned. Sure, this boy – or man she figured – was *similar* to the Elmer she knew. But Elmer Wadscott had always been a pale and skinny boy. The man that stood before her was anything but that. They had grown up and gone to school together, but he had always been rather sickly most of the time and absent from classes. She knew him more from partying out in the meadows as a teenager. It was hard for her to believe that the spindly and ghost white little boy had truly transformed into the tanned, built man in front of her. "No," she shook her head, "it can't be.

His smile widened even more. "Sure is." He waggled his eyebrows for good measure. It seemed he had also gained a silly amount of self-confidence.

Iowyn giggled. "Well then, I guess the years have been kind to you too."

Elmer went back to making her tea, but talked over his shoulder. "I have your dad to thank really. Burke, that is. He ordered a book for my mom without her even asking, and it had a few home remedies for most of my breathing problems. I take tonics twice a week, and can work out in the fields with my dad like I always wanted to."

So that explained the tan and the muscles. Iowyn couldn't help but let a soft smile spread across her face. Burke had always used his access to knowledge to help the people in town. He even helped the teachers at school when it came to reading and writing lessons. To know that he had some part in expanding Elmer's quality of life, it made her rather proud of her father.

"Now, don't leave me in suspense," Elmer paused, setting a fresh cup of tea in front of Iowyn and a small bowl of sugar, "tell me about you?"

Iowyn scoffed lightly, "What about me?" she asked, adding a few spoonfuls of sugar to her cup.

Elmer rolled his eyes. "Come on, Morgnah! You left town for Petra? Went to University? You've had to have *something* interesting happen to you along the way. At least more interesting than this place."

Iowyn smirked. "I don't really know what to tell you, Elmer. I spent a lot of time studying."

He shot her a look of skepticism.

Iowyn was only partly lying, she had done a lot of studying, but she had also gone out with her friend Loyla to the taverns and dancing clubs almost every weekend that she could. They'd gotten in plenty of trouble together, but Elmer didn't need to know about all that. "Really, Elmer, University isn't as wild as people make it seem."

"Oh, I think you're selling yourself short." He shot her a wink, and Iowyn felt the tiniest blush rise in her cheeks.

Was he flirting with her?

She didn't know what to say. Elmer looked her over again and blew out a breath. "You look good, Iowyn. Really good."

Her blush grew a bit. She couldn't believe that Elmer Wadscott of all people was making her blush. From what she remembered, she'd thought him to be just a little cute when they were growing up. But he had done some growing himself since she left. Dare she say it, he was pretty attractive. Almost as attractive as Maddox.

The silence between them was killing her slowly, so she decided to change the subject. "I'm in the Hunter's Guild now. Here on assignment."

Elmer's face dropped. "Fuck, that's right. You're here about the kids."

Iowyn was about to ask Elmer to expand on his comment, when Ulric came up to the bar, interrupting their conversation. "You didn't have to come after me, you know. I was going to go by your place."

Iowyn didn't even look at the grumpy hunter as she waved her hand dismissively at him. "I know my way around here just fine.

And I was already ready to go." She focused back on Elmer, trying to salvage whatever information he was about to give her before the interruption. "Pardon my colleague," she gave Elmer an apologetic smile, "he has terrible manners."

Elmer returned her smile and gave a sideways glance towards Ulric. "Yeah, we met last night."

"You were saying?" Iowyn prodded. "About the kids?"

Elmer's smile fell, and Iowyn almost felt bad for asking. He let out a breath that made his shoulders sink a bit. "Kids have been going missing every so often around town. They go out and play – like we used to at that age – and then they don't come back. The town's been doing searches, but no one has turned up."

"How long has this been going on?" Ulric asked.

Iowyn rolled her eyes. Of course he would take over her interrogation. Was that even the right word to use? Elmer was in no way a suspect, but he had information. Maybe inquiry was a better word for it? Whatever it was, it was typical of Ulric to think she couldn't do it herself.

"Since the spring thaw. Parents are trying to keep a better eye on their kids, but you know how kids are. They sneak off, thinking they know better."

"How many have gone missing?" Iowyn asked, and braced herself for the answer.

"Four."

Ulric swore under his breath.

Elmer continued, "But a lot of the mothers have taken their kids a few towns over to stay at the old monastery. They figured it would be safer there than to let their kids stay here." Elmer brushed the hair out of his face. "So the Guild thinks some creature is behind it? That's why you're here right?"

Ulric nodded. "Yes, but we'd like to keep a low profile until we know what we're dealing with."

Elmer swallowed. "Yeah, of course. I'll help anyway I can. If you want me to, I can ask around, discreetly of course."

She hadn't been close with Elmer when they were growing up, but she knew that he was personable and kind-hearted. Two things most people weren't these days.

Iowyn gave a kind smile. "That would be helpful."

Elmer gave them a few leads, mainly the parents of the kids who disappeared. Thankfully, enough hadn't changed in the past six years that Iowyn still knew where they all lived.

They had left Elmer at the Itchy Badger and were out on the main cobblestone road. Iowyn had been right, a few side streets were now paved with the same cobblestones. An uneasiness settled in her as she looked around the town that she had grown up in. It was weird to think how similar yet so different everything had become.

"Are you going to flirt with every man in town?" Ulric abruptly asked. He seemed oddly annoyed.

Iowyn blinked at him. "And you're referring to?"

"Elmer, and the dark-haired one on the street."

Her mouth dropped open. "Were you watching me?"

He scoffed. "I didn't need to. The blush on your cheeks was red enough that a blind man could see it."

Was he serious right now? Iowyn let out a huff of frustration. "If you must know, they're old friends. I haven't seen them in a while, and let's just say, they've grown up, and I noticed."

Ulric grunted in a way that it almost sounded like a short laugh.

"Why do you care if I flirt anyways?" she asked. It was none of his business what she did outside of the assignment. The fact that he was scolding her for doing something as innocent as talking to men other than him was absurd.

"I really don't, but we have a job to do, Beastie. Just make sure you remember that."

Her hands went to her hips. "Remember that four kids from my hometown are missing and probably dead? Thanks for reminding me," she sneered.

Ulric let out a long breath and looked up to the sky. "I don't have the patience for this today."

Typical. He started this whole fight and now it was her fault that he felt exasperated by it. "Then why don't you do yourself a favor and just stay out of my personal life, Ornthalas." She started walking in a different direction.

Before she could get more than a few steps away, Ulric grabbed her forearm and spun her around to face him. "Where do you think you're going?"

Iowyn rolled her eyes from sheer annoyance. "You said it yourself. You don't have the patience for me." Iowyn pulled away from his grasp, and took out a small notepad and pen that she'd stashed in her back pocket that morning. She drew a rough map of Calluna and circled where two of the four families lived, tore it out and shoved it into Ulric's chest. "I think it's best if we split up. You go do your thing, and I'll do mine." Iowyn turned back on her heels and went in the direction of where the Washburnes lived. She didn't wait to hear Ulric's protest before hollering over her shoulder, "We'll compare notes tonight."

CHAPTER

14

The sun sank low in the west by the time Ulric made his way back to the bookshop. Lantern light spilled through the shelves and book stacks to illuminate the otherwise darkened shop. The front door was left open, but Ulric still rapped his knuckles against the doorframe to announce his presence.

"Over here." Iowyn's voice sounded from the back corner of the shop. Ulric followed the sound, weaving his way through the labyrinth of bookshelves to find her seated at a large round table. Books and papers were splayed open in front of her, her long black hair tossed up into a messy bun and half-moon spectacles perched on her nose.

He was a little taken aback by her appearance. She looked so natural and simple, and yet she was altogether spectacular. He would have thought that the messy hair and the addition of spectacles would have detracted from her appearance, but it had the opposite effect. Something about them was just...

Ulric shook the thoughts away. No. She was his partner and nothing else. And besides, she was absolutely annoying, and not to mention the biggest pain in his ass. He most certainly did not think that she was cute.

Iowyn didn't look up at Ulric as he sat in the chair across the table from her. Her attention was on the book in front of her, while her right hand wrote down notes on a scratch piece of paper. Her eyes never left the words on the page, yet she was able to write flawless notes on the paper to her side, moving to a new line when she came to the edge.

Iowyn finished a sentence of her notes, punctuating the end of the sentence with a dot of the pen, and finally let her eyes drift up to Ulric. "I talked to the Washburnes and the Lawlers. They didn't know much. I hope for both our sakes that you had better luck than me," she muttered.

Ulric exhaled, like he had been holding in a breath while waiting for her to acknowledge him, and ran a hand through his curls. "No. Neither the Calloways, nor the Bowmans had anything of importance to say. They have no clue where their children would have gone to play that wouldn't have been safe. It seems no one in this town can even bring themselves to believe that anything bad can happen here."

Iowyn lowered her gaze from him, a slight frown on her face.

Ulric motioned towards her notes and the books on the table. "What's all this for?"

Iowyn gathered up a few papers. "My dad and I went to the town archive and looked for anything relating to missing persons."

Ulric raised a brow. She'd gone and went to look for other leads without any prompting. It wasn't what he'd expected from her, especially with her so new to fieldwork.

She handed the papers across the table to Ulric. "This was all we could find in one day. I tried my best to dumb it down for you."

Ulric's newfound esteem for her crumpled as he narrowed his eyes at her. "How thoughtful of you."

She smirked at his annoyance and sat back in her chair. "We had to go back fifty years, but we found a string of reports of a few missing children and young girls that sounded pretty similar to what's happening now."

"And?"

Iowyn shrugged. "Don't know. Looks like they didn't figure it out back then either." She grabbed a different book off the top of the stack. "But I thought fifty years was almost too exact to be nothing. We're either dealing with an old creep that decided to come out of retirement or a creature that acts out habitually or has a long dormancy period."

Ulric cocked a brow again. He would probably never tell her outright, but the way she thought was intriguing to him. Her mind was quick to put together things that he wouldn't even think of being a possibility. "Anything jumping out at you?"

Iowyn took off her spectacles and lightly rubbed her eyes. "Not anything that I could see being around here, but maybe that's the problem. I'm going to take a deeper dive in the archives tomorrow, see if there's anything farther back in the timeline."

Ulric gave a nod, a silent sign of approval, when an idea sprouted in his mind "How many townspeople do you think are over the age of fifty?"

Iowyn's eyes searched the ceiling, as if the answer she was looking for would be up there. "I don't know if I can really say for sure, but it couldn't be more than forty or so. Why?"

Ulric blew out a breath. "People were disappearing in Calluna fifty years ago. Maybe it wouldn't hurt to ask them if they remember anything about this string of disappearances when they were younger."

Her eyes flickered with surprise. "Not a half bad idea, Ornthalas."

Ulric held back a smirk. "I have those sometimes. I'll ask Elmer for any older folks he thinks would be willing to talk to me."

Iowyn looked back down at the books and papers in front of her and crossed her arms. "Despite that, we still don't have much to go on." She opened her mouth to say something more, but her eyes shot to something behind him. As she stood from the table, Ulric turned in his chair to see the dark-haired man from the street.

"Maddox." Iowyn straightened her linen shirt and tucked a stray piece of hair behind her ear. Was she fixing herself up for him? Ulric had to stop himself from rolling his eyes.

Maddox shifted his weight and looked between Ulric and Iowyn. "Am I interrupting something?"

"No, no! We were just finishing." Iowyn waved her hand dismissively at the table and pulling her spectacles off her face.

Ulric smirked, and leaned back in his chair. "Were we?"

He could tell from Iowyn's angered stare that she wanted to set him on fire, but he just smiled back at her.

"You'll have to excuse him," she said. "He's a bit lacking when it comes to manners."

It was the second time that day she'd made a dig at his manners. If only she knew how Ulric had grown up, and what manners *she* lacked compared to him. It would have been enough to irk him, but he was having too much fun embarrassing her. Ulric ignored Maddox as he stood from the table and feigned hurt. "Is that any way to talk about your partner?"

Maddox pursed his lips, but cleared his throat and held out a hand. "Nice to officially meet you. Maddox Varkin, town constable."

Ulric looked Maddox over closely for the first time. He'd met plenty of constables in his time working in the Guild, and he'd never met one that presented themselves quite like Maddox. His dark blue uniform was pristine, as if it was his first time wearing it. The flintlock pistol in his belt glinted in the light of the bookshop. From what Ulric could see, there wasn't a speck of powder residue on it. He took Maddox's hand, possibly squeezing a bit harder than he needed to. It was soft in his – even the staunch grip couldn't conceal that.

Everything about the man in front of Ulric screamed trouble as he shook his hand. Even the man's smile seemed too perfect, too practiced.

"Ulric Ornthalas."

Maddox gave him a small smile with a nod. "As town constable, I'll be happy to help you in any way possible."

Ulric returned the smile, although he didn't let it reach his eyes. He would play nice, even with every instinct telling him that something was off about the man in front of him. "We'll be sure to let you know if we need you."

Maddox's jaw clenched. Just like it had at every other mention of Ulric and Iowyn together. Maddox looked past Ulric. "I'll wait for you outside."

Ulric stood still and said nothing. He kept his eyes trained on Maddox's back as he left the way he'd come in.

Iowyn rounded the table to follow, but Ulric was quick to grab her forearm. "Not so fast, Beastie."

She huffed. "What now, Ornthalas? We have no leads, therefore, nothing left to discuss. Now can I go and enjoy my night?" She stared up at him in a challenge, like she'd already seen the future and knew that she was going to win this fight.

Ulric held her amber gaze, his grip on her arm unyielding. "I just find it fascinating that you're so quick to trust him." His voice carried a note of skepticism. "Something you care to tell me?"

Iowyn pulled her arm free from his grasp, annoyance flashing across her features. "He's been a friend for a long time. Not to mention he's the fucking constable? He's trustworthy."

Ulric's lips curled into a half-smile, his tone dripping with irony. "How well do you *really* know him?"

Iowyn's brow furrowed as she narrowed her eyes. "What exactly are you implying?"

Ulric leaned in slightly, his voice lowering. "Just that people have layers, Beastie. Sometimes the surface is just a façade."

Iowyn rolled her eyes, crossing her arms over her chest. "You've known him for all of five minutes."

Ulric chuckled, unfazed by her reaction. "You'd be surprised what you can learn about someone in five minutes."

She sighed, shaking her head in exasperation. "You're impossible."

"And *you* have the uncanny ability of getting into trouble." He took a step closer, his gaze intense. "I just want you to be careful. That's all."

Iowyn's expression softened as she searched his face. She swallowed slightly before speaking. "I appreciate your concern – really – but I can take care of myself."

They stood there for a moment, neither saying anything. It was the closest they had ever come to a peaceful resolution.

Iowyn cleared her throat, breaking the momentary silence. "Anyways, I should probably catch up with Maddox. We have… plans."

Ulric's eyebrow arched, a knowing smirk playing on his lips. "Plans, huh?"

Iowyn's cheeks flushed slightly, and she jabbed a finger at Ulric's chest. "Don't get any ideas, Ornthalas. We're just friends." She rolled her eyes again, turning to head for the door. "Goodnight, Ornthalas."

"Goodnight, Beastie."

"Oh, come on. I knew who it was by the tenth chapter," Iowyn admitted.

Maddox's jaw dropped. "You did not."

She smiled. "Did too. It was pretty obvious."

Maddox shoved her over onto the picnic blanket. "You're just saying that because I chose the book this time."

Iowyn laughed. "I am not! It was pretty clear to me that it was the ex-military doctor as soon as the untraceable poison and antidote was discovered. He had the medal for exemplary service in the face of danger, which just screams *espionage, where he'd have to use poisons like that." She sat back up and Maddox pushed her again.*

"You're such a little know-it-all." He grinned at her, and Iowyn's heart leapt in her chest, just like it did every single time he had looked at her like that the past two years.

"You're just pissed cause you're the one out of school and you didn't figure it out until the end."

Maddox shrugged. "At least I got the whole experience from the book."

Iowyn stayed down on the blanket, her eyes searching the clouds for any discernible shapes. When all she saw was tufts of white cotton candy in the sky, she refocused on Maddox, only to find him staring back at her intently.

"What are you looking at?" she asked. She wondered if maybe her hair was lying in a funny way, or if she had somehow gotten sauce from one of the sandwiches they had packed on her face when eating.

The corner of his mouth upturned slightly. "You," he said, matter of factly.

She rolled her eyes and scoffed. "Thanks, Maddox. I can tell that you're looking at me. But why?"

"Because," he started, moving to lay next to her and propping himself up with his elbow. He reached out to tuck a piece of hair behind her ear. "You're beautiful."

Her heart and stomach both flipped simultaneously. Holy shit, was this really happening?

Iowyn swallowed, trying her best to keep her face and body neutral. The last thing she wanted was for him to know how freaked out and absolutely ecstatic she was. She could play it off like his words didn't mean anything, like it wasn't the first time a boy had said those words to her. But that would be a lie, and it felt wrong to lie to him.

"You really think that?" she asked.

He traced the back of his finger along her jaw. "I've always *thought that,* Iowyn."

Iowyn was glad that the butterflies in her stomach couldn't actually make her sick, because she was experiencing an entire swarm of them. And their activity only hastened when Maddox dipped his head down and placed his lips on hers.

Her heart pounded in her chest like a drum, a cacophony of excitement and nervousness. She hadn't allowed herself to want this. They were friends who talked about books, and for a long time, she had accepted that that was all they ever would be.

The softness of his lips against hers sent shivers down her spine, and she couldn't help but close her eyes, savoring the sensation. His breath was warm, his touch gentle, and in that moment, the meadow around them seemed to fade away. It was just her and him, lost in a world of their own.

Time seemed to slow down as they continued to kiss, and she wondered if he could hear the rapid beating of her heart. Every second felt like an eternity, and she never wanted it to end.

Maddox pulled away slowly, smiling. His beautiful blue eyes sparkling. For a moment, the meadow was silent, save for the soft sounds of their breathing and the distant chirping of birds. Then, Iowyn found her voice, her words coming out in a gentle whisper. "Maddox…"

He leaned in closer, his forehead resting against hers. "I've wanted to do that for a long time."

He kissed her again, a little deeper than before, and Iowyn found her hands flying up to cup Maddox's face.

She couldn't believe how good it felt to finally be kissing him. All the tension that had built up between them over the past few years seemed to melt away as their lips interlocked. The world seemed to fade away, leaving just the two of them in this moment of pure bliss. She had never felt so alive.

Iowyn she wanted more. She wanted to feel Maddox's hands on her body, to explore the depths of his desires. Without thinking, she reached up and began to unbutton his shirt, exposing his bare chest. Maddox broke them apart, and Iowyn took a deep breath. Had she gone too far? Done too much? She couldn't help herself. It was impossible to deny the way she felt about Maddox, but she wasn't ready to say anything just yet. The words were just too big, too complex for her to fully comprehend.

Maddox brushed his thumb against her cheek. "Iowyn… I don't want to rush you into anything—"

"Shh," Iowyn interrupted, placing a finger on his lips. "I want this. I want you," she whispered.

Maddox's eyes widened with surprise for a moment, before they darkened and he leaned in to kiss her again. Maddox broke away from the kiss and let out a frustrated sigh, looking deeply into Iowyn's eyes. "Are you sure about this?" he asked, his voice thick.

Iowyn nodded, unable to form words. He opened his mouth to ask something else, but Iowyn cut him off with another deep kiss. She wanted him to know that she was ready for whatever he had in mind. She grabbed his collar and pulled him closer. Maddox's hands ran down her back, sending shivers through her body. It felt as though they were in their own little world, and nothing else mattered.

Iowyn pressed herself up against Maddox's chest, his body hard and warm against hers. She let out a small gasp as he trailed kisses down her neck, his hands roaming over her body, seeking out every inch of her skin.

Desire coursed through her veins as Maddox pulled her closer, their bodies molding together as they moved in perfect harmony. Iowyn felt herself losing control, her body responding to Maddox's every touch — every kiss — in ways she didn't even know were possible. She moaned softly as he nipped at her earlobe, his hands moving more urgently over her body.

In that very moment, she was ready to give Maddox every part of her. So she did.

CHAPTER

16

"Sorry about that." Iowyn blushed from the embarrassment and made a mental note to make Ulric pay later for being an intimidating asshole.

Maddox leaned against the cedar-sided building with his arms crossed. His face was hard, and he looked anything but happy. "Is there something going on between you two?"

"Between me and who?" she asked, shocked at the pointedness of the question.

"You and your *partner.*"

Iowyn snorted. "What? Gods, no. I can't stand him."

It was a ludicrous thought. Ulric and her? They could barely tolerate each other long enough to get through a single conversation without picking a fight. Not to mention all the times she wanted to slap Ulric's stupid smirks off his face – whenever he actually decided to smirk that is.

Maddox's face didn't lighten. His blue eyes were icy. "Are you sure about that?"

She was taken aback. He didn't believe her, and for some reason, that made Iowyn's heart grow heavy in her chest. "Maddox, if I say there's nothing between me and Ornthalas, then there's nothing."

Maddox searched her face then relaxed, letting out a breath and unfolding his arms. "Okay." He took her hand and started to lead her away from the bookshop and out of town.

"Where are we going?" she asked. The sun had given way to the waning moon. Its silvery light illuminated the paths where there was no lamplight.

Maddox smirked, and Iowyn felt her heart jump in her chest at the sight. It was as if she were a stupid teenager again. "You'll see."

She followed him out of town and into the forest that led towards the meadows. Lantern bugs twinkled and blinked as they fluttered among the tall trees and long grasses. A light breeze brought along the scent of citrus blooms and dewdrops. The night was peaceful. Iowyn and Maddox's footsteps were the only sounds to be heard besides the chirping of crickets and the ripple of foliage in the breeze.

Maddox led Iowyn out of the trees and into a small clearing. A large quilt waited in the middle with a few pillows and two bottles of wine.

"You set this up?" Iowyn asked.

Maddox looked away sheepishly and rubbed the back of his neck. "Do you like it?"

Iowyn sat down on the quilt. It was pillowy and made of soft textiles. She almost felt bad the thing was getting dirty from being on the ground. "It's been a long time since someone's done something like this for me."

"Really?"

Iowyn smiled. "You sound surprised."

Maddox sat down next to her. "Well, yeah. Did the guys at University not have eyes or something?"

She shrugged. "Maybe I just wasn't their type."

Maddox uncorked both bottles of wine and offered one to her. "So... there hasn't been anyone?"

Iowyn grabbed the open bottle and swallowed the slight lump in her throat before taking a short drink. "I didn't say that." She plastered on a playful smile. "What about you?"

Maddox averted his gaze. "No one worth mentioning."

Iowyn laughed. "Oh, I'm sure there was a line of girls at your door as soon as I left."

Their relationship had never been anything very public, but once word had gotten out around school that Maddox Varkin was hanging out with Iowyn Morgnah – well – she had gotten nothing but dirty looks from all the other girls at school. Her leaving for University would have reopened the door for any of them to try and have Maddox for themselves.

Maddox smirked, taking a swig of his own bottle of wine. "You have no idea how boring this place got after you left."

"Well, that's Calluna for you." Iowyn took another drink. The warmth of the wine settled in her stomach and moved through her body. "I'm sure it's a pretty easy gig for you as a constable."

"Well, I definitely haven't had the need to solve any murders, if that's what you're saying."

She was surprised how easily the two of them had gone back to their casual selves. She hadn't expected to run into Maddox. And to be honest, the thought of him hadn't even been at the top of her list when she knew that she was coming back home. In fact, he hadn't even crossed her mind until she'd seen him in the road that morning.

They had ended things before she left, and Iowyn had been in a few relationships since Maddox, and she was sure that he had done the same. But part of her had expected things to be awkward between them. The fact that he had been happy to see her and had gone through the trouble to set something like this up for her – it was nice. It had been a long time since Iowyn had had something nice.

"So," he paused, "you really did it. You're working for the Guild now."

Iowyn nodded. "I've been working for them for a while now, but I just started fieldwork a week ago."

"So, you don't even know this partner of yours very well, then?"

Iowyn shook her head. "Not really."

"Are you sure you can trust him?"

She almost laughed at the parallel of Maddox's question to Ulric's, but she sighed instead. "Honestly? I don't know. I think so? Sure, he might be an ass sometimes, but he's kept me safe." Iowyn didn't go into detail – didn't want to go into detail.

But Maddox's question rattled in her brain. Could she trust Ulric? The best she could come up with was a big fat maybe. Had he quite possibly saved her life on the Druid? Yes. Did she know what awful thing he did to be put on probation? No. Did that mean that he could still possibly be a danger to her. Maybe?

Maddox's face softened. "I just want you to be careful. That's all."

"Funny," Iowyn scoffed, "he said the same thing about you."

Maddox tore his eyes from her face and looked at the bottle as he twirled it in his hands. "But, you're happy? You like what you do?"

"Yeah, I like it. It's better than sitting in a dark archive, that's for sure."

Maddox frowned, a slight crease forming between his dark brows. "But it's dangerous to be out in the field."

Iowyn's jaw tightened. She stopped herself from rolling her eyes in agitation. She hated whenever someone made it seem as if she didn't understand how oddly dangerous her dreams were. Working in the field meant being put in front of some of the most dangerous creatures in all of Phyrra. Perhaps it was foolish to want to be a field monstralogist to anyone else, but if Blake Ophedian could do it, so could she.

"I know that. That's why I have Ulric to protect me."

Maddox's face hardened a bit at the mention of her partner, which just made her want to roll her eyes even more. She decided a change of subject would be best. "What do you know about the disappearances?"

It was a simple question, and one she probably should have asked him sooner rather than catching up. She was here to do a job after all, and he was the town constable. If anyone knew anything, he would.

Maddox pursed his lips. "Not as much as I'd ultimately like to. Kids go off to play, then a few come running back to town crying and saying that one of the friends was taken."

"Taken by what?"

He shook his head. "Honestly, I'm not even sure that they have any idea what it is. All I know is that it isn't some sick psycho taking kids. It's something else. Something dark." He took his eyes off of her, focusing back on the bottle in his hands. "None of the kids have shown back up. I think…" he took a deep breath. "I think that they might never come back."

Maddox took in a shaky breath. "When Albilot sent out the request to the Guild, a lot of mothers took their kids to the monastery a few towns over. They didn't want to risk their kid being the next one to go missing. I tried to convince everyone with children to go, but not everyone can afford to just up and leave everything."

Iowyn reached out her hand, placing it on his forearm. "We're going to find whatever it is."

"I know." He gave her a sad smile. "If anyone can figure it out, it'll be you."

An intense silence fell between them. A bit of heat rose slowly to Iowyn's cheeks at the compliment, and she became overly aware of the thudding of her heartbeat in her chest. Maddox's blue stare was fixed on the bottle in his hands. His voice dripped with longing and regret as he softly said, "I've missed you, Iowyn."

She took another drink of wine. It was all too serious, and she hadn't expected it. "I've been known to have that effect." She winked in the hopes to lighten the mood.

Maddox grabbed the bottle from her hands and set it down on the ground with his. "You're not hearing me," he said.

She stared at him, a bit dazed. Her heart seemed to thud louder.

Maddox let out an exasperated sigh. "I've missed you since the day you left. I haven't been able to get you out of my head. I couldn't just forget you and move on. I tried, Iowyn. Gods, did I try." His hand rested on top of hers. "But we had something that I just can't find with anyone else."

Iowyn's face flushed, though she couldn't be sure if it was from Maddox's words or the wine. "Maddox–"

He cupped her cheek. "It doesn't matter. I don't want you to apologize. You're back now. We can start over…" He trailed off, his eyes leaving hers for a split second to dart down to her lips. He leaned in to touch his forehead to hers. Maddox closed his eyes. "I want you, Iowyn," he breathed.

The words set her insides ablaze. The heat rose, and she closed her eyes as Maddox closed the distance between their lips.

The kiss was a collision of emotions and memories, a convergence of longing and familiarity. Iowyn's heart raced. Maddox's lips were warm and gentle against hers. As their lips parted, they stayed close, their foreheads still touching and their breaths mingling in the cool night air.

Iowyn opened her eyes, her gaze meeting Maddox's intense blue stare. The moonlight painted a soft glow on his cheekbones. He looked every bit the boy that she'd been head over heels in love with as a teenager, yet so different. His jawline was more defined, chiseled with the passage of time and adorned with a shadow of stubble. His eyes held a deep, mature intensity that was new, yet hauntingly familiar. They were the same eyes she had fallen for all those years ago, only now they were laden with experiences that she wasn't a part of.

"Maddox," Iowyn whispered, her voice soft yet conflicted. "I don't know if we can just pick up where we left off."

He sighed, his hand still cupping her cheek. "I know that things have changed Iowyn. I'm not asking for an instant fix. I just… I need you to know how I feel."

She couldn't help but lean into his touch, torn between the past and the present. "And?"

Maddox's thumb caressed her cheek gently. "I've spent years trying to fill a void that you left behind. And no matter how hard I've tried, no one else has been able to fill it."

Iowyn's heart ached, her emotions swirling like a storm within her. She had thought that she had moved on from Maddox, that their time together was just a simple chapter of her life that had closed. But now – in the midst of this quiet night – she wasn't so sure.

"Maddox, it's complicated," she said, her voice tinged with what she could only characterize as regret. She was a member of the Hunter's Guild now – a field monstralogist. She was finally doing what she had always dreamt of. She wasn't so sure that she was ready to give it up to settle down, if that's what he wanted. When this assignment was over, she would be leaving.

Maddox nodded, his gaze still locked onto hers. "I know. But maybe it's time we stop overthinking things and just let ourselves feel."

Iowyn's breath caught in her throat. Maddox's thumb continued to trace patterns on her cheek, his touch gentle and reassuring. "We can talk about all that later," he whispered. "Right now… I just want you…"

She couldn't help herself. Iowyn closed the remaining distance between them, pressing her lips to Maddox's once again.

In that moment, in the quiet of the meadow illuminated by moonlight, Iowyn surrendered to the pull of her heart, allowing herself to feel, to explore, and to rediscover the connection that had once defined her small world.

Their kiss deepened, the intensity growing with each passing moment. Maddox's hands roamed over her body, tracing the curves of her hips and waist, pulling her closer to him. Iowyn's own hands found their way into his dark hair, tangling in the strands as she leaned into him. The hunger between them was palpable, their bodies moving in sync as they explored each other.

Maddox broke the kiss, leaning his forehead against hers once again, his breath coming in rough and ragged. "I've missed you so much," he whispered, his lips brushing against hers.

Iowyn's heart swelled, her own breaths coming in short gasps. "I've missed you too," she breathed. Her eyes locked onto his before she brought her mouth to his again.

Maddox's hands trailed down Iowyn's back, pulling her closer. The feel of his muscled body against hers ignited a fire within her. She felt alive once again, her heart pounding in her chest as she lost herself in the moment. At that moment, Iowyn knew that she wanted him. She wanted him with a fierceness that she hadn't felt in nearly a year. It was a primal desire that consumed her, and she knew that she couldn't fight it any longer.

Breaking their kiss, Iowyn cupped Maddox's face with both her hands, her gaze filled with raw desire. "Take me," she whispered, her voice low and husky.

Maddox's eyes widened slightly at her words. The last time they had been together, she had still been very new to all of this. But she wasn't that shy girl anymore. His hands trailed up her back, and released her hair from its messy updo. The long raven strands tumbled over her shoulders and down her back. A few strands fell into her face, and Maddox softly tucked them behind her ears. "You're so beautiful," he whispered.

Iowyn couldn't help the smile that spread across her face and the heat in her cheeks. It was something so sweet to say in the midst of something so arousing. She kissed him again, taking his bottom lip between her teeth as she pulled away, lightly raking them against the soft skin.

Maddox's hands delved under her shirt, finding her bra and unclasping it. The cups fell away from her breast, her bare skin pressed against her shirt. A moan escaped Iowyn's lips as Maddox's hands found her breasts, his fingers kneading the soft flesh. She leaned into him, pressing her lips against his, her tongue sliding into his mouth.

His fingers trailed down her body, leaving a burning path across her skin as he wrapped an arm around her waist and pulled her firmly onto his lap. Iowyn rocked her hips lightly against his, savoring the friction and heat that came with it. Her hand moved to his thigh, tracing the bulge underneath his pants before she reached her fingers underneath and touched him. Maddox shivered as her fingertips wrapped around him. She felt him twitch underneath her as she moved, gently massaging him. His lips moved down to her neck, his teeth nibbling at the sensitive skin.

Iowyn moaned as his kisses moved across her neck while she continued to stroke him. His hands moved over her body, fingers tugging at her shirt, pulling it up at the hem. She raised her arms over her head and let him pull the shirt off, tossing it away to the forest floor. Maddox moved his lips back to hers, kissing her gently while his hands found her breasts, his fingers teasing across her nipples. Iowyn moaned into Maddox's mouth as she pulled his own shirt off of him. Maddox moved, holding Iowyn up enough to lay her down upon the quilt.

Her hips ached for him, needing him to be buried inside of her. He moved down her body, lips and tongue teasing across her skin. Iowyn sighed as his lips found her belly. Maddox reached out, unbuttoning her pants and pulling them off of her. She blushed as he tossed them away with the rest of their clothing, laying before him, completely naked.

Maddox undid his own pants, freeing himself from the confines, and was quick to nestle himself between her parted thighs. He slanted his mouth over hers before pushing himself inside of her – slowly, carefully, in a sweet, sweet torment. He was gentle, moving slowly as he kissed her. Iowyn moaned against Maddox's lips, the feeling of him sinking into her a wonderful sensation that sent waves through her. Her hips moved upward, meeting his thrust, pulling him deeper and deeper inside her, her hands pulling him closer. Maddox's lips found her neck again while he moved inside her. Iowyn's hands moved down his back, her fingers caressing the muscular lines of his body. Her fingernails teased, scratching lightly across his back, moaning in his ear as he moved.

Maddox's thrusts started to change, from slow and gentle to hard and fast. His body ground against hers, making her gasp with every thrust. Iowyn moved against him, her hips moving to the new rhythm, responding to his movements. She arched against the ground, her hips rising upward, meeting Maddox thrust for thrust. She could feel herself winding tighter, just starting to near the point of pure bliss. So close and so far at the same time.

Maddox's body tensed under her fingers as he released himself, his body shuddered, and he pulled himself from her, lying down on the quilt next to her.

Iowyn blinked. The stars in the night sky were all that twinkled back at her.

That was it?

Maddox cleared his throat, a flush of red coming up his neck and over his cheeks. "I'm sorry… it's – uh, well – it's been a while."

Iowyn felt heat rise in her own cheeks, partly embarrassed at herself for being so quick to disappoint. "That's okay," she paused. "It's been a while for me too."

Iowyn hadn't been with anyone for a little over a year. She hadn't wanted to. Not when her last relationship had left so much to be desired and almost ruined her. But seeing Maddox again – being with him again – it was almost like turning back a clock and reliving a better time in her life. She would enjoy it, even if it was only for a little while.

A coy smile overtook the flush on Maddox's face, and he leaned down to kiss her softly on the lips. "I'll make it up to you," he murmured against her lips.

"Better sooner, rather than later," Iowyn teased.

"Oh yeah? Why's that?" He tucked a stray strand behind her ear.

Iowyn gave him her own flirty smile. "Would hate for you to leave me wanting when I go away."

Any amusement on Maddox's face was wiped away.

Maddox swallowed. "Right… of course."

Iowyn's brow creased in confusion. Had she said the wrong thing? She couldn't help herself asking, "What's wrong?"

Maddox shook his head, the sadness on his face was gone, replaced with a small grin. "Nothing." He looked up to the moon, as if he could tell the time by its position in the sky. "We should probably head back."

CHAPTER

17

Maddox got up, and retrieved their clothes that had been scattered about. They dressed in silence, and left the blanket behind, walking back towards town. Maddox took her hand as they walked through the trees, but something was still off with him.

Truth be told, the silence wouldn't have bothered Iowyn, had it not been for her noticing the tightness in Maddox's jaw. She couldn't stand the thought of ruining what had otherwise been a great night with some stupid comment. She'd meant nothing terrible with anything she'd said, but obviously something had dampened Maddox's mood.

Before they broke through the tree line, Iowyn planted her feet and pulled Maddox to a stop. "What's wrong?"

Maddox looked back at her, like it was a silly question. "Nothing's wrong."

She let go of his hand and crossed her arms. "Don't do that."

"Do what?"

"Pretend like I didn't just ruin the whole night."

Maddox's face softened, and he turned fully to face her, placing a hand on each of her shoulders. "Iowyn—"

"Don't," she cut him off. "You know how I feel about lying."

She'd given him a piece of her mind when they had started their book club. He had denied that he was even talking to Iowyn to a group of his friends one day at school, saying that it was preposterous. It had not only pissed her off, but she could have sworn she had felt her heart crack when he'd said it.

Maddox sighed, as if he was remembering it too. "You didn't do anything wrong."

"Then what?"

He looked up at the sky, shutting his eyes and blowing out a breath. "You just reminded me that you're not here to stay."

Iowyn's heart became stone and sunk in her chest. "Maddox—"

"I know," he said. His hands came to cup her face. "I know, I just…" Maddox swallowed, running a thumb across her cheek. "Let's just enjoy what time we do have?"

Iowyn couldn't think of what to say, and for fear of saying something that would just make things worse, she simply nodded.

Iowyn rounded the corner of the building and almost jumped out of her skin when she saw someone waiting for her.

Ulric leaned up against the building next to the back door of the bakery, his large arms crossed against his chest, and one foot perched on the wall behind him. She clutched her chest as her heart threatened to leap from it.

"Genova's sake, you fucking scared me." Iowyn let out a slight chuckle of relief that it was just her partner.

Ulric looked anything but amused. "Have fun?"

Iowyn straightened and braced herself for whatever onslaught Ulric had prepared for her. She shrugged nonchalantly. "Just catching up with an old friend."

"In the woods in the middle of the night?" Ulric scoffed, and rolled his eyes. "If that's what you call catching up," he muttered.

"How would you know?" Iowyn asked. "Were you following me?" Iowyn's heart raced at the thought of Ulric seeing what she and Maddox had just done out in the meadow.

Ulric huffed a laughed. "I'm a grown man, Beastie. I can piece together what you were doing just fine without being a stalker."

Iowyn scoffed. He had some nerve judging her. Sure, she'd never seen Ulric take a girl to his room, or entertain one at a tavern, but even if she had, she wouldn't ridicule him about it. "Well, what I do with my free time is none of your business."

"It *is* my business when there's some unknown creature on the loose. You could have been in danger."

"Maddox was with me."

Ulric scowled and pushed off of the wall, coming face to face with her. "If you think that he would be able to protect you, then you are sorely mistaken."

Iowyn narrowed her gaze. That was it. He could attack her all he wanted. Really, she could care less. But Maddox? Someone he didn't even know? Someone that she knew would take care of her? That was too far. "You don't even know him."

"I don't need to know him when I know everything else. You said it yourself. This town has never had run-ins with magical creatures. Ergo, Maddox has zero experience. Just. Like. You." He pointed a finger into her chest.

Iowyn slapped his hand away from her. "I have experience now. I killed a werewolf."

As if to prove a point, Ulric grabbed the wrist of the hand that swatted his own away, and leant down so his face was level with hers. His voice was dangerously low. "You were *lucky*, Beastie. Without me there, you would have been eviscerated, and came here in a pine box instead of riding in on your beast."

Iowyn opened her mouth to lodge a protest at him, but Ulric stopped her, squeezing her wrist tighter.

"Do *not* argue with me about that. It's the truth. You know it. And I know it."

She shut her mouth.

Ulric heaved an annoyed sigh and dropped her arm. "Like it or not, we're in this together. Your actions have the potential to get one of us killed. Could quite literally sign my death certificate. So *grow up.*" He ground out the last two words. He was so close, his breath fanned across her face.

Iowyn swallowed, biting down the curses and expletives that she wanted to shout at him. But even she could logically see that she was in the wrong for leaving tonight. She hadn't thought it through – hadn't thought of the consequences that could have befallen her. As much as it pained her to admit to herself, Ulric was right.

Iowyn looked at the door to the bakery, the door that Ulric was standing in front of. She looked past him as she asked quietly, "Can I go now?"

Ulric's face shifted from one of anger to something else. She might have found it concerning, but as far as she knew, Ulric wasn't capable of such a thing when it came to her. His body untensed, and he stepped aside.

Iowyn walked past him and stooped down to grab the back door key from underneath a loose piece of siding near the bottom of the doorframe. She unlocked the door and stepped inside without even saying goodnight.

CHAPTER

18

Ulric had woken up later than usual, which he blamed on the late-night babysitting, and the cold shower he took before bed. He had been nothing but restless after getting back to his room, and had only finally fallen asleep from sheer exhaustion.

His first destination was the town hall. An old haggard man with a wispy white beard down to his belt led Ulric down into the town archives. The dark subterranean rooms held large bookcases with numerous tomes and old bindings of crumbling documents. At the bottom of the stairs the old man simply pointed in a general direction, and then left to go back up the stairs.

"Thanks for all your help," Ulric murmured under his breath. He lifted his lantern in front of him to shed some light on the narrow passages. It made the most sense to him that the oldest records would be farther back in the archives, so he started his search for Iowyn.

He mentally prepared himself for seeing her after their exchange last night. She had been in the wrong, and he knew that, but another part of him felt as though perhaps he'd been just a little too harsh about it. But nothing else had gotten through her otherwise brilliant brain, so he had decided before she showed up that he would give her nothing but the cold hard truth. Perhaps then she would listen to reason, instead of doing things to spite him. With the way she left him last night, it seemed she had finally realized something, but he still wasn't sure how she'd be this morning.

134

Ulric weaved his way through the bookshelves, looking at the age of books and scrolls to try and pinpoint how far back in time the records hailed from, but he was a hunter, not a scriven. His guess was as good as horseshit when it came to records and books. Luckily for him, after a few twists and turns, he came upon the faint glow of another light.

In a corner on the floor, surrounded by stacks of books and piles of loose records, sat Iowyn. Her half-moon spectacles perched on her nose. The lantern light made her amber eyes more akin to glowing embers. Her hair sat atop her head again in a messy bun.

Ulric swallowed, whether in anticipation of the bombardment Iowyn had prepared when she saw him or from the way she looked – so studious and in her element – he wasn't one hundred percent sure.

His presence cast a shadow over the documents Iowyn was reading, and she looked up to see what was blocking her light. Her eyebrows knit together. "What are you doing here?"

Ulric rubbed the back of his neck. What was he doing here? There wasn't really a good reason for him to be down in the archives, other than to check up on her. He wasn't a researcher. He wouldn't even know what to look for. "With a lack of leads, I didn't know if you needed any help," he supplied.

Surprisingly, a sly smile curled her lips. "You want to help me? With research?"

He stifled the urge to roll his eyes by clenching his jaw. "No, not really. We both know I'm probably not the best at that, but…" He trailed off, not quite sure what to say.

"But?" Amused intrigue lilted in her tone.

Shit, now he'd really need a reason. He cleared his throat. "I could help with getting you books and records, or at least putting them back." It felt like such a silly offer. He was a hunter, reduced to worm work because nothing else had turned up with his usual methods of investigation. He was used to hunting creatures that made themselves known or that at least someone has seen. This working from nothing was new. Helping Iowyn out, even as a retriever, meant that they could get closer to finding whatever was taking those kids, he would do it.

Her smile broadened. "You want to be my gopher, Ornthalas?"

Ulric let out a huff and turned around to leave. "Forget it."

"Oh, come on! I was just teasing!"

He kept walking. If she couldn't take him seriously for wanting to help, then why even bother?

A hand grabbed his forearm. "I'm sorry, okay? Come on, I'll show you what I'm looking for, and maybe even teach you a thing or two." She punctuated her sentence by winking at him.

Ulric rarely knew what to say, especially when someone acted out of character. Firstly, she had apologized, which she had never really done before. Secondly, she was rather chipper after the fight they'd had last night. Throwing a wink at him seemed weird, even for her at her sunniest. And thirdly, she was throwing him a bone to not be a jerk for once.

His mother had always told him when he was young, *"It is better to keep your mouth closed and let people think you are a fool, than to open it and remove all doubt."* With no real clue as to what to say, he just stared back at her.

Iowyn tugged on his arm and led him back to her spot on the floor. "Come on, I promise, I won't bite."

Ulric tensed a bit. Now he really couldn't tell if she was flirting with him or not.

"Are you okay?"

Ulric looked down at her to find a look of concern across her face.

"Fine," he assured. "I'm fine."

Her amber eyes assessed him up and down. "Okay… Uh, well, you can start by putting this stack back. I didn't find anything there. I can show you where the shelf is." Iowyn let go of Ulric's arm, and he became suddenly aware of the absence of warmth.

He followed Iowyn as she explained how the archives were laid out and how records were normally categorized and shelved. "Where did you learn all of this?"

She cocked a brow. "You do realize that my dad owns a bookshop, and I was a scriven for two years after university, right? Besides, almost all libraries and archives abide by the Phyrran Categorical System."

Ulric paused and cleared his throat. "Right, my bad."

They circled back to the corner that Iowyn had made into her makeshift workspace, and Ulric took off his sword belt, leaning it against the wall. There would be no real need to have it strapped to his hip down here. Not unless there were some monstrous rats to kill.

He started putting tomes away on the shelves where he surmised they must go. How many people actually ever used the records this old? He figured it wouldn't be the end of the world if he accidentally put a book away on the wrong shelf. Someone would find it eventually.

Each time he came back to Iowyn, there were more books in the return stack. Her posture seemed to degrade with every hour that passed, and her sunnier temperament dimmed with every book that failed to give her any answers.

Ulric started taking larger loads with him, until he noticed her nose stuck in the same book for multiple trips. He no longer had any books or scrolls to return, so he sat down on the cold stone floor next to her and rested his back against the wall.

She was deeply engrossed in whatever she had found. So much so, that she hadn't even noticed how close Ulric was sitting next to her. There was less than an inch of space between them.

Ulric peered over her shoulder, looking at the scribbled text. No wonder it was taking her so long to read it. It was almost illegible. "Care to share with the class?"

Iowyn startled at the sound of his voice, and let out a sigh with the slightest edge of agitation. "I'm not sure, it could be nothing—"

Iowyn's voice was cut off by her own scream. She jumped higher than Ulric would have thought possible from her sitting position and right into his lap.

Ulric shot up to his feet, but Iowyn clung to him like a scared cat in a tree. Her arms wrapped around his neck and her legs hooked together around his torso. Ulric grabbed the back of her legs instinctively to steady her. "What? What is it?" he asked apprehensively, still not seeing any danger to alert him.

Iowyn pointed down at the floor by the book that she had been reading, which was now flipped upside down. A fat and hairy spider the size of her fist moseyed along the floor.

Iowyn scrambled in Ulric's arms as it got closer. "Kill it! Oh my gods, *kill it!*"

Ulric couldn't help the smile erupting on his face as he bit back a shred of laughter. "Is Beastie scared of a little spider?" he couldn't help but tease.

Iowyn's head whipped towards him and she smacked his shoulder. "Don't call me that," she said through gritted teeth. "And little? You call *that* little? That thing is *huge!*"

Ulric looked to the spider on the floor and then back to Iowyn's wide eyes with a shrug. "I've seen bigger."

The spider ambled its way across the floor unbothered, coming closer to Ulric's boot. Iowyn's hands fisted the back of Ulric's shirt and her legs tightened around his hips. She was trying her best to get as far off the floor as possible. "For fuck's sake," she yelled, "you're a hunter! Kill it!"

Ulric smirked at her before lifting his boot and lowering it onto the unsuspecting arachnid with a satisfying crunch. He patted the top of Iowyn's messy bun. "There, there, Beastie. The terrible monster had been slain."

Iowyn looked down at the floor to confirm his words then looked back at his face. His self-congratulatory smile dropped. Her amber eyes stared into his, their noses almost touching. Not only that, but Ulric had just become increasingly aware of where his body met hers.

His heart fluttered like a butterfly in a garden on a full moon. Iowyn's gaze remained fixed on his. Ulric's instinct to move away from her warred with a strange pull he felt, telling him to pull her closer. Her breath fanned against his skin, and his fingers tightened involuntarily on the backs of her legs. The sweet scent of vanilla swathed around him, threatening to cloud his better judgment.

How many times had Ulric held a lover like this?

He managed to speak, his voice coming out huskier than he would have ever intended. "You can let me go now."

Iowyn blinked, as if snapping herself out of a daze, and slowly released her hold on him. She slid down to stand on her own two feet, but took a second before stepping away. Ulric stepped back from her as well, clearing his throat and trying to regain whatever composure he could muster.

Iowyn's pale cheeks were a rosy shade of pink. She looked down at the squashed spider, like she was expecting it to keep moving. "Thank you," she mumbled, her voice a tad bit shaky.

Ulric couldn't help but chuckle, trying to ease the tension that had seemed to settle thick in the air. "No need to thank me for saving you from the terrible monster. It's my job."

She shot him a half-amused, half-annoyed glare, playfully swatting at his arm. "You're insufferable, Ornthalas."

He grinned, a strange warmth growing in his chest. "And you're easily scared by spiders, it seems."

Iowyn huffed, but a hint of a smile tugged at the corner of her lips. "I am not."

Ulric folded his arms across his chest. "Could have fooled me."

She cleared her throat and opened her mouth to say something, no doubt a sly quip or sarcastic comment, but Iowyn was interrupted by the sound of frantic footsteps.

Ulric instinctively moved to stand in front of Iowyn, pushing her back between him and the wall. Elmer came out from behind a bookshelf with a lantern in hand. He looked relieved to have found them, but his face was white as a ghost's. He managed to speak while panting hard. "A kid's been taken by the bridge."

Ulric took no time to react, grabbing his sword and fastening the belted scabbard to his waist. He started following Elmer out of the archives. Iowyn's mind struggled to process everything that had just gone on in the short span of time, and had hardly even registered Elmer's words before he and Ulric were gone.

A child had been taken, and Ulric was on his way to face whatever it was that had done it.

"Shit," Iowyn cursed under her breath, grabbing the book she had been reading so intently and hurrying to get out of the archive. She was close to finding something. She knew it. Everything was starting to line up with what they already knew. A string of disappearances a hundred years back. Children missing while playing outside of town. The spring thaw. And she'd be damned if she was going to lose the one potential lead they had.

She would also be damned if she was going to let Ulric go off
and find an unknown creature on his own without her. If she saw
it, even just a glimpse of it, perhaps she could identify whatever it
was and end this assignment faster.

The fact that Ulric had left her without a second thought was
more than a little inconsiderate in her opinion. Though she
supposed it could be easily explained by the fact that there was a
child's life in the balance.

Iowyn broke out of the town hall and into the street just in
time to see Elmer and Ulric on horseback as they both raced off in
the direction of the river. Shadowfoot was easily pulling away from
the blue roan quarter horse that Elmer rode. Holding the book in
the crook of her arm, Iowyn tucked her fingers into her mouth and
let out a shrill whistle.

She only had to wait a few seconds before Dren bounded from
the back of the bookshop and bakery at the end of the road and
came to a halt in front of her. He wasn't saddled or bridled which
meant Iowyn was going to have to ride her beast bareback for the
first time in years.

She heaved herself up and over his back. Ulric's figure on the
back of Shadowfoot was just cresting over the far hill.

Iowyn leaned down beside Dren's face and pointed towards
them on the horizon. "Follow! Fast!"

Dren was all too happy to oblige.

Iowyn's fingers fisted the longer hair of Dren's mane and
squeezed his middle with her legs so hard that it hurt. She clamped
down on the book underneath her arm to keep it from falling. Her
whole body was tense to keep herself from bouncing off of Dren's
back as he galloped.

Iowyn's hair came loose from the haphazard bun she had
fastened earlier that morning. Dren ran like he was the wind itself,

like he had something to prove. He was racing with Shadowfoot, who already had an immense lead.

Inch by inch, stride by stride, the distance between Dren and Shadowfoot closed in, until they were neck and neck. Iowyn risked giving Dren a reassuring pat to let her beast know that he'd done a good job. He followed Shadowfoot's every move until they came to a halt at the stone bridge.

Ulric dismounted and rounded Shadowfoot before Iowyn could do the same. "What are you doing?"

"My job?" She went to get off of Dren's back, but Ulric held her leg down against Dren's body with his large hand. His strength was enough to easily keep her from moving. She leveled a glare at him. "I'm your partner. You aren't leaving me out of this."

"I think it went upriver!" Elmer shouted from the bank of the river.

Ulric let out a long exhale and gritted his teeth. He released his grip on her leg. "Fine, but you do what I tell you. Got it?"

Iowyn swallowed. He was actually going to let her go with him. She nodded eagerly and tried to keep back the smile that threatened to widen across her face. There was a kid in danger. Smiling wasn't the most appropriate thing to be doing right now.

She jumped down to the ground. Elmer was making his way up the river bank. Ulric placed a hand on his sword hilt. "Grab the horses. Stay behind us, and stay close. Keep your dagger ready, just in case. Don't wander off, and if you see something, say something. Got it?"

Iowyn nodded again. For once, she didn't want to answer him with some snarky quip. Iowyn placed the book against the bridge. No reason to bring it with her. Dren followed closely behind as she grabbed the reins of the two horses, placed her hand on the handle of her dagger at her belt, and followed Ulric's lead.

Elmer pointed off in the distance, yelling back at them. "The screams were coming from farther north."

"North?" Iowyn questioned out loud. "That leads back to the lake."

Ulric looked back over his shoulder, his legs eating up the distance between him and Elmer. "Is that important?"

Iowyn wasn't altogether sure, but still supplied, "Well if the creature's heading towards the lake, then maybe it lives there, not the river."

Ulric said nothing. As they moved along the riverbank, his head moved back and forth, scanning the area around them. "If it did, would that make a huge difference?"

Iowyn nodded. "Astronomically."

"How far is the lake from here?" Ulric's attention went back to Elmer.

"About a mile or so—"

A faint but horrifying scream resounded from far off in the north, towards the lake. Ulric and Elmer looked at each other. "Move," was all Ulric said before he rushed to mount Shadowfoot, wrenching the reins from Iowyn's hands.

Iowyn's feet were moving before her brain had any real time to catch up as she jumped onto Dren's back. They were running towards a screaming child being dragged off by gods only knew what. At least she wouldn't be happening upon the creature by herself.

The screams and wails continued, growing louder the farther she ran. She willed Dren to continue and only wished that her lungs would stop screaming for air. They burned as if she were the one running with all her might. The trees along the riverbank passed by her in a blur. Branches whipped at her face. The screams were becoming less frequent and losing veracity. Were they even running fast enough? Maybe Ulric would get there in time. She'd lost sight of him, but who knew how much closer he'd be? Gods, she hoped she would get there in time.

Iowyn finally broke through the tree line to find the rocky lakeshore in front of her. Ulric stood at the edge of the water, already dismounted from his black mare. His emerald eyes were trained upon the water while Elmer was scanning the surrounding trees. The surface was as smooth as glass. Not a ripple in sight.

It didn't make sense. The screams were coming from here, so where was the kid? Where was the creature? There were no signs of life besides Iowyn, Elmer, and Ulric and their mounts, so where had the thing gone? Had they somehow gotten to the lake before the creature?

She wanted to ask Ulric, but the way his jaw was set, she figured it best not to. She dismounted and looked down at her feet, at the tracks she and Dren had both made in the pebbled beach. There had to be *something. Anything.*

Ulric backed away from the water's edge, but his eyes stayed on the lake's surface. His eyes seemed to be taking in everything, calculating, trying to figure out the same thing that she was. He came to stand beside her and drew his sword. Iowyn's heart raced, grabbing the hilt of her dagger tighter.

Twigs snapped behind them, and Ulric was quick to whirl around at the sound. Iowyn did the same a second later to see Ulric's sword pointed at Maddox's throat.

"Fuck, you're fast," Maddox breathed, his hands raised by his head. "Would you mind lowering that thing?"

Ulric kept his sword where it was, not saying a word.

Iowyn looked between the two. "What are you doing?" she hissed between her teeth.

Ulric ignored her questions, asking his own. "What are you doing here?" It was much more of a command than a question.

Maddox scoffed. "My job? I heard the commotion in town."

Ulric still didn't lower his sword. Iowyn looked across the blade to where Elmer was now standing on the other side.

Elmer cleared his throat. "As much as I'd love to see Varkin get stuck, I think there are more important things to be worried about right now."

Ulric's emerald eyes flashed over to Elmer, then back to Maddox. His sword lowered, but Ulric's jaw was still tense as he said, "Don't get in the way, Constable."

Ulric turned, and Iowyn expected him to walk right past her, but he grabbed her forearm and pulled her with him, away from Maddox and Elmer and towards the lake. "Stay close to me. Got it?" he murmured to her.

She opened her mouth to protest but stopped herself as she noted the slight uneasiness in Ulric's usually solid tone. He was worried about something. The obvious culprit was of course the missing child and unknown creature, but even before they had gotten to the lake, Ulric had been cool and reserved. No, it was something else.

They began walking around the edge of the lake, and Iowyn tried her best to set her mind to the task at hand. If it really was a creature taking children – and at this point, it seemed as though it almost had to be – then it would have to leave tracks of some kind.

Evidence. They needed evidence. A simple clue. *Anything.*

As she walked the perimeter, a recurring anomaly began to stand out amongst the rocks and mud. Not tracks, but long and consistent drag marks, like a wet broom had been used on the shore to obscure any trace of something being there.

Iowyn tugged on Ulric's sleeve and pointed out the weird trails. He looked them over, a curious and concerned look on his face, before following them with Iowyn close behind. They skirted the edge of the lake, and the trail took them almost halfway around before leading into the water.

Ulric scanned the shallow waters in front of them and then tensed. "Shit," he breathed, his sword coming down to his side.

Iowyn moved to his side so that she could see what had elicited such a reaction from him. Floating only a few yards out from the shore, entangled in pondweeds, was the small shoe of a child.

CHAPTER

19

When they all returned to town, Maddox called the town magistrate to the bookshop. Ulric recounted what they had discovered, much to everyone's horror. It was decided that a town meeting would be called tonight, to make everyone aware of what had happened, and hopefully keep more children from suffering the same fate. Elmer left with Maddox to go see the child's family to give them the terrible news. They would be going to the other families as well to let them know that it was very likely that their children were never coming back.

While everyone else seemingly found something to do amidst the terrible news, Iowyn seemed to be frozen in place. Five children had been killed by some beast that she still had yet to identify, and although she knew that she needed to start researching, she just couldn't. Seeing that tiny shoe just floating on the surface of the lake had shattered her.

Their names rang through her head.

Ada Washburne.

Claire Lawler

Elsie Calloway

Wally Bowman

And now, Toby Thomas

Five children that had gone out to play and would never come back home.

She had no idea how long she had been sitting at the front counter of the bookshop, staring at the small clock above the front door that ticked away without a care in the world. Burke set a cup of tea in front of her, taking a seat next to her.

"I thought you might want some company."

Iowyn grabbed the cup. Heat seeped from the porcelain into her fingers and palms. "Thanks."

Burke placed a hesitant hand on her shoulder. "Are you okay?"

Iowyn couldn't help but scoff. She didn't look up from the cup. "I'm fine. I'm not the one that's dead."

Burke was silent, and Iowyn knew it wasn't because he didn't know what to say, but because he was thinking of just the right way to say what he wanted to. Her father was always eloquent, always had the right things to say, even if it took him some time to come up with them.

"It wasn't your fault, Wynnie."

Iowyn took a deep breath at the words. It was true, and she knew it. There was quite possibly nothing that could have been done for Toby. They had been too far away. Dren and Shadowfoot had run with all their might. Even if she or Ulric or even Elmer had gotten to the lake in time, what were the chances they would have been able to save him then?

It wasn't her fault, true. But someone's child – someone who had barely even begun to live – had died.

"I know, Dad… I just wish we could've done something."

Burke took her hand. "Wynnie… You should know better than anyone that you can't save everyone. Not even Blake Ophedian and Ird Smildenn could."

Leave it to Burke to bring up her hero to make a point. There were a few passages in Blake Ophedian's books that Bearen had neglected to read to her when she was younger. It was only when Iowyn had grown to reading by herself did she learn about Ophedian and Smildenn's shortcomings while on the job, the assignments that didn't go their way.

Burke continued, "Today was something beyond your control. It's natural to want to control everything, to try and bend the universe to our will. But that's not how life works."

A tear fell down her cheek. "I know, Dad. But… I guess I always thought that I'd be better than them. That if I was smart enough, I would be able to save people before the monsters could get to them."

Burke pulled Iowyn into a hug. The gesture put her on the brink of breaking down. But she held back the cascade. She needed to be stronger than this.

However, her resolve was no match for Burke's next words. "I know – without a shadow of a doubt in my mind – that if anything is going to bring justice to those children, it's you."

There wasn't a single empty seat to be found in the Itchy Badger. Every single person left in Calluna was inside, standing room only. The town magistrate, Ellis Albilot, stood on the stage talking to Maddox. His once salt and pepper hair and beard were now completely gray. His dark skin held more wrinkles, the most gathering beside his eyes.

Albilot had been the magistrate in Calluna since Iowyn was a child., the man that had let her keep Dren all those years ago. He was wise and knew just what made Calluna tick. As a magistrate, he was more than fair when it came to passing judgment and ending disputes between neighbors, and Iowyn never once doubted that he truly cared for each and every person who lived in Calluna.

He had never married, never had children of his own. But he was a regular at the school, helping out teachers and giving lessons about government and Phyrran history whenever he had the time. She had remembered him saying once that the children of Calluna were as good to him as if they were his own. She could only imagine how he felt knowing they were all in danger now.

A small table served as a makeshift pulpit for Albilot to announce from. He banged a wooden gavel against the table, silencing the crowd and garnering everyone's attention.

"Ladies, gentlemen! Thank you all for coming tonight." Albilot smiled out at the crowd, but it was dropped as soon as he came to the matter at hand. "I'm sure by now that you are all aware of why this meeting has been called. We have been besieged by something unknown. It has been taking out children and," he paused, as if trying to find the best way to put the rest of his sentence as delicately as possible, "we now know that they will most likely never come back."

Gasps and slight outrage sounded from the crowd. Iowyn shifted uneasily in her seat. Their anger and sadness were reasonable, so she tried her best to ignore the pinching pain in her chest.

Albilot raised a hand, and the crowd quieted down. "As some of you know, after the third disappearance, I sent a letter to the Hunter's Guild, asking for help. They have answered and sent us two of their proxies." He gestured down towards Ulric and Iowyn in the crowd. Thankfully, most people could see only Ulric due to his height.

"But the main reason for this meeting is to implore you all to be diligent in keeping the remaining children in town. Do not allow them to go off on their own. Do your best to explain to your children the dangers surrounding our town at the moment. And if you see any go off on their own, please alert the constable right away. Perhaps by working together in this time of hardship, we can spare another family the heartbreak of losing a child."

Ulric stood from his seat in the front, went up the stairs onto the stage, and turned towards the crowd. "I realize that what you want are answers right now. What we ask is that you remain helpful to us during our investigation."

A woman's voice sounded from the crowd. "But what creature is it?"

Ulric's eyes darted down to Iowyn. He took a breath in before answering. "We still don't know."

Furor erupted. The townspeople yelled and shouted, bombarding Ulric with questions. Everyone's voices melded together in a cacophony of anger, as if Ikris, the god of chaos himself, had been in the room.

Albilot pounded his gavel on the table to settle everyone down. "Let the man speak!"

Ulric gave the magistrate a nod of thanks, then continued. "What we do know is that this beast, whatever it is, is connected to the water. So it would be best to keep the children from going near the river or the lake."

"How many different water monsters could there be?" one person asked.

"How do you expect to kill something you don't know anything about?" another questioned.

Iowyn looked from the crowd behind her, to Ulric on the stage as more questions came. Questions that she wasn't even sure that *she* could answer with all her background knowledge on creatures. To his credit, Ulric stood his ground on stage, not looking the least bit bothered by the bombardment. His eyes darted to Iowyn, and she waited for him to show her any sign that he wanted her help, but he turned his attention back to the crowd, and let them yell and shout their questions at him.

He didn't know what to tell them. What could he? They still knew virtually nothing about the creature, and didn't even have it narrowed down to a species. They were going to eat him alive. A week ago, she would have relished the sight. But now, she felt like she had to bail him out. She was his partner after all, and he had saved her life. The least she could do was take the heat from an angry crowd.

Iowyn blew out a breath and stood, but found herself too short, so she stepped up onto her chair to look out into the crowd. The crowd's attention turned to her, and a few people murmured among the congregation with recognition of who she was. Iowyn had never been nervous when it came to addressing crowds. She most certainly hadn't felt like this when she had cussed out the crowd in Leeside. But something about the way everyone was looking at her with a mixture of anger and disdain, it made her heart race and her palms sweaty.

She took in another deep breath before speaking out. "We believe that whatever is responsible has terrorized Calluna in the past. Records show a disturbing amount of child abductions every fifty years or so. That, coupled with the connection to water, narrows down what creature it could be."

An angry male's voice piped up from the far side of the crowd. "Could be? That's the best you can do?"

Iowyn's heartbeat quickened. "We only have so much evidence to go off of at this point. I–"

"How can you say that when our children are dying?"

More angered shouts and questions rose in the air, and Iowyn only wished that she could shrink down into nothing. One word seemed to ring out amongst the others from the back of the congregation. "Bitch!"

Bearen stood up so quickly that the force knocked his chair back, quieting the room immediately. His hands were balled into fists at his sides, and his chest rose and fell slowly with deep breaths.

Attention went back to the magistrate as he slammed the gavel repeatedly on the table. "I want order in here!"

Bearen helped Iowyn down from her chair and they both sat down. Ulric remained on the stage next to Albilot, but he gave a tiny nod to Iowyn when she looked up at him.

Maddox stepped forward on the stage. "Everyone here wants the same thing. To bring justice to these lost children, and prevent any other loss of life. Now the Hunter's Guild has sent us two capable people to help us in our time of need. They need our help to hunt this creature down. As your constable, I implore you to do what they ask, and be forthcoming with any information you might have."

There were quiet murmurs of agreement along with grumbles of discontent, but if anyone had qualms with what Maddox had asked, no one was piping up about it.

The meeting continued with Albilot taking time to shift to other town matters before concluding. People filtered out of the tavern slowly, with most staying around to partake in the food and drink that the Badger had to offer. Iowyn left out of the side door by the stage that led behind the inn, rather than walk through the mass of people who had just heckled and degraded her.

The cool night air felt refreshing compared to the hot and stuffy room she had just been in. She leaned against the back wall, breathing deep, and trying her best to keep everything together.

"You okay?" A larger hand grabbed hers, and when Iowyn looked up, she had half expected to see emerald eyes, instead of the blue ones looking down at her. She couldn't place the heaviness in her heart as she pulled her hand from his and took a step away from the wall.

"Oh, Maddox. You startled me."

Maddox grinned sheepishly. "Sorry, I saw you leave and wanted to make sure you were okay."

Iowyn looked away from him and into the distance, focusing on the line of trees nestled behind the building. "Sure – yeah – I'm fine. Why wouldn't I be okay?"

Maddox stepped in front of her and tilted her head up with a hand under her chin. "You've been through a lot today. You don't have to lie to me."

"I'm not."

He looked down at her skeptically.

Iowyn took a deep breath and let it out, shaking her head. "I just don't know how to feel right now."

Maddox took a step closer. "Don't think then."

Iowyn rolled her eyes, stepping back from him. "You know that's not how my brain works."

He took another step. Iowyn's back met with the back wall of the tavern. Maddox's mouth dipped to be in line with hers. "Let me help you, then."

Maddox closed the short distance between them, one hand gripping Iowyn's waist, the other tangling in her hair. Iowyn tensed at the sudden move. She placed her hands on Maddox's chest, intending to push him away, but her resolve faltered as his tongue delved into her mouth. While it wasn't the most appropriate thing to be doing at the moment, if this could help her forget all the bad things – even for just a while – then she would welcome it.

But the sound of the back door to the tavern opening caused Iowyn to break away. Her head turned to see Ulric, and her hands dropped away from Maddox.

Her stomach seemed to drop to the ground and her cheeks heated, though why, Iowyn didn't really know. She was a grown woman. She could kiss Maddox if she wanted to. And she certainly didn't care what Ulric thought about her romantic endeavors. But for some reason, her first reaction was to move away from

Maddox. He however, didn't move away from her, and kept her pinned against the wall.

Ulric cleared his throat, his eyes flitting from Iowyn to Maddox. "I'm sorry. I just… wanted to see if you were alright."

"She's fine," Maddox answered curtly.

Ulric's jaw clenched, and fire lit in his eyes as he stared at Maddox. "I wasn't asking you."

Iowyn swallowed. "I'm okay."

Her voice sounded foreign to her. It was small and mousy, but perhaps being caught in such a compromising situation had made her embarrassed enough to affect her tone.

The tension in the air was palpable, like a storm threatened to open up the sky above them at a moment's notice. Iowyn's heart raced. Ulric's gaze bore into Maddox.

Maddox took a step away from Iowyn, but his eyes never left Ulric's. Iowyn stood there, unable to move.

Ulric just thinks he's protecting you because you're his partner, she told herself. She wished she could find her voice again, to defuse the tension, but it was like her vocal cords had been pulled from her throat.

Ulric's gaze flicked to Iowyn, and for a fleeting moment, a hint of something softer than anger crossed his expression. It was quickly masked, replaced by a forced smile. "Well, if you're alright, Beastie."

Maddox's jaw tightened at Ulric's nickname for her, his hands curling into fists at his sides. Iowyn felt a knot in her stomach, seemingly torn between the two men ready to collide like opposing forces of nature.

Iowyn took a deep breath, attempting to diffuse the mounting tension. "I just needed some fresh air. It was getting a bit overwhelming inside."

Ulric nodded; his eyes still locked onto Maddox's. "Well, if you need anything, you know where to find me." With that, he turned and retreated back into the Badger, the door closing behind him.

The cool night air, which had initially been a source of relief, now felt stifling. Iowyn turned her attention back to Maddox.

"I can speak for myself," Iowyn finally said, her voice barely above a whisper.

Maddox looked up, his expression softer now than it had been just a moment ago. "I know. I just…" His voice trailed off.

"Just what?"

"I just can't stand *him*," he finished.

"You don't even know him."

Maddox brushed a strand of hair from her face. "I know that he gets to spend time with you. Travel the continent with you. And that drives me crazy."

Iowyn offered a small, sad smile. "Maddox, when all of this is done, I'll be leaving again." She knew that bringing it up might make him upset, but it was the truth. She bit her lip. "I don't want things to get complicated."

Maddox's fingers lingered on her cheek, his gaze locked onto hers. "Maybe complications aren't always a bad thing. Maybe they're just a reminder that we're afraid to lose something."

Iowyn felt her heart ache at his words, a bittersweet warmth spreading through her chest as Maddox lowered his lips to her again.

Iowyn repacked her bag for about the eighth time that night, constantly rearranging and reassessing what she could go without until she made it to Petra. What inexpensive things could she leave behind? What sentimental things did she want to bring with? It was a huge puzzle in her mind, and one she was having more trouble solving that she had originally thought possible.

"You're really leaving." The voice caught Iowyn off guard and made her almost jump out of her skin. She turned to her door to see Maddox standing there.

Iowyn let out a huge breath and placed her hand over her racing heart. "My gods, Maddox. You scared the shit out of me." She smiled, but he didn't return it.

He shut the door behind him, then came to the side of her bed.

"How did you even get in here?" she asked. There was only one way into the upper part of the building that served as her home. At least, only one conventional way up. A skilled climber could scale the oak tree in the backyard and shimmy through an unlocked window if they wished – gods only knew Iowyn had a time or two.

Maddox ignored her question and grabbed her hands. "Don't leave."

All the amusement left her face.

Maddox continued to plead. "Don't go." His eyes were wide with desperation.

"Maddox–""

He ran a hand through his hair. "Why do you want to leave? Why?"

"You know why." She had told him many times about her dream to be a monstralogist. He was one of the only people besides her fathers who knew the true extent of her love of magical creatures. It was something she had been terrified of telling him because she thought he would see her as nothing more than a complete nerd, but he had instead thought it endearing.

Maddox sighed and cupped her face. "Am I terrible for wanting you to stay?" he asked.

Iowyn's heart raced as she looked into his eyes, seeing the pain and conflict etched into his every feature. Part of her wanted to stay, to forget about her dreams, but her heart yearned for something more, to become something more.

Iowyn shook her head. "No, you aren't terrible."

He swallowed. "There's no way to convince you to stay?"

She shook her head again, tears welling up in her eyes. "I have to go, Maddox. This is my dream. I can't let it just pass me by."

Maddox's fingers tightened around her face, his eyes searching hers. "But what about us?"

"I don't know." Her voice wavered.

"What if—

"No." Iowyn shook her head free of his grip. "No 'what ifs.' I'm leaving Maddox."

She could see his heart shatter right in front of her.

"This wasn't supposed to happen," she whispered, squeezing her eyes shut.

Maddox stepped back, his hands falling to his sides. "I know," he replied, his voice heavy. "But it did happen, Iowyn. And now I can't imagine my life without you. I don't know how I'm just supposed to say goodbye to you."

Iowyn's heart ached at the words.

"I'm sorry," Iowyn whispered, tears streaming down her face. Maddox took a step forward and wrapped his arms around her, pulling her into a tight embrace. Iowyn buried her face into his chest. The tears flowed from her eyes, leaving a wet spot on Maddox's shirt.

Maddox's hands roamed down her back, clutching tightly at her shirt as if she would vanish right then and there. Maddox's heart pounded against her chest, his warmth seeping into her skin. She wanted to stay in his embrace, to never let go, but she knew she couldn't stay. She had to leave, to chase after her dreams, no matter how much it hurt.

"I'll miss you," Maddox whispered, his lips brushing against her forehead.

"I'll miss you too," Iowyn replied, her voice muffled against his chest.

They stayed like that for what felt like an eternity, until Iowyn pulled away from Maddox's arms, wiping the tears from her eyes.

Iowyn took in a deep breath and leaned in, kissing him gently on the lips. He kissed her back harder, and she could swear she could hear him pleading through the way his lips played against hers.

Don't go.

Stay.

Stay with me.

Iowyn broke away, and looked at the floor, unable to look him in the eyes. She grabbed her bag and slung it over her shoulder, taking one last look at the room she had grown up in.

"Goodbye, Maddox," she said, her voice barely above a whisper.

Maddox didn't say anything, but the look on his face said it all.

CHAPTER

20

Iowyn flipped through her old journal. She had notes on almost every creature she had ever read about inside of its pages, and she was beginning to kick herself for not having a better way to organize her notes. One page would talk about phoenixes, the next would have a drawing of a yeti's anatomy. There was no rhyme or reason to it, and it was becoming increasingly difficult for her to be able to find anything of use.

With every moment that went by, Iowyn felt the ire inside of her begin to bubble.

Ulric took a seat next to her at the table, and cleared his throat. "Good morning."

She glanced up from her journal briefly. "I haven't found anything yet."

"That's fine." The uncharacteristic softness of his voice was enough to tip her over the edge.

Iowyn snapped her book shut. "No, it's not. You know it. I know it. Everybody in this town knows that it's *not fine*."

Ulric stared at her.

Iowyn found the loose sheet of paper that she had been writing short notes on and tossed it at Ulric. "We don't know enough for me to know exactly what *it* is."

His eyes didn't even look at the paper. They didn't leave her face. "How long have you been up?"

She went back to thumbing through her journal. "Never went to sleep." Between the threat of another death and her own

inability to figure out what the creature was, Iowyn had no desire
for sleep. She wanted answers.

Ulric scowled. "Beastie—"

"I don't want to hear it," she snapped. Iowyn balled her hands
into fists on the table and shut her eyes tight. "I'm *better* than this. I
shouldn't be struggling to figure this out. I—"

"You're human," Ulric interrupted. He placed his hand over
one of her fists. "You aren't perfect."

Iowyn pursed her lips. There was never a time in all of her life
where she couldn't figure something out with the clues given to
her. There was always something in the back of her mind that
seemingly always gave her the right answer. It spoke from the far
reaches of her memory and gave her a slight twinge in her gut,
letting her always know that it was correct. Whether in her classes,
given a riddle by Burke, or reading a mystery novel, she had always
had that faint little voice and pinch in her stomach that let her
know that she had landed on the right answer.

As she pored over the books on the table last night, she hadn't
gotten that feeling once. Not even a whisper of it. It was wrong. So
wrong not to feel it for once.

"Well, that doesn't help change the fact that people – *children* –
are dying."

"Nothing about that is your fault." Ulric's voice was softer than
she had ever heard it before. "Let me help you. Maybe two minds
will be better than one."

"With yours it'll be more like one and a half," she muttered.

One corner of Ulric's mouth turned down farther than the
other. "I'm trying to help you, so I'm going to pretend that I didn't
just hear that." He gazed over the records and books on the table.
"What happened to that book from the archives? You thought you
were onto something with it before."

Iowyn shook her head. It had been her one hope, their only lead. But as she had combed through it last night, the hundred-year-old text had only soured her mood more. "It only confirmed what we already know. They tracked whatever it was to the lake, but no one ever saw it and lived to talk about it."

Ulric sighed, agitated. "So, then we go through whatever it could be one by one until we figure it out."

"*No*, really?" Iowyn mocked. "That thought never occurred to me. What do you think I've been trying to do all night?"

Ulric threw up his hands. "For fuck's sake, I'm just trying to help. What do you want from me?"

"I don't want anything from you! I want the fucking answer!"

Ulric shook his head. "That's it."

He stood up and grabbed Iowyn's forearm. His grasp dug into her skin.

"Ow! What are you doing?"

He dragged her out of her seat and out from the back of the bookshop and into the street.

"Let me go!" Iowyn tried her best to pull herself out of his grasp, like she had so many times before, but she was like a mouse trying to free herself from a bear trap. Ulric kept walking, dragging Iowyn behind him. He led her into the woods, practically unfazed by any of her struggling, until he finally stopped and released her.

"What the fuck is wrong with you!" Iowyn yelled, rubbing the sore part of her forearm. It wasn't really a question that she was asking, more of an accusation.

Ulric crossed his arms and leaned against a tree. "You aren't mad at me."

"I beg to fucking differ," she scoffed. "I've been more than mad at you since we met."

"You're angry with yourself right now, and it's getting us nowhere." He pushed off from the tree, taking a wide stance. "So hit me."

Iowyn blinked.

What did he just say?

"Hit me," he repeated in her silence.

"What?"

He took a few steps forward until he was standing right in front of her. "All that pent up anger you have at yourself for not finding the answer? It's hindering you, not helping. So get it out. Hit. Me."

There was no way he could be serious. Iowyn searched his face, trying to find any kind of bluff, but reading Ulric Ornthalas was like trying to read a dead language. This had to be a test of some kind, but much like identifying the creature, Iowyn was coming up short with figuring out what kind of test it could be.

"I'm not going to hit you." Iowyn turned on her heel to head back to town. Test or not, this was a massive waste of time. Time that she could be using to figure out what creature was killing innocent children.

Ulric grabbed her arm again and spun her back around before she could even get two steps away from him. "You aren't going anywhere until you deal with this," he said through gritted teeth.

"Let me go." Iowyn did her best to pull her arm out of his grasp, but he simply held on tighter, and it was starting to hurt. "Let me go, Ornthalas," she said again, louder this time.

Ulric smirked, like this was fun for him. "Make me," he challenged.

Iowyn had learned at a young age not to physically react with her anger. It had only taken a few times being summoned to the school after hours for Bearen and Burke to take things into their own hands. It wasn't her fault that Carter Cormick was a bully and needed to be taken down a few pegs. Or that Assandra Rochere wouldn't stop telling lies about her to everyone. In Iowyn's defense, she'd given them both ample warning. It was easy to lash out – Bearen had told her – it was harder to have control.

So, under Burke's own tutelage, she had learned how to use her words more than her fists when it came to her anger. And Bearen had supplied her with ample swear words she'd used to bolster her turns of phrase. It had been the way she'd lived her life since she was ten, and now Ulric was basically just telling her to forget all of that. To lash out. To hit him. She wouldn't deny that she had thought about hitting him more than a few times since meeting him. And now? Now he was asking for it. So, she supposed if she was dumb enough to do so, the least she could do was oblige.

Iowyn breathed in slowly through her nose and planted her feet. Her free hand curled up into a fist. And she swung.

Her knuckles collided with the side of Ulric's jaw, stunning him just enough that his grip loosened and she could pull her arms away. Ulric took a full step back, his hand flying up to where he'd been struck.

Iowyn flexed her hand as a light pain pulsed through her fingers. She let out her breath and turned on her heel to walk back to the bookshop. "You were right," she called back, a small smile on her face. "I do feel better."

Ulric rubbed the side of his jaw. Iowyn – it seemed – had been holding out on him. When he had baited her into hitting him, he thought that he would easily absorb whatever blow she threw at him, considering he had taken punches from guy's twice her size. The right hook she had just thrown at him was a nasty one. Enough to make him think twice about telling her to hit him again, and instead let her get back to her research.

Ulric took his time getting back to the bookshop, but when he entered, Burke stopped him. "She isn't back there. She came in and went straight up to her room, so what did you do?"

Ulric raised his brows at the accusation and the sternness in the otherwise demure man. "I didn't do anything to upset her. In fact, she left me rather pleased with herself."

Burke's eyes widened.

Ulric realized all too late how what he had just said to Iowyn's father sounded. His hands came up quickly in defense. "I didn't mean anything like that. She was upset. I let her hit me. That's all."

A low chuckle came from the doorway that connected the bookshop and bakery. Bearen was taking up almost all of the empty space in the void, his shoulders just barely fitting in the doorframe. "You *let* her hit you? Seems you're braver than I thought."

Burke turned around on Bearen. "She shouldn't be *hitting* anyone! We agreed on that."

Bearen sighed. "She isn't ten anymore, Burkey. I'm not so sure we have any control over what she does anymore."

A large crash sounded from upstairs, followed by a sound that Ulric could only liken to an avalanche. All three men looked at each other, then hurried up the stairs to figure out what in the world could have made the racket.

Ulric had yet to be inside the Morgnah's home above the shops, and he was surprised at how small the living quarters were, especially when considering Bearen's size alone. He was sure for both him and Burke, the quarters were a little more than cozy, but to add in a growing child to such a small space?

Bearen was first to the door that Ulric assumed was Iowyn's room. He knocked and pressed his ear to the door. "Iowyn? Are you okay?"

She opened the door a crack, an embarrassed smile on her face. "Sorry," she grimaced, "was that loud?"

"What on earth are you doing in there?" Burke piped up. He stood on his tip toes to try and look past Iowyn and into the room.

She bit her lip. The gesture was small, but it caused the slightest jump of Ulric's stomach.

Not the time, or the place, or the girl, he silently chided himself.

"My bookshelves fell. I'm really sorry." She kept the door only slightly ajar. "I promise nothing's broken. I just need to clean it up."

Ulric found it funny how even though she was a grown woman, Iowyn was still behaving like a child with her hand caught in the cookie jar about to be disciplined.

Bearen moved away from the door, pulling Burke away as well. "Well, your friend can help you with that."

Iowyn finally locked eyes with Ulric standing behind her parents. "No thanks." She went to shut the door, but Bearen was quick enough to stop it with his hand.

"Your friend *will* help you," Bearen repeated, his voice laced with an uncompromising tone. It took Ulric aback somewhat. He'd only ever heard the baker talk to his daughter with such a lightness to his otherwise sonorous voice.

Iowyn sighed. "Fine."

She opened the door fully and Burke gasped at what Ulric could only guess was a bookshop owner's worst nightmare. Books of every size lay haphazardly all over the floor, the bookshelves piled on top of them. Bearen dragged him away from the awful sight, and both went back downstairs.

Iowyn knelt to start picking up the numerous books on the floor. "I must not have hit you hard enough if you're already back to bug me."

Ulric stepped into her room slowly. Besides the absolute mess of books on the floor, it was exactly how he would have pictured her childhood bedroom to be. A large desk sat by the window with countless ink bottle stains and pillar candles burnt down to nothing. Any blank space on the walls were plastered with sketches and paintings of creatures. She'd been allowed to explore her interests and dream of becoming whatever she wanted to be. It was quaint and cozy – nothing like what he remembered his own room being like as a child.

Ulric looked down to read the titles of some of the books: *The Ultimate Field Guide to the Fantastic Beasts and Monsters of Our World*, *The Encyclopedia of the Unknown: An Exploration of Mythical Monsters*, *The Complete Compendium of Magical Creatures and Monsters*, and *Mythical World: Demystifying the Creatures of Legend and Folklore*, to name a few.

"Well, if you wanted me to leave you alone for longer, you should have knocked me out." He knelt down beside her and began stacking books.

"That could always be arranged," she smiled.

Ulric couldn't fight the upturn of his own lips. He cleared his throat. "What were you doing up here?"

"Well, I don't know if you've noticed," she gestured to the books all around them, "but I have just about every book about magical creatures I could get my hands on up here. I thought I remembered one that might have the answer we're looking for."

"And that caused all the books to fall?"

Iowyn pursed her lips. "No…"

"So, what happened?"

She sighed and pointed to the only blank wall in the room. "These shelves were stacked on that wall. And the book I wanted was on the very top shelf, so instead of just doing the smart thing and grabbing a chair to stand on, I did the dumb thing and just climbed on the bookshelf." Red creeped up her neck and towards her cheeks.

"You mean to tell me that you did something *dumb*, Beastie?"
Ulric feigned surprised.

She punched his shoulder. A dull ache spread outward from the
impact. "Leave the sarcasm to me, Ornthalas. Your delivery is
terrible."

He smirked. When things were less tense like this between
them, Ulric really didn't mind her. He actually could admit that
there were times that he did genuinely like her.

"So then, you know what book it is we're looking for?" he
asked.

Iowyn gave a defeated sigh. "More like a specific chapter is
what I remember." She flipped through the pages of each book as
she stacked them.

Ulric looked at the massive pile of books in front of them. If
she would have to flip through all of them, it could take hours.
"Would you like me to put the books aside for you to look
through?"

Iowyn looked at Ulric, as if his politeness was as odd to her as
finding an iceberg in the desert. "That would be helpful, yes."

He started stacking books and righting the bookshelves. Iowyn
directed him to where they each went, and it was a wonder that the
shelves hadn't fallen before. Each had its own unique dimension,
and she had them stacked on top of her other as precariously as
possible. "Some nails would really help solve this problem, you
know," Ulric commented.

Iowyn shrugged. "The weight usually holds them down."

When there were no more books to pick up and stack, Ulric
started to put the books that Iowyn had already combed through
back on the shelves. As he filled the shelves, he found that Iowyn
was right. The added weight of the books seemed to help with the
shelves' wobbliness.

After a while, Ulric found himself leaning against the wall, watching Iowyn as she sat on the floor and flitted through the pages of each book.

"Do you find the floor comfortable or something?" he asked finally.

She stopped rifling through the pages at his comment. "What?"

He motioned to her position on the floor. "You're always on the floor when you're reading."

Iowyn scoffed. "I'm not *always* on the floor."

Ulric raised a brow.

"I use tables sometimes," she added begrudgingly, moving onto the next book.

Ulric picked up a new stack of books to put away, the title of the book on top catching his attention: *Odea: The Mother of All.*

"Well, this is surprising," he said out loud.

Iowyn looked up from the book in her hands. "What is?"

Ulric picked the book off the top of the stack with a free hand and showed her the cover. "You know, now that I'm older, the gods are really messed up when you think about it."

"What do you mean?" she asked, curiosity peaking in her voice.

Ulric continued to put the other books on the shelves as he talked. "I mean, if you think about it, it's all pretty fucked up. Odea created everything and everyone. She hated seeing her creations die, so she created Mortem to be her equal but opposite, the god of death and the underworld."

He picked the book back up and thumbed through it himself, stopping on a spread that showed the most famous drawing of Odea and Mortem, thought to be drawn by Genova, the first human. Odea on the one side, her skin as dark as the earth and her eyes not one, but all colors. Her long white hair was twisted intricately in hundreds, if not thousands, of braids with ribbons of silver and gold intertwined. A white gown hugged her full body, and she stood with her arms open, as if prepared to embrace the entire world.

Mortem, on the other side, was a stark contrast to his wife. His hair and eyes were black as night, his skin as white as snow. Shadows and other wisps of darkness surrounded him. Everyone who died would face the god of death and judgment before being ushered into the underworld. Whether you went to Paradise or the Pit was all up to him. In his hands were the tools of a craftsman, the very ones that he used to build those deemed worthy enough their own personal Paradise.

Ulric could stop himself from talking. "But if Odea created him and she's the Mother of All, wouldn't that technically make him her son? Yet they are married in almost every iteration of the Word that you can find. And then they have their two sons together, Ikris and Temphon. And Odea creates for them two goddesses as their perfect matches, which if you think about it, makes them all siblings. It's all very incestuous and creepy when you break it all down."

Iowyn huffed a laugh out of her nose and gave him smile. "They're *gods*. Normal rules don't really apply where deity is concerned. And you know what? I think that this is the most I've ever heard you talk about anything."

Ulric paused. He supposed it was true. He wasn't much for conversation. What had possessed him to even start talking about the gods in the first place? It was very unlike him, but the book seemed so out of place among all the other volumes in Iowyn's collection. "Why do you even have this book? It doesn't fit with the rest?"

Iowyn shrugged. "It sort of does if you think about it. Some scholars think that the creation tale is wrong and that the magical creatures that dwell in the world came from another place farther away, while the Traditionalists posit that it's quite possible that

Odea *did* create everything and everyone, and the creatures have always been here."

She held out a book to Ulric, and he took it from her to place on the shelf. "What do you think?" he asked.

Iowyn looked up at the ceiling, as if the answer was somehow up there. "I don't really know. I think both schools of thought have some merit. Maybe Odea was made up to explain what we still think of as unexplainable. Or maybe we actually were all made by some benevolent Mother who just loves to create."

Ulric sat down next to her, and took a new book off of an untouched stack to hand back to her. "That's not a very straight forward answer."

She leveled her amber eyes at him. "Just because I know a lot, doesn't mean I know everything."

He didn't say anything, just held her gaze. He found it made her talk more when he didn't say anything in return, like she couldn't help but fill the empty space with her own words.

Iowyn sighed. "Okay, so *maybe* I lean a little more towards the idea that creatures weren't always here. I mean, why have the different classification between animals and creatures if we weren't used to one over the other before? Think about it. Dren technically doesn't have any magical powers or mysticality to him at all, yet deupins are *creatures* and not animals?"

Ulric let her words sink in. She had a point, and one that Ulric hadn't ever really thought about. Growing up, he learned that some beasts were animals and some were creatures. It had never occurred to him where the classification had come from. It was just something everyone accepted as fact.

Iowyn turned her attention back to the book in front of her, and Ulric felt a heaviness settle in his chest. He didn't want the conversation to end. He *liked* that they were actually talking for once and getting along. When she was actually talking about what she was passionate about and not badgering him for information about his personal life, he found her quite agreeable, even pleasant. He needed to think of something else to ask her. Anything.

She furled the pages, and stopped. Her body went still and her eyes widened at the spread in front of her. "I found it," she breathed.

Ulric sat down next to her and leaned over to see the book for himself. "What does it say—"

Iowyn raised a hand blindly to Ulric's mouth. He scowled at her, but her attention was focused solely on the book in her lap. Her amber eyes raked across the pages, seemingly lit from within with intrigue and anticipation. She removed her hand from his face only to turn the page.

Iowyn took a sharp intake of breath, and she began reading:

When considering creatures of lakes and the deep in general, one must keep in mind the kelpie. Though rare and barely documented, kelpies are not confined to one region of Phyrra. They are known for their great adaptability, surviving for centuries in unfavorable conditions, and have been recorded in climates of all extremes.

Kelpies, at their base, are shape-shifting spirits that most commonly manifest as large, black horse-like creatures. These supernatural beings can be easily distinguished from actual horses by their telltale features—backwards hooves and pointed teeth. These distinctive physical traits serve as cautionary markers to those who may encounter these alluring creatures, acting as harbingers of the danger they pose.

The kelpie's shape-shifting ability extends to assuming human form, a deception that has long been the preferred tactic in their dark endeavors. This ability to take on a human appearance enhances their seductive charm and enables them to better ensnare unsuspecting victims. It is worth noting that the kelpie's preferred sources of sustenance are young children and beautiful women. The manner in which they capture their prey remains consistent with the mythological narratives — luring their targets away and entrapping them in the depths of water bodies. Once ensnared, the kelpie proceeds to consume its victim before discarding the entrails and other non-nutritious bits, such as clothing, at the water's edge, further perpetuating the cycle of danger and deception.

Part of what contributes to the elusiveness and rarity of kelpies is their propensity to enter long periods of dormancy following their feedings. This aspect of their behavior is not only intriguing, but also adds to the challenge of documenting their existence. Dormancy periods vary greatly among individuals, spanning from as short as a year to potentially stretching across several centuries. With study of these creatures being almost impossible, it is hard to understand what factors play into the length of the kelpie's dormancy period, whether it be age, climate, diet, etc. Each kelpie's dormancy pattern and frequency of feeding before entering dormancy are believed to be unique to the individual.

Interestingly, historical records indicate that kelpies can be bested by weapons crafted from specific materials. Silver-tipped weapons and those entirely made of iron have been noted as effective means of countering the kelpie's formidable power. These traditional weaknesses have been woven into the tales surrounding the creatures, adding a layer of folklore and strategy for those who would venture to face these aquatic enigmas.

"Holy shit," Ulric muttered. "You did it. You found the answer."

A smile blossomed over Iowyn's face, and Ulric's heart seemed to stumble at the look of pure joy. Iowyn's gaze met Ulric's, and it was at that moment that Ulric realized just how close they were sitting.

Ulric's eyes dipped to Iowyn's lips for just a fraction of a second. It would be all too easy for him — he realized — to lean down and bring her mouth to his. But that was preposterous. He didn't even want to kiss her.

Did he?

A knock at the bedroom door broke his trance, and quickly brought him back to reality.

21

"Hope I wasn't interrupting anything?" Elmer whispered, giving Ulric a sly smile as they stood in the doorway of Iowyn's room.

"What is it?" Ulric asked, trying his best to change the subject and not sound irritated.

Elmer shook his head, but his smile didn't go away. "You said you wanted to go riding today, remember?"

Ulric looked back at Iowyn on the floor, her nose still in the book that they'd read the passage about kelpies. "Change of plans," he said quickly to Elmer. "We're doing a stakeout."

"Stakeout?" Elmer asked, much louder than Ulric would have liked. Iowyn's head was pulled out of the book immediately.

"What?"

Ulric turned to her. "We need to get proper identification, right?"

She nodded.

"So, Elmer and I will stake out the lake and wait for whatever it is to either come out of the lake or return to it."

Iowyn shut the book and got to her feet, all the while shaking her head. "No, I'm going with you." She started walking towards the door, making for a way to get around Ulric, but he stepped in front of her.

"Not this time, Beastie. You need to stay here and–"

"And what, exactly?" she asked, placing a hand on her hip. "What if the thing that you see isn't what we think? What if it is something completely different? You need me there to see it firsthand. I'm your best shot at identifying it.

Elmer cleared his throat from behind Ulric. "She kind of has a point there."

Ulric clenched a fist, but released it almost as soon as it had formed. She was right. Worst of all, he *knew* that she was right. She'd have to come with, which meant that he was willfully putting her in danger.

Ulric let out a breath. "Fine."

Iowyn smiled.

"*But*," he held up a finger and pointed it at her, "you stay with me and do whatever I say."

Iowyn bit her lip and nodded. She quite poor at hiding her excitement.

Elmer clasped his hands together. "I'll go fetch the mounts then–"

"No," Ulric shook his head. "If we go, we go on foot. I don't want the presence of other creatures to deter whatever it is from showing up."

Elmer grimaced slightly, but put on a smile with a sigh. "I guess it isn't a terrible day for a walk."

The distance to the lake hadn't seemed all that far before, but it was slow, and Iowyn found herself almost wishing she'd stayed back to read in bed for the afternoon. The only thing helping to make the time fly by was Elmer.

"What's Petra like?" he asked. He'd been asking lots of questions about the Guild, University, and just traveling Phyrra in general.

Iowyn blew out a breath as she tried to think of how to explain the capital of Rathian. "Honestly, it's one big stone maze. You turn a corner and suddenly you're in a quiet courtyard, or some ancient temple, or an artisan's workshop. The streets are a maze of narrow, winding paths packed with people from all over. Merchants are everywhere, shouting out the prices of their goods — everything from fine silks and spices to rare gems and handcrafted weapons. Every street has a stall or a shop, and the variety is just mind-blowing. It's like the whole of Phyrra has gathered in one place. And I mean people are just everywhere. Street performers are on just about every corner, playing music, dancing, and doing acrobatics to make a living. You'll find scholars and scribes having lively debates in open-air forums, and priests and priestesses offering blessings. The inns and taverns are always full of people, most nights it's standing room only."

Elmer's eyes seemed to sparkle as he hung on every word.

"You should go sometime," Iowyn said. "That or to Kence. It's no Petra, but it's still a bustling city."

Elmer shook his head. "I don't know about that."

"Why not?" Ulric asked. Iowyn's head swiveled to her partner, a little at a loss for words at Ulric's sudden interest in their conversation.

"I... well..." Elmer stuttered, suddenly finding his boots very interesting. "I don't think I'd fit in," he finally admitted, looking up at Iowyn with a vulnerable glint in his eye.

Iowyn went to tell Elmer that that certainly wouldn't be the case. Petra was quite possibly the one place where anyone could belong. But Ulric stopped in his tracks and held up a hand. The command was quite clear.

Quiet.

They'd discussed that silence would be necessary the closer they got to the lake. Their presence should be minimal in order to allow for the creature to surface. Iowyn made a mental note to say something to Elmer later, when she wouldn't be chided for speaking.

A few minutes later, the lake shore came into view, and Ulric whispered directions to Elmer, no doubt telling him what area he should be surveying and the best ways to stay out of sight. Elmer gave Ulric a firm nod, then went off in the opposite direction.

Iowyn followed Ulric as he made a path through the trees. For such a large guy, it amazed her how quietly he could walk through the underbrush, without so much as snapping a twig. He stopped at a large cedar, one that Iowyn was sure was more than a hundred feet tall. Ulric looked at the tree, then to Iowyn, and she could see the thoughts racing through his head. He was wondering how he was going to get her up the tree.

Iowyn couldn't help but roll her eyes, and without a sound, found a good starting foothold and a sturdy bottom branch, and started climbing the tree herself. Had Ulric ever decided to ask her, he might have known that Iowyn grew up climbing trees like this one. She'd climb the oak tree behind her parents' building to reach the roof late at night, whenever she needed a change of scenery or to clear her head.

Iowyn kept climbing, her focus the next foothold, the next branch to grab. She could hear Ulric beneath her, not nearly as stealthy once off the ground. Branches snapped and there was the occasional swear under his breath. Iowyn stopped climbing as she reached a large bough that cleared the rest of canopy, swinging her leg over the branch and finding a seat.

Ulric clambered up after her, sitting on the bough next to her, his breath labored. Iowyn decided to stay quiet and keep any biting remarks to herself.

"You're rather good at climbing trees," he said finally, his voice hushed.

"Thank you," she replied, her gaze sweeping over the lake. "You're quite terrible at it."

"Oh?" The slightest bit of amusement lilted his tone at the jab. A week ago, such a comment would have sent them spiraling into an argument. But now…

"Yes," she affirmed.

"And just how did you acquire such a useless skill?"

Iowyn shot him a pointed look. Weren't they supposed to be silent right now?

"I used to climb trees like this all the time. The one in our backyard especially." Iowyn finally tore her eyes away from the water's edge. "And it isn't useless. In fact, I think that it's rather useful to us now, isn't it?" Iowyn thought about punctuating her statement with a stuck-out tongue, but she settled instead for crossing her arms across her chest.

Ulric shook his head slightly. "You always focus on the negative things I say, you know that?"

Iowyn clenched her own jaw. "You know, I really never thought I would *ever* need to say this to you, but do shut up, Ornthalas," she hissed. Iowyn turned her gaze back to the lake and the surrounding rocky beach. She must have been imagining things, because she could have sworn that she saw Ulric smile from the edge of her vision.

They sat in silence, waiting for any chance that the creature might appear. It was a long shot at best. If they had more people, they could stake out along the river leading to town as well. It was a gamble to spend so much time waiting, but they would be grasping at straws until they knew for certain what the creature was.

Hours passed by as they sat on the bough. Iowyn's back cried out with every small movement. She didn't have the luxury of sitting next to the trunk of the tree. She hadn't thought of the advantage of needing something to lean back against until her lower back began to burn and ache.

The silence rang in her ears. The urge to say something was like an itch begging for the relief of being scratched. But she held her tongue. They had to blend in with their surroundings, and being quiet was one of the best ways to do so.

The only thing that seemed to help her pass the time was studying the surroundings. How many leaves were on the bough they sat on? How many birds flew past them in the sky? How many trees between them and the water? It helped, but only for so long. She was running out of things to count. She needed something more interesting to study.

Iowyn cursed herself for not bringing a book to read, something to take her mind off the waiting, while also stimulating her brain at the same time. Ulric shifted slightly next to her. His back leaned against the trunk of the tree. One of his long legs hung off to the side, the other propped and bent at the knee.

Perhaps there was something else to study in the vicinity.

She didn't look directly at him, but more so stole sideways glances at him. His own emerald gaze was locked on target, surveying every movement, every ripple of water, like a wolf ready to attack.

His attire was rugged, much like himself. His tunic, strained at the seams with the bulk of his muscles, was worn and frayed around the edges. It was the same green shirt he had worn the night they went after the werewolf, and she noted the mending stitches where there had been tears before. They had been expertly sewn back together with tent stitches; the thread matched the green fabric of his shirt almost perfectly. The sleeves were rolled up to his elbows, revealing sinewy forearms peppered with small scars and scratches.

His hands were another story altogether. They were strong, calloused from years of handling weapons and equipment. They could effortlessly swing a sword or pull back the tough string of a bow, and she remembered how they felt whenever he'd picked her up or taken her hand.

His hair was a stark contrast to the lush green foliage around them - a rich chocolate brown that gleamed under the soft filtering sunlight, rustling slightly as he shifted his weight against the bark. Tousled tendrils danced across his forehead in no particular order, and Iowyn felt an uncharacteristic urge to brush them back into place.

His jawline was chiseled like a statue carved by skilled hands. There was something animalistic about the stubble tracing the contours of his face. As Iowyn thought about it, she realized she'd never seen the hunter before her without the shadow of stubble on his face. Would he look younger without it? More boyish? Looking at the man before her, she quite doubted it possible.

The jagged slash across his cheek was beginning to heal at the edges, leaving light pink skin on his otherwise tan face. His lips were almost always in an unwelcoming expression. Either pressed together, or in what seemed to be a permanent kind of frown, yet as she looked at them now, she found herself wondering how they would feel... She hastily chased that thought away, puzzled as to why it even occurred to her in the first place.

Ulric's eyes shifted, glancing her way, and Iowyn couldn't help the thump of her heart at the idea of being caught looking at him. Her eyes went right back to the water. From her periphery, she saw Ulric turn his head toward her and open his mouth, but the sound of sloshing water caused her to reach out and grab his forearm.

Ulric's head snapped back to the lake, and Iowyn's grip on his arm tightened with every second that passed. The sound grew louder, and finally, from the mouth of the river below them, a creature stepped out from the trees.

Before Iowyn's heart could leap from her chest, Ulric's hand came over her mouth, and his other arm snaked around her middle. He pulled her right against him and the trunk of the tree. Iowyn gripped his arm tightly with both hands as she did her best to calm her breathing as her mind raced. They'd expected the creature to come from the lake, not the river. Did this mean another child had been taken while they'd been here?

No, that couldn't be. There was no screaming, no cries for help. She shut her eyes tightly for a second, taking in a deep but silent breath, then opened her eyes to focus on the creature.

A massive black horse trudged through the water where the shallows of the lake met the mouth of the river. Had Iowyn not known any better, she would have thought Shadowfoot had somehow made a break from the stables and found her way back to Ulric. But as the creature passed below them, it wasn't a black coat of fur that covered its body, but thick and twining black vines. With each step, a leg with a backward hoof came up from the water. The creature stepped up onto the rocky beach, and started its way around the perimeter of the lake. Its large, long tail – longer than any horse's tail she'd ever seen – made up of what looked like pondweeds and lake kelp, swayed behind it, disrupting the rocky pebbles of the beach. As it walked further away, it was clear that this was the creature that had made the trail they'd followed the day before, right to the child's shoe.

The kelpie.

It walked almost halfway around the lake, and then turned to walk back into the water.

Ulric's breath hitched for a moment, then released in a barely audible sigh. His green eyes glimmered with something that Iowyn couldn't quite decipher. Was it relief? Anticipation? Perhaps, even a hint of fear?

As the creature turned, the kelpie's head tilted upwards. For a heartbeat, its eyes - swirling orbs of murky green - met with theirs. Iowyn's blood turned to ice. There was an eerie intelligence lurking in those eyes; it was as if the beast recognized their presence high up in the tree, or worse, felt their gaze upon it

But then, as abruptly as it had happened, the moment ended. The kelpie dipped its head and waded deeper into the water until it vanished beneath the surface with barely a ripple disturbing the tranquility of the lake.

The silence that followed was deafening. Iowyn felt her heart thudding against her ribcage like a wild bird trapped within a cage, and she only realized she had been holding her breath when she felt the need to gasp for air.

Iowyn peeled Ulric's hand from her mouth. "Did...did it see us?" she whispered. Her voice felt strange in the echoing silence that followed the monstrous horse's departure.

Ulric didn't answer right away, his gaze still fixed on where the creature had dived under the water's surface. His voice was low next to her ear. "We need to leave. Climb down, slowly and quietly."

"What about Elmer?"

"He knows what to do," Ulric assured. "Go."

His hold on her slackened. She turned to face the tree, slowly beginning her descent, each hand and foot moving with an almost silent precision that she was quite proud of. She was midway when she heard the minimal creaking of the bark above her. Ulric was making his own way down, albeit noisier than she was.

Reaching the ground, Iowyn took a moment to steady herself, looking around for signs of movement. It was eerily quiet. Her heart still pounded in her chest, and she felt like it was trying to match her audibility with its thudding rhythm.

Ulric landed lightly next to her, a ghost of a sound amidst the silence. She felt his hand on her shoulder, his thumb brushing against her skin in a comforting circular motion. "Stay close," he murmured, his voice barely more than a whisper in the breeze.

The forest seemed forbidding now, even in daylight. The shadows appeared deeper and more menacing. The tall trees swaying gently in the wind looked like sentinels guarding the dark creature of the lake.

They moved cautiously through the forest, Ulric leading while Iowyn followed closely behind him. She scanned the ground for twigs and sticks that could easily snap under her feet. It felt like ages until they broke through the trees and into a meadow clearing.

"Wait," Ulric instructed. He held his hand up to stop her from proceeding further. Her heart pounded fiercely in her chest, echoing in her ears as she searched the open expanse for any sign of danger.

She could see nothing out of place. The meadow was just as she remembered it – a large, picturesque expanse of swaying grasses and wildflowers with the mountains as its backdrop. The breeze rustled through the stalks, creating waves in the sea of green. It was beautiful, serene even.

Ulric's grip on her shoulder tightened imperceptibly. "Listen," he whispered.

She strained to hear what he was hearing. The wind rustling against her ear made it difficult until she heard it - movement in the trees not far from them. Before either of them could react, something broke through the trees on the far side of the clearing. Iowyn released the breath clenched in her chest at the sight of Elmer.

His hands hit his knees as he doubled over, gasping for breath. Iowyn stepped forward and into the clearing, rushing over to him. "Are you okay?"

Elmer held up an upturned thumb, still breathing heavily.

Ulric was soon at Elmer's side, and even offered the young bartender a pat on the back.

Elmer looked up at Ulric. "That... that *thing* was nasty."

Ulric just gave him a smirk. "Welcome to Guild work."

Iowyn stared at him with wide eyes.

Ulric Ornthalas had just made a sarcastic comment. Which meant either she was beginning to rub off on him, or they were fucking doomed.

Elmer and Ulric saw Iowyn home, then walked together on the cobbled street back to the other end of town. Elmer was apparently due for his shift at the Badger any minute, and Ulric wanted more than anything to have a quick rest before making any kind of plan.

"What the hell is that thing?" Elmer pointed at the large blue bird that stood at the stables entrance. It walked back and forth in the open door, like it was *pacing*.

Ulric sighed and walked towards the bird, much to Elmer's alarm. As he approached, the falcon's head swiveled, and its eyes glowed a bright yellow. It offered out its foot, and Ulric knelt down to untie the top of the leather tube and retrieve whatever was inside.

Ulric unfurled the parchment to find a blank page, save for the top of the missive, which stated:

Status report requested for Assignment #43895

Ulric's eyes rolled back into his head as he read it. He had hoped that the status report he'd been asked to relay on the last assignment was just a one-off thing. He should have known better. Now that he was on probation, it wasn't enough to just check in with the Guardsmen whenever he came to an outpost. No. They needed to be sure he was where he was meant to be. Not out on the lama trying to avoid Smokheim, but actually doing the assignment that was set before him.

Ulric folded the message and stuffed it into the back pocket of his pants. The seeking falcon screeched, waiting impatiently for Ulric to return the report.

"Give me five minutes, birdbrain," Ulric grumbled.

The falcon, apparently not happy with that answer, flapped its wings and alighted enough to perch on the hitching post outside. It glared at Ulric like it wanted to pluck out his eyes with its black beak. It screeched again when Ulric walked past the hitching post, its impatience practically palpable. Ulric turned on his heels to walk backwards toward the inn. "I need a fucking pen!" he yelled at the avian beast.

Great, he thought, *now I'm talking to fucking birds.*

Ulric turned back around and entered the Itchy Badger. A few of the same patrons from nights before were already in their spots, and a large man was serving them their drinks of choice from behind the bar. Ulric walked past them all, up the stairs and into his room. He found a spare fountain pen in a drawer of the desk that sat in the corner of the small room.

Ulric looked down at the piece of paper in front of him. He'd been on assignments for months at a time before his probation, and never once been asked to give a status report. He and Iowyn had barely been in Calluna for three days. Had news of the other child's disappearance made it back to an outpost?

Ulric picked up the pen.

Short and sweet. If the Guild didn't like it, then that wasn't his problem. Besides, that damned bird wasn't going to wait for him to take his time to be more eloquent about it. Ulric set the pen back in the desk drawer and rerolled the scroll tightly before walking out of the Badger and back to the hitching post.

The seeking falcon screeched at the sight of Ulric, even splaying its wings out on either side, as if to say, *"Hurry up and let me fly!"*

"Yeah, yeah," Ulric grumbled. Despite his flippancy with the bird, he was still wary of his hand as he reached for the leather tube strapped to its leg. He carefully inserted the scroll into the open tube, and tied it shut, ever mindful of how close he was getting to the bird. A seeking falcon's beak and talons were no joke, and the last thing Ulric wanted was to add another scar to his face.

When Ulric backed away from the beast, the falcon screeched once more before flapping its wings and taking to the sky. Ulric shielded his eyes from the cloud of dirt and dust that the falcon's large wings kicked up around the hitching post, and watched as the bird flew west, not letting his eyes leave it until it was nothing but a speck in the sky.

"Are you going to tell me what that was all about?"

Elmer's sudden appearance at his side made Ulric half jump. He'd figured the young barkeep had gone inside. He felt ridiculous as soon as he did it, and hoped that Elmer hadn't noticed, but his mouth quirked up to one side.

"Didn't take you for the jumpy type, Ornthalas."

Ulric scowled. "I'm *not* jumpy."

He sighed. "Let's hope not, for all our sakes." Elmer's gaze went back to the sky. "That's quite possibly the biggest bird I've ever seen. What was it?"

Ulric's brows raised. "You mean, you've really never seen a seeking falcon?"

"Seeking falcon?" Elmer whispered. "*That* was a seeking falcon?"

Ulric nodded.

Elmer let out a little whistle. "I mean, I've heard of them, sure. But I thought they'd be just like other falcons and hawks around here. Not large enough to spill my guts on the floor."

Ulric clapped a hand on Elmer's shoulder. "They're harmless, for the most part. So long as you don't test their patience." He started to lead them both in the direction of the Badger. "Besides, if you really want to know a bird you should be scared of, a giantyta would be much more formidable."

"A gian-what-a?"

Ulric huffed a laugh at Elmer's perplexed look. "Think of a snowy owl, but the size of two bears standing on top of each other."

Elmer's hazel eyes widened like saucers as he imagined it. "My gods, you mean something like that exists?"

"Nowhere around here, thankfully enough for you. They live high up in the Severni Mountains that span from Oqira to Acantia."

"So, you've never had to deal with one?"

"I didn't say that."

Elmer smiled a bit. "Tell me about it?"

Ulric sighed. He wasn't really one for telling stories, but for some reason, he really didn't mind telling Elmer. Something lit up in his eyes when Ulric told him even the most boring stories of assignments. Perhaps he felt some pity for the young man, who'd never traveled farther than a few miles in either direction of Calluna.

Ulric opened his mouth to answer Elmer, but a flash of white in the trees at the edge of town caught his attention, giving him pause. A man stepped out from the tree line, his dark hair shining with droplets of water in the midafternoon sun. As he tugged on his dark blue jacket, even from a distance, Ulric knew who had just emerged from the forest, walking away from the direction of the lake.

Maddox.

22

Iowyn had fallen asleep almost as soon as her body had hit her mattress, still in her clothes from the stakeout. It had been hours of sitting in an uncomfortable position. Her backside ached more than she could ever remember, and her body screamed out for rest.

She wasn't sure how long she had been in the realm of sleep before being roused from it.

Clink! Clink!

Iowyn popped open an eye, the sun threatened to shine through the curtains that covered her window, but she could see the avian silhouette outside as clear as day.

Clink! Clink! Clinkity-clink!

She groaned, loud enough that she hoped the seeking falcon outside could hear how perturbed she felt by the interruption of her late afternoon nap. She rose from the bed, and even went so far as to stomp over to the window before throwing open the curtains.

The seeking falcon was not moved by any of Iowyn's griping. Its eyes glowed yellow as they fell upon her, and it held out its taloned foot for her to extract the message from its carrier tube.

Iowyn opened the latch on the window, and had barely gotten the paper in her hands before the falcon let out an ear-splitting shriek, and alighted back into the sky. She sighed, pulling the curtains back shut, and making her way back to her bed, flopping onto the mattress.

She unfurled the paper, a familiar feminine scrawl almost leaping off the page at her.

Dear Wyn,

Where are you now? You could be anywhere. Though I know that you aren't in Rathian because I'm sure I would have heard about it. Or you would have least come say hi.

My new partner is still annoying, thanks for asking. I'm pretty sure he got us kicked off of night duty from talking too much, and I don't know whether that was on purpose or not. But now, we get to go on assignments rather than patrols.

I will say, he has the ability to drive Dad absolutely bonkers, which is only one pro next to the huge list of cons of being this man's partner. Thorn in Dad's side or not, I would have still preferred to have you over him as my partner in a heartbeat.

Dad still isn't letting me go anywhere outside of Rathian. The man simply can't fathom not being in control of my life in one way or another. All of our assignments have been more or less open and shut: a couple chupacabras near the Holithan border and a cave wyrm between the North and East outposts. We almost got handed an assignment to track down a cockatrice in Vrig, but Dad put a stop to that before we gained any traction.

I won't lie, knowing that you are out in the field is a little unsettling to me. At least when you were a scriven, I knew where you were at all times, and that you were safe behind outpost walls.

NOT that I don't think that you can handle fieldwork. That's not what I'm saying. I'm saying I don't know if I can handle you doing fieldwork.

Write to me as soon as possible. If only to let me know that you're safe. I want to hear everything! (Especially about your terrible partner.)

Love,

Loyla

Iowyn smiled, and walked over to her desk, found a pen and paper, then started to write her reply.

Dear Loyla,

Iowyn stopped her writing, and looked up at the window. The falcon was gone, and she realized there would be no way to send her letter until they were finished with their assignment.

Iowyn put the pen down and folded up the letter. She tucked the small paper square in the inside pocket of her leather bag. She could finish it later, when all was said and done, just like she'd promised in her sentences.

Iowyn sighed and looked towards her bed. It would be nice to return to her nap, but her letter to Loyla had reminded her that

there was a much more pressing matter at hand. She had a job to
do.

The falcon Ulric received back from his status report was clear.

*Body retrieval of kelpie of utmost importance. Bring to Central Arondiran
outpost with the utmost haste.*
- Guild Master Pedar Foxe

Ulric was surprised when he came down the stairs from his
room to see Iowyn seated at the bar, talking idly with Elmer. The
barkeep, as if almost sensing Ulric's presence, waved him over and
set out a glass of whiskey.

"What are you doing here?" Ulric asked.

Iowyn sighed. "I can't come to the only tavern in town?"

Ulric shook his head, realizing how harsh his tone had
sounded. "I hadn't meant that you couldn't. I just figured you'd be
at home, resting."

A small crease formed between Iowyn's brows. She seemed
surprised, but any indication of it quickly left her face. "I thought
we might try to formulate a plan. Together."

Ulric jutted a thumb in Elmer's direction. "You want to include
the bartender with zero hunting skills?"

Iowyn crossed her arms, and then said, almost as if in a
challenge, "You sure seem to."

Ulric held her gaze, but the fire in her amber eyes seemed less
scorching than it had ever seemed before. It was more docile, more
playful.

He hadn't realized how long he'd been staring until Elmer
cleared his throat.

"Do I get a say in my involvement?"

Ulric looked away from Iowyn to the young man behind the bar. Ulric had been years younger than him on his first assignment with the Guild. But he had also been trained at University. Elmer, while most likely a strong and capable hand on the farm, was as green as they came.

Ulric held out his hand. "The choice is yours, Elmer. You can help, or you can sit it out. I won't fault you for either choice."

Elmer looked down at Ulric's outstretched hand, tapping his own fingers on the bar as he thought about the offer. "I've come this far, haven't I?" He gave a small smirk, and clasped his hand with Ulric's.

Iowyn took her glass – from what Ulric could see, it was just filled with water – and took a long drink. "Good, now that we have that settled. We know what the creature is, and now we just need to kill the thing."

Ulric corrected her. "We need to get a weapon, find the thing, and then kill it. What did your research say kills kelpies?"

"Silver, or pure iron."

"Well, you had a silver tipped bolt to kill that werewolf. Don't you have any more of those?" Elmer asked.

Iowyn frowned in confusion. "How do you know about the werewolf?"

Elmer pointed to Ulric. "He told me last night."

Iowyn looked at Ulric. "You told him about that?"

He shrugged. "I guess after a few drinks, I tell stories. And no, I don't have any more of those. You wouldn't want to even know how expensive the last one was."

"You know," Iowyn started, "with how many creatures have a weakness to silver, you'd think you hunters would wise up and start carrying silver swords or something."

"Silver is heavier than steel," Ulric supplied.

Iowyn gave a lopsided frown as she looked up at nothing in particular. Her eyes flitted about like she was seeing something in the space above her head. "Only by about three grams per cubic. And you're strong enough to deal with that."

Ulric looked at her dubiously. "You did not just do the math for that in your head."

"Look it up." she challenged, crossing her arms. A small defiant smile spread across her face. "Tell me I'm wrong."

Ulric rolled his eyes. "Regardless of density, a silver sword would be expensive and terrible for any defensive fighting. Steel is much harder and better for weapons."

"Not if they can't kill the thing," she pointed out in a sing-songy voice.

Ulric sighed, turning to the only other person in the conversation. "Elmer, help me out here."

Elmer held up a hand. "Don't look at me. She's making some good points."

"Don't encourage her." He scowled.

"What if you just had a silver sword for hunting certain beasts?" she went on. "No one says you have to ditch your old reliable, but just have the silver one on hand."

Elmer chimed in. "Why not just have a sword made of every metal?"

Iowyn snapped her fingers. "Now you're thinking, Elmer."

Ulric ran a hand over his face.

"Face it, Ornthalas. If you had a silver or even an iron sword, then we wouldn't need to take the time to have a blacksmith make one."

"I would rather waste a day or two than have to lug around umpteen different swords with me on every assignment. And," he countered, "by that logic, I should have a set of armor in every metal imaginable as well."

Iowyn scrunched her nose. "You don't wear armor."

Ulric cocked a brow, albeit a bit triumphantly. "Exactly, Beastie."

"Why don't you?" Elmer asked.

Ulric sighed, leaning more onto the bar. "Because armor is a great way to get you killed. It's impractical and slows you down." He could see the confusion on the barkeep's face. "A hunter survives by their skill alone, not because of some fancy plate of metal protecting them."

Elmer tapped the table as he thought. "Okay, so no special swords or armor. What about a bolt made of solid iron then? The kelpie shows up, then you shoot it from a safe distance."

Ulric shook his head. "Wouldn't work. Too heavy. My crossbow is pretty robust, but the weight of the bolt wouldn't allow it to fly right."

"Well, if a sword is out of the question, what about a knife?" Iowyn asked.

Ulric thought about the suggestion. A knife would be light enough to wield, but limit his range. "I would have to get pretty close to the thing for a killing blow. From what your books say, this thing is good at ensnaring people. The more distance I have, the better."

Iowyn rolled her eyes. "Then what do you suggest, Hunter?"

Ulric thought about it for a few moments.

The weapon would have to be able to work both as a ranged weapon and in close combat just in case. It couldn't be something that would have too much weight. Ulric was strong, but iron was dense. The weapon being made out of such a heavy material would affect how he could fight with it. "You do have a blacksmith in town, don't you?" he asked finally.

Elmer scoffed. "Of course we do."

Ulric downed his glass and stood from the table. "Take me to him."

Elmer rose from the table and walked to the door, and Iowyn went to follow suit, but Ulric placed a hand on her shoulder. "Not you, Beastie. You have to figure out a way to draw that kelpie out." He turned to leave, then stopped himself. There had been something that had yet to sit right with him. "Can you do me a favor? No questions asked?"

Iowyn looked up at him with a tiny crease between her eyebrows. "I think so?"

Ulric swallowed, knowing that his next words had the potential to blow up in his face. "Stay away from Maddox, just for the time being."

The crease between her eyes grew deeper, and she crossed her arms. "Why?"

Ulric sat back down in the chair next to hers. He'd had a bad feeling about Maddox since their first meeting. And the way he'd shown up at the lake the other day, as soon as the screaming had seemingly ended. Coupled with what they knew of the creature now – its ability to shapeshift into human form. And Ulric seeing him come from the forest… It all just seemed too coincidental for him to ignore. "I'll explain later."

Iowyn scoffed, and put on a smile, but it dropped when she studied Ulric's face. He wasn't smiling. "You can't be serious. You can't just ask me to stay away from someone and then not explain."

"I will, explain," Ulric assured. "Later, and if it turns out that I'm wrong, I'll admit it."

"He's the *constable*, Ornthalas. He–"

"Please, Iowyn." Ulric interjected. "I promise, I will explain later."

Iowyn's amber eyes searched his face, and he hoped that she would be able to see what she needed to agree with him. Maybe he was being overcautious. She looked at him for a few seconds, then nodded. "Okay," she said. "You can explain later tonight."

Elmer and Ulric left Iowyn. She was a bit put out by being told to go back to research, but that was quickly dissipated by Ulric's other ask.

Stay away from Maddox? For what possible reason?

Ulric hadn't liked Maddox from the second he met him. She knew that. He'd told her himself. She hadn't known Ulric long enough to discern if he was a good judge of character. Maybe he was just seeing things. But then again, he'd been right about the men on the ship…

It would do her no good to stew on it. She would just see things that weren't there, much like the detectives in a Nathaniel Cipher novel when a suspect just happened to be someone close to them. She would just keep away from Maddox like Ulric asked, until he explained, not because she thought Maddox was dangerous by any means. Certainly not because of that.

As Iowyn walked back to the bookshop, she couldn't help but feel a little relieved to have some distance from her partner. Twice now she had found herself in close proximity to Ulric, and each time, her mind seemed to go completely blank until someone or something was able to snap her out of it. There was no denying that things were changing between them. They still bickered from time to time, but at least Ulric seemed to be warming up to her a bit. That had been her goal all along, hadn't it?

Iowyn shook away all the distracting thoughts bouncing around her head as she walked into the bookshop. Burke was behind the front counter working on his ledgers. She walked past him and up into their home above. Her room was tidier than it had been, but there were still plenty of books on the floor that had yet to be put away.

She would put them back on the shelves, looking for any mention of kelpies as she did. One resource's information was great, but multiple never hurt. The more knowledge they had, the better off they would be when finally coming face to face with the creature. Iowyn only wished that there was some organization to her personal library, or that the book she needed would just jump out to her.

Iowyn went to work, taking her place on the floor, doing her best to organize the books as she went. When the sun began to dip below the horizon, she lit some candles and lanterns around the room. She kept working, focusing on the task in front of her.

A light knock sounded at her door, and she turned to find Ulric's tall figure standing outside of her room. "Just wanted to check in."

Iowyn gestured to the multiple books around her. "Just researching."

Ulric kept outside of her room, staying just outside her doorway, like he was waiting for her to invite him in again. "Find anything?"

"Maybe, what about you?" She changed the subject. Her research was boring, and wasn't nearly as important at the moment as securing a weapon to kill the kelpie.

Ulric rubbed the back of his neck. "The blacksmith will start working on the spear in the morning."

"Spear?" she questioned. "You know how to use one of those?"

Ulric smirked. "I know how to use a lot of deadly weapons, Beastie." He lingered in the doorway for a moment longer. "May I come in?" he asked.

It was rather cordial of him, considering he had just been inside her room earlier that day. Iowyn thought about making a sarcastic comment, but instead came back with a request. "If you explain what you meant earlier, then yes."

Ulric nodded, his hands folding behind his back. He came into the room, far enough to shut the door behind him, then leaned against the door. His eyes roved the room, like it had when he'd first entered that morning, but this time, it felt more avoidant than inquisitive. He blew out a breath, looking down at the floor. "I think Maddox is involved in this somehow."

Iowyn blinked. "You what?"

Ulric looked up at her. "Do you promise to hear me out?"

"Yes." She folded her arms against her chest. "But I don't promise that I'll stay away just because you ask."

Ulric's throat bobbed. "Fair enough." He looked towards her desk at the edge of the room and gestured to the mahogany stool. "May I?"

Iowyn nodded, and realized just how tired Ulric looked as he took his seat. He ran a hand through his hair. "I really haven't liked Maddox from the start," he began. "But this isn't just about what I think of him."

"How so?"

Ulric stayed silent for a moment, studying her. His eyes were like a wolf assessing a doe in the middle of a meadow. "I think Maddox could be the kelpie."

Iowyn couldn't help but scoff at the insanity of the. "That's absurd—"

"Kelpies can shapeshift, can't they?" he asked.

"Yes," Iowyn affirmed, "But that doesn't mean—"

"You didn't find it odd that he showed up at the lake almost at the same moment that the screaming stopped?" Ulric asked, his emerald eyes locked onto her face.

Iowyn's heart seemed to jolt. It was absurd.

Right?

Sure, kelpies could shapeshift into human form, but just because they could, didn't mean that they would. They had only ever seen the kelpie as a horse, and as far as they knew, that was all the children had seen.

But Maddox had been at the lake when Toby Thomas had been taken. He had shown up right when the screaming had stopped…

But like she'd said to Ulric, Maddox was the constable. It made sense for him to show up when news of a child being taken would have surely gotten to him as quickly as it had gotten to them. Him being there wasn't anything out of the ordinary. There had to be an explanation for it. Poor timing didn't mean anything. "Technically, so did we. It could just be that we were all too far away when we found out the child was taken."

Ulric took a deep breath. "I saw him today, Beastie. He came from the direction of the lake, after we came back to town. He came out of the trees, with no horse, and wet hair."

Iowyn froze, the words registering in her mind one by one. "He," she began, but the rest of her sentence didn't seem to follow. There was an explanation. There had to be. "He could have just been out in the water. Taking a dip in the river."

Even the excuse seemed weak to her. Maddox had told everyone in town to stay away from the river and the lake. Sure, he was the constable, but shouldn't he have been leading by example? To go to the river by himself was insane, if not extremely careless.

She shook her head. It didn't make sense. None of it made any sense. "So what? This thing has been pretending to be Maddox since we were kids? That doesn't make any sense."

Ulric seemed calm as ever, and it unnerved her, especially when her mind seemed so frazzled, trying to piece together an explanation. "I don't know if it's him, or if its pretending to be him, but," he paused, looking her over, "if I am right, then that means you being near him, or anything that appears to be him is dangerous."

Iowyn stared at Ulric, but it was like she was looking through him. Kelpies were tricksters, taking forms that would get people to trust them, to follow them into the water. Who better to masquerade as then the town constable? No one would be the wiser.

She shook her head again, as if it would jumble up the doubting thoughts springing up in her mind like spreading weeds. "It can't be." She looked at Ulric dead in his eyes. "I would've noticed it if it was true." But her heart thundered in her chest. "Wouldn't I?" she whispered, more to herself than to Ulric.

Ulric let out a long breath through his nose. "Okay, Beastie. Fair enough." He stood up, and Iowyn couldn't believe how easily Ulric was giving up on trying to convince her.

"That's it?" she asked, almost dumbfounded.

Ulric ran a hand through his curls. "Would arguing really convince you?"

"No but," she uncrossed her arms, "I guess I thought that you would be more adamant, is all."

Ulric frowned slightly. "I think we both know that you'll most likely do what you want anyways."

His words struck Iowyn like an arrow to the chest. She couldn't place it, why, of all the things, that this seemed to wound her most. Perhaps she wanted him to try to convince her more, to try and win her to his side. Perhaps she wanted him to want her to trust him, just a little bit.

Ulric walked to the door, and paused as he opened the door. "I'll check in with you tomorrow. Try to get some sleep, okay?"

She could have sworn she heard a tinge of concern in his voice, but she supposed the fact that she hadn't had a full night's rest in the past forty-eight hours was cause enough for that.

"Goodnight, Beastie." He turned to walk away, but Iowyn called out to him.

"Ornthalas?"

She'd thought about using his first name, but it seemed bizarre on her tongue. She'd almost never called him by his first name. Not to his face anyways, and almost never without his surname accompanying it.

Iowyn swallowed as he looked at her with those piercing green eyes. "I'll stay away from him," she said. "Maddox."

Ulric continued to stare at her, like he couldn't believe what he was hearing, but nodded and walked out.

CHAPTER

23

The next morning, Ulric and Elmer weren't big fans of Iowyn's plan.

"You want to do *what?*"

Iowyn huffed. So, this is how it would be today. "Let's face the facts. The kelpie likes one of two things: children and ladies. We all know we aren't putting a kid out there as bait, so that leaves me."

Ulric started pacing and shaking his head. "You can't."

Elmer nodded. "I agree."

She scowled and crossed her arms. "I *can.* And we don't have any other choice."

Ulric pinched the bridge of his nose. "It's insane."

"So is letting this thing go unchecked for another fifty years!"

Burke and Bearen had followed Ulric and Iowyn's raised voices to the back of the bookshop. "What's the matter?" Burke asked.

Elmer turned to the both of them. "Your daughter thinks it's a great idea to offer herself up as bait to the creature to draw it out."

Burke's eyes went wide as his head whipped towards Iowyn. "Absolutely not! Are you crazy?"

Iowyn rolled her eyes. It was the umpteenth time she'd been asked that today. "It's the only way!"

"You can't be serious," Burke said.

"She is," Ulric commented.

That seemed to be the consensus today. Iowyn was crazy and couldn't be at all serious about risking her own life to help keep the children in Calluna safe. But she was serious, and if that made her crazy, then fine. She'd be crazy.

"I am serious. Unless you want to use another kid as bait?" she challenged.

Burke opened his mouth, but Bearen spoke first. "Of course we don't want that."

Everyone's attention was torn from Iowyn at a slight rapping of knuckles against the bookshelf. Maddox stood in his uniform and cleared his throat. "I'm sorry, I heard a commotion."

Iowyn couldn't believe it when she saw Ulric roll his eyes at the constable. She also couldn't believe how her heart seemed to thunder at the sight of him, but not in the usual way it did. No, her heart wasn't beating from excitement, it was beating from fear.

"No need to be sorry, Constable," Bearen replied.

Maddox's eyes traveled over each person in the corner of the bookshop. "Sorry, was I interrupting something?"

"Only Iowyn's plan to become creature food," Elmer muttered, and Ulric was quick to elbow the bartender in the ribs.

Ulric then leveled a look at Iowyn. She was the only one in the room aware of his suspicions. Maddox being here while they were planning wasn't the greatest idea. That is, if it wasn't really Maddox.

Maddox locked his blue eyes onto her. "You can't be serious."

"Oh, for fuck's sake, will you all stop saying that?"

Iowyn pushed the few open books in front of her across the table towards her parents. She didn't need Ulric's permission, or Maddox's for that matter. But she wouldn't go through with this if they didn't want her to. She was their only child – their chosen daughter. If they said no, she would respect that.

She was overly aware of Ulric's eyes burning into her as she explained to them, "The literature is pretty clear. This thing only goes after kids and young maidens. If we want to stop it, you're going to have to let me go out there."

Burke's eyes roved over the pages in front of him, and he gave an unsure glance to Bearen. "She's right…"

Iowyn knew that by showing the proof in the pages, Burke would concede. Knowledge was powerful. Burke had been the one to teach her that, and he couldn't deny the facts when they were right in front of his face. Now, she just needed to convince Bearen.

Bearen swallowed at the look in Burke's eyes and nodded. "Fine, but you aren't doing anything without him," he pointed to Ulric, "teaching you how to keep yourself alive."

Iowyn bristled. "I know how to take care of myself, Bear. You made sure of that."

He gave her a stern glare. "Iowyn. You're going to do this."

She sighed. If this was Bearen's one condition to let her do this, then she guessed that she could stand to have a lesson or two from Ulric on self-defense. Not that she'd enjoy it any. "Fine," she agreed.

Elmer pulled one of the books from off the table and started reading it for himself. He looked up with a smirk. "Don't creatures like this normally go for virgins?"

Iowyn's eyes went wide. Maddox stiffened from where he stood behind Bearen and Burke.

Elmer did *not* just say that in front of both of her fathers.

Burke's eyes had mirrored hers, going wider than saucers, while Bearen's had narrowed at Elmer. Burke was almost turning red as he spluttered, "And just what exactly are you trying to insinuate about my daughter, Elmer Wadscott?"

Elmer went white, not so much because of Burke, but because of the death glare being leveled at him by Bearen behind him. He was quick to hold up his hands as a sign of defense. "Nothing at all, Mr. Morgnah. I swear. I just thought I remembered that that was usually the case in the old tales. I wasn't saying that Iowyn—"

Bearen's low voice cut him off. "Stop talking, Elmer."

Elmer's throat bobbed. "Yes, sir."

She looked over to Ulric. He was still standing, his arms now crossed, but he wasn't looking at her, nor was he enjoying the exchange between Bearen, Burke, and Elmer. His eyes were fixed on Maddox, like if he blinked, he would miss something, some clue that would key him into whether or not his theory was correct. His gaze turned to her, and all she could see on his face was annoyance. Whether it was because of her or Maddox, she couldn't really tell. But she could only guess that he wasn't happy with her, for saying anything about their plan in front of Maddox. Or maybe he was just as displeased as her with having to teach her self-defense.

She could take care of herself. But if she was being completely honest with herself, the idea – although all her own – of being served up to the kelpie on a silver platter churned her stomach a little.

Ulric sighed. "Let's get to it then."

Ulric had taken Iowyn out into the forest until they reached a small ring of trees that provided a private little area. "How did you find this place?" she asked.

"On a walk," was all he replied with.

Over the past few days, Ulric had seemed to be opening up – if even just the slightest – but now he was just as short with her as he'd been during their werewolf assignment.

He set a small pack down against one of the trees, then made his way to the center of the circle. His arms were crossed, but he still said nothing. He simply stared at her with leveled eyes.

"What?" Iowyn asked finally.

Ulric's jaw clenched. "You've just made things very complicated."

"Excuse me?"

"Your constable knows the plan."

Iowyn was taken aback at Ulric's choice of words. *Your constable.*

"What else was I supposed to do? He's the *constable*. Not telling him about our plan – especially in front of everyone else – would have been suspicious."

Ulric dropped his arms. "I know."

Iowyn furrowed her brow at the admittance.

"You had no choice. But I don't think our plan has to change. We just need to surmise whether my theory is right before we try anything else."

"And just how in the world do you suppose we do that? If there really are two Maddox's walking around."

Ulric smirked. "You got us into this mess. You'll figure it out."

Iowyn placed a hand on her hip. "And if I don't?"

Ulric's face fell. "Then we will most likely fail and someone else will die."

Iowyn looked at him, gobsmacked. Was he really putting this all on her? She shook her head.

Ulric spoke softly. "You'll figure it out, Iowyn."

His tone took her aback. It was the sincerest she'd ever heard him, like he believed in her. That he believed that she could – no, *would* – succeed. That they would both succeed, together. She couldn't place the feeling that was swirling around her as he looked at her, his normally icy features thawing in front of her eyes.

Before Iowyn could respond, Ulric cleared his throat and started his lesson.

"So, I know you can throw a punch," he said, rubbing the side of his jaw.

Iowyn allowed herself not to worry about the task Ulric had just put before her. Focusing on not dying was a bit more important at present.

"Sure can." She shot him a self-congratulatory smile.

"But have you ever been in a real fight?"

Iowyn thought about it. "Define real?"

Sure, she had punched a few people in her life – most of whom deserved it – but would she call that a fight? Most times she hit them, and they either went down, or someone else got in the middle of it before anything could escalate further.

"Have you ever been hit before?"

Iowyn looked to the ground as the uncomfortable memories came back. She swallowed. "Yes." Her voice came out as little more than a whisper. "The guy on the boat, and…"

Ulric took a step closer. "And?"

She turned away from Ulric's green gaze. Her heart beat uncomfortably in her chest and she could hear each thump inside her ears. Her breath wasn't filling her lungs as well as it should have. "And I don't want to talk about it."

She heard Ulric take another step towards her. "Beastie—"

"*Please*," she blurted, turning back around on Ulric. "Please. Just drop it."

Something in her tone made a flicker of worry flash across Ulric's face before it vanished. He went back to asking questions. "Okay, so you're more offensive than defensive. That's good to know. We'll work on defense then."

And just like that, Ulric ran towards her. Iowyn's first reaction was to shriek and turn and run herself. Running away was defensive, right? At least that's what she told herself in the moment to feel a little less ridiculous. The problem was that Ulric was taller than her and had a much larger stride. She barely made it ten feet before Ulric had his arms wrapped around her middle and picked her up.

Iowyn thrashed outwardly, swinging her fists at his hands and arms and kicking her feet backwards to try and make him release her. "Not fast enough, Beastie," he whispered in her ear. Iowyn could hear the hint of a smile in his words. Like he was enjoying this.

A shiver jolted down her spine.

That was most certainly not *a shiver inducing thing,* she thought. *Get it together, Iowyn.*

The fact that her body reacted that way to Ulric Ornthalas of all people? It was enough to give her an idea, one that she might very well regret later. She continued her thrashing with her arms, but more precisely aimed a backwards kick towards Ulric's groin.

Ulric dropped one of his arms from where it held her against his chest, dropping his hand to catch her leg before it could make any contact. "Fighting dirty now?" He tsked his teeth. "I thought your father would have taught you better than that."

"Shut up!" Iowyn yelled out. She looked down at where Ulric was holding her. One arm came around her chest where his hand grasped her shoulder, and the other held her right leg down against him. Another idea sparked in her head, and she acted before she could overthink it. Iowyn bit down hard on Ulric's hand where it held her shoulder.

Ulric let out a short cry of pain as he pulled his hand from Iowyn's mouth and dropped her to the ground. As soon as her feet hit the ground, she scrambled far enough away from him that she felt safe to turn around. "Ha!" Iowyn laughed. "Got you there, Ornthalas." She crossed her arms and stood up a little taller with the confidence of having bested him this once.

Ulric was bent over slightly holding his hand. He let out a long breath and looked up, a slight twinkle of mischief and anger in his eyes. He stood back up to his full height, shaking out his hand, and for once, Iowyn was a little afraid of him. Before this, Ulric's one job had been to protect her, so why would she ever feel threatened by him? But now, it was his job to do basically the opposite. He wouldn't actually hurt her – she was sure of that – but something in him at this very moment seemed predatory, wolf-like almost.

He began circling her. And Iowyn did her best to not let him out of her sight. "Running should be a last resort, not your first option," he lectured. "Most creatures you'll deal with on assignments are much faster than any human, and will strike you as soon as you turn your back."

Iowyn watched him and noted every small movement Ulric made, from each step he took, to where his eyes flitted and focused. She wasn't sure if it would do her any good. Ulric had been trained on how to do this kind of thing, while she had learned on how archives were most commonly laid out and how to find the most pertinent information.

Ulric lunged forward, and Iowyn did her best to side step out of his way before he could grab her. "Not bad," he commented. "Now try that again, and hit me when I least expect it."

"By telling me to do it, won't you be expecting it?"

Ulric let out a frustrated sigh. "Just try, okay?"

"Don't get mad at me for pointing out the flaws in your plan," Iowyn muttered.

"I'm not mad."

"Could have fooled me—"

Her snappy comeback was cut off by Ulric lunging for her again. She dodged out of the way, and because she figured he was probably expecting her to punch, she kicked his rump instead. He stumbled a few extra steps from the added momentum, but he didn't fall.

Ulric turned around, his face unreadable. "Okay. Now? I'm not going to let you get away."

Iowyn's brow furrowed. "What do you—" Iowyn started, but Ulric lunged again. She tried to dodge him again, but Ulric was much quicker this time. Had he been holding back? He looped a leg behind hers and pushed. Iowyn fell onto the ground, right on her ass. "Ouch! That was uncalled for."

Ulric crossed his arms, a smirk playing on his face as he looked down at her. He shrugged. "You push me, I push you."

Ulric held out a hand for her to take, but Iowyn pushed it aside and got up by herself. She dusted off her clothes and shot Ulric an annoyed look. "You're enjoying this a little too much, Ornthalas."

"Have to make sure you're prepared for anything, Beastie. The kelpie won't go easy on you just because you're bait."

Fine then. If he wasn't going to go easy on her, then there was no reason for her to do the same.

Ulric began demonstrating a blocking move. "When your opponent strikes, you need to block like this."

Iowyn raised an eyebrow, a smirk playing on her lips. "Oh, really? Because I thought I was supposed to just stand there and let them hit me."

Ulric clenched his jaw, trying to maintain his composure.

Iowyn sighed dramatically. "Fine, fine, Professor Ornthalas. I'll do it your way."

They continued the lesson, with Ulric patiently correcting Iowyn's form and technique. But her smart remarks persisted, and she could see Ulric's frustration grow with each one.

"Now, when you're in a tight spot," Ulric explained, "you can use your surroundings to your advantage. Look for objects you can use as improvised weapons."

Iowyn glanced around and then picked up a small stick. "This is the best I can do."

In a flash, Iowyn was picked up, her back against a tree and her arms pinned above her head with one hand. Ulric's temper had flared. "Can you stop being a sarcastic pain in my ass for one fucking minute and just listen to me?"

His face was inches from hers, his body flush against her. She could feel every muscle that lingered underneath the front of his tunic. A flicker shot behind his piercing eyes. They were staring daggers at her, but Iowyn found that only excited her body more. The warmth that spread from her cheeks downwards made her even madder.

She scoffed, doing her best to push away how her body was reacting. "I'll stop being a sarcastic pain when you stop being a domineering asshole."

"Domineering? I'm trying to keep you alive, something which you make *extremely* difficult!"

She struggled to free her wrists. Damn him for being so large and strong.

"Then why bother?" she yelled back.

Ulric breathed heavily, then did the last thing Iowyn expected. He let her go.

Iowyn stumbled away from the tree, rubbing her wrists and giving Ulric a surprised look. He turned away, running a hand through his hair in frustration. "I bother because if something happens to you, I lose everything."

Iowyn's brows knitted together. What was he saying?

"What do you mean?" she asked.

He sighed, sitting down against a tree on the opposite side of the clearing. "The other term of my probation. If anything happens to you, I get a one-way ticket to Smokheim."

She stood there silent, her heart dropping into her stomach.

The stories about Smokheim were told in every duchy in Phyrra. It was an unknown frontier. The only people who knew the true horrors of the island never lived long enough to tell them. Hunters that made the voyage to Smokheim, never came back.

She shook her head. "They can't do that."

"Of course they can," Ulric huffed. "They're the fucking Guild. Who's going to tell them no?"

Iowyn's mind reeled. The Guild held almost as much power in Phyrra as the dukes themselves. They provided an invaluable service to every person on the continent. The only people who could question their authority were the dukes, and why would they care about one hunter?

"And you're on probation," she thought aloud, "so you can't just leave to save your own skin."

Ulric rested his head against the bark of the tree. He didn't need to answer her. She knew she was right. "Even if I could leave, I don't think I would."

"Why?"

He sighed. "I left home when I turned eighteen, never went back." he continued. "I went to University and studied venatology, and got into the Guild all on my own. The Guild is all I have."

Iowyn took a few steps forward and knelt down next to Ulric, placing a hand on his arm. "I… I didn't know."

"Not your fault," he grumbled. "You've been trying to get me to talk about myself for weeks now. I could have told you at any time."

"So why didn't you?"

He leaned his head back against the trunk of the tree, staring up at the sky above. "I've never been good at *this*."

"Being human?" she smirked. But her joke did nothing to change the look on Ulric's face. Iowyn sat next to him, their shoulders touching.

She waited for Ulric to say something, but then again, it seemed rather fruitless at this point. Besides, the silence emanating from Ulric was different this time. Usually, it had been charged with something more volatile, like anger. But this? This was unlike anything Iowyn had ever experienced with the hunter before. It seemed emptier, desolate even.

Iowyn took a deep breath. "I'm sorry, that I make things difficult for you," she said softly, looking straight ahead at the trees in front of her, instead of at her partner. Ulric's head moved to look at her, but she kept her gaze forward as she continued. "I should know by now that *this*," she made a slight gesture towards him, "is just how you are. And no amount of sarcastic quips or prying is going to change that."

She sighed, her own head resting on the tree behind them. "I know that you don't want to be my partner, you never have. But I did think that sooner or later, you'd realize that I'm stuck with you just as much as you're stuck with me, and – I don't know – maybe we'd just make the best of it?"

The silence stretched on, and still Iowyn didn't look at Ulric. If he didn't want to talk, then she'd allow it. If he wanted to stay in the silence, then the least she could do was be there with him. Minutes seemed to stretch on as they sat underneath the tree, and Iowyn silently wondered what could possibly be going on in her partner's head.

"How about this?" She nudged his arm lightly. "We both try to be better. I won't be such a pain in the ass, and you can start opening up at your own pace, bit by bit. We start trusting each other, and actually start working as partners."

Ulric's eyes glanced down at her. She figured this would just be another time where he just went silent, and didn't reply, but he surprised her. "I promise to try."

She held out her hand to him. "And I promise to try and not get myself killed."

Ulric's large hand enveloped hers. It squeezed hers gently as they shook. "Good enough."

CHAPTER

24

Ulric had given Iowyn as much of a crash course in self-defense as he could muster in one day. He had picked up the spear from the blacksmith later that day, and added another item to his order to be done the next morning. Tomorrow would be the day they decided. It would give them the best chance of surprise if Maddox was in fact the kelpie, or had some association with it, and Iowyn had seemed confident that she could figure it out before the morning, although Ulric wasn't completely sure how. He wasn't even sure he wanted to know her plan.

Besides, if everything went according to Ulric's own plan, Iowyn wouldn't even need most of what she had learned. He sent up a silent prayer to Odea, and sorely hoped that it would be answered.

Ulric went downstairs from his room and took a seat at the bar. The innkeeper's wife came over. She was a plump lady with dark skin and thick coiled hair, with the uncanny ability to know who needed what at any time. Ulric supposed that that was just how things went when someone owned an establishment like the Itchy Badger.

"Some food for you tonight, dear?" she asked.

Ulric gave her a slight nod, and she walked away, all the while waving for Elmer to serve him some alcohol.

Elmer came over shortly with a bottle of whiskey and some glasses. "What's new? He asked nonchalantly, leaning across the bar.

Ulric thought for a second about not telling Elmer the plan, but he had been nothing but helpful with their endeavors. Ulric had even started to think of him as a friend – or at least some semblance of one – which wasn't usually the case when it came to Ulric and people in general. Elmer could have been a great hunter in the Guild had he gone to University. He had a way with people that Ulric didn't possess, and would be a great asset to any party trying to get information from locals and about the goings on. It was a shame, he thought, that such a natural talent was wasted in a small town like Calluna, serving drinks behind a bar.

"We're going after it tomorrow."

Elmer's eyes widened. "Tomorrow? So soon?"

"You rather we wait?" Ulric asked.

He poured a glass for Ulric and himself. "No, gods no. Does Maddox know?"

Ulric pursed his lips and looked Elmer over. "Why should Maddox know?"

A crease formed between Elmer's brows. "Because," he explained. "He's the constable."

Ulric brought his drink to his lips. "That's what everyone keeps saying."

Elmer lowered his voice. "You don't trust him?"

"How did he get the job, Elmer?" Ulric asked, matching Elmer's hushed tone.

"I–" Elmer stopped himself. He blinked. Then blinked again. "I'm not all that sure, to be honest. I mean, he shadowed Constable Rosen a few times when we were kids in school but…" his words trailed off. Elmer washed down his own drink. "I'll be honest. I never really liked Varkin when we were kids. He was a spoiled brat. Always got everything he wanted because his daddy made big money and all the girls were crazy about him. But he hasn't been so bad since becoming constable."

"So besides trailing after the old constable, he had no experience?'

Elmer shook his head. "Not that I know of."

Ulric cocked his brow. "You think he might have been able to buy the position?"

"No," Elmer scoffed. "Albilot wouldn't take money to make Maddox constable. He cares about this town too much."

Ulric ran a hand through his hair. He stared at his glass as Elmer poured him another drink. It didn't make sense for a town to allow someone with no experience to help protect them. But then again, he supposed Calluna was a bit of an outlier with its lack of history with creatures. Still, something about it all didn't sit right with Ulric the more he thought about it.

"You're really going to go after that thing tomorrow? It just seems a bit rushed" Elmer asked

Ulric blew out a breath. "Iowyn will be fine."

"Why wouldn't Iowyn be fine?" A voice from behind Ulric asked.

He turned in his seat to find Maddox standing behind him. "No reason," Ulric explained. "Elmer here just noticed she seemed a little stressed this morning is all."

Maddox narrowed his eyes at the hunter. "Is that right, Wadscott?" he asked, his blue eyes not leaving Ulric.

Elmer looked at Ulric before shrugging. "She's been hitting the books pretty hard. I was just worried about her."

Ulric couldn't believe how quickly Elmer had caught on to lie to the constable, but he was glad for Elmer's sharpness. Maddox's attention remained fixed on Ulric. A fire lit behind his eyes that Ulric had seen many a time, and only ever meant one thing: trouble. Not that Ulric wouldn't love to get in a fight and go toe-to-toe with Maddox, but he also didn't need to make any more trouble for himself. Beating up a town constable wouldn't help his probation case one bit.

"Do we have a problem here, Constable?"

Maddox looked down his nose at Ulric. "I don't know, Hunter. Do we?"

Ulric rolled his eyes, but couldn't help smirking a tiny bit. "Trust me, you don't want to do this."

"Leave Iowyn alone," Maddox warned, taking another step forward. It was then that Ulric smelled the liquor on Maddox's breath. He had been drinking enough to make reckless decisions, but not enough yet to slur his speech or give away any physical indicators.

Ulric wanted more than anything to take Maddox outside and show him what for, and maybe even see what the constable was made of. But something other than his better judgment stopped him. Instead, he thought of Iowyn. What would she do when faced with something she didn't like and wanted to piss off? Besides – of course – throw a nasty right hook at their jaw?

Ulric tilted his head. "That's a little impossible at the moment, considering she's my partner, and it's my job *not* to leave her alone."

Maddox's jaw ticked.

Elmer couldn't help but join in. "Didn't you two break up ages ago? What's got a dead bug like that crawling up your ass, Varkin?"

Maddox's eyes flickered to Elmer behind the bar. "Shut up, Wadscott."

Ulric's smile broadened. "Oh, I think you hit a nerve there, Elmer."

Maddox took another step closer, getting up in Ulric's face. "If so much as a hair on her head is harmed, I swear to Ikris, I'll—"

Ulric's face turned to stone and he stood up, towering a head above Maddox. "You'll what? Hurt me?"

Maddox's throat bobbed, and part of Ulric's ego puffed up at the sight.

"Let's face it, Maddox." Ulric lowered his voice. "You couldn't take me down even if you tried. And as for Beastie, she can more than take care of herself. And if for some reason she can't, then I'll be there to save her. *Not you.*"

Maddox bristled at the use of Iowyn's nickname. He must have hated the familiarity and closeness the moniker implied. Ulric waited for Maddox to say something more, to take the bait, to give him a reason, but he just grumbled something under his breath as he finally turned and walked away and out of the tavern.

Ulric sat back down, and Elmer stared at the door. "Pretentious prick," he muttered.

The corner of Ulric's mouth upturned. At least he wasn't the only person who couldn't stand the constable.

CHAPTER

25

The small clinking of something hitting against Iowyn's bedroom window was enough to draw her attention out of the book she was reading. For a brief moment, she thought perhaps it had begun to rain outside. It was midspring after all. But the clinking wasn't as steady as a hard rain hitting the glass panes. In fact, the unrhythmic frequency of the clinks was quite grating.

It wasn't a falcon. They were insistent with their pecking at the window. Maybe it had been the wind hitting the branches of the tall oak tree behind the building against her window? But Iowyn couldn't remember the oak tree being close enough to reach her window.

Another clink was the final straw. Iowyn's curiosity had gotten the better of her, and she needed to know just what it was making that annoying sound. Perhaps once she knew what it was, she could go back to reading her book in peace.

She padded to the window above her desk and looked out, but all she saw was the little shed where Dren and Josephine were kept, and the remnants of Burke's vegetable garden.

Clink!

A small pebble hit the top left pane of her window.

Clink!

Another pebble struck the bottom right pane.

Iowyn cleared off a spot on her desk that she could climb onto, and then opened the window. She peered down to see who was crazy enough to be throwing pebbles at her window at gods only knew what hour in the night.

Enough moonlight shone on the ground to illuminate where he was standing. His black hair and pristine uniform gave him away.

"Maddox?" she asked in a hushed tone. "What are you doing?"

He smiled, that small dimple making an appearance. "I had to see you."

Iowyn's heart sank. Maddox might have thought he was being romantic, and although Iowyn had never had someone throw pebbles at her window, her thoughts went to Ulric's own hypothesis about the constable.

"Well," she said. "You've seen me now."

Maddox's smile broadened "Come down!"

Now her heart beat erratically in her chest. She knew she would have to. It was the only way she would be able to figure out if Maddox was a man or kelpie. The thought was still seemingly preposterous to her.

She'd known Maddox her whole life. Would a creature like the kelpie play such a long con? Or perhaps, were there two Maddoxes running around town. One, the man she knew and had loved, and another, the mere form taken on by the kelpie. Her mind swirled with possibilities. But she tamped them all down.

Maddox's grin turned mischievous. "Come down, or I'm coming up!" He made for the oak tree, but there was no way he would be able to make it to her room even if he climbed the farthest-reaching branches. The only window the tree reached was the one to her parents' room.

"Stop, stop!" she hissed in frustration. "Fine, I'm coming down."

Better for her to go down knowing all the creaky floorboards and squeaky hinges in the house than Maddox flopping into her parents' room.

Iowyn could see the triumphant smile on his face as she shut her window. She placed a hand over her racing heart.

You'll be fine, she told herself.

Iowyn slipped on her boots. She left her belted dagger draped across her desk chair. It wouldn't do her any good, it wasn't made of anything that would hurt a kelpie.

She made her way down, going the long way around the recliner in the living room and hopping over the third to last step on the stairs. She went out the bakery's back door, and not the bookshop's, since Bearen oiled the hinges on it more regularly.

She came outside, and was puzzled to find no one standing outside. Her hand went to her hip, but her one form of protection wasn't there. Iowyn swallowed. Had she made the whole thing up? Maddox had been right next to the oak tree when she'd been in her room, so she went to look around the back of it.

In the shadow of the oak tree, a pair of hands grabbed her middle, spun her around, and pressed her up against the rough bark of the trunk. It wasn't too unlike the way Ulric had held her against the tree that afternoon, except Maddox wasn't trying to hold her down. Iowyn was just glad she hadn't shrieked when he had grabbed her.

Maddox smiled. "Come with me," he whispered. His breath fanned across her face. It smelled undeniably like alcohol.

"Have you been drinking?" she asked.

The romanticism of his actions was dulling by the second.

"Come to the river with me," he said as he came to whisper in her ear. "We can skinny dip like we used to."

Iowyn hoped that the fear that was overtaking every inch of her body wasn't conveyed through her face. "Maddox, I can't. I–"

Maddox gave her a wry smirk. "Come on. It'd be just you and me. Nobody else around." His eyes darkened as they dipped from her eyes to her lips and then farther down to her body.

Iowyn let out a breath through her mouth. "I can't, Maddox." Although part of her wanted to give Maddox the benefit of the doubt, she couldn't help the panic in her racing mind. He wanted her to go to the river with him. Any other time, that wouldn't have set off alarm bells for her. But the fact that Maddox knew about the creature and the tie the creature had to the water, to the very river that he wanted to take her to? It didn't bode well.

She had made up her mind, that she would only really test Ulric's theory if Maddox was acting suspicious, as she still didn't quite believe it herself. And it seemed like this was as good of time as any.

His hands moved slowly over the sides of her hips as his fingers drew tiny circles over the fabric of her pants. "Why not?"

Was he pouting? Because if so, it was definitely not something she was into.

His blue gaze locked with her own eyes. Her mind whirled. She needed an out, or at least some way to confirm what Maddox was – man or creature posing as man. She had nothing close to her that was iron. The closest thing she could think of was Burke's gardening tools, which were all in the small shed with Dren and Josephine. She needed something, anything that she could make Maddox touch that was iron or silver.

Silver.

Iowyn reached into her pocket. Her fingers enclosing over the cold metal of her pocket watch. "It's pretty late, Maddox–"

She fumbled with the watch as it came out of her pocket, dropping it at their feet.

Maddox looked down at the shiny watch as it lay on the ground. He stared at it for a moment, and Iowyn held her breath. He bent down, his fingers effortlessly wrapped around the silver timepiece. Iowyn stared at it as he clicked open the front cover of the watch, reading the face of the clock in his palm.

"I suppose it is," Maddox agreed, before handing the watch back to her. "But that's never stopped you before."

She took the watch back from him, and an uneasy feeling began to twist in her gut. Was it embarrassment? Guilt? Perhaps both. She'd lost all trust in Maddox, all because of the words of a man she hardly knew.

Part of her wanted to tell him. Tell him that she was sorry for thinking he was even capable of something so monstrous. Tell him that she would be bait tomorrow for the terrible thing that was plaguing their town. But the other part of her, the logical part, knew that that was probably the worst thing she could do. Because Maddox was drunk firstly, and obviously not thinking straight. And secondly, she knew more than anything that Maddox would try to stop her in his right mind. He, unlike Ulric, would be unable to let her risk herself. Because deep down, she knew how he felt about her, and people who felt like that about someone didn't let them do something as stupid as play decoy for a murderous creature.

She decided she would tell him a half truth, to at least save him from worrying and herself from the headache of dealing with a domineering and very drunk Maddox. "We're hunting it tomorrow."

"You can't be bait for that thing, Iowyn."

"I'm not," she lied. "After you left, we figured out a better way. Well – not me – but Ornthalas did."

Maddox pushed away from the tree and ran a hand through his dark hair and down the back of his neck. "Why does that brute even need you?" He scoffed, "Some hunter he is if he can't take a single creature down by himself."

She shushed him. "He's my partner, and two pairs of eyes and ears are better than one," she supplied, hoping it was a good enough reason for him. "Besides, I stay hidden for the most part."

Maddox didn't seem at all convinced, but he still came back to stand in front of her. "Promise me you'll be safe," he said.

Iowyn swallowed. She really couldn't promise that, but sometimes lying was a necessary evil. Besides, what were the chances he would even remember this in the morning? "I promise."

Maddox got even closer to her, which she hadn't thought possible. Her back was fully pressed against the tree trunk and all of him was in full contact with her. Something within her felt conflicted about how close he was. A few nights ago, this would have driven her crazy with want, but now, she just felt a little suffocated by his proximity.

"I want you, Iowyn," he whispered, running the back of his finger against her cheek.

Iowyn sighed, and ducked underneath his arm to get out from between him and the tree, a movement Ulric had just shown her that day. "Maddox, I can't do this. Not tonight."

"Why not?" he asked.

Iowyn gave another sigh. "Because you're drunk, Maddox, and I don't like feeling like just a hookup."

She turned away from him to go back into the bakery, but Maddox grabbed her wrist. "Iowyn, you're not just a hookup to me."

He actually sounded hurt from her words.

She just looked at him. While a distraction was probably what she needed most, she really didn't want anything that Maddox was looking for tonight. "Go home, Maddox," she said.

Maddox's grip tightened on her wrist. "Iowyn, please."

Iowyn sighed again and paused. She took a deep breath, and attempted to lightly pull her wrist out of Maddox's grip. When he didn't release it, she changed her stance ever so slightly to give herself a better base. She thrust the hand Maddox was holding forward, and grabbed her fist with her other hand, and used the leverage to pull up and out of Maddox's grasp.

It was another maneuver Ulric had only taught her just that day, and she had executed it flawlessly. Maddox was a little stunned by the action. He went to grab her again. "Iowyn–"

"Maddox." Her voice was firm and it caused him to stop in place. "Go home."

She turned her back on him, though she opened her ears to listen if he tried to follow her, but she made it all the way back to the bakery's back door, and shut it quietly behind her, latching the lock. She sank to the floor, leaning her head against the door. She didn't want to go back to her room, but she needed to at least wait until Maddox had left to go where she really did want to go, the place she always went when she felt lost.

CHAPTER

26

Ulric lay in bed, staring at the ceiling. He went through everything he had planned out in his mind, over and over and over again. Everything needed to go perfectly, or else Iowyn stood a chance of being in real danger. He went through every contingency as well. What would he be able to do if something went awry? What would he even be capable of?

Ulric sat up from bed, and began putting his clothes back on. He needed something to get his mind off of tomorrow. Anything. A walk should be enough to clear it before going to sleep because gods only knew he needed sleep.

The tavern below was quiet, but still inhabited by those patrons with nowhere else to go. Elmer was no longer behind the bar, replaced by a large man. Ulric gave him a short nod before heading out the front door.

Calluna was peacefully asleep, swathed in laternlight. The only sounds to accompany Ulric were his boots on the cobblestone road and his own thoughts.

It was a beautiful little town. Ulric could admit that to himself. It was so different to where he'd grown up. Illeross was a booming city with people and commerce of every kind coming and going each day. Taking a walk at this time of night in Illeross was a surefire way to get yourself mugged, if not killed. Perhaps this town was where Iowyn had gotten her sunnier disposition – at least sunnier compared to him.

It made sense now, her blissful ignorance when it came to the common dangers of the world. Being from a place like Calluna,

228

where nothing bad ever happened, she must have had no idea of the terrible things that creatures and even people were capable of outside of the books she read.

As if his thoughts of her had been some kind of dowsing rod, Ulric found himself stopped in front of the Morgnah's joint bakery and bookshop. He shook his head, and went to turn around and walk back to the Itchy Badger, when a figure sitting atop the roof caught his eye and seemingly took his breath away.

In the moonlight, she was unmistakable. Her pale skin seemed illuminated from within, giving off a soft glow. Her hair was unbound, falling in waves around her shoulders. She sat with her knees pressed against her chest, her head and amber eyes upturned to the night sky.

Ulric rounded the back of the building keeping his eyes on her. There was only one way he could find up to where she sat. Suddenly, her talent of climbing trees made more sense. The bark of the oak tree bit into Ulric's palms as he found holds and footings to climb up to the roof.

She didn't say anything when he came to sit beside her. There wasn't even an inkling to tell him that she had even noticed his presence. Her gaze was focused on the night sky and the hills beyond her quiet town.

"Couldn't sleep?" he asked finally, clearing his throat.

Iowyn didn't acknowledge the question. "It's not him," she said.

Ulric blinked at her. "Pardon?"

Iowyn clutched her knees closer to her chest. "Maddox, he isn't the kelpie. He picked up my pocket watch."

Ulric studied her face, expecting to see some arrogant look on her face, as well as to hear a triumphant, "*I told you so,*" from the monstralogist. But she didn't look the least bit happy about the revelation. He waited for her to say something – anything.

He tried himself to come up with something. Would it be better to ask her about her sudden melancholy? About why she seemed so troubled? These were the kind of conversations that Ulric strayed away from. He felt like he never really knew what to say, and was so afraid to say the wrong thing that he always felt it better to say nothing at all.

Ulric swallowed, as he asked, "What's wrong?"

Iowyn laughed at the question. "Nothing, besides the fact that I could die tomorrow."

"That's not going to happen." Ulric didn't mean for it to come out so sternly.

She looked up at him, her amber eyes swimming with a kind of urgency. "How can you know that?"

Ulric moved without thinking, and placed his hand over hers where it rested between them on the roof. "I won't let anything happen to you, Beastie. Believe me."

Iowyn's throat bobbed slightly. But she nodded, looking away from him. "Okay," she whispered. Iowyn took a deep breath and let it out, her body relaxing with it. "You probably think I'm a coward, considering I asked for this."

Ulric let out a breath of his own. "Honestly, I'd be more concerned if you weren't worried about it." His gaze turned to the stars and he leaned back on his hands.

The stars shimmered like distant diamonds. He searched for the constellations, ancient patterns etched by human imagination across eons. Ikris, the god of chaos and the mighty hunter, stood tall and proud in the sky with his arrow of five bright stars. The Gorgons, a cluster of delicate sisters, sparkled like a luminous bouquet. Each constellation told a story of gods, hunters, and magical creatures. He had learned all about them with his father many years ago – one of the few pleasant memories he had with the otherwise callous man.

"Do you know any constellations?" He wasn't sure what had possessed him to ask her the question, but it changed the subject. Perhaps she simply needed a distraction. He could do that much for her.

Iowyn's head turned slightly towards him. Her brow furrowed but she answered. "Not really, no."

Ulric cocked a brow. "Seriously?"

Her amber eyes narrowed at him. "Yes, seriously."

"But you're a—" He stopped himself from finishing the sentence. Calling her a worm wouldn't do him any favors. "I mean, you're smart. You've never learned about them?"

Iowyn's gaze returned to the world in front of her. "I know some of the legends behind them, sure. But I couldn't point them out to you, if that's what you're asking."

"Really?" It didn't make sense. He'd only known her for a few weeks, but he knew that she was brilliant. Anyone who had a simple conversation with her would be able to tell that. Ulric had grown up learning about the constellations, and he had thought that everyone else had done the same thing.

Iowyn sighed. "Really."

Her frown seemed to deepen, and Ulric felt like something was slipping away with every second that they sat in silence. He'd promised to try. To try and open up. Perhaps now was the perfect time to show her that he could uphold his promise.

He cleared his throat. "Do you – I mean – would you like to?"

"Like to what?"

"To learn?"

Iowyn chuffed and then went silent when she looked at Ulric's face. "Are you offering to teach me about the stars, Ornthalas?"

He nodded and offered her a small smirk.

She blinked and her lips parted slightly. He knew that face. She was thinking something through in her head. He had noticed she got the same kind of expression on her face when going through a problem and all the best ways to solve it. Her eyes became just a little distant, the tiniest crease formed in between her dark eyebrows, and her lips parted ever so slightly.

She blinked, and the distant look was gone. "Okay," she said finally.

Iowyn sat up taller and looked at him expectantly, waiting for him to start. It was then that Ulric realized that he hadn't thought his offer through this far. He wasn't exactly sure where to start.

"Uh, well, first I guess you should look up. See if you see any groups of stars that are brighter than the others." He didn't look away from Iowyn as her face turned skyward, the light of the moon illuminating her pale skin again.

Iowyn lifted her hand. Her slender finger pointed, and Ulric followed the direction. "There? I think?" Her voice was unsure. Off to the east was a grouping of six bright stars in the shape of an upright rectangle with another three above in an arc. "Is that anything?" she asked, turning her head towards Ulric.

Ulric came closer to her side, pretending he hadn't seen the constellation. He brought his own head closer to hers, so as to look down the sight of her arm. It was a shameless excuse to get closer to her. Something he most certainly should *not* have been doing. But he couldn't help himself.

"The Door to Paradise," he supplied. "Not bad for your first time, Beastie."

A faint smirk curled her lips. "Show me more?" she asked.

Ulric stayed close as he pointed out the constellations and navigational stars to her. She listened intently to every word, every explanation, even asking her own questions and talking about the myths as to why the constellations were put into the sky by Odea. It seemed funny to him that she knew the stories, but had never been able to find them herself in the sky. "It's like looking for a bunch of needles in haystacks," she explained.

He pointed to the last constellation he could find. Off to the west, it was barely peeking up over the horizon. "You see that fainter cluster there? The three in a triangle and the eight rays of stars coming off from it?"

Iowyn squinted, then nodded.

"That is Dral'goth the Devourer."

"I don't know that one," Iowyn said.

The admittance surprised him, but also gave him a small feeling of triumph. He sighed, resting back on his arms. "Not surprising," he gave a sly smirk, "knowing you."

"What's that supposed to mean?" Iowyn's tone became abrasive, but Ulric's smirk didn't fall. Knowing something that she didn't was a little fun.

"Dral'goth was the first creation that Odea regretted. A gargantula." He paused, and Iowyn's reaction was all that he needed to see. Her eyes widened in recognition.

"I would hope she would regret making a huge fucking spider!"

Ulric couldn't help but chuckle slightly. "Odea sent Mortem himself to kill Dral'goth, for her insatiable hunger and killing any living thing that crossed her path. And he did. But Mortem was also too late. Dral'goth had laid eggs and continued her lineage. Odea put Dral'goth in the sky as a reminder of the destruction she wrought, and as a warning to kill gargantulas before they can reproduce."

Iowyn shut her eyes as a shiver racked her whole body. "I fucking hate spiders."

Ulric let the corner of his mouth turn up. "I've noticed."

Another silence fell over them, but this one felt different. It was a comfortable silence, one that Ulric would have stayed in forever if he could. They sat together for a while, until Ulric felt the tingling sensation of goosebumps on his arms. He stole his gaze away from the sky to find Iowyn looking at him, a small smile on her face. "What?" he asked.

Iowyn shook her head slowly, her amber eyes assessing Ulric as they looked him up and down. "Nothing," she said. "I just have this feeling."

Ulric's mouth went slightly dry. "What kind of feeling?"

Iowyn's gaze went back to the sky, her smile now reaching her eyes. "That we might just be friends after tomorrow."

Ulric knocked on the blacksmith's door, and was surprised to find it open. He walked inside the front of the forge where a fire was already roaring.

"Hello?" he asked aloud. He didn't see anyone in the immediate vicinity.

The blacksmith, a much younger man than Ulric had originally expected to see behind the anvil with countless burn scars across his forearms, came out from the back room. Elmer had introduced him as Henry, and he had taken the forge over from his father the year before.

"You're out quite early," he commented. His blond hair was muddied from soot and smoke, but his brown eyes burned brightly. They reminded Ulric of Iowyn's eyes, how they seemed to shine from within when exposed to firelight.

"Just wanted to see if my additional request had been finished or not."

Henry nodded. "It's in the back. Though I still think you should go with one of my finer blades." His eyes flitted to the far wall, where a few tools and weapons hung on display.

Ulric shook his head. "No, whatever you've made will be perfect."

The blacksmith went into the back room and came back out with a small parcel wrapped up in burlap. He held it out to Ulric.

Ulric fished out some coins from his pocket and traded them for the parcel. Henry looked at Ulric's outstretched hand a little puzzled. "You already paid me, sir."

"Call it a tip, then," Ulric said. "A thank you for working so fast."

Henry smiled and took the coins from Ulric's hand. "It was my pleasure, sir. It's not every day I get to make something for a hunter."

Ulric nodded. "Hopefully, when the Guild's work is finished here, you won't need to for a very long time."

Ulric left the forge to make his way to Iowyn's house. His footsteps echoed on the cobblestones as he made his way through the quiet morning streets of the town. The first rays of sunlight began to peek over the horizon, casting a warm golden glow on the quaint houses and shops. It was a peaceful moment before the bustle of the day began in earnest. Even from halfway across town, he could smell the treats being freshly baked by Bearen.

It was still early when he finally made it to the front steps of the bakery, but the door was wide open and inviting. Ulric sat at one of the tables inside the small shop, content to wait. Considering the severity of today, he decided it wasn't the best idea to rush Iowyn.

Bearen gave him a curt nod from behind the counter. "Anything I could get for you?"

Ulric shook his head. "No, but thank you. I'm sure I'll be much more open to sweets once this is all over," he said.

As Bearen left him to go back to work, Burke entered the bakery. "I hope you got plenty of sleep," he said.

"Of course," Ulric replied, and noted the way that Burke was wringing his hands. He was obviously worried about his daughter. Ulric found it sweet. He and Burke had brought Iowyn into their life without so much as a second thought. They were quite possibly two of the most amazing parents Ulric had ever met, and not at all what he was used to. Gods only knew his own father had left much to be desired. Keeping Iowyn safe was a part of his job, yes, but now it was more than that. He would do it for them as well, to make sure their daughter came home again.

"It's her birthday today – you know. Well – not her *birthday* exactly – but the day we found her. The 21st day of Midspring. We made it her birthday considering there were no records to go off of. I don't even know if she realized it was today with everything else going on," he rambled.

Her birthday.

She hadn't made any mention of it to him ever, so it was quite possible that Burke was right in his assumption. Truth be told, even he couldn't tell what day it was. Days got away from you in this line of work.

"How old is she then?" Ulric asked.

Burke sighed. "Oh, twenty-four we suppose. We took her to a doctor when we first found her, and he guessed that she was around three years old." Burke rubbed the back of his neck. "All I know is that it sure doesn't feel like it's been that long. It feels just like yesterday…" His voice was bittersweet as he trailed off. His eyes went distant, and there was no doubt in Ulric's mind that Burke was reminiscing silently to himself.

Ulric wished that he could think of something to say. Anything really to make Burke worry less, but he simply couldn't. So he said the only thing that sprang to mind. "You both did a fine job raising her."

Burke snapped from his pensiveness, and the side of his mouth turned up into a small smile. "We certainly tried our best," he joked, his smile broadening. The comment had been enough, it seemed, to turn the book merchant's mood.

Bearen called out from the kitchen, "Burkey! Come give me a hand, will you?"

Burke rolled his eyes playfully, then sighed. "Duty calls," he mused before leaving Ulric at the table to help Bearen in the next room.

Ulric looked out the window and watched as the people of Calluna started their days, going about to different shops, a few even stepping into the bakery. He sat at the table watching people live their everyday lives, until he felt two abrupt taps on his shoulder from behind. He turned in his stool, and the sight before him was more than surprising.

It took his brain a few moments to realize that it was Iowyn. She looked the same and yet completely different. Instead of her normal garb of a linen shirt, pants, and boots, she wore a dress. It was a simple cornflower blue color and fit her snugly. She probably hadn't worn it since she had left for University, and had no doubt filled out a bit more since then.

Wavy black hair cascaded around her shoulders, with only the top half pulled away from her face. From the moment he had met her, she had always worn her hair up or braided back. Save for last night, this was the first time that he had actually seen it down. And she had taken the time to put on a touch more makeup than usual. She more than looked the part of a beautiful young lady. Though Ulric wondered how she would look with the addition of her half-moon spectacles perched upon her nose as well.

"Is it too much?" she asked, looking down at herself. She ran her hands down her skirt.

Ulric stood up from his seat. "No, not at all."

Her mouth twisted. "I feel a little foolish."

"Don't," Ulric said immediately. Iowyn's eyes shot up to meet his. "You look—"

"Oh, Wynnie! You look beautiful!" Burke came back out from the back of the bakery.

Her cheeks reddened at the compliment. "Thanks, Dad."

Burke came and gave her a hug, and Ulric was surprised that he said nothing of it being her birthday. Ulric met his eyes, and something in them said: *Not now. After.*

Burke looked at the gold pocket watch attached to his vest. "I need to open the bookshop. I will see you later." He hugged his daughter again, holding on for a little longer than normal before walking through to his own bookshop. Ulric didn't miss Burke's pause at the doorway, his eyes lingering on Iowyn's back before turning away.

He would make sure that it wouldn't be the last time Burke saw his daughter.

Iowyn pointed to the parcel on the table. "What's that?" she asked.

Ulric grabbed the wrapped burlap and handed it to her. "I had it made for you at the blacksmith."

Carefully, Iowyn untied the twine and unfolded the burlap to reveal a blackened dagger. Its handle was made of the same metal as its blade, but tightly twisted together in a unique spiral pattern."What is it?"

Ulric cleared his throat. "It's a dagger."

Iowyn looked up at Ulric through narrowed eyes. He could tell she was doing her best not to roll them as well. "Yeah, I know it's a dagger, but what is it made of?"

"Iron," Ulric replied. "I had the blacksmith make it for you as soon as you made it clear that you were going to be the one to lure the kelpie out."

She smirked. "But, you said a dagger would be useless."

"For me, yes. But the more I thought about it, it would be stupid to have you go out there with nothing."

Iowyn's smile grew. "So, you do care, Ornthalas."

Iowyn tested the weight of the dagger in her hands. It was much heavier than the one she usually carried. It was made entirely of pure iron, from the tip of the blade to the end of the handle, and although Ulric said that he doubted it would be able to kill the kelpie itself, for her sake, she hoped it would be able to do some damage if needed.

"Thank you, Ulric."

His face stayed the same, but she caught the slightest movement of his eyebrows at the use of his first name. She waited for him to say you're welcome, but he never did. Instead, he simply motioned to the door and followed her out into the street.

CHAPTER

28

"Do you want to go over the plan again?"

Iowyn gave a frustrated sigh. "No, but I think you certainly do."

Ulric crossed his arms. The sideways glance he gave Elmer was all she needed to see.

She waved in his direction. "Yeah, yeah, I know. Now is not the time to be snarky."

Ulric let out a long breath. "One more time."

Iowyn put her hands on her hips. "I go over to the bridge, and do whatever until the kelpie comes. I do my best to get it out of the water and as close to you as possible, then I run to Elmer who will be waiting on horseback to whisk me off to safety."

Ulric nodded. "Good." He looked behind him, then hesitated. "Shadowfoot isn't far off either if…" His words trailed off.

Iowyn shook her head. "That won't happen."

She wasn't completely sure if the comment was meant to bolster his confidence or her own. But she was right. It wouldn't happen. It *couldn't* happen.

"Beastie," he said softly.

His tone caught her a bit off guard. She looked up into his emerald green eyes, eyes that had been eerie to her only a week ago, but now felt somewhat reassuring. "What?"

He stared down at her, then put his hands on either side of her. It was a bit more intimate than Iowyn was used to from the stoic hunter. "If things go wrong, I will come after you."

Iowyn closed her eyes and shook her head. She really didn't want to think about what would happen if the kelpie was able to take her. What horrors would await her? What had those poor children gone through?

"Hey," Ulric squeezed her arms. "I promise."

Iowyn looked back up to study his face. The gash from the werewolf just a week ago was starting to heal over, leaving fresh pink skin around the edges. That night felt like a lifetime ago. Ulric had gone from a man she couldn't stand to someone she had come to trust with her life in such a short amount of time. She focused in on his eyes, and something inside them, despite everything, told her that he was telling the truth. He would come after her.

Iowyn nodded, looking into his emerald eyes. "I know," she whispered. "I trust you."

Elmer cleared his throat. "Let's get this over with, shall we?"

Elmer took his horse and Shadowfoot by the reins and started walking away to wherever he was going to stash them all away. Iowyn found herself wishing she'd brought Dren, but Ulric was adamant that another creature could deter the kelpie from even showing up.

Still, Iowyn couldn't move. She felt somewhat rooted to the spot. The first step she took would be one step closer to danger, and she wasn't altogether sure whether or not she was brave enough to do this.

"Hey," Ulric said again. He took one more step closer to her, and his hand came under her chin to tilt her head back up to his. "You've got this."

And then Ulric Ornthalas did the most un-Ulric thing. He smiled at her.

Not some half smirk, or a slight upturn of the corner of his mouth. But a full smile.

Iowyn, taken aback, blinked in disbelief. She had seen Ulric in countless dire situations—face grim, voice steely, always the epitome of stoic resolve. This smile, however, was like sunlight breaking through storm clouds.

Without another word, he pulled away from her, and walked away. Like he hadn't just shattered every preconceived notion Iowyn had ever had about him.

Iowyn, in a bit of a daze, walked to the river alone. But the closer she got, the more her heart grew heavy in her chest. There was of course a chance that the kelpie wouldn't show, but there was an even larger chance that it would. It had been days since the last child was taken, and Iowyn bet if anything, that the beast was hungry and waiting for anything to make into a meal.

Iowyn sat down at the river's edge against the side of the stone bridge. The drop leg sheath around her thigh tightened as she bent her leg. She had replaced her usual dagger with the iron one as soon as they had left the bakery. The pressure of the sheath against her skin was a comfort. She had something that could harm the kelpie if she needed to. That is, so long as the lore about kelpies and iron was true.

Iowyn looked at the large sycamore tree that Ulric was supposed to be in, and she searched the upper boughs for any trace of him, but saw none. Either he wasn't up there, or he was well-camouflaged. For her sake, Iowyn hoped it was the latter.

She pulled out her journal and pen from her deep skirt pocket and opened to a blank page. She figured now would be as good of time as any to jot down her notes about werewolves and kelpies. It was the first time she was able to just sit down and write since getting her journal back.

Iowyn silently wondered to herself how the kelpie would know how to come for her. Could it smell her? Or was it drawn in another way? What if it didn't come today? Would they try again tomorrow? Her stomach flipped at the thought of being put on display for a murderous creature day after day until it finally decided it wanted to feast on her.

Iowyn pushed the thoughts away. Dreading would get her nowhere, especially considering the fact that she was the one to put herself in this situation. And why? For multiple reasons she supposed. The first – of course – being that she didn't want to risk the life of another child. Maybe she wanted to prove to herself and to Ulric that she could be much more than a worm doing research. That she could do whatever was necessary. That she deserved her place in the Guild and as his partner.

Ulric sat on a high bough of the sycamore. From his high vantage point, he could see everything, and he was close enough that he felt more than confident in his ability to throw the spear in his hands. Everything would go perfectly fine, so long as Iowyn stuck to the plan and got out of the way as soon as the kelpie was on the bank of the river and out of the water.

His tailbone had started to go numb from sitting on the hard tree branch. It had been nearly an hour, and nothing had appeared out of the river. He'd spent that hour watching Iowyn jot down notes in her journal, while also surveying the surrounding water, and simply waiting for anything out of the ordinary to happen.

Iowyn put down her journal, apparently finished with whatever entry she had been writing. He studied her from his perch. Her raven hair danced in the light breeze, and her pale skin was ever on display, even in the slight shade of the bridge. Her chest heaved in a sigh, and Ulric did his best not to look too long at the low cut of her dress bodice. The whole thing had to be at least a size too small, but it was the perfect amount of constriction to hug each and every curve of her body. He couldn't help but admit what he had been denying since the first day he met her.

He thought she was breathtaking.

Iowyn looked around at her surroundings, even scanning the treetops, but her amber gaze never settled on him. She stopped and took a long look at the river as it flowed past her. Her chest heaved again and her mouth opened. Ulric gripped the spear tight, ready to see the kelpie rise out of the water. But instead of a scream or call for help, Iowyn began singing.

He couldn't make out the words, just the lilting melody. It sounded old, like something passed down for generations. Iowyn's voice carried the tune effortlessly. Ulric listened as Iowyn's voice filled the air, each phrase echoing through and across the serene landscape.

The song came to a natural conclusion, and as the final note hung in the air, a moment of silence lingered, leaving only the gentle rustling of leaves and the soft gurgle of the river to fill the void.

Iowyn's eyes reopened and fixed on the water.

Minutes passed, and the stillness of the scene was broken only by the occasional call of a distant bird. Ulric's muscles tensed as his patience began to wear thin.

Then, just when he was beginning to doubt their plan, a ripple formed on the river's surface. It started as a faint disturbance, but it grew steadily. A dark shadow waited just underneath the surface.

Ulric's heart pounded in his chest as he readied himself for the moment of truth. The kelpie was rising from the water, lured by Iowyn's sweet voice, and it was now up to him to ensure that their plan succeeded. Up to him to ensure that Iowyn remained safe.

29

Iowyn scrambled to her feet as the first ripples formed on the surface of the water. The large black head of the beast rose first, and Iowyn held back the urge to scream. How any child could look at this thing and think that it was friendly was beyond her.

The kelpie's entire body was a mass of black and dark green kelp and pondweeds. Serrated and pointed teeth, like that of a saw blade, protruded from its mouth. As it stepped onto the bank with its leading leg, Iowyn could see the twisted, backwards hooves. It was mere feet in front of her, and it was time for Iowyn to put on the show of her life.

She couldn't let the kelpie think that she feared it, or knew exactly what it was. It needed to think that she was a dumb and helpless girl that was out by the river alone. She wasn't sure of the creature's intelligence, but she thought it better to be safe than sorry and assume it might sense a trap.

"Oh my," Iowyn said, trying to rid her voice of any shakiness. "What are you?"

The kelpie whinnied in reply, but it was more like a shrill shriek, grating to her ears like nails against a chalkboard. She looked the monster up and down. She couldn't pretend that she thought it was a real horse. It had come up from the water right in front of her. So Iowyn went with her second option.

She swallowed. "Are you… magic?"

Another whinny from the beast, this time paired with a rearing and nodding of its head.

The kelpie was still standing in the shallows of the river. She needed to get it further down the river and up onto the bank, where Ulric would have a clearer shot for his one throw.

Iowyn backed away from the kelpie slowly, trying her best to act as if she were in a daze at the thought of being in the presence of a magical creature. Everything she'd read about kelpies had one thing in common: they acted friendly until they ensnared you. If she could stall and stay far enough away from it, maybe she could lead it further onto land.

"What kind of magic?" she asked.

The kelpie took a step forward, but gave no response.

"Obviously not a magical *and* talking horse then," she commented, taking another slight step back as she tapped a finger on her chin. "Yes or no questions, then?"

Another eerie whinny.

With each question she asked, she did her best to take another step backwards, closer to the sycamore tree.

"Can you fly?"

The kelpie remained silent.

"Can you grant wishes?"

It whinnied, and nodded its head fervently.

Iowyn's brows shot up from the response.

"Wishes?"

The monster neighed again, coming as close as it had ever been to her. It was a good teen feet from the edge of the bank, but its face was right in Iowyn's. The musty and earthy smell of the lake water attacked her senses, and it took everything in her not to retch at the scent. The kelpie's eyes, like wet green marbles, stared into her, and – as if she could hear them speaking to her – they said one thing:

Touch me.

Iowyn raised her hand. She had done it. It was on the bank and out of the water. It was in the perfect position, now all that was left was for her to run.

Touch me.

The eyes pleaded. But Iowyn had no intention of becoming dinner. She let her hand come within inches of the kelpie's face. And as the creature closed its eyes to revel in her touch, Iowyn bolted.

Ulric raised the spear, poised to hurl it at the beast.

"Come on," he muttered under his breath. The kelpie was only feet away from Iowyn, still halfway in the water and had the cover of the bridge.

He sent up a silent plea to Odea. Iowyn could do this. She'd have to. There was no going back now.

His eyes trained on his target as Iowyn stepped back slowly. She led it further and further up the bank, step by step, until the creature finally came up to her face. Even from this far away, he could tell the thing was nasty.

Iowyn raised her hand. What was she thinking? Was she going to touch it? He reaffirmed his grip on the spear. She wouldn't do that.

"Move, Beastie. *Move.*"

Her hand came closer to the kelpie's face, and just before touching it, she turned and ran towards the trees.

The kelpie screeched at the trickery, and reared up onto its back legs, ready to charge. It was Ulric's perfect opening. His arm cocked back, and flung forward. The spear whizzed by the leaves and down towards the target.

Ulric held his breath, only letting it out once the spear hit the kelpie in its side, and the kelpie let out a sharp wail.

But the spear didn't sink into the kelpie's flesh like it should have. By all accounts, and Ulric's own experience, the spear should have stopped halfway through and remained lodged inside the kelpie's abdomen. But the spear continued clean through the kelpie, and sunk into the ground about ten feet away from the creature. The gaping burnt hole left from the spear was only left agape for a moment, before it was closed over by new kelp and pondweeds as the kelpie lowered to the ground. The kelpie looked over at the iron spear, then traced its head towards the trees. Ulric could have sworn it looked right at him and narrowed its eyes before darting for Iowyn.

"Fuck," Ulric grunted.

The kelpie hadn't been slowed. Its murky green eyes were trained on Iowyn as she ran, and it was gaining on her.

Ulric didn't have time to think. He needed to get down to the ground. Iowyn had the iron dagger with her, somewhere, but it wasn't enough. A whole fucking spear hadn't been enough.

His palms scraped against the bark of the sycamore as he haphazardly climbed down as fast as he could, but the pain didn't matter.

Once again, Ulric sent up a plea to Odea under his breath. "Don't let her die, please. She can't die. She *can't.*" His heart had turned into a heavy stone, and it was sinking further into his stomach as each second ticked by without his eyes on her. "She can't fucking die," he said louder.

Finally, his boots hit the ground, sending skittering bolts of pain up his legs. He took no time to start running in the direction that he had seen both Iowyn and the beast run. Branches reached out at him, blocking his view. All he could hear was the snapping of twigs and wild hoofbeats. Ulric finally broke through the trees to find the road. Iowyn was still running, but the kelpie was just behind her, its jaws snapping wildly at her back. Ulric willed his legs

to move faster as he unsheathed his sword at his side. He was
silently wishing he'd taken Iowyn's advice of having a silver sword
instead of steel. He wouldn't be able to kill the kelpie with it, but
maybe he could still hurt it.

The kelpie caught up to Iowyn, and used its head as a battering
ram to shunt Iowyn forward and stop her from running any
farther. She fell onto the road, kicking up a small cloud of dirt.
Ulric was still at least fifty feet away. There was no way he could get
to her in time.

The kelpie stood over her as she tried to stumble back onto her
feet. A few vines of pondweed from the beast's wild mane
articulated, as if becoming sentient. They grew longer, and Iowyn
let out a scream as they grew long enough to wrap around her
wrists and waist. She kicked and screamed wildly as it hauled her up
onto its back, and several more vines from the creature's body
entwined themselves around her.

The kelpie reared on his hind legs, victorious. But it was
enough to give Ulric the extra time he had needed. As it stood on
its hind legs, Ulric slid on the dirt road and sliced with his sword.
The metal collided with the botanical mass that made up the
creature, severing its back limbs from the rest of the body. The
kelpie cried out with an ear-splitting shriek. As Ulric came to stand
on the other side of the creature, he had hoped to see it rendered
immobile. But the vines from the back quarters of the kelpie simply
grew to reattach to the severed stumps of its back feet.

A thundering of hooves sounded behind him. Elmer was
coming with Shadowfoot.

The kelpie swung its head to stare at Ulric, and he could have
sworn it gave him a crooked smile before breaking out into a run,
back towards the river with Iowyn in tow.

CHAPTER

30

As the kelpie raced for the river, there was only one coherent thing that Iowyn could think to scream.

"Ulric!"

This wasn't happening. It wasn't supposed to be happening. She cursed herself for her foolish idea, for thinking she was even cut out for this in the first place, for risking her life.

She clawed at the vines holding her to the kelpie's wet, vegetal body, trying her best to get any part of her free. The pressure of the sheath dug in against her thigh, her possible salvation.

Riding on the back of the kelpie was disorienting. Iowyn was used to fast travel on the back of Dren, but as soon as they had hit the river water, the kelpie had taken on a supernatural kind of speed. Her stomach pressed back into her spine, and the wind stung her face. Even if Ulric was already on Shadowfoot, would he be fast enough to even catch up to her? He hadn't been the last time the kelpie had taken someone.

Iowyn knew deep down that nothing was for certain, and despite his promise, she couldn't count on Ulric to be there in time to save her. No, she would need to do her best to save herself.

A loud and familiar howl sounded from off in the trees to Iowyn's left, and her heart leapt in her chest. From up on the bank, a flash of black and silver fur raced beside them.

Dren.

The deupin must have raced all the way from town at the sound of Iowyn's screams. Tears welled in her eyes at the sight of him. His paws thundered against the ground, and he brayed again,

251

more frantically at the sight of Iowyn atop the monstrous creature, and the kelpie let out its terrible whinny in response.

Iowyn's free hand patted over her skirt, and grabbed a fistful of fabric. She pulled downward with all of her might, and felt the taut fabric rip. Iowyn was quick to grab the dagger that still waited in the drop leg sheath.

She cut the vine wrapped around her other wrist first. The dagger sliced through the weedy vine like butter, and the severed ends were burnt from the iron. The kelpie cried out in pain, its fluid strides faltering slightly. Iowyn grabbed the vine that encircled her waist, and lightly touched the dagger to the tendril. It sizzled at the contact, slowly burning away. The thick black vine burned scarlet like an ember before falling away as ash. The kelpie shrieked again, and Dren charged into the river, head down and antlers forward.

Iowyn, still very much attached to the kelpie's back, clutched the dagger tight and inhaled a deep breath as Dren struck the front quarter of the beast, knocking it onto its side under the cold current of the river.

Pain shot through Iowyn's bare leg as the kelpie hit the river's bottom. The weight of the monster crushed her leg and it dug into the rocks of the river bed. She let out a garbled scream below the water, all the air from her lungs escaping in a flurry of bubbles.

The kelpie regained its footing and lifted them both out of the water. Iowyn sputtered, coughing up water. Before she could get her bearings, the kelpie was struck again from the other side, and they were plunged back into the water.

The kelpie gained its footing before its body could slam back down into the riverbed. It stood up and whirled around to face the deupin head on, stomping its front leg into the water in a challenge.

Iowyn grabbed wildly at the vines and weeds that held her onto the kelpie's back. Freeing herself would help keep her out of harm's way and also help give Dren an edge until Ulric could catch up to them.

Her fingers wrapped around the girth of one of the larger vines, and when she was sure she wouldn't harm herself, she slashed it. The kelpie reared, and Iowyn grabbed a handful of other vines ensnaring her covered leg, and slashed again. The vines sizzled as they died and fell into the churning water below.

As Iowyn made to cut more vines, Dren charged once more. His antlers hit the kelpie square in the chest, knocking the creature backwards. The iron dagger flew from Iowyn's hand, and onto the bank behind her. She clutched to the creature's back as it began losing its balance and threatened to topple backwards. If it did, she would surely be crushed, and it wouldn't matter that she only had one leg left to free. It wouldn't matter that Dren had come to her rescue. She would die.

Vines shot out from the kelpie's body, grappling onto the larger rocks in the water and steadying it. It regained its balance and lowered back onto its four backwards hooves. Without warning, it charged at Dren and headbutted him in the ribs with preternatural strength. It was enough force to launch the deupin out of the water and back onto the bank of the river. Dren let out a yowl that made Iowyn's heart shatter in her chest. It was the sound only made by dying things.

The kelpie stalked towards Dren's limp body on the bank, but then cocked its head unnaturally down river. Iowyn strained her own ears to try and hear what it could possibly be, and was met with the rhythmic sound of galloping hooves.

"Ulric," she breathed.

The kelpie huffed, then broke off in a run upstream. Iowyn only had a few seconds to glance back at Dren, her eyes honed in on his chest and ribs as she searched for any movement in the creature she loved so dearly. But the kelpie's movement was so sporadic and jostled that there was no way to discern between her own movement and any signs of life.

Iowyn blinked tears away as she lost sight of Dren. With each stride, the kelpie brought them closer to the lake. There was no sign of Ulric. It was quite possible that these would be some of her last moments alive. Knowing that was not at all a comfort.

Without the iron dagger, she was unable to free herself. She tried everything she could think of. Clawing at the vines with her fingernails had just made them constrict around her other leg, and hitting at the creature did nothing to slow its pace. Still, she couldn't accept giving up.

If there was any chance of living, Iowyn wanted it.

Ulric pushed Shadowfoot harder than he ever had before. He knew the end destination, but he hoped to catch up to the kelpie and Iowyn before they got that far. Who knew how long she had once the kelpie made it to the lake?

Elmer rode behind them on his own horse. Ulric held the spear under his arm, not too unlike a knight holding a lance in a joust.

Even now, with a million thoughts racing through his head, he chided himself for not aiming more precisely. He should have known, should have expected, that such an elusive creature would need to be dealt a killing blow and nothing less.

It was his fault it was still alive. His fault that Iowyn's life was now in danger. His fault if she died. Her blood would be on his hands.

At that moment, he didn't care about his place in the Guild, or going to Smokheim. All he cared about was her, returning home alive.

The lake came into full view. This was it. Her last moments of peace before being dragged to a watery death. Iowyn tried to take in the scenery. Tried to memorize it as best as she could. The highlands to the north still had snow on their caps. The trees grew taller and thinner the farther up the face they went. The blue sky and pristine cotton clouds reflected beautifully off the lake's surface. Wildflowers of every color blossomed where the rocky beach met the edge of the forest.

She took it all in, for what else could she do?

As the creature stepped from the river and into the lake, panic set in immediately. The water rose to meet her as the kelpie trudged farther away from the shore. As the water engulfed her, she let out one last cry.

"Ulric!"

She barely got in another breath before her head went under. The world blurred into a chaotic frenzy. She couldn't breathe. The air had been replaced by the relentless grip of the chilled water. Her body instinctively fought to stay afloat, but it was a futile struggle against the kelpie that pulled her down.

Was this it? Was this how it would end?

Memories flashed before Iowyn's eyes – moments of laughter, of love, of life. Sitting on Burke's lap learning to read. Bearen sneakily placing a dollop of frosting on her nose. Maddox leaning forward to give her her first kiss. Galloping through the hills with Dren for the first time. Long hours in the archives. Throwing a drink in Ulric's face. Shooting the werewolf. It seemed strange to her how, in these dire moments, the mind raced through a lifetime of experiences in mere seconds.

Her lungs burned. Her limbs began to grow heavy, as if they were made of lead. With each moment, the underwater world around her grew darker and colder.

She looked up to the surface. It was so far away.

Ulric. Where was Ulric? He had promised to save her.

Her eyes stung as she continued to search for his figure in the water, but the water had distorted everything into a blurry, shifting mosaic.

Her chest tightened, and deep down, Iowyn began to accept it. She had read about the experience of drowning once. She knew she wouldn't be able to stay awake much longer. Soon she would drift away, like she was falling asleep – at least that was how the book had explained it. Every ounce of strength was draining from her body.

The world was fading further into darkness. Time seemed to stretch on, and the sound of her own heartbeat echoed in her ears as each beat took longer than the last.

Iowyn let her last bit of breath out, and marveled at the small bubble as it floated towards the surface. She instinctively inhaled, nothing but water entering her body. Her eyelids began to droop, and she could hear nothing as the darkness finally clouded her vision.

CHAPTER

31

The last ripples from the kelpie's descent were disappearing when Ulric dismounted.

"Shit," Elmer cursed under his breath.

Ulric wasted no time. He threw the iron spear down and quickly removed his boots and shirt. Picking the spear back up, he dove into the icy water.

The shock of the cold did nothing to slow his descent. He was more afraid of the kelpie swimming out of reach. If it swam too deep, then there was nothing he would be able to do to save Iowyn. The weight of the spear – for once – was welcomed. Ulric held on tightly to his only useful weapon as its weight helped drag him further down into the depths.

He saw her first in the inky black water. Iowyn was still on the creature's back, unmoving. Her raven hair floated around her like a shroud, but even in the dark depths, her pale skin shone like the moon on a clear night. Her arms were suspended in the water, and she looked as if she were in a peaceful sleep atop the murderous beast. Its back half had transformed. The black vines had rearticulated into a fish-like tail, making it faster in the water.

Ulric kicked his legs harder, pushing through the cold water. The kelpie, sensing his approach, turned to face him. Its green eyes now glowing under the water with some eerie, otherworldly light. As Ulric drew nearer, he could see the kelpie's sharp teeth and the wicked smile on its horse-like face. Perhaps it would get two meals today.

The kelpie's tail propelled it forward with greater speed. Ulric knew he only had minutes, maybe seconds to get Iowyn from the kelpie's back and onto land. If he was going to kill it, it would have to be now.

The beast gnashed its teeth as it came closer, and Ulric braced himself. He would likely only get one shot, and if he missed, then both he and Iowyn would be dead.

Ulric's lungs burned as the creature raced towards him, poised to strike. Its jaws opened wide, unhinging like a snake as it reached nearer. With a powerful stroke of his arm, Ulric thrust the iron spear up at the last second, skewering the kelpie's head.

The beast stopped mid strike, mouth still open. From inside of its mouth, Ulric could see sparks crackling, despite them being underwater. The kelpie went limp, its body seemingly setting itself ablaze and burning itself from the inside out.

Ulric let go of the spear, allowing it to sink to the bottom of the lake as he reached out and grabbed Iowyn, pulling her free from the kelpie's back as the last vines that held her burned away. She was limp and unconscious, but alive. She had to be alive. Her being dead wasn't an option. With all his remaining strength, Ulric kicked back towards the surface, dragging Iowyn with him.

Air. He needed air. *She* needed air. He didn't even let himself think of the possibility that she could be dead. It wasn't an option.

Gasping for air, Ulric finally broke the surface.

From the shore, he could hear Elmer cursing repeatedly as he waded into the shallows. Elmer lifted Iowyn's body out of the water, taking her onto the beach. Ulric collapsed on the rocky shore, panting and shivering from the cold. With every breath, his muscles seized.

Ulric pushed himself up off the ground and crawled over to where Iowyn lay. He wrapped his arms around her, trying to warm her chilled body with his own. As he looked down at her pale and lifeless face, his heart dropped.

"She isn't breathing!" Elmer hollered.

Ulric shook her. "Wake up, Beastie. Wake. Up."

Nothing. Her arms were limp at her sides. Her lips parted, but no breath escaped them. She was so cold. Too cold.

"Beastie, *please*. Wake up!"

She'd been in the water too long. He knew it deep down, but he didn't want to accept it.

Ulric laid her down on the pebbles and rocks on the beach, and wiped away the wet strands of hair that clung to her face. Desperation clawed at him as he gazed down at her. Her skin wasn't just pale but ashen. Her lips were tinged with a deadly shade of blue. The bitter cold of the water had stolen the warmth from her body.

Ulric shook her again, more urgently this time. "Beastie, please," he pleaded. "You can't leave me. Not like this. Wake up!"

Ulric could hear the timbre of Elmer's voice, but it was like he was miles away. No words registered to him.

Iowyn remained motionless, her chest disturbingly still.

Trembling, Ulric placed his hands over her heart. With each compression, he prayed to Odea for a sign, a flicker of hope to cling onto amidst the overwhelming despair. His muscles screamed with exertion, but he refused to relent. Each second brought a new, desperate plea to bring her back from the abyss, to defy the cold grip of death. He leaned down and breathed life into her chilled lungs, pressing his own lips to hers, willing her to come back.

"Come on, breathe. Breathe, breathe…"

"Ulric," Elmer's hand grabbed his arm. "I think she's—"

"*Don't* even finish that sentence, Elmer," Ulric warned.

Time seemed to blur as Ulric continued his desperate efforts, refusing to give up. All that mattered was Iowyn's life, hanging in the balance.

"Ulric." Elmer's voice was soft.

He ignored it. He couldn't stop.

A hand gently rested on his shoulder. "Ulric, she's—"

He swatted the hand away. One more. He would try one more time. He had to try.

Ulric placed his hands on top of each other, and pressed lightly but forcibly down on Iowyn's chest. He counted to five, then took in a breath before lowering his mouth to hers one last time. He blew his breath into her, but her body stayed still.

He hovered over her face, taking it in. Her eyes were shut. No longer would those amber orbs of hers try to burn into him. He would never see them roll in annoyance, or see her half-moon spectacles perched on her nose while she read. Her lips would never say his last name spitefully, or utter another curse. And it was all his fault.

Elmer knelt beside him and placed his hand on Ulric's bare shoulder again. "You did everything you could."

Ulric let out a shaky breath. He knew Elmer was simply trying to be comforting, but it wasn't. He would have to go back into town with her body and tell her parents. Bearen would most likely try to kill him, especially when he told them that he would have to take her to the nearest outpost. All the bodies of Guild members that died on assignment were given to the Guild before being released to family. They would have to perform an autopsy to confirm her cause of death and assure no foul play. Ulric would bring her back. He owed her that much. Besides, it wasn't like he'd have a next assignment to get to afterwards.

Ulric leaned down to her ear. "I'm sorry, Beastie," he whispered. The words were like a vise around his heart. He looked into her face once more, and bent to place a gentle kiss on her lips.

Iowyn's body seized, and she sputtered to life as she coughed up mouthfuls of water. Ulric couldn't bring himself to believe it as her eyelids fluttered open, revealing dazed, unfocused eyes.

Iowyn's gaze slowly fixed on him, and a weak smile tugged at the corners of her lips. "Ulric," she whispered, her voice barely audible.

Ulric picked her up off the ground and held her cold body tightly to him.

Iowyn drearily blinked her eyes as the world came back into focus. She was alive.

As she looked around at her surroundings, she could swear the sky was bluer and the trees were greener than she remembered. Her body shivered as the heat from Ulric's body wrapped around her, thawing the ice that had gripped her limbs. It should have bothered her that he was holding her so closely, especially without a shirt, but she was so cold it was miserable.

Coherent thought eluded her as recent memories came to the surface. The kelpie's vines wrapped around her, the chill of the water, the sight of Dren on the bank.

A soft rumble echoed in the distance. Ulric's eyes darted toward the source of the sound, and Iowyn followed his gaze. On the horizon, dark clouds were gathering, and the rumble grew louder, like a distant thunderstorm.

"Dren," she breathed. Iowyn weakly pushed Ulric away, and tried to stand. Her exposed leg screamed in pain as she did her best to put weight on it.

"What's wrong?" Ulric asked, taking her arm to steady her.

Iowyn looked towards the river that flowed from the lake. "We need to find Dren." She tried to take a step, but she was still too weak and didn't have feeling back in all of her extremities. She stumbled, and Ulric's arms caught her at her waist.

"Beastie, he's at home. We have to get you back to town."

Iowyn pushed at Ulric's chest with all her might. "No! We have to find Dren! He came for me. He fought the kelpie. He's hurt and could be dying!"

She could see a dissonance in Ulric's eyes as he looked to Elmer, a mixture of worry and doubt. Did he not believe her? Did he think she was making this up?

She pointed down the river. "He was lying on the bank. He wasn't *moving*." Tears began to stream down her face. "Please, we-we-we have to go find him."

Ulric grabbed his shirt and boots from the ground and put them on. Without hesitation, Ulric scooped Iowyn up into his arms, cradling her gently despite the icy water that still clung to her skin. Her weak protests faded as she clung to him for support. He lifted her onto Shadowfoot's back as if she weighed nothing.

Ulric went over to Elmer. "See if you can find any sign of Dren. We'll be close behind. If we get separated and the storm becomes too much, get back to town and let the Morgnah's know their daughter is safe"

Ulric climbed into the saddle himself behind her as Elmer rode off. "Alright, Beastie," he said with determination. "We'll find Dren. I promise."

They rode swiftly along the riverbank. Iowyn's eyes scanned everywhere for any sign of Dren. Rain began to fall in light sprinkles. With every passing moment, her heart sank farther.

A low and groaning bellow sounded in the trees, and Iowyn grabbed Ulric's thigh beside her at the sound. Ulric stopped Shadowfoot to listen. Her heartbeat thud loudly in her chest as she waited for the sound again. Echoing through the trees, the low bellow resonated through the forest.

Iowyn couldn't tell where the sound was coming from, but Ulric quickly spurred his horse away from the river. Iowyn whistled for Dren. If he had moved away from the river, perhaps he was alright to meet them halfway in the forest.

Another low sound emitted from the thick of trees, closer this time, but it was more of a groan than the others before. The sound was sad and haunting.

Ulric urged Shadowfoot deeper into the forest, following the direction from which the eerie sounds were emanating. Iowyn kept whistling and calling out for Dren, her voice carrying through the trees in the hopes that he would hear and respond. She couldn't bear the thought of losing him. He was more than a mount to her or a pet. He had been her closest companion in the years since leaving home. He was hers, but she was also his.

Then, just as hope began to wane, a faint response came from the depths of the forest. It was a weak sound, barely audible over the rumbling of thunder and the rain pelting the leaves.

"Dren!" she called out, her voice trembling with emotion.

The response came again, closer this time, and they continued to follow the sound until they finally spotted Dren, huddled under the cover of a massive oak tree.

Iowyn jumped down from Shadowfoot's back, the pain in her leg disappearing at the sight of Dren. His fur was damp and cold to the touch. He was weak and shivering, but alive.

She ran to him and knelt beside him, taking his large head in her hands. Dren's eyes lit up at the sight of her, and he let out a soft bray. His chest heaved with difficulty where the kelpie had struck him. Broken ribs were most likely the cause.

Ulric brought Shadowfoot closer as a bolt of lightning streaked across the sky, accompanied by a loud thunder clap. "We need to find shelter," he said.

Iowyn looked up at him from where she knelt beside Dren and shook her head. "I'm not leaving him."

Ulric opened his mouth to say something, and Iowyn braced herself for the argument to come, but he closed his mouth before any words came out and pursed his lips. He took a breath, then said, "I know."

Iowyn gently stroked Dren's fur, offering him what comfort she could. Despite the pain he was in, he nuzzled her affectionately.

Ulric dismounted and joined them, his eyes filled with concern. She knew he was right. They needed shelter, and the storm showed no signs of letting up.

"We'll find shelter, but we won't leave Dren," Ulric affirmed, his voice unwavering. "We'll ride out the storm. Together."

With that decision made, Ulric began to search for a suitable place to wait out the storm. They all could use a bit of rest before heading back into town, especially with an injured beast the size of Dren.

It didn't take long before he stumbled upon a cave nestled at the base of a rocky hill about half a mile from where he had left Iowyn. After making sure it was uninhabited, Ulric was sure it would provide ample protection from the rain and wind, and would be large enough for him, Iowyn, the deupin, and his horse.

He traveled back quickly to the large oak tree where Iowyn had already devised a plan to help move Dren. Using Shadowfoot as a kind of crutch, Dren moved much easier than walking on his own. Ulric and Iowyn walked together, leading their animals to the cave.

Iowyn said nothing the whole time, and constantly checked to make sure Dren wasn't overexerting himself.

By the time the cave came into view, both Ulric and Iowyn were completely soaked through to the bone. Together, they carefully guided Dren into the cave, laying him down on a bed of moss and leaves. Iowyn continued to soothe him, her touch gentle and reassuring.

Ulric set about gathering whatever dry wood and leaves he could find to start a fire. Soon, a small, flickering flame danced in the darkness of the cave, casting a warm and comforting glow. Dren eventually fell asleep, his breathing still labored, but better now that he was dry and warm by the fire.

They didn't speak for the longest time. The crackling fire was all that kept the silence from being unbearable. He couldn't help but feel overly responsible for the way things had gone, for Iowyn being taken and almost killed, and now for the state of Dren. If Dren died, he was certain that Iowyn would never forgive him. But what could he say to her? *I'm sorry*, just didn't seem to be enough.

He studied Iowyn as she cradled Dren's head in her lap, and Ulric had to keep telling himself that she was real and alive. He was almost certain that she was dead not even an hour ago, and had come to terms with the fact that she was never waking up on that rocky beach. But she *had*. She was sitting three feet away from him, alive and breathing, with little more than a few scratches and bruises.

Iowyn reached across the distance between them to grab Ulric's hand. Her amber eyes were aglow in the flickering firelight. "Thank you."

The words felt like a knife in his heart. Ulric pulled his hand away. "You shouldn't thank me."

Iowyn's eyes widened. "But–"

"You shouldn't thank me," Ulric repeated, his voice heavy. He stared at the fire, unable to bring himself to look at her. She shouldn't be giving him any gratitude. He had been too late in getting to the lake. By all accounts, she should have been dead.

Iowyn closed her mouth and let out a heavy sigh through her nose. "I'm too tired to fight with you right now." She reached out, and her hand came to the side of his face, urging him to look at her. "Just let me thank you because I want to, Ulric, whether you think you deserve it or not."

Ulric finally met her gaze. "That's the second time you've called me by my name today."

Iowyn smirked. "I think you've more than earned it."

A stray piece of her black hair fell into her face, and Ulric's hand raised slightly to put it behind her ear. But Ulric pulled it back, stopping himself and letting go of her hand.

The cackling of the fire filled the silence, until Iowyn finally asked. "How long was I – what even is the right word? Out?" She paused. "Unconscious?"

Dead, Ulric's mind finished for her.

His gaze refocused on the fire. The dancing flames were easier to look at than her. Even from the corner of his eye, he could see her. The faint beginnings of what would become blue and purple bruises stuck out against the pale skin of her exposed leg. They weren't too much unlike the blue tint of her lips when Ulric had pulled her from the water.

"I'm not sure. You'd have to ask Elmer." Ulric stood up. The walls seemed to be closing in around him. "I'm going to find more firewood."

The rain drenched Ulric as he ventured out into the storm. Every step he took was heavy with the weight of his thought. He had gone from accepting that Iowyn was gone forever to getting her back from the dead. She was alive, and every fiber in his body told him that it shouldn't be possible.

He had lied when he said that he wasn't sure how long she'd been gone. He'd counted every second since he had pulled her from the water in his head. He had only stopped when he had accepted that she was dead, and even then, he had reached an impossible number. Anyone else would have joined Mortem in eternity.

Twelve hundred and fifty-two.

As they took their first steps onto the cobbled main street of Calluna, Iowyn couldn't help but feel drained. The events of the day had sapped every bit of energy from her.

Burke was the first out of the shops and out onto the street. He looked horrified as he raced to Iowyn's side. "Wynnie? Oh, my gods, we thought the worst! What happened?"

Iowyn gave a weak smile as she realized the state of her torn dress. "I'm okay, Dad. We killed the kelpie, but Dren got hurt."

Bearen had slipped out of the building and was standing a good twenty feet away, listening to Ulric. Burke continued his fussing over her, but Iowyn didn't hear much of what her father was saying. She was too focused on trying to figure out what Ulric was saying to Bearen to be concerned with listening to Burke. He talked in a hushed tone to her father, and she wondered what on earth the hunter could be relaying to the baker. Perhaps he was trying to make sure at least the more sensible of her parents had the whole story.

Bearen held out his hand for Ulric to shake. When Ulric grasped the baker's large hand, Bearen pulled him into a hug. Iowyn watched Ulric's eyes widen at the sudden gesture, and had to suppress a laugh at his overall awkwardness.

Burke threw up his hands in exasperation. "What are you laughing at?" he asked, then followed Iowyn's gaze to where Bearen and Ulric were standing, no longer hugging. He tugged at her arm. "Come inside, let's get you cleaned up."

Iowyn was quick to protest. "But, Dad. Dren—"

"I'll take care of him," Ulric said, coming to her side and taking Dren's lead from her. She opened her mouth to argue, but Ulric insisted. "I've got him. Go. Be with your family."

There was a sincerity in his eyes that made Iowyn let go of the reins. He would make sure Dren was okay. Even though she believed that, Iowyn still raised a finger. "Anything happens to him, and I'll kill you."

Ulric's mouth twitched up into an amused smirk. "Got it."

Iowyn let Burke and Bearen lead her up to the shop. Each step was heavier than the last.

"Oh, and Beastie?"

Iowyn turned, locking eyes with Ulric.

He was still smirking as he started to walk away. "Happy birthday," he said over his shoulder.

Her brow furrowed. Birthday? No. It wasn't her birthday. It couldn't be.

She looked at Burke, who shrugged rather sheepishly. "We figured we should wait to tell you until after you got back."

It was a slow ascent up the stairs to their home. Bearen and Burke left Iowyn in her room where she could wash and change. She looked at herself in the mirror and could now understand Burke's horrified face. She looked like she'd been down to the Pit and back.

The skirt of her dress was torn from the hem nearly up to the waist. Her cheeks heated. How had she not noticed the large slit in her skirt before this? Her leg was completely exposed, the tender skin blossoming with bruises. Her hair was tangled and matted from the water, wind, and mud. Iowyn groaned at the thought of how much time it would take to detangle all of the strands.

As she undressed, her thoughts wandered to Ulric, who had returned to town looking remarkably unscathed compared to her disheveled state. It was a curious contrast that didn't escape her notice, and a part of her wondered how he managed to maintain his composure through it all. However, as she continued to shower and let the warm water wash away the mud and grime of the day, her thoughts took a darker turn.

She almost died today. On her birthday of all days. And what's worse was she hadn't even realized that it was her birthday this morning. She supposed that with the excitement and stress of recent assignments that she had simply lost track of time.

Her mind kept going back to the moment she had woken up on the beach, coughing up lake water, and how the world seemed so vibrant and new.

As Iowyn got out of the shower, she realized how exhausted she was. The adrenaline from the day's events had long since worn off, leaving her drained and emotionally spent. She wrapped a towel around herself and stepped out of the bathroom, heading to her room to find some clean clothes.

She dressed in her usual choice of pants and blouse, when a knock came at her door.

"Come in," she called to the closed door.

Burke hesitantly opened the door. When he saw Iowyn standing next to her bed, he relaxed. "Dinner's ready." He smiled, and Iowyn knew the smile all too well.

They had planned something for her birthday, and Iowyn's heart swelled. She never took them for granted, her parents. They had chosen to keep her when no one had asked them to. Their family was an unconventional one, forged not by blood but by an unspoken acceptance of each other. And that acceptance was everything.

Iowyn followed Burke out to the dining table, where three plates had been set. A casserole dish sat in the center, the familiar scent wafting in the air. "Shepherd's pie?"

"It's still your favorite, right?" Burke asked, a hint of nervousness in his tone.

Iowyn's eyes glistened with the light watering of tears. All she could do was nod her head as she sat.

Bearen came up the stairs with a plate covered by a light towel in his hands and set it down on the table. He pulled the cloth up to reveal a small cake with white frosting and twenty-four light blue, unlit candles.

"We won't sing happy birthday, since you've always hated that, but you can still make a wish." Bearen winked as he struck a match to light each candle.

Iowyn's eyes filled with tears as she gazed at the cake. For a moment, she forgot about the events of the day, and focused on the warmth and love that surrounded her.

"Thank you," she whispered, a lump forming in her throat. Iowyn smiled gratefully at her parents, noting a warmth in her chest that she couldn't quite explain. They had always known her so well, and yet there was so much about her that they didn't know. All the secrets that she kept locked away within herself, the ones that made her feel like an imposter in her own skin. Were they even aware of how close she came to not coming back to them? It was strange, to be surrounded by love and yet feel so far away from it. She wondered if anyone else ever felt that way with their own families.

As she blew out the candles, Iowyn made her wish. She wished for courage, for the kind of bravery that would allow her to face the things that terrified her the most. The things that kept her up at night, that made her heart race and her palms sweat. She wished for the ability to let go of the past, and to move forward with a sense of purpose. When she opened her eyes, her fathers were looking at her expectantly. She smiled at them.

Bearen cleared the table when they were all finished eating, and Burke pulled out a yellow garment box from under his chair. She hadn't even noticed it when she came out of her room, which seemed odd to her considering the garish color of it. She must have just been so in her own thoughts that she missed it.

"Oh, you didn't have to get me anything," Iowyn protested lightly as she took the box from him.

Burke waved the comment away. "Nonsense. Just open it!"

In the moment in between lifting the lid of the box and seeing what it held inside, Iowyn secretly hoped that whatever was inside wasn't the same color that the box was. Yellow could be a beautiful color, but this shade had the slightest tinge of green to it, making it absolutely repulsive. When she could see inside, she was relieved to see a beautiful hue of maroon.

Iowyn ran her hands over the fabric. From the top, she could only see a hood of soft merino wool trimmed with velvet of the same color. She pulled it out of the box, yards of fabric falling to the floor, to reveal a beautiful riding cloak.

It was made of the same soft merino wool as the hood and was lined with a thick, luxurious black silk. The edges of the cloak were trimmed with velvet of the same color as the hood, and it fastened with a simple brass clasp.

Iowyn was speechless at the beauty of it. She wrapped the cloak around her shoulders, its warmth and weight settled around her. It was soft and comforting, and she felt like she could lose herself in it.

"Thank you," she whispered again, looking up at her parents with tears in her eyes.

"It's just what you need now that you'll be traveling more often," Bearen said with a twinkle in his eye.

Iowyn turned around and admired the cloak in the mirror that hung on the wall. The velvet trim gave it an elegant touch. She felt like royalty.

Ulric sat down at the bar, finding a tense Elmer.

"How is she?" he asked.

"Exhausted, but fine. I wouldn't be here if she weren't."

Elmer let out a heavy sigh. "Thank the gods." He reached down and pulled out two glasses, and poured them both a drink.

"We might just have Odea herself to thank for this one," Ulric said as he lifted the glass to his lips.

"Where is she, then?" Elmer asked.

"At home with her parents. It's her birthday, actually."

Elmer's eyes widened as he leaned onto the bar. "You made me help her play bait for some murderous creature on her *birthday*?"

Ulric pointed at Elmer. "You and I both know that we didn't make her do anything that she didn't want to."

Elmer scoffed. "Well, yeah, but on her birthday? Come on, even you can admit that's kind of fucked up."

Ulric took another sip, savoring the burn and warmth on his tongue. "I didn't know it was her birthday until this morning, and she didn't know until," he turned to look at the large clock that hung above the fireplace, "a few hours ago."

Elmer raised a brow. "She forgot her own birthday? Seriously?"

Ulric nodded. "Time can get away from you in this job."

"Have you ever forgotten yours?" Elmer asked.

The corner of Ulric's lip curled up into a soft smile. "No. My little brother writes to me for every holiday and birthday."

Elmer looked surprised. "Huh, didn't take you for the type."

Ulric set his glass down on the bar. "What's that supposed to mean?"

Elmer laughed. "You can't be serious. Come on, you're like the epitome of a lone wolf."

"Ain't that the truth," Iowyn commented, sliding onto the barstool next to Ulric. She looked better than when he had left her with her parents. The color had returned to her face. Her hair was pulled back into a long braid over her shoulder, and she was back to wearing a long sleeve blouse and pants.

"What are you doing here?" Ulric asked.

"What? I can't come to a bar on my birthday?"

"But you don't even drink," he added.

Iowyn and Elmer gave each other a look, then burst out laughing. Elmer clapped a hand on Ulric's shoulder. "Oh, my friend. You must not have grown up in a small town."

He hadn't, but he didn't understand what was so funny.

"It's basically a rite of passage for teenagers to steal a bottle from their parents and bring it to the woods for a party," Iowyn explained.

Elmer smiled. "Well, what will it be then for the birthday girl?"

"Phoenix sunrise, if you don't mind."

Elmer clapped his hands together. "Coming right up." He went off to start making Iowyn's drink, leaving Ulric and her alone at the bar. The silence between them hung heavy in the air, and Ulric noticed that Iowyn began picking at her fingernails.

"Are you alright?" he asked, placing his hand lightly on her forearm.

He expected her to pull away and snap at him, or start an argument about treating her like a child or a worm. But she didn't. She simply sighed, and it seemed like the kind of weary sigh that let everything go. "My leg hurts like hell but besides that, I'm more than alright, Ulric. I'm alive." She gave him a small smile.

"I'm surprised your parents let you out of the house after the day you've had."

She shrugged. "We did the cake and candles, and spent some time together, but then they went to bed, and I didn't quite feel like sleeping just yet. I figured you might be here so I made my way over." She looked down at her hands. "To be honest, I needed to just get away for a little bit. It was all so... overwhelming."

Ulric wanted to ask what she meant, but she continued talking.

"I checked on Dren. He seems like he's doing much better. Thanks for looking after him."

Ulric nodded. "I know you'd do the same for me with Shadowfoot if the roles were reversed."

Elmer came back with Iowyn's drink, and Ulric pulled his hand away from her. "The first birthday drink is always on the house." Elmer gave her a wink, and a rosy tinge came to her cheeks. Was she just not used to male attention? It seemed any would make her normally pallid skin flush.

Elmer turned to attend to another customer, leaving Ulric and Iowyn in a moment of quiet. "I was able to tell the magistrate of our success. Hopefully he can send for the mothers and children at the monastery in the morning and tell them to return to town."

Iowyn took a sip of her sunset-colored drink. "That will be good."

Ulric nodded. "I also thought that we could postpone traveling until after they returned. That way, Dren could have extra time to recover. With no creature carcass to return, there is no need to hurry off to an outpost right away."

Her eyes lit up. "You'd do that?"

"Well, I can't leave without you, and you won't leave without Dren, so, it seemed the best course of—"

Ulric's words were cut off by Iowyn lunging forward and wrapping her arms around him. Her sweet scent of vanilla curled around him. Ulric went rigid at the sudden embrace. She was... hugging him?

"Thank you," she whispered before pulling away. "I actually have one more thing to ask you." Her focus went back to picking at her fingernails. "I was wondering if you would let me take out Shadowfoot tomorrow?"

Ulric's brow furrowed. "I don't see why not. But… why?"

She shrugged. "It's nothing really. I just left my journal by the bridge."

"Your journal is that important?" he asked.

"I've been taking notes in it since I was a kid. It has everything I know about creatures in it. It wouldn't be a terrible thing to have when we go back on the road."

Ulric nodded grimly. "I don't know if you'll have much luck with the storm, but I'll have Shadowfoot ready for you in the morning."

Elmer returned, bringing a newer conversation with him. It was nice, Ulric thought, to sit for a while and just talk with nothing pressing hanging over him. He hoped to find some solace in the next few days, with nowhere to go and nowhere to be, he could actually relax and take his time.

What he would do exactly, he wasn't entirely sure, but the idea of doing nothing was tantalizing. After almost six years of constantly being on the road traveling, it would be nice to kick his feet up, or do anything other than hunt. So, Ulric paid for a few rounds of drinks, and just enjoyed having good company around.

The cool midspring night was a brisk change from the warm tavern as Iowyn walked home.

She wasn't sure what had spurred Ulric's change in demeanor, and she noted that they had barely fought all day, even during the most stressful of situations. Perhaps they were becoming friends? They surely weren't strangers to each other anymore. Though, it still bothered her that it seemed that Ulric knew more about her than she did about him.

She would need to find a way to remedy that, because she couldn't stand not knowing even the most basic things about him. She could count almost everything she knew about him on one hand.

What would be so bad about telling her even just one personal thing about him? Even tonight, when Elmer and her were reminiscing about school and childhood antics, he barely offered anything up himself, just sat and listened. If she didn't know any better, she would have thought him a mute tonight, incapable of any speech.

Getting to know Ulric was going to be a challenge – she knew that – and he had promised to try. And she had promised to be the patient one, and allow him to open up on his own terms. The night on the roof had been nice, and she'd learned that Ulric had a vast knowledge of the stars. She hadn't asked for him to tell her that, and maybe that's why he had offered it up to her. Maybe she had been going about it all wrong from the beginning.

"Iowyn?" someone called from behind her.

She turned, and Maddox stood in the street. He quickly closed the distance between them, holding her head between his hands. His eyes raked over her, assessing her wildly. "Are you okay? I heard from Albilot. It took you and–"

"I'm fine, Maddox," she interrupted, a small smile curling her lips. The concern was rather sweet of him.

Maddox swallowed, and shifted on his feet. "Uh, look, I shouldn't have shown up to your house drunk, I know that. I also know that it was very insensitive to try and get you to sleep with me while intoxicated." Maddox ran a hand through his hair. "It wasn't my best moment. And I hope to the gods that we can just forget that it happened. But…" His eyes roamed across the ground, as if the words he was looking for were there. He sighed. "You just drive me crazy, Iowyn."

She wrinkled her nose. It wasn't a very nice thing to say. Maddox saw her reaction and held out his hands. "Not like that, I mean…" The words seemed to evade him. He groaned and pinched the bridge of his nose. "I mean, I can't stop thinking about you," he whispered.

Iowyn's expression softened. "Oh."

Maddox gave her a small, albeit bashful, smile. "Yeah."

Heat rose in her cheeks.

"I know I messed up, Iowyn. And I'm willing to do whatever it takes to make it up to you. Just please don't shut me out."

Iowyn felt her head spin. What even were they to each other? Considering Iowyn's place in the Guild, it was unlikely anything would continue between them once she and Ulric had to leave, which would be in a few days. But damn her if she didn't want to have someone – someone good – even just for a little while.

Iowyn looked into Maddox's eyes, searching for something. Anything. Sure, this thing – whatever it was – between them wouldn't last. Their time together was, but Iowyn couldn't help but want to be selfish. She wanted him. Wanted him in a way she hadn't wanted anyone for over a year.

Without a word, she leaned in to kiss him. Maddox did not hesitate, wrapping his arms around her and pulling her close. His hands roamed over her body, tracing the lines of her curves and pulling her in tighter.

When they finally broke apart, Maddox looked at Iowyn with a mixture of wonder and awe. "I don't want to let you go," he whispered.

Iowyn felt a lump form in her throat. "I know," she said softly. "But–"

Maddox shook his head. "No. No buts. Come home with me."

Iowyn knew it was a bad idea, but the thought of spending a few more hours with him, even if it was just for physical pleasure and not to feel alone, was too tempting to resist. She nodded slowly, and Maddox took her hand.

The walk to Maddox's house was short but silent, and Iowyn found herself comfortable with the quiet. They passed the house that Maddox grew up in, and it dawned on Iowyn that it wasn't their final destination. Maddox was a grown man now and had his own place. They walked a few blocks more until they came to a stop.

The house was small and quaint. White shutters contrasted faintly with the pale-yellow siding. It had a nice porch with a small path leading to a tiny garden. The grass was well-trimmed, and a small flower bed brimmed with red tulips. Maddox squeezed Iowyn's hand, his skin was warm, and he led her up the stone steps to his door.

Inside, the home seemed quite warm and welcoming, not anything that Iowyn would expect a bachelor's house to look like. Though, she supposed Maddox's mother might have had a hand in the curtains that hung in the windows, and the matching rug on the floor of the living room, as well as the beautiful dishes that sat on the exposed shelving in the kitchen.

Iowyn didn't have long to observe the rest of the house. Maddox led her by the hand into the bedroom. He gave her that smile that always seemed to make her knees go weak. Heat rose in her cheeks. She couldn't help feeling like a teenager again whenever she was with Maddox.

Maddox turned to face her, his hands coming up to cup her face. He leaned in to kiss her gently, taking his time to explore her mouth as if memorizing every inch of it. Iowyn wrapped her arms around his neck, pulling him closer to deepen the kiss.

Maddox's hands moved down to her hips and his hardness pressed against her. Iowyn's heart jumped at the thought that it was because of her. Maddox broke the kiss, his forehead pressed against hers as he panted for air.

"I could do that forever," he murmured, his lips brushing against hers.

"Maddox," she breathed.

"I'm serious."

"Shut up and kiss me."

Maddox grinned and pulled her in for another kiss. His hands tugged at the bottom of her shirt, the soft material sliding over her skin. The slight chill in the air sent goosebumps across her body. Maddox bit his lip and leaned down to press his lips against her neck. Iowyn sighed softly, her hands resting on his shoulders as he kissed his way down her collarbone.

His hands moved from her hips to the front lacings of her pants. His fingers fumbled with the strings as he continued to kiss her neck. Once he had them untied, he hooked his fingers into the waistband and pulled them down. Iowyn stepped out from them, her hands reaching for the bottom of Maddox's shirt, but his hands grabbed her wrists, stopping her.

His eyes were fixed on the large bruises forming all over her thigh. Maddox looked up at her, a worried question lingering there. "I'm fine, Maddox." A dull ache radiated from the bruises, but nothing so debilitating that she couldn't enjoy herself.

She pulled the shirt over his head and dropped it to the floor. Her hands roved over his chest as she kissed him again, pushing him back towards the bed. His legs hit the foot of the mattress first, and she pushed him back gently to fall onto his back.

His chest heaved up and down with want. Her eyes wandered to his pants, and she could see the outline of his erection through them. She leaned down and kissed him, her hand wandering to the buckle of his belt. Maddox grinned up at her and pulled back slightly.

Iowyn smiled and kissed him again. She finished undoing his belt and tugged at the waistband of his pants. Maddox raised his hips off the bed so she could pull them off. His erection was straining against his boxers.

She took off her own underwear, and Maddox did the same until they were both completely naked. Maddox gripped Iowyn's hips and pulled her in close until she was sitting on his lap, her legs straddling his waist. Iowyn sank down onto his erection, her hands gripping his shoulders tightly as he filled her up.

Iowyn kissed him again, holding his face in her hands, and Maddox's fingers became tangled in her hair as she began to move.

He gripped her tightly and pulled her in close, rocking his hips up to meet hers. She gasped as he ground up against her, their groins rubbing together and sending sparks shooting up between her thighs. She kissed him, biting his lip as she gripped his shoulders tightly. Maddox's hands started roaming up and down her back, his fingertips digging in as he pulled her in close.

They were both panting and gasping with each movement of Iowyn's hips. Maddox kissed the hollow of her throat and her head fell back, giving him more access to her neck, which he took advantage of. He held her hips tightly and thrust upwards as she bounced against him.

Iowyn moaned a little louder each time Maddox moved against her. Jolts of electricity pulsed through her body, but there was something else under the surface, winding tighter and tighter with every movement. She continued to rock over him, her body silently urging her to go harder and faster. The pressure in her stomach kept building, her fingers digging into Maddox's shoulders.

Iowyn's head fell back as the pressure inside her grew. Her body was tense, her muscles tight, as she rocked over Maddox. He was kissing her neck, his warm breath sending shivers through her body and leaving goosebumps in its wake. She gasped and put her forehead against his, closing her eyes tightly. The world fell away from her, and all she could feel was Maddox moving beneath her.

Her body was a tense coil, well and truly wound. Maddox held her tightly, his fingers digging into her skin as he began to move faster beneath her. Her movements started to become more frantic as she rode him harder and harder.

Iowyn's head fell back and she let out a long moan, the bounce of his cock inside her hitting her in just the right way. Maddox grinned against her neck and pressed her against his chest.

The sensations welled up inside her, all her muscles tightening. She breathed out her nose, the pressure finally snapping as she gasped and let out a long moan. Maddox's lips pressed against her neck. She felt him stiffen beneath her, his cock twitching as he came inside her. She gasped as it sent her over the edge, her body tensing up and then releasing.

Iowyn collapsed against Maddox and he wrapped his arms around her as wave after wave rolled over her. She was still panting, her body covered in a thin layer of sweat. Her chest heaved as she caught her breath, her hair sticking to her forehead.

One of Maddox's hands reached up to stroke her hair as he held her close. Iowyn closed her eyes, reveling in the feeling of his arms around her. She wanted to stay there forever, but she couldn't.

When she caught her breath she lifted her head, looking at Maddox. He smiled at her and kissed her gently.

"I…" Iowyn struggled to find words, eventually giving up. Maddox chuckled.

"What?"

Iowyn paused and smiled at Maddox.

The two of them were silent for a while, just holding each other. After a time Maddox spoke. "What are you thinking about?"

"I was just thinking that…that it's been a long time since I felt like this." It had been years since she had ever felt this safe with someone. Yet, with Maddox, everything was different. It scared her to feel this way again, because it meant she had something to lose.

Iowyn leaned up and kissed Maddox. They lay together for a while longer in silence, simply enjoying the afterglow.

Maddox was the first to break the silence. "You know, I was going to ask you to marry me."

Iowyn lifted her head from his chest. "What?"

His eyes were focused on the ceiling. "When you told me you were thinking about going to University. I thought about it. I was ready to do anything to keep you here."

"Why didn't you?" she asked. It was a valid question, and a million reasons popped into her own head as to what he was going to say. Because they were too young. Because, in all their time together, neither of them had ever said those three little words. Because he had thought about it and decided he wasn't ready. Because he had decided to put her dreams ahead of his.

Maddox swallowed. "When I was little, my mom used to read me this story about a batterfly who was in love with his favorite flower. As winter approached, it did everything in its power to keep the flower alive, but eventually it had to let it go and it died. The batterfly was terrified that it would never see the flower it loved ever again, but when spring came around, its flower came back."

Iowyn furrowed her brow, not quite comprehending what Maddox was saying. He looked down at her and gave her a small smile. "The moral of the story was, if you love somebody, let them go. If they return, they were always yours. If they don't, then they never were."

Iowyn took a deep breath and let it out. "You let me go."

"And now you're back." He smiled, and the dimple of his right cheek came to the surface.

Iowyn pushed herself off Maddox and sat up, wrapping the top blanket around her body.

She felt a knot form in her stomach at Maddox's words. She had come back, but only because she was working for the Guild and had been assigned here. She had never intended to stay for long, let alone forever.

"Maddox, I–" she started, but he cut her off.

"I know you didn't come back for me," he said, his voice softening. "But I'm glad you're here."

Iowyn felt a pang of guilt as she looked at Maddox.

His eyes softened. "I never stopped loving you."

Iowyn looked away. She couldn't bear it. "Maddox, I can't stay here. As soon as the rest of the town gets back from the monastery, I'm leaving."

Maddox clenched his jaw and sat up, facing Iowyn. He took her hands in his. "No, you can stay. This could be your home. We could be together."

Her heart ached at his words. Part of her wanted to stay, but another part just couldn't. Not when she was finally out in the field.

She couldn't just let her dreams go. "I can't stay, Maddox," she said, her voice barely above a whisper.

Maddox placed a hand on her cheek and made her look him in the eyes. "You *can*, Iowyn. Please, I–" he hesitated, "I love you."

At one point, Iowyn would have given anything to hear Maddox say those words to her. They would have quite possibly made her heart soar clear out of her chest. But now, all she felt was her heart sinking.

She opened her mouth, but Maddox continued on. "You don't have to say it yet, if you don't want to. But I do. I have to say it, Iowyn. I didn't say it when you left and it's one of the biggest regrets of my life." He leaned forward, placing a delicate kiss on her lips. "I love you, and I want to be with you."

Iowyn swallowed the small lump forming in her throat. "Maddox. In three days, I'm leaving town."

His face had hardened. Iowyn couldn't help the beat of her heart quickening at that look. She'd seen it before, a face full of tender love turn cold and sour in a heartbeat. "Does this have something to do with him?"

Him? Who was him? Iowyn racked her brain until it landed on the only person it could possibly be. She shook her head. "Maddox, I told you, Ulric is just my partner."

"I'm not a fool, Iowyn," he said. "And I'm not blind. I see how he looks at you."

"Maddox, that's ridiculous," she said, trying to keep her voice steady. "Ulric and I are just friends. Nothing more. Even if Ulric did have feelings for me, which he doesn't, it wouldn't change anything. I don't have feelings for him."

That was ridiculous, Maddox was being delusional.

"But you're going to leave with him." Maddox's voice was strained.

"Maddox, that's not fair," she said softly. "I'm here now, with you. We're not together, so how can you expect me to stay? The Guild is my job. It's been my dream since I can remember. You can't expect me to stay here just because you want me to."

Maddox shook his head, gritted his teeth and looked her in the eye. "Fine," he said after a few moments of silence. "Then go. Be with him instead."

"For the last time, there is nothing between me and Ulric! None of this has anything to do with him!" she shouted.

"I don't believe you," he growled.

Iowyn pulled away and climbed off the bed. She started to gather her clothes. "I can't do this. Especially if you're not even going to listen to me."

As soon as her feet hit the floor, Maddox's face fell. He moved for her as she slipped her shirt over her head. "*Don't* come near me," Iowyn warned.

"Iowyn," Maddox breathed. "I'm sorry. Don't do this. Don't go."

Iowyn quickly put on her clothes. She tried to ignore the way her hands were shaking as she fumbled to tie the laces of her pants. "I think we can both see that this," she gestured to the space between them, "was a mistake."

Maddox stood from the bed. "Don't say that." He stopped right in front of her, grabbing her hands gently. "Iowyn, I'm sorry, I didn't mean it."

Iowyn wanted to believe him, that this was just a misunderstanding, but she knew better. Had promised to never let herself fall into this kind of trap again.

And she couldn't ignore the nagging in her gut. That Maddox would always be too afraid to let her go. That she would never be able to pursue her dreams if she stayed in Calluna town. She gently pulled her hands from his grip and took a step back.

"I have to go," she said, her voice shaking.

She didn't wait to hear him protest and ran out of the house.

CHAPTER

34

Ulric had been true to his word. Iowyn met him at the stables in the early morning, and he was readying Shadowfoot to ride.

She was still tired after the long night, and had thought about not showing up. But when she thought about it more, she figured it would be best to just pull herself out of bed. If she hadn't shown, there was a chance that Ulric would go looking for her, and she wasn't in the mood for all that could entail.

Ulric was unexpectedly cordial. "How did you sleep?"

Iowyn shrugged. "Alright, I guess."

His brow furrowed as he continued to check Shadowfoot's saddle and bridle. "Long night?"

She sighed, and thought about what telling him about her extracurriculars last night would accomplish. Not a whole lot, she figured, so she decided instead to ignore the question. "Anything special I should know?" she asked, gesturing to the black mare.

Ulric absentmindedly stroked the side of the black mare's neck. "She doesn't spook easily, if that's what you mean." He handed her the reins. "If she starts off running or disobeying, it's probably for a good reason."

"Good to know." She reached up for the pommel of the saddle, and was surprised to see Ulric bending over with his hands together to make a step for her. It was a chivalrous gesture, one that Iowyn had never actually seen in practice and only read about in books. "Oh, um, you don't have to do that."

Ulric stood up. "Sorry, force of habit, I guess."

Iowyn raised a quizzical brow. "You help ladies into saddles often?" She gave him a playful smile.

Ulric glanced away and sighed. "Nevermind."

Iowyn placed her left foot in the stirrup and pulled herself into the saddle. "It won't take long," she said.

"Take as long as you need," Ulric replied, giving Shadowfoot a light pat on the hind quarter, and setting the beast into motion.

As she settled into the seat, Iowyn noted small differences between riding Dren and Shadowfoot. Dren's back sat higher, and his paws made the ride much smoother than hard hooves. Iowyn had to admit deep down, she did enjoy the sound of clipping hooves on the cobblestones. She was interested to see how fast Shadowfoot could actually run. She urged Shadowfoot faster, and the black mare happily obliged.

The cool air bit at her cheeks, sending shivers down her spine. She tightened her new maroon riding cloak around herself as she took in the vast expanse of the rolling hills that spread out before her. The grass was still covered in dew, and the sun was barely peeking over the horizon, casting long shadows across the landscape.

They quickly came upon the stone bridge, and Iowyn dismounted.

The ground was spongy from the hard rain of the storm. She retraced her steps with Shadowfoot following close behind her. She found the spot where she had sat while waiting for the kelpie to appear and looked around for any sign of her journal. The area looked about the same as it had the day before, but she noted the appearance of a few clover blossoms among the greenery that hadn't been there before. Iowyn picked a few and held them out in her open palm for Shadowfoot. The horse's velvet lips scooped up the blossoms gingerly. Shadowfoot let out a content snuffle, and Iowyn climbed back into the saddle.

Her journal had most likely been washed into the river during the storm. The water would have ruined the pages and bled the ink she had made most of her notes in. Her heart sank at the thought of all those years of knowledge lost and the hours spent compiling it all by dim candlelight. Her childhood and dreams had all been poured into that journal. It was different now, knowing her journal was truly lost and not just forgotten under her mattress. She would never get it back. Although the thought pained her, in some ways, she felt content. Perhaps now, Iowyn could start over, start fresh.

The fresh morning air felt refreshing in her lungs. Riding with Dren had always been a way for Iowyn to escape her feelings for a little while and be more present. Maybe taking Shadowfoot out for a bit longer wouldn't hurt.

Iowyn pressed Shadowfoot forward once more, her mind now free from the weight of the lost journal. She let the mare carry her further into the rolling hills, the rhythm of hooves against the earth providing a comforting background to her thoughts.

The landscape around them began to change; they left behind the lush green hills and entered the dense forest, where tall trees created a canopy of leaves overhead. The woods seemed alive with the sounds of nature: birds singing their morning songs, leaves rustling in the gentle breeze, and the distant churning of the river.

The forest, with its vibrant hues and the symphony of nature's sounds, felt more alive than ever. The scent of wildflowers along the riverbank was sweeter, and the gentle breeze on her face was more invigorating. The sun peeked through the canopy, shedding dappled rays across the banks of the river and the water's surface. As they rode, a glint caught her eye in the grass a few feet away. Iowyn dismounted Shadowfoot and walked towards it. A faint smile came across her lips, and she picked up the object. The blackened iron dagger with its twisted handle was warm from the sun in her hand.

It was odd to think that had she not lost it, she might have been able to free herself from the kelpie before they had made it to the lake. That one simple variable of holding on tighter to the dagger could have made all the difference. With a wistful smile, Iowyn tucked the dagger into her belt.

Returning to Shadowfoot, she patted the mare's sleek neck affectionately. The horse snorted softly in response, as if sensing the shift in her mood. Together, they made their way back to town, finding Ulric hadn't really moved from where they had left him in the stables. He was sitting on a hay bale, his back against a stall door, reading a small book.

Iowyn dismounted and gestured to the book in his hands. "You read?"

"When I have time, yes." Ulric put the book behind his back, and rose to take Shadowfoot's reins.

Iowyn's curiosity was too much for her to subdue. She switched spots with Ulric and went around his back, swiping the book from his hands. Iowyn studied the cover. She almost burst out laughing when she read the title. "An Enchanted Rose?"

Ulric plucked the book back from her hands and tucked it into his back pocket. "So I like to read a romance novel every now and then."

Iowyn crossed her arms and smiled. Ulric Ornthalas was embarrassed? "No need to blush on my account."

"I'm not–" He began to protest but cut himself off, taking Shadowfoot into an empty stall. Iowyn could hear him grumbling as he took off the bridle and saddle. "Did you find your journal?" he asked from the stall.

Although Iowyn wanted to continue grilling Ulric about reading romance novels, she decided to give him a break. He had allowed her to take Shadowfoot for the morning after all. "No. You're probably right about it getting washed into the river."

Ulric came out of the stall and latched the door behind him. "I'm sorry."

Iowyn waved his apology away. "It was just a bunch of notes."

Ulric's eyes flicked to Iowyn's belt. "You found the dagger."

She took it from her belt. "Oh, yeah. I wasn't trying to, or anything, it just kind of jumped out at me." She held the dagger out to Ulric.

He took the dagger from her, but then shook his head. His fingers hooked into her belt as he tucked the knife back into the band. "Keep it. It was a gift."

An air of silence floated between them. Iowyn's mind raced to find something to say, but Ulric was quicker to break it. "The mothers and children will most likely be returning in two days."

"That's wonderful," Iowyn replied.

Ulric cleared his throat. "You should spend as much time as you can with your parents – while you can – and help Dren recover."

Iowyn nodded. "Burke had the farrier come over and take a look at Dren. He's no veterinarian, but he said Dren should be fine in a couple of days, so long as he doesn't exert himself."

"I'm glad to hear that," Ulric smiled softly.

"So what exactly does Ulric Ornthalas do with his free time?" Iowyn asked. "Besides reading the occasional romance novel?"

Ulric shook his head, but the smile remained on his face. "If you must know, I'll be helping Elmer's family with plowing."

"You're going to do what now?" Iowyn asked.

"Their plow horse has an infected hoof, so I'm lending them Shadowfoot to help them out while we're still in town." As if responding to her name, Shadowfoot let out a snuffle from her stall.

"That's," Iowyn blinked, "rather kind of you to offer."

"I've never worked on a farm before. It will be nice to have the experience."

She cocked a brow. "Thinking of having a farm in retirement or something?"

Ulric shrugged. "You never know."

"So, I guess I won't be seeing much of you around then," Iowyn commented.

"No, I don't suppose you will," Ulric agreed. "But I'm sure your constable will be happy about that." Iowyn couldn't help but notice the change in Ulric's tone and demeanor. The slight warmth and friendliness that had been floating throughout their conversation had vanished, and there was a distant look in his eyes. It was as if a shadow had passed over him.

"Oh, Maddox and I–"

"You don't need to explain, Beastie," Ulric interrupted. He said a curt goodbye and then left the stables.

Iowyn stared at Ulric's back as he walked towards the Itchy Badger. She sighed, and resigned herself to the cold hard truth. That she may never truly understand the man that was her partner.

CHAPTER

35

Three days had passed since the kelpie had been slain. Iowyn had done what Ulric had suggested and spent most of her time tending to Dren as he recovered from his injuries and enjoying some quality time with her fathers. She hadn't seen Ulric at all during those two days, but he had shown up this morning with the news that the mothers and children would be returning.

The small crowd gathered on the cobblestone main street as those who had been living in the monastery for close to two months finally came back home. Iowyn and Ulric stood in the doorway of the bookshop, watching families reunite. She looked over to see a soft smile on Ulric's face. It was an unusual sight to see his emerald eyes dancing behind a smile.

Iowyn lightly punched his arm. "You're telling me that all this time, Ulric Ornthalas can actually smile?"

He rolled his eyes, but it was more playful than she'd ever seen the reaction. "What can I say?" Ulric gestured to the happy crowd. "This is why I joined the Guild. For happy endings like this."

She cocked an eyebrow. "Big, bad Ornthalas believes in happy endings?"

He leaned against the door jamb, his smile still not fading. "I think you'd be rather surprised by what I believe in, Beastie."

Iowyn smiled back at him, and they turned their attention to the crowd. She couldn't help but feel warmth spread in her chest each time she saw a little boy or girl reunited with their parents and grandparents. She had helped make her town safe again, and there was a sense of pride inside of her that she hadn't quite felt before.

"Daddy!" A little girl no older than four years old with a splash of freckles across her nose ran out from the crowd. Her little strawberry blonde pigtails bounced up and down as she ran hurriedly and jumped into the arms of a dark-haired man.

Not just any man, but a man in the uniform of a constable. Maddox.

Realization hit Iowyn like a phantom punch to the gut, and she even felt Ulric tense next to her.

It couldn't be. The child had to be mistaken.

But Maddox hugged the little girl tightly as he held her in his arms and smiled up at her.

Maddox had a child. And that meant…

A woman with similar strawberry blond curls emerged next from the crowd of people, walking straight over to Maddox. "Oh, Elora, don't run away from Mommy like that."

It was Assandra. It had to be. No one else in Calluna had ever had hair like that.

Assandra Rochere had always been the girl in town that every other girl wished she could be. Effortlessly beautiful and popular. She'd been anything but nice to Iowyn growing up, especially when her and Maddox's secret meetings in the meadows had been exposed to the rest of the school. Assandra had always gotten everything else she'd ever wanted in life. Why not Maddox too?

Assandra looked up at Maddox and smiled. "Hello, darling," she said before kissing him.

Iowyn's heart dropped. As Assandra reached up to cup his cheek, a fancy gold band with a small white jewel sparkled in the sun on her left hand.

Wife. She was definitely his wife.

Another phantom punch to the gut as Iowyn came to terms with the truth. Firstly, Maddox had lied to her about almost everything since she had arrived in Calluna. Secondly, she was the other woman, and she had unknowingly allowed Maddox to be unfaithful to his wife. It didn't matter who his wife was, Maddox had cheated, and lied to do it. Thirdly, Maddox had asked her to be with him, not two nights ago. Had that been a farce? Just a way to get more from her?

Iowyn stood frozen as her head spun. Ulric's hand rested on her shoulder. "Are you alright?" he asked. His eyes flicked between her face and where Maddox and Assandra stood out in the street with their daughter.

He had a fucking daughter with her.

Maddox was still holding Elora in his arms when he looked over his shoulder, as if he could sense Iowyn and Ulric's eyes on him. His blue eyes locked on hers, and she saw the faintest flicker of panic in his eyes. He gave Elora and Assandra each a kiss on the cheek and excused himself. They walked away, probably on their way home to the small yellow house. The same yellow house that Iowyn had been in not two nights ago – in his and Assandra's bed, no less.

Maddox walked right up to Iowyn, ignoring Ulric entirely. "Iowyn, I can explain," he whispered.

Iowyn's hands curled into fists at her sides. "You have a wife," she breathed, doing her best to keep her composure. "You have a wife and a daughter?"

Maddox went to grab her hand. "Iowyn, please I–"

She stepped back from him, not wanting him to touch her.

Maddox swallowed, his eyes flicked back to the crowd behind him. "Can we go somewhere private to talk?"

"Why?" Iowyn spat. "Afraid someone will find out?"

"Iowyn–"

"You lied to me. About *everything*."

"No!" He grimaced. "Some thing's, yes, but I meant everything I said when it came to you. That was all true." He reached out to touch her face, but Iowyn recoiled again. "Please, Iowyn. I meant what I said. I tried to move on, but I just couldn't. Assandra means nothing to me."

"You *married* her, Maddox, how can you say that?"

"Because she isn't you!"

Iowyn scoffed. "I can't believe you, right now." She turned her back on Maddox and started heading farther into the bookshop. Ulric blocked the rest of the doorway, leaving Maddox outside.

"Iowyn! Please I —" he stammered.

Iowyn was just a few feet from leaving his sight in the bookshop. "I'll leave them!" Maddox blurted.

Iowyn's steps halted, and she turned slowly back to Maddox.

"You'll what?" she asked, half hoping that she had misheard him.

Maddox swallowed. "I'll leave them. If it means being with you, I'll leave them."

From the corner of her vision, Iowyn saw Ulric's entire body tense. His jaw clenched, hands balled into fists, and his eyes looked like a blazing forest fire.

Maddox's eyes were filled with desperation as he continued, "Iowyn, I love you. I never stopped loving you. Assandra was a mistake, a misguided attempt to move on when I thought you were gone for good. But being with you now, seeing you again, it's like a dream come true. Please, give me a chance to make things right."

Before he could move, Iowyn stormed back up to Maddox. Her hand moved faster than Maddox could think, and it smacked right across his cheek. Her hand stung from the impact. As soon as she'd done it, she'd regretted making the hit a slap and not a punch. A slap was too soft for the amount of rage boiling inside of her.

Iowyn's voice was low. "If you think that I would ever take a father away from his daughter, then you don't know me at all." She took in a deep breath that seemed to burn her lungs with all the anger it contained. "Go home, Maddox. Go home to your wife, and kid." Maddox stood there, holding his cheeks, his eyes wide. "For your sake – for the sake of your marriage and family – I won't say a word to them. In exchange for my silence, I never want to see you again." She turned her back on him. "Come on, Ulric," she called behind her.

Ulric shut the door to the bookshop and flipped the "open" sign in the window to "closed." Footsteps followed behind her, and Ulric made it to her side within a few steps.

Iowyn sighed, resting her back against the closest bookshelf out of sight from the front window. She closed her eyes. "Go ahead and say it. I told you so."

Because he had, in fact, thought something was untrustworthy of Maddox the first night he met him, the night that they had gone out to the meadow and she had allowed herself to feel wanted for the first time in a long time. He had known Maddox for less than five minutes and was wary of him. What had he seen that she hadn't? Perhaps she would ask him at some other time. And maybe she would try to get him to teach her how to see those things in everyone, so she could avoid getting hurt like this again.

"Are you alright?" Ulric asked instead.

The sudden concern for her was a bit more than she could take right now. The swarm of emotions were finally hitting her in succession. Anger for being lied to. Guilt for what she'd unknowingly done. Regret for not listening to her partner's intuition. Sadness for Assandra and Elora.

Iowyn squeezed her eyes shut tighter. "Don't get mushy on me, I'm fine." Her voice was level and monotonous. With a myriad of emotions swirling within her, she couldn't focus on one to let loose, and she didn't feel like doing that just now, especially in front of Ulric. She would wait until she was in the privacy of her own room, and then she'd see what came to the surface.

Iowyn opened her eyes, her gaze meeting Ulric's concerned face. "I'll be fine," she answered, her voice tinged with a mix of anger, hurt and disbelief. "I just…" She couldn't find the words.

Ulric stared at her in silence for a moment before he spoke. His words were sure and unwavering. "You deserve better."

She nodded, her eyes stinging with unshed tears. "I know."

CHAPTER

36

After leaving Iowyn at home, Ulric had gone back to the Itchy Badger to get a head start on writing his report for the Guild and take the rest of the day a little easier.

Part of him hadn't wanted to leave her alone, not when she was vulnerable, but he wasn't sure what help he would be to her in such a situation. They were partners. Personal stuff like breakups – or whatever she wanted to call what had happened between her and Maddox – didn't really fall under his purview. Not that he would even know how to comfort her. Men were much easier to deal with in these kinds of situations. He could just take them to a bar and drink with them. They'd play darts or billiards, and just have fun until they forgot about the girl making them sad. If he could help them get with someone else that night, even better. Ulric had a sneaking suspicion that those things, however, wouldn't help Iowyn feel any better.

When he had finally finished writing a good portion of his report to the Guild, Ulric walked downstairs to the main floor of the Itchy Badger, and was surprised to find Iowyn sitting across the room at the bar. Ulric walked up to the opposite side of the bar where Elmer was working.

"Has she been here long?" he asked. From what he could tell, she hadn't seen him yet.

Elmer cast a worried look down the bar. "She's been hitting the bottle pretty hard. What happened out there?"

300

Ulric clapped a hand on Elmer's shoulder. "I'd tell you, but it's not my place to." Elmer gave him a solemn nod and went about serving a tray of drinks to a large gathering in the corner.

Ulric took a seat next to Iowyn. Her hair was loose around her face, and she didn't even deign to look at him. She just stared into the glass in her hands.

Ulric tried his best to think of something to say. *Hello,* just seemed too simple and trivial. But Iowyn spoke before he could even open his mouth.

"Maddox was my first everything. First crush, first kiss, first love." Iowyn smirked. "The funny thing is, he never even crossed my mind when I found out we were coming home. Not a single thought. But then, I saw him in the street and all these feelings came rushing back." She downed the last of the amber liquid in her glass, and motioned for Elmer to pour her another. He gave Ulric a wary gaze before Ulric nodded, and he came over to fill her glass. She didn't continue talking until Elmer was out of earshot.

"You know, had I not gone to University and stayed here, he might have married me. I'd be his wife. We'd have a kid together." Her nose crinkled at the last part.

Ulric suppressed a chuckle. "Do you not like kids?"

"Oh, I love kids. I mean, I risked my own life to save all the kids in Calluna for the gods' sake. But," she shrugged, "I don't. I don't think I'd be a good mother."

The statement surprised him. "Why do you think that?"

"I never had a mother. Well – strike that – I never knew what it was like to have a mother. I wouldn't know the first thing about it."

Ulric smiled at her, and Iowyn leveled her gaze at him. "What? You think that's funny?"

Ulric placed a hand on her shoulder. "You know how worried Burke gets about you? And how Bearen was ready to more or less beat me into the ground when he thought I had hurt you? From what I can tell, you have two amazing parents. You know from them what it takes to be a good mother."

Iowyn looked back down at her glass. Ulric thought they had left the topic of Maddox behind, but she took another drink and continued on her drunken rant. "You know, I've been mulling it over in my head. Maddox never really spoke to me or even approached me once this whole time unless we were alone. No one in town ever saw us." Her voice went quiet. "I guess I wanted to feel wanted by someone so badly, that I didn't think to think. Does that make sense?"

Ulric nodded. Although he was beginning to notice her slurring speech and the way she was speaking her mind more than she probably meant to.

She ran a hand through her long hair. "Gods, am I really that stupid?"

Ulric grimaced. "You aren't responsible for his actions, Beastie."

She smirked again. "I sure know how to pick them, huh? First Xander, now Maddox."

"Who's Xander?" Ulric asked. He had never heard the name before.

Iowyn blew out a long breath."

Ulric was curious. "Did he cheat on you too? Or were you the other woman?"

Iowyn's eyes widened. "Cheat on me? Pfft, no." She pushed Ulric's shoulder.

"Then what'd he do that was so bad?"

Iowyn took another pull from the bottle in front of her. "When I got out of University, I became a scriven for the Guild. I got placed in an outpost in Acantia. That's where I met Xander."

"He was a scriven too?".

She shook her head. "No, he worked for the Guild. He's a big tall guy, like you."

For some reason, Ulric didn't like the comparison.

A faint smile played on her lips as she continued. "He was great, at first. Really, really great. Made me feel like a princess, which was a nice change compared to the idiots I dealt with in University."

Ulric was confused. She had made it sound like this guy was the worst, but the other boot hadn't dropped yet in the story, he guessed. "But?"

Iowyn took another drink. "But then one day, my friend Loyla came into the outpost fresh off an assignment. And Loyla's like, my *best* friend. We had no idea the other would be there, and it was so good to see her again, so we went out together to get some drinks in the nearest town."

Ulric still didn't see where the story was going, and this was the first time he was hearing of this Loyla. He felt a pang in his chest as he realized that he was a little hurt that she hadn't said anything about her before, and another pang at the thought that maybe she had, but he hadn't been listening.

"Xander found out and lost it. Came into town and found me. I was drunk, *obviously*, and that made him *really* mad. I mean come on, I was out having fun with my best friend. What? Was I not supposed to have fun and get a little drunk? He found me, and automatically started accusing me of fucking around with all the guys in the bar, just because Loyla had been kissing some guy when he came in. I told him I hadn't but he didn't believe me, so he took me back to the outpost, and then he…" Iowyn hiccupped, stopping her story.

Ulric froze, his mind processing her speech and his own imagination filling in the blank. "He what?" When she didn't answer, he grabbed her shoulder and turned her in her seat towards him. "What did he do, Beastie?"

Her eyes went distant for a while, and Ulric wondered where she went in her mind. Iowyn blinked, and smiled, rolling her eyes at the same time. "He was an ass. I wasted a whole year on him and he was a total ass." She waved off his grip on her shoulder. "Oh, but who am I even kidding? You've probably never dealt with anything like this before."

His eyes narrowed at her, there was something she wasn't saying, but who was he to lecture her about secrets? Drunk or not, he knew when someone wanted something left buried.

"I've had lovers before, Beastie," Ulric replied.

Her mouth twisted in a dubious expression. "Oh really?"

Ulric took a deep breath and rolled his eyes. He guessed he had walked right into that one. What harm would it be to tell her? There was a chance that she wouldn't even remember most of the conversation anyways, and after the week they'd had, part of him felt like she almost deserved a glimpse into his life. "The first girl I ever loved, Marjorie, left me for my older brother as soon as I left home."

Iowyn let out a breath that came out more like a raspberry. "Ouch."

Ulric took a drink of his whiskey. He feigned a smile. "Last I heard, they were engaged."

"That must make family dinners awkward." She took a swig of her own glass. Iowyn's eyes widened, and Ulric prepared himself to have her spit her drink all over him, but she swallowed it in a drunken hiccup before asking, "Wait, you have a brother?"

He smirked. "I have three, actually. They're all back home in Vrig."

Iowyn blinked. Then blinked again and held up her hands. "Hold up. Hold up. Are you telling me that all this time, all I needed to do to get you to tell me things was get *drunk?*"

Ulric took the glass from her hands with a smirk. "I told you, Beastie. I tell stories when I drink." He winked, and finished the drink, then picked up his own and finished that one too. Ulric gestured down the bar for Elmer to bring two more for the both of them.

Iowyn tapped her forehead several times. "I'm going to remember that." She paused, looking Ulric up and down, then down and up. "You're a lot nicer drinking too."

Elmer came over with another glass for Ulric, and poured them each a glass. Ulric fished out a gold coin and set it on the bar. "You can leave the bottle, Elmer."

Elmer raised his brow at the coin, and looked between the two of them before picking up the coin off of the bar. He set the bottle down, and opened his mouth to say something, but his attention was snagged by another thirsty patron hollering from across the room.

Iowyn took a sip from her new glass. "Marjorie sounds like a bitch."

The sudden comment made Ulric laugh — *actually* laugh — out loud. Iowyn jumped in her seat and looked at him like she had no idea who the person sitting next to her was. The shock on her face was replaced with a full smile soon after. "He can laugh too? Who are you and what have you done with Ulric Ornthalas?"

He pushed her — lightly enough that she wouldn't lose her balance. "Can we stop this narrative that I'm some kind of sociopath?"

She held up a finger. "To be fair, you don't really do much to even attempt to be sociable. Why is that?"

Ulric shook his head, but kept smiling. "Nice try, Beastie, but I'm not nearly drunk enough for that conversation."

Iowyn pointed to herself. "But I am."

His smile widened. "Nice try."

She tilted her head. "You have a nice smile."

Ulric blinked in surprise at the compliment. "Thank you."

Soon, they were the only two left in the tavern.

Iowyn stood up from the stool, and Ulric almost fell out of his seat as he shot forward to grab her forearm before she hit the floor.

"I really don't think you're in any shape to walk across town."

"You could just take me," Iowyn offered.

Any other time, that would have been exactly what Ulric would have done, but he'd been drinking himself, and Iowyn could barely stand up. He would basically have to carry her, and he wasn't very surefooted himself at the moment. "You can stay in my room. I'll sleep on the floor."

"Such a gentleman," Iowyn teased. "But I'm good." She took a step forward and her back foot caught on the leg of her stool. Iowyn stumbled, catching herself against the bar.

"Sure you are," he laughed. Ulric pulled Iowyn back onto her feet and steadied her. "Come on, up you go."

Ulric gestured to the stairs, but Iowyn's amber eyes narrowed at him. "What about rule number three?"

"Sleeping together and near each other are two completely different things." He twirled her around, and steered her towards the stairs.

"You're kinda bossy, you know that?"

Ulric smirked. "So you've said."

They came to the stairs, and Ulric stayed behind Iowyn as she started to climb up to the second floor. He braced himself to have to catch her if she lost her balance and decidedly fell backwards down the stairs. Leave it to her to survive being drowned by a kelpie, only to die from a drunken tumble down a flight of stairs.

Iowyn did fall, but forward onto her hands. Her foot caught on a step and flung her forward. Ulric bit back a laugh at the creative expletives that fell from her mouth. "Are you alright?" he dared to ask.

"I'm great," she said, her words still slurring. "It's like a whole new world down here."

Ulric sighed and bent down. He angled himself to place one of Iowyn's arm across his shoulders and hoisted her up to his side. His other hand came to rest on her hip. "What am I going to do with you?" he mumbled to himself.

"Hopefully keep me alive," Iowyn jested.

Ulric took each step up the stairs one at a time, careful to focus on his balance. "You do tend to make that difficult for me."

"I'm sorry," Iowyn slurred. "Really, I'm not trying to get myself killed. It just sorta happens."

"Sorta?"

"I ate some berries on a picnic when I was little, apparently, they were poisonous. Then I fell out of a tree when I was seven and hit my head on a rock. My dads thought I was a goner, but I ended up waking up with just a bad bump on my head. And…" Iowyn's voice trailed off.

"And?" Ulric asked. They were almost at the top of the stairs.

Iowyn's head lolled to one side to look at him. "And I guess there have been a few other close calls."

"You piss off Ydall as a child or something?"

Iowyn frowned at him, then her eyes flitted to the ceiling above, like she was racking her brain to remember. "I don't think so."

Ulric's boot hit the top of the landing, but he didn't let go of Iowyn as they continued down the hallway. Iowyn's feet were dragging with every step she took. He counted the doors as they passed, until they came to the seventh door on the left. Ulric set Iowyn against the wall, and reached into his pocket to find his room key.

"You know, I've never been up here before," Iowyn mused as she looked down the hallway. "I guess I never really had a reason to."

"There's a first time for everything, Beastie." Ulric inserted the key into the lock and opened the door. He gestured for Iowyn to go in first.

Iowyn looked up at him, and he could have sworn her eyes were shimmering. "I used to hate you calling me that."

"Used to?"

Iowyn shrugged, her shoulders practically touching her ears with the exaggerated movement. "I guess it's grown on me."

Ulric followed Iowyn into the room and shut the door. He fumbled with the small lantern on the table for a bit before lighting it. He hissed as the match burnt down to his fingertips, swearing under his breath. Hopefully their next assignment would take them somewhere with power.

"You make your bed?" she asked, staring at the neatly made bed in the middle of the room.

"I'm not an animal."

Iowyn sat on the bed, and Ulric felt an uneasy tightness in his body. They were alone and drunk – one of them exceptionally so.

Iowyn reached over to the bedside table, almost flopping over as she reached for the small book. She eyed the cover. "This isn't *An Enchanted Rose*."

"Very good, Beastie," Ulric let the sarcasm drip from his tongue. He leaned against the wall, crossing his arms against his chest.

"*Fire and Flame*," she read aloud. Her brow scrunched. "That's a terrible title. Fire and flame are the same thing."

Iowyn opened the book to a random page, squinting slightly as she read. Her lips parted and moved as her eyes rived the page. Iowyn's eyes widened suddenly, and a gasp left her lips as she shut the book, looking up at Ulric. "This isn't just a romance book! This is a *naughty* book!"

Ulric bit back his smile, doing his best to keep his features neutral. "I'm an adult. I can read naughty books if I want." He walked over to her, taking the book from her hands and setting it back down on the nightstand.

Her mouth hung open, like the statement was preposterous. And Ulric finally allowed a full smile to overtake his face and a deep laugh reverberated from his chest.

Iowyn seemed to freeze as she stared at him.

"What?"

A soft smile spread across her lips. "You should laugh more. You have a nice laugh."

Ulric blinked down at her and the sudden compliment. Iowyn stood up from the bed and looked from it and back to Ulric. "Sorry, I should probably let you have your bed, huh?"

Ulric shook his head. "No, you can sleep there. I just need a blanket." He grabbed the top cover from the bed, and the extra pillow from the sitting chair, and threw them both on the floor below the window.

Iowyn sat back down on the bed. "Are you sure?"

Ulric nodded. "I've slept in worse spots."

"Okie dokie," Iowyn yawned, stretching her arms above her head and flopping over onto the bed.

Ulric chuckled to himself as he saw her curl up into a ball, not even under the covers, her boots still on her feet. "Sit up, Beastie. Your boots are still on."

He pulled her back up to sitting, moving her legs off the bed. Ulric knelt in front of her. His fingers struggled with the laces of her boots, but soon he had one boot off, then the other. Ulric sighed, placing his hands on his thighs, and looking up at her. "There," he said, "now you can go to—"

Ulric barely had any time to react before Iowyn leaned down and pressed her lips to his.

Ulric froze for a moment, taken by surprise. But her lips were so soft against his, and instinct overrode his shock. He leaned into her, a hand resting at the small of her back. The sweet taste of the alcohol she'd been drinking lingered on her tongue, and the fragrant smell of vanilla swirled around him.

Iowyn's hands fumbled to find purchase on Ulric's chest, her fingers clutching onto the fabric of his shirt. The room around them seemed to spin in slow motion. Time stopped for the few moments that stretched on into a graceful standstill.

But then, as her hands went behind his neck to tangle into his hair, Ulric grabbed her wrists and pulled away. "I don't think this is a good idea," he breathed.

It most certainly wasn't. He knew that. But he couldn't help the pull he felt to close the small distance between them and kiss her again. He wanted more than anything to bridge that gap, to taste the sweetness of her lips once more.

In that moment Ulric could only think of the many reasons why he should let go. They were partners, paired together to do a job – one full of uncertainty and danger. Adding something more to the mix would make things messy and, in the worst cases of scenarios, fatal. Besides, he was not a man made for romance. His past was one filled with shadows that he didn't wish to cast over someone as bright as her. Yet as he cataloged all these rational reasons, there came unbidden but impossible to ignore, and overwhelming desire to cast them all aside.

Iowyn's eyes were still closed as she bit her bottom lip.

The warmth radiating from her was intoxicating, drawing Ulric in like a moth to a flame. But then, just as he was about to fall over the precipice and surrender to his desires, Iowyn's eyes flew open wide and the color drained from her face.

Before Ulric could ask what was wrong, she jerked out of his grip with a gasp, clutching at her stomach. It happened so fast that for a moment, Ulric could only stare in horror as Iowyn's body convulsed painfully. Her hand went to her mouth, and Ulric scrambled to grab the wastebasket by the desk for her. He placed it in front of her, and Iowyn doubled over, her body heaving with violent retches. Her fingers tightened around the edges of the bin, knuckles going white from the exertion.

Iowyn let out a groan as she wiped her mouth with the back of her hand and laid back on the bed, tucking herself away under the covers. Her eyes closed, and her breath fell into a shallow rhythm, signaling that she had drifted into unconsciousness. Her face was as white as the pillowcase she rested her head upon, her lips devoid of their usual vibrant color.

He moved to sit on the edge of the bed, his hand reaching out to brush away an errant lock of hair from her forehead. She made no movement, no indication of waking.

With one last glance back at Iowyn's still form, Ulric got up from the bed and left the room quietly. Distance. He needed distance. And enough time to sober up – maybe a cold shower for good measure. Ulric couldn't get out of the room fast enough.

CHAPTER

37

Iowyn's head pounded as she opened her eyes. The bright sunlight pierced through the crack in the curtains that shielded the window. She groaned, trying to sit up, but quickly regretted it as pounding waves of nausea hit her. Memories of the previous night came in fragments and she winced, wondering what kind of mess she must have made.

She looked around the room, realizing that she wasn't in her room above the bakery and bookshop. Ulric's large black duffel bag sat up against the far wall, his sword and crossbow in the sitting chair. Panic set in as she tried to remember what had happened – how she had gotten there – but her mind drew a blank.

Did they sleep together? Would Ulric have broken his own rule?

She couldn't remember anything beyond what had happened at the bar. Looking down at herself, she was still in her clothes from the night before, which was a good sign. The only thing missing were her boots, which she found on the floor next to the nightstand.

The door to the room opened, and Ulric walked into the room with a tray of food and a large glass of water. Iowyn spied a large leather-bound book tucked under his arm. "Good morning," he greeted her with a small smile. "How are you feeling?"

The smell of food wafted towards her, causing her stomach to perform little feats of acrobatics. She was certainly hungry, but her stomach was not prepared for the sustenance quite yet. As he sat the tray on the foot of the bed, she took the glass to drink some water. "I'm okay," she said apprehensively, her voice hoarse. "How did I end up here?"

Ulric moved his crossbow and sword to the floor to sit in the chair. "You got a little too drunk last night. I thought it would be better if you stayed here instead of trying to get you across town."

Iowyn nodded slowly. It seemed her plan to get blackout drunk had succeeded. She sucked in a breath before asking her next question. "We didn't… you know?"

Ulric's jaw clenched. "No," he said sternly. "I slept on the floor." He gestured down to a pile of blankets on the floor at the foot of the bed. "I'm not the kind to take advantage of anyone like that, Beastie."

Iowyn swallowed at his callous tone. She had assumed the worst, even though deep down, she didn't think it possible, but he was obviously bothered at the fact that she felt the need to ask.

"I know that, I just," she paused. "I don't remember much, and I just wanted to make sure."

Ulric's brow ticked up, but he didn't say anything. Soon his features reset and his face gave nothing away. It bothered her – especially now – how he could so easily slip on that mask of pure indifference and simply become emotionless. She wished that she had the power to just look at him and know what he was feeling at any moment.

Instead of sitting in silence, Iowyn decided to ask another question. She smiled, somewhat sheepishly. "Please at least tell me that I didn't do anything to make a complete fool of myself did I?"

Ulric's face softened a bit. "Nothing that I'll hold against you."

Her eyes widened. "What does that mean?" She ran a hand over her face. "Oh gods, what did I do?"

Ulric shook his head, a slight smirk on his lips. "Nothing, but you did throw up. And it was almost all over me."

Iowyn covered her face with her hands and groaned. She peered through her fingers, and was surprised to see Ulric smiling. Not a smirk, or a slight grin, but a full smile. She studied his face in this rare expression. Was he only smiling because he thought she couldn't see him? Was her embarrassment that amusing?

Ulric's fleeting smile vanished as Iowyn dropped her hands, and she couldn't help but feel a pang of disappointment. Iowyn pushed herself to sit up more fully, finally able to handle the smell of the food without becoming queasy. She picked up a piece of bread from the tray and nibbled on it, her thoughts swirling like her stomach.

"What do you remember about last night?" he asked.

The question filled her with worry. "Why? What happened?"

"Nothing," Ulric shook his head, "I'm just curious."

She looked at Ulric apprehensively, then thought about the night before. "I remember going to the bar and drinking – a lot. I remember you coming over to sit with me. I remember you telling me about your own shitty love life, and that you have three brothers. And…"

"And?" Ulric asked.

Iowyn thought hard to remember but it was as if she were trying to grab hold of a shadow. She could see Ulric, sitting in front of her at the bar. His mouth moved but no words reached her ears.

Iowyn blew out a breath. "I know we talked more after that but it's all fuzzy. Why? What else did we talk about?"

Ulric waved off her question. "Nothing important."

She didn't believe him. Why would he ask if there was nothing to ask about? "Did you tell me more about you?" She cocked an eyebrow and gave a sly grin. "Stuff you're embarrassed about? Or did something else happen?"

Ulric grimaced before smirking himself. "Nothing you can remember it seems." He stood up and set the leather-bound book he had walked in the room with on the bed next to Iowyn.

"What's that?" she asked.

"Your journal."

Her brows knitted together. The leather book before her was about the same size as her old one, but the cover was bound in brown leather, not black. "That's not my journal."

"It's your new journal."

Iowyn looked up at Ulric, towering over her. She could see the slightest hint of uncertainty behind his emerald eyes. She picked up the journal and furled through its pages. Each one was completely blank.

Ulric scratched the back of his neck. "I figured since your other one was likely washed down the river, you could use a new one."

She couldn't tear her eyes away from the book in her hands. "You got me a gift?"

Ulric cleared his throat, his usual stoic demeanor wavering slightly under Iowyn's surprised gaze. "It's not really a gift, more like a practical replacement. I thought you might need it for whatever it is you like to keep track of."

Iowyn couldn't help but smile, touched by Ulric's gesture. She traced her fingers over the smooth brown leather cover of the journal. It might not have been a grand or extravagant gift, but the thought behind it meant the world to her.

Iowyn left Ulric's room after quickly washing her face and combing through her hair with her fingers. She would have a proper soak in the tub when she got home. She shut the door to his room, her brand new journal in tow, and turned on her heels to head downstairs.

"Iowyn?"

She stopped dead in her tracks.

A hand grabbed her forearm and spun her around.

Iowyn could all but keep her eyes from rolling out of her head. She held up her hand as he started to speak. "Maddox, I don't want to talk. I don't want an explanation. I don't want *anything* from you. Just leave me alone."

Maddox's eyes narrowed, and he tightened his grip on Iowyn's arm. "You think it's just that simple? I didn't lie to you."

"Didn't *lie* to me?!" Iowyn exclaimed, her voice rising like the anger inside of her. "You led me on, Maddox. You made me believe that there was no one else. And now, you're trying to justify your actions by saying that you were unhappy in your marriage? That doesn't give you the right to cheat on your wife or play with me."

Maddox opened his mouth to speak, but Iowyn cut him off.

"Save it, Maddox. I'm done with you. Now let me go."

The door to Ulric's room opened. He saw Iowyn first, a quizzical look on his face. "What–"

His question stopped when he opened the door fully and saw Maddox with his hand tightened around Iowyn's arm.

Maddox looked from Iowyn to Ulric, and into the room that she had come out of.

Ulric's room.

Hurt blazed in Maddox's eyes, but the sight made Iowyn feel nothing. "You slept with him?" he seethed. "You said that there was nothing between you two!"

Ulric went to speak, but Iowyn held up a finger, stopping the words in his mouth before they could fall out. "So what if I slept with him. At least he doesn't have a fucking wife and kid!"

Maddox's face turned red with fury, and he released Iowyn's arm with a hard shove. She stumbled back. "Slut."

Iowyn took in a deep breath to calm herself, but it was no use. Everything inside of her exploded. "Fuck you, Maddox. You can go back to your miserable life and pretend that you never cheated on your wife. But don't you *dare* talk to me like that. I am not some weak woman that you can belittle and insult. I'm done with you. And I hope that I never have to see your sorry face again."

Maddox's jaw clenched, and his hand rose up suddenly.

Iowyn's eyes widened. It couldn't be. Maddox wouldn't hit her. Sure, she had said things to piss him off, but that wasn't Maddox.

He wouldn't hit her. He *wouldn't* hit her.

The thought repeated in her head as his hand began to fly downward towards her. Iowyn found herself raising her hands in defense and shrinking away.

Ulric stepped in front of her, grabbing Maddox's wrist out of the air. His voice was unlike anything she had ever heard come out of him before. Rough, gravelly, and deadly serious. "You touch her again, you die."

Iowyn's breath seemed to catch in her throat at the words.

Maddox's eyes grew wide as saucers from the threat. "I'm sorry," he sputtered. "I didn't mean it. I just–"

"Go," Ulric growled, pushing Maddox back. "Before I change my mind."

Maddox nodded, and with a last sorrowful look at Iowyn, turned on his heel and left. Iowyn watched him go, unsure of what she was feeling.

She had trusted Maddox in multiple ways. She had trusted him to be some of her many firsts, to not take advantage of her or break her heart. That trust made the idea that he would resort to striking her, whether in his right mind or not, hurt all the more.

Ulric turned to face her, his eyes soft with concern. "Are you alright?"

She wrapped her arms around herself and nodded. Her whole body was still shaking. She looked at Ulric. "I'm…" she stopped, unsure. "I think I just need to go home."

"Do you want me to walk with you?"

She appreciated the offer, but an awkward and silent walk home with Ulric was the last thing she wanted. "No, I'll be fine."

"Are you sure? It's not–"

"I'm fine!" She shut her eyes as she snapped. Iowyn regretted it as soon as she heard herself.

She hurried past him. As she came to the top of the stairs, she turned around to see Ulric watching her from the doorway to his room. She wanted to say something to him, to thank him for stepping in front of her, but nothing that came to her mind seemed adequate enough.

CHAPTER

38

Ulric shut himself in his room. He wanted nothing more than to track down where Maddox lived and give him more than just a piece of his mind. His muscles strained as he clenched his hands into tight fists.

It wasn't worth it. *He* wasn't worth it.

If it got back to the Guild that Ulric beat a constable to a pulp, then he could very well sign his own transfer to Smokheim.

Ulric blew out a long breath and laid down on the bed. The pillow still smelled like vanilla, coupled with the other scent that he couldn't quite place. He inhaled deeply, shutting his eyes. She just had to smell like something so comforting, didn't she?

It was becoming clearer in Ulric's mind that Iowyn was very well on her way to turning into someone that he cared about.

He would've stepped in front of any girl about to be struck. It wouldn't matter if they were a complete stranger to him. He knew that. But the leftover rage that bubbled under the surface, that wasn't something he felt for just anyone.

He could let go and go back to being indifferent as ever, pretending that the past few weeks didn't have any effect on him. Or he could let her in.

Ulric groaned and flipped over in bed. His head nestled in the pillow, and Iowyn's sweet scent invaded his nostrils. He took one last breath in before chucking the pillow across the room and grabbing the one he had used last night from the floor.

Clink! Clink! Clink!

The sound came from the window.

Clink! Clink! Clink!

The tapping came again. With a heavy sigh, Ulric rolled out of bed and pulled back the curtains. The light from outside temporarily blinded him. As his eyes adjusted, Ulric saw the source of the clinking. The vibrant jewel tones of the seeking falcon's plumage shimmered in the sunlight.

Clink! Clink! Clink!

Ulric silently wondered if all seeking falcons were impatient, or just the one's the Guild decided to use. He unlatched the lock of the window and lifted the inside sash. The seeking falcon's talons gripped into the wood of the window sill. Ulric reached for the leather tube strapped to the falcon's leg. The falcon's eyes glowed as his hand undid the leather straps and took the message.

The seeking falcon lifted up into the air as Ulric shut the window. He undid the seal of the scroll, a faint smile coming across his lips as he read the inside.

This was one missive he wouldn't wait to give. He pulled his boots back on, and went down the stairs to the bar.

Elmer saw him coming as soon as he reached the bottom step. "You just missed Iowyn."

"Didn't miss her. She came from my room. Listen, Elmer—"

Elmer's eyes widened. "She what? You mean – you two?"

Ulric shook his head and sighed. "No, not like that. I took her up to my room to sleep it off last night, remember?"

"No, I thought you took her home." Elmer lowered his voice. "So… you two didn't?"

Ulric clenched his jaw. "No. *Nothing* happened."

Elmer raised his hands in defense. "Alright, alright. I mean, I wouldn't blame you if you did, but it's good to know there's still good guys out there. You know, I—"

"Elmer, shut up for two seconds," Ulric interrupted. It wasn't the nicest way to get Elmer's attention, but it was the quickest. He put the letter on the bar.

"What's that?" Elmer asked. He looked at the paper dubiously.

"That," Ulric stated, "is my gift to you. A little thank you, for all you've done to help."

Elmer's forehead creased. He still didn't reach for the letter.

"Go on," Ulric prompted. "Read it."

Elmer picked up the letter and unfolded it. "Mr. Ornthalas. I was more than happy to receive your letter. It has been some years since your time here at University, but your accolades still hold true – with myself and many other faculty.

"I am delighted to hear of you finally taking up my offer to…" Elmer's words trailed off. He looked up at Ulric, his eyes wide.

Ulric nudged him on. "Keep going."

Elmer took a breath. "To sponsor a student of your choosing in the venatology program. Elmer Wadscott – from what you've written – sounds like a perfect candidate. We would be happy to accept him into the University for the coming autumn term." Elmer set down the letter. His face gave away nothing of what he was feeling, it was as blank as a fresh sheet of paper.

"Well?" Ulric asked.

"I don't know what to say."

"You don't have to say anything."

Elmer's eyes went back and forth from the letter to Ulric until he finally held it out in front of him. "I can't accept this."

"Elmer, I wouldn't have recommended you if I didn't think you deserved it."

Elmer scoffed. "I'm a bartender. I'm not like you."

"You're more like me than you think. Better even."

Elmer rolled his eyes.

"It's true, Elmer. You have a way with people. You could help a lot of people going into the Guild. Don't you want to get out of here? Be more than just a bartender?"

"I can't afford University."

"You don't have to. I'm sponsoring you."

"I won't take your money."

"You won't. The University will."

"What if they fail me?"

Ulric couldn't hold back a smirk. "Trust me, if University is anything like when I went, you'll be one of the top students."

Elmer ran out of excuses.

"Elmer, you can do this and be one of the few people that helps make Phyrra a better place, or you can stay in Calluna forever, and be content with never reaching for more."

"Is that why you joined the Guild?" he asked.

Ulric swallowed. It wasn't far from the truth, but he never told anyone the whole truth. He trusted Elmer, and part of him thought of telling him, but he decided a long time ago that no one could know the whole story. "I joined the Guild because I wanted to be a part of the solution, not the problem. I wanted to help and protect people. The Guild was my way to do it."

Elmer leaned on the bar and took a deep breath. As he looked up at the ceiling, Ulric could see the cogs turning in Elmer's brain. "Okay," he breathed, "I'll do it."

Ulric slapped a silver coin on the bar. "I'll drink to that." He had never recommended anyone since leaving University. He had never met anyone on his assignments that he thought could cut it, let alone be good for the Guild.

But Elmer was.

Iowyn was in the middle of rechecking her pack for the third time when someone knocked on the door. "Come in," she called out.

Bearen entered and came over to sit on Iowyn's bed. She could see his eyes studying her as she placed each item into her bag. He wouldn't speak first. He rarely did unless he had something that he needed to say or she needed to hear. He was similar to Ulric in that way, but her father's silence never seemed to bother her. She had found a coziness in Bearen's silence. Perhaps because she had grown up in it, she never felt uncomfortable in it.

"We don't need to have a sappy goodbye, Pa."

He let out a short huff of a laugh. "I know. Just figured, I'd get mine in before Burke makes a mess of things."

She smirked. "I promise to write this time. I have a feeling I'll have much more to write about now being in the field."

"Just do us both a favor and leave out all the dangerous parts?" Bearen asked.

She finished fastening the buckle on the outside of the bag and sat down next to Bearen on the bed. "Already way ahead of you on that front. I figured I could just write Burke the nice stuff, and you all the exciting parts."

Bearen wrapped an arm around her and hugged her into his side body. "That's my smart girl."

She put her arms around her father and gave him a light squeeze. They sat in silence for a bit before Iowyn found something to ask. "How come it seems you don't worry about me as much?"

Bearen let out a laugh, deep and loud. "Trust me, Iowyn, I worry." He paused, looking down at her. "I knew when we took you in that things were going to be different. I was going to be a parent, a *father*. To say I was scared was an understatement."

"You don't seem scared now."

He smiled. "Well, you're an adult now. The hard part's over. Part of my job was to protect you, yes, but my real job was to prepare you to be able to survive in the world on your own when I couldn't be there. I worry about you – like any parent would – but I also know that the girl I raised? She can handle anything this world throws at her."

A tear slid down Iowyn's cheek. She lightly wiped it away. "You said nothing sappy, Pa."

Bearen pulled her to a tight hug. The smell of sugar and flour enveloped her, and she found the warmth of the embrace comforting. She would miss this, she realized. Even as independent as she had become over the past six years, she still would miss her parents, her home, her childhood.

Burke's plummy voice sounded faintly from the kitchen. "Bear? Wynnie? Where on earth–" He appeared in the doorway of her room. "Oh, I'm sorry. Am I interrupting?"

Bearen didn't let go of Iowyn but shook his head. Burke came to sit on the other side of her. "Your friend is outside," he said softly.

Iowyn took a big breath before letting go of Bearen and turning to hug Burke, nestling her head in the crook of his shoulder. His hugs were never nearly as warm as Bearen's, but they were comforting to her all the same. "I will write this time. I promise."

She could hear the faint smile in Burke's voice. "I know you will."

"And I'll visit more often. Whenever I'm in Arondir." It wasn't a promise that she could always keep, but she would try.

Burke patted her back softly. His voice was softer, a little shakier. "That will be nice."

CHAPTER

39

The warm rays of the sun kissed Iowyn's pale skin. She took a deep breath of the fresh air. The wind was picking up, bringing with it scents of pine trees and wildflowers.

Iowyn felt a contradiction of emotions as they headed out of town. She was upset about leaving her parents again. She had no way of knowing the next time she would even see them again. Part of her was glad to have had the time she did with them, even if it was only for a few days. Anything was better than nothing.

Despite the sorrow she felt leaving her family, she couldn't help but feel excited when it came to thinking about what adventure was coming next. She felt confident, especially with Ulric by her side. Together, they had already bested two harrowing creatures, and had saved each other's lives in the process.

As silence drifted between them with only the accompanying sounds of nature to fill it, Iowyn snuck a sideways glance at her partner. Ulric's chiseled jawline was sharp against the sunlight. The wind ruffled through his hair, sending locks of his dark curls across his forehead. His eyes were focused on the road in front of him. How was he always so serious? It seemed criminal at times, along with the fact that although they had been together now for almost three weeks, she still knew close to nothing about him.

He had definitely come out of his shell a bit, but he was still a stranger to her. The most she knew was that he was from Vrig, went to University, and had three brothers. While he knew a wealth of information about her and her personal life now that they had been to Calluna. Perhaps now she could ask him some questions without him being so cross about it.

"What are you thinking so hard about?" Ulric asked.

The sudden question caught her off guard. "What do you mean?"

Ulric motioned to his own face. "You get this look on your face when you're thinking something through."

Iowyn scrunched her features. "I do not."

A playful smirk appeared on Ulric's face. "Come on, Beastie. Out with it."

Iowyn sighed. There was no use in lying to him, it would be better to just tell him the truth. "I was just trying to think of something to ask you."

"You mean you have more questions for me?" He sounded as though that couldn't even be a possibility.

Iowyn scoffed, "You can't possibly think that I don't" He gave her a sideways glance again. "Look," she continued, "I feel like I don't know you as well as you know me. It's like you said before, if we're going to be partners, you're going to have to tell me everything. Well, not everything, but I'm definitely going to want to know the basics."

"Which are?"

She slapped his arm. "Come on, you know! What are your favorite things? Your pet peeves? Those kinds of things."

Ulric looked at her skeptically.

"You act like you've never tried to get to know someone before, or be someone's friend."

"So, you want to be my friend?" he asked.

"Yes, don't you want to be mine?"

He stared at her for what seemed like an eternity, then shook his head, his focus back on the road. She waited for him to say nothing. To ignore the question completely, as if she'd never even asked it in the first place.

"Alright," he answered, his voice low. "Ask away."

Iowyn blinked in surprise. She hadn't expected him to agree so easily.

She cleared her throat before starting with an innocent query. "What's your favorite color?"

A small smile played on Ulric's lips as he answered, "Blue, like the ocean."

Iowyn nodded, storing the information away. Her next question was more personal. "Why did you leave Vrig?"

His smile faded and was replaced with a far-off look. His gaze turned to the horizon, brow furrowing slightly as if dredging up memories that lay hidden in recesses of his mind.

"I had my reasons," he answered. And Iowyn wanted to ask for more information, but something in his tone told her it wasn't the right time. His mouth was set in a stern line. He was waiting for her to ask more, but she wanted to prove to him that he could trust her as well.

"See? That wasn't so hard." She let out a small laugh, and started Dren into a light run.

Ulric was soon riding next to her, and she tried her best to gauge his feelings from her periphery. He didn't look mad, but he didn't look happy either.

He had seemingly slipped on that permanent mask of being somewhere between indifferent and pissed off. She knew he had the ability to smile and to laugh, yet it seemed he would never let himself.

It seems her goal still stood from her first meeting Ulric, although with one more provision:

She would break down those walls, become his friend. And she would find a way to take away that mask of his, one way or another.

After a few hours, they slowed to take a short rest at a nearby lake. Ulric couldn't help but notice Iowyn dismounting from Dren a good twenty feet from the lake's edge, letting the beast walk to the water himself. She sat in the shade of a nearby tree, and Ulric came to sit by her out in the sun. An impending weight settled over him that threatened to drop at any moment.

Since the day they met, Ulric could tell that there was a lingering question in Iowyn's eyes. It was the most obvious question that someone in her position would ask. And yet, she hadn't. In all her time of babbling and bickering, she'd never let the one question he'd seen behind her eyes fall from her lips.

He took a seat in the grass next to her, lying back. "So?"

The space between Iowyn's brows wrinkled. "So what?"

Ulric sighed. "Ask the question you've wanted to ask me since the beginning."

Iowyn looked out over the lake, her eyes going a little distant. Ulric felt his heart beat harder with every second she thought. She was silent for longer than he liked, as if she were weighing the advantages and disadvantages of knowing the answer in her head.

"I never asked before because part of me didn't want to know," she started. "It was terrifying getting partnered with someone and being told that they were on probation. There's countless things that a hunter can do – unwarranted lethal force, endangering civilians, sheer recklessness – the list goes on." She looked him in the eye, her amber eyes swimming with uncertainty. "But now that I've been your partner for a bit longer, I can't imagine what you could have done that was so bad to warrant it. You've saved my life several times now, and although I know now that keeping me alive is part of it, I also think you would have done it anyway, probation or not."

He would have. Even without the Guild's direction, he would have done the exact same thing. It wasn't a question, but he nodded in confirmation anyways.

"So, what did you do?"

Ulric took a deep breath through his nose. He was honestly surprised she hadn't asked before this, and part of him wanted to lie, to give a harmless reason instead of the truth, but if he lied and she found out? Ulric knew it would be better to tell the truth and deal with the consequences of that then the repercussions of lying. He had promised to try, and although he was unsure of how she would react, he wanted her to trust him.

"I was on a bounty hunt in Beor." His eyes focused on the clouds in the sky. "There were a few minotaurs rampaging and pillaging some of the smaller villages in the mountains. I joined another group of hunters who were tracking the minotaurs' movements. We were able to trap two and bring them down with little problems. But the last one was bigger than the others – huge even by minotaur standards. Turns out we were the ones really being tracked." Ulric shut his eyes, the scene from that night playing in his head. "It ambushed us as we slept, grabbed one of the men in the party.

"I had my crossbow, and everyone was shouting at me to take a shot, so I did. It was like the damn thing saw it coming, and–" Ulric opened his eyes. The blinding light shocked his senses and erased the moment from his mind's eye. "And it used him as a shield. My arrow killed him."

Ulric turned his head, away from the sky and away from Iowyn. He focused on the blades of grass as they jittered in the breeze. "When all was said and done, we brought his body back to the nearest outpost. There was an investigation, and despite it being an accident, his mates blamed me for his death. So, I was brought in front of all the Masters and was put on probation, since they couldn't definitively prove it wasn't an accident."

"But it *was* an accident." Iowyn argued. "That isn't fair."

Ulric sighed, turning his head back over to her. "It was my word against the word of four other people."

She shook her head. "But it was an accident. You shouldn't be punished for it."

Ulric's gaze went to his hands. "Accident or not, I killed him, Beastie."

"That's bullshit and you know it," she huffed.

"Beastie—"

"Did you aim for him or the minotaur?"

"I—"

"No, you don't even have to answer that. I already know the answer, and so do you."

He sat up, not looking her in the eye. He knew if he looked into her eyes that he would see it. See everything that she felt, that she was thinking. He couldn't bring himself to look

Lantern bugs flashed in the dwindling light of dusk as they approached the Central Arondiran outpost. Leaves of ivy climbed across the great stone wall, and the air thrummed with the sounds of people enjoying their night.

Iowyn and Ulric dropped off their animals with the stablemaster, and Iowyn gave extra instruction for Dren. He had done well with the ride, but she wanted to be sure that she hadn't pushed him too far. Hopefully, they would at least have a day or two before having to go off on their next assignment.

Iowyn was more than ready for rest and Ulric offered to grab her some food if she secured them both a room. He would need to check in at the Guardsmen's post anyways. The deal was easily struck, and they both went their separate ways.

Iowyn made her way to the barracks and talked with the man at the front desk. She flashed her golden pin, proof that she was part of the Guild and therefore deserved free lodging. He handed over two brass keys, and Iowyn told him to let the man who fit Ulric's description that came in with food know which rooms he'd given her. She even gave the man a silver coin for his trouble.

She went up the stairs and found the first of the two rooms, left her door unlocked, dropped her bag on the floor, put both keys on the bedside table, and flopped face down onto the bed with her boots still on.

Iowyn had drifted into the lightest of sleeps when a knock came at her door. She knew who it was, and so she didn't even bother getting up or opening her eyes. A few beats later, Ulric walked into the room. She expected him to scold her for leaving the door unlocked, but he didn't. The tray clinked as he set it down on the bedside table. He let out the faintest of sighs, and then Iowyn felt a tugging at her feet, followed by the sound of her boots falling to the floor, then the scraping of a brass key against the wood of the bedside table. Ulric's footsteps retreated, and then the door clicked as it opened and latched shut.

Iowyn peeled her eyes open to see a steaming plate of potatoes, pork and carrots on the tray. She sat up and grabbed the tray. She would thank Ulric in the morning. For now, she just wanted to eat and go back to sleep.

She had been relieved to finally know the story behind Ulric's probation. It had been circling in her mind since she had been assigned as his partner, and planted a seed of doubt in her she hadn't known how to uproot. She had been more than assured that

Ulric would take care of her, and he had proven it himself several times, but not knowing – him not telling her – had made her think the worst.

It angered her – even now when thinking about it – to know that Ulric was being punished for simply being unlucky. It was the minotaur that had used the man as a human shield, not Ulric. She could see – she supposed – how the others in the party could see it as Ulric's fault, but that didn't make them right. Being a hunter was a deadly profession, and accidents happened all the time. Why had this one been any different? Maybe her report to the Guild on their latest assignment would gain him some favor with the Masters. He had saved her life. Wouldn't that count for something?

But what would happen once Ulric was off probation and reinstated as a full member of the Guild? Would he still be her partner? Or would he be free to go back to being a solitary? Would he even *want* her to be his partner anymore? She had meant what she had said to him on the roof of her parents' building. She saw him as a friend, but did he see her that way too?

All the thoughts swirled in her brain, trying to deduce just what would be the most likely to happen. As far as she knew, she and Ulric would still be partners for a while. There would be plenty of time to discuss it with him, whenever he was ready to.

Iowyn finished her meal and rose to set her tray outside in the hall. A faint smile curled her lips as she reached for the doorknob. Ulric had locked the door on his way out. It was such a trivial little thing, but for some reason, it meant something more to her.

Iowyn set the tray outside, and shut the door, double and triple checking that she locked it behind her before she made her way back to bed. She was asleep as soon as her head hit the pillow.

CHAPTER

40

Ulric knocked on Iowyn's door in the morning, but she didn't answer. Her door was locked, so she was either still asleep, or she had already left for the morning. He went down to breakfast in the mess hall, and found her at a table alone, writing on loose sheets of paper while eating with her other hand.

Ulric grabbed his own food and sat next to her, peering over her shoulder to try and read some of what she was writing. He had to admit, she had some of the nicest handwriting that he had ever seen. He had seen the hand of countless government officials and nobility, but hers was something special. What perplexed him was the fact that she was able to write so fast and still keep her penmanship so neat. Her lettering was mostly print, but devolved to connective cursive slightly when she wrote fast enough not to pick up the pen. The faintest of connections could be seen between the common combinations of letters, like her s's and e's.

Ulric read the sentence at the top of the page as he sat down.

The fact remains, that although Ulric Ornthalas can be completely reluctant to teamwork at times, he's saved my life —

Iowyn signed her name at the bottom of the page and reorganized the papers in the correct order. She folded up her report and set it to the side, finally putting all of her focus onto the food in front of her. "Thank you for grabbing me dinner last night."

"Not a problem."

"How did you sleep?" Iowyn asked.

"Fine," Ulric answered, taking his eyes off the folded-up report. The pleasantry that existed between them since leaving Calluna was still a little odd to him. A part of him was still waiting for the other boot to drop, or for him to mistakenly say something that would set her off like a match to gunpowder. "What about you?"

Iowyn took a bite of scrambled eggs and nodded. "Good. Is your report done?"

Ulric took his own folded up report out of his back pocket and set it on the table. "Care to read it?" he asked, his tone a bit teasing.

Iowyn gave him a sideways glance. It was the first time she'd looked at him since he sat down. "I'm good. But thanks for offering."

"Really?" Ulric was a little surprised. She had all but jumped at the chance to read his report the last time.

She shrugged. "I trust you."

Ulric blinked at her as she went back to eating her breakfast.

He couldn't help but notice she didn't offer for him to read her report. Perhaps because he hadn't read her first one. He also couldn't help but notice the way he felt hearing those words. *I trust you.*

The words rang in his head. She'd said them to him before, right before the kelpie had taken her. Right before she had drowned in the lake. They had been a comfort to him before, but now? The words were like snakes ready to strike. He couldn't help but feel the weight of them settle in his chest.

Ulric shoved them all away, back into a deep corner of his mind. "That's too bad." He picked up his report and put it back into his pocket. "You'll miss out on all the compliments I gave you."

Iowyn sat back in her chair and crossed her arms. "Or – and you'll have to hear me out on this one – you could just say them to me out loud like a normal person."

Well, Ulric had definitely walked into that one. He had complimented Iowyn multiple times in the report, but probably not in the ways she would prefer. Ulric did his best to always keep his reports short and to the point, and he found himself on multiple occasions last night, writing more about Iowyn than the assignment itself. It was a pain to have to restart as many times as he did. He finally decided the best way to go about it was to keep her out of it unless she was directly involved. It seemed to help.

Ulric thought about the crumpled-up pages in the wastebasket upstairs in his room. He wished he could just hand those over to her now, it was easier than saying anything out loud.

He cursed himself silently before speaking. "What you did was brave, Beastie."

Iowyn's amber eyes looked him over apprehensively. Ulric felt a growing uneasiness settle over him that was only lifted when she replied. "Thank you."

The message had come as they ate. A Guardsman had walked up to their table, scarlet caplet and all. Master Foxe was ready for his audience to go over their most recent assignment.

On the top floor of the garrison, Ulric and Iowyn stood in front of the Arondiran Guild Master's office. Ulric had met him before for his probation hearing, but he noticed Iowyn wringing her hands as they waited.

Ulric leaned down slightly. "You have nothing to worry about," he said in a low voice.

When Ulric had met him, Master Foxe seemed like an all-around nice guy, and it was hard to believe that he had ever been a hunter himself. In his time as Guild Master, he had grown quite fat and happy. He was the only one of the Master's Council to talk to Ulric after the hearing, and had even apologized to him about the outcome.

A pair of Guardsmen came down the hall, their scarlet capelets draped over their shoulders. These Guardsmen must have been held in high regard, as they wore plated armor as they strode down the hall to whatever post they were to take up in the Garrison. Ulric didn't miss their gaze on him as they passed.

"I'm not too fond of Guardsmen either," Iowyn muttered.

Ulric couldn't help but ask, "Why?"

Most women in the Guild saw the Guardsmen as a good thing — a way to keep the rowdier and more degenerate hunters in check.

She shook her head and gestured to the door. "It's a long story."

Ulric studied her, but he couldn't discern anything besides her evident nervousness. He rapped his knuckles on the door.

"Come in!"

Ulric opened the door and held it open for Iowyn to walk in first. Iowyn shot him a look as she walked past that screamed, *Coward!* But he had meant what he said. She had nothing to worry about when it came to the Arondiran Guild Master.

Foxe sat behind his large desk with papers strewn all about. His clothes were much nicer than most hunters could ever afford and on par with what most nobility wore these days, a definite perk of being at the top of the ladder inside of the Guild. His jacket was black silk, and trimmed with gold and silver embroidery from the way it gleamed in the light. The sheer amount of fabric needed to clothe such a large man alone would have cost a small fortune.

His plump face lit up when Iowyn and Ulric walked in. "Ah, Mr. Ornthalas, Ms. Morgnah! Just the people I wanted to see. Come in! Come in! Sit, please!"

The enthusiasm was enough to put Ulric on edge. Sure, Foxe was a nice guy, but even this was a little *too* nice. Ulric waited for Iowyn to sit first, then took the seat next to her. The chairs were plush, and reminded him of the kind of chairs his mother was fond of having out for guests.

Ulric pulled out his and Iowyn's reports from his inner vest pocket, and Foxe had them out of his hands before Ulric could set them on the desk. He flipped through them excitedly, humming to himself as he skimmed over the words. Ulric studied him closely, trying to gauge whether or not the Guild Master was satisfied with their work.

Foxe came to the last pages of both of their reports. He flipped them over, as if he was looking for more information to be hidden on the back of the pages. His overgrown eyebrows knitted together. "You didn't retrieve the body?" he asked.

"There wasn't a body to retrieve," Ulric stated. "As I said in my report, the kelpie disintegrated when it was killed."

Foxe turned his attention to Iowyn. "Is this true?"

Ulric kept his features neutral despite the slight. Foxe – it seemed – didn't believe him.

Iowyn looked to Ulric nervously then back to Master Foxe. "Um, well I assume it is. I was unconscious when it all happened, sir."

Foxe let out an irritated sigh, his enthusiasm from before dwindling. "So you didn't see the kelpie *disintegrate,*" he used air quotes, "as your partner says."

Ulric clenched his teeth. Why would he lie? He was already on probation. Or maybe his probation was why Foxe was asking these questions?

Iowyn wrung her hands, shaking her head. "No, I didn't see it disintegrate. But if Ulric said it did, then I believe him."

Foxe leaned back in his chair, steepling his fingers together. "Very well," he said. "I suppose we'll have to take your word for it, Mr. Ornthalas. But let me remind you, we take our work very seriously here. Failure to follow protocol can lead to dire consequences."

The veiled threat was clear to Ulric. *Smokheim.*

Ulric nodded respectfully, trying his best not to clench his fists in frustration. He'd done his job, and even risked his own life to save Iowyn. Yet here he was, being treated like a criminal.

Foxe stood and made his way over to a large standing cabinet on the far wall of his office. He opened it, revealing an assortment of ledgers, as well as a large steel safe. He expertly turned the dial this way and that, until the door clicked and swung open. Foxe leaned over, and Ulric braced himself in the case the seams of the Guild master's fancy pants decided to give way.

He stood back up with two bags in his hands, each about the size of an apple. One was handed to Ulric, and the other was given to Iowyn.

"Your payment – as always." Foxe smiled, but Ulric was beginning to find the niceties off putting.

Foxe cleared his throat as he went to sit back behind his desk. "You'll be happy to know that I've cleared you for your next assignment." He opened a side drawer of his desk and fished out a new venture scroll. "Mr. Ornthalas has been requested in Rathian."

Requested? Ulric had almost always worked alone in the past. There were only a handful of people he had ever worked with out of the pure necessity of the moment. It was a short list of possible hunters, but it had also been years since he'd seen any of them.

"Miss Morgnah is of course cleared to go with you, as your partner and all."

Ulric rose and took the scroll from Foxe. "Thank you, sir."

Iowyn gave her own thanks to the Guild Master. He let her walk out of the room first and was about to follow her out when Foxe spoke up behind him. "Mr. Ornthalas?"

Ulric turned in the doorway. "Yes, sir?"

"Do you mind if we have a little chat?" Foxe asked, a smile still tugging at his lips.

Ulric looked back in the hall where Iowyn was waiting. "I'll be here," she said.

Ulric nodded, and walked back inside the Guild Master's office. Foxe sat back in his chair, kicking his feet up on the desk. Ulric shut the door to the office behind him, and Foxe's smile dropped. The kind and cordial man that Ulric thought Foxe to be was nowhere to be seen. "Let me be the one to remind you to do what you're told."

An unspoken *or else* was hidden in his tone.

Ulric's brow furrowed. "Sir?"

Foxe's face hardened. "After you identified the kelpie in your status report, you were given instructions to bring the beast's body back here."

Ulric shook his head. "But, sir —"

Foxe held up a hand, and although Ulric had never felt intimidated by the Guild Master before, Ulric thought it wisest to shut his mouth. This was not the same Guild Master who had talked to him outside of the probation hearing. Or maybe it was? Had the jolly, fat man been just a persona all this time? Ulric had always silently wondered how a man like Foxe came to such a high standing in the Guild. Perhaps he was getting a glimpse of the real Foxe, the hardened hunter, and not the mask he put on to appease his constituents.

"Might I remind you of your current standing?"

Ulric swallowed. "I don't need a reminder, sir."

Foxe smiled, but it wasn't jovial. "Good, because I would *hate* to lose such a capable man in our ranks to some gods-forsaken island across the Epottum." Foxe sighed, running a hand over his face, like Ulric's presence in his office annoyed him. "From now on, you follow your orders to the letter. From me, or any of the other Guild Masters. We say 'Jump,' you say, 'How high'? They say 'Bring back a body,' you say, 'Where and when'? Understand?"

Ulric squared his shoulders and met Master Foxe's hard gaze. "I always follow orders, sir," he said evenly.

Foxe nodded once, and his face changed again. He gave Ulric a bright smile. "Good. I'm counting on it."

Ulric left the office, the weight of Foxe's warning like a stone in his stomach.

Ulric caught up to Iowyn down the hall and handed her the scroll. Something about him felt different. He was confident going into the office, but came out more rigid than ever.

Iowyn looked down at the unopened scroll in her hands. "You didn't open it," she said, holding it back out for him.

He pushed it back to her, giving a backwards glance at Foxe's office. "You can."

Something was definitely wrong. "Are you spooked because of what Foxe said?"

Ulric tensed as his attention snapped back to her. "What?"

"He said there'd be consequences if you failed to follow protocol."

Ulric relaxed a bit. "Oh, no. I'm fine."

Iowyn studied him and waited for him to go on and tell her what it was that Foxe had wanted, but ultimately ended up rolling her eyes when he didn't. She turned her attention to the scroll in her hand and unfurled it.

Request for Assistance
Location: Western Rathian Outpost
Guild Member(s) Requested: Ulric Ornthalas
Requested by: Daegan Baarde
Report:
Meet at the Western Rathian Outpost for more information.

"Well," Iowyn scoffed, "that's not very helpful."

Ulric smirked. "Yeah, sounds like Daegan alright."

"So, you know this guy?" she asked as they started down the stairs.

"Daegan and I have helped each other on and off through the years. He's a good friend, you'll like him."

Iowyn raised a brow. "You have friends?"

Ulric let out a small but agitated sigh. "Yes, Beastie. I suppose I do."

APPENDIX

From the field journal of Iowyn Morgnah

DEUPINS

The deupin, a remarkable creature of myth and legend, exists as a bridge between the worlds of the majestic wolf and the graceful deer. Residing in the rugged terrain of mountainous Vrig, Rathian, Acantia, and Beor, these enigmatic beings are renowned for their unique blend of characteristics, combining the attributes of canines and cervids.

Deupins display a striking amalgamation of physical features. These creatures are notably larger than a typical horse, their massive frames facilitating their survival in the challenging mountainous environments they inhabit. Their most distinctive features include large, splayed paws and robust hind and forelimbs, which provide them with remarkable agility and strength.

Male deupins are particularly distinguished by their antlers. These antlers can be formidable, with impressive branching structures that serve both as a means of defense and a symbol of dominance within their herds.

Deupins exhibit canine-like ears and sharp teeth. These adaptations contribute to their exceptional sensory perception and hunting prowess. Their noses, though reminiscent of bovine creatures, are highly sensitive, aiding them in tracking prey and navigating their mountainous habitats.

One of the most captivating aspects of deupins lies in the diversity of their fur patterns and coloration, reminiscent of both horses and dogs. Their fur can display a wide array of hues, including earthy tones like browns, grays, and blacks, often adorned with intricate spots and markings. This variability in coloration not only serves as camouflage in the rocky terrain but also reflects the adaptability and genetic diversity of the deupin species.

Deupins are known to be highly social creatures, living in tight-knit packs or herds. These groups are characterized by a complex hierarchy, with dominant individuals, often males with the largest antlers, leading the way. The pack dynamic extends to hunting, as deupins cooperate to bring down prey, combining their strength and cunning to secure sustenance in their challenging environment.

Their social structure also plays a crucial role in their reproduction and rearing of offspring. Mating rituals are marked by elaborate displays of strength and dominance, with the alpha males vying for the attention of the females. Once offspring are born, the entire pack takes part in their care and protection, ensuring the survival of the next generation.

Beyond their enigmatic presence in the wild, deupins have shown themselves to be remarkably adaptable and capable of forming deep bonds with humans. Much like domesticated dogs, and other large creatures, such as horses or cerlines, deupins have proven to be loyal companions and reliable mounts when trust is established.

Deupins, with their intelligence and social nature, readily form bonds with humans they trust. These bonds are characterized by unwavering loyalty and a deep sense of companionship. Human-deupin pairs often exhibit a profound mutual understanding, built on shared experiences and trust.

Much like dogs, deupins display affection and protective instincts toward their human companions. They are known to be highly attentive to their human's emotions and are quick to respond to cues, whether it be a gesture, a spoken command, or a subtle change in body language. This keen sense of empathy makes them not only reliable companions but also excellent support animals, offering comfort during moments of distress.

The impressive physical attributes of deupins, including their size, strength, and agility, make them well-suited to serve as mounts for trusted humans. Once the bond of trust is established, deupins can be trained to carry riders across diverse terrains, navigating rugged mountains with remarkable ease.

Deupins' powerful hind and forelimbs provide stability and strength, ensuring a comfortable and secure riding experience. Their large paws offer excellent traction, making them well-suited for challenging landscapes. Additionally, their canine-like ears and keen senses contribute to heightened awareness, enhancing safety during rides.

SEEKING FALCONS

The seeking falcon, a majestic avian species of considerable size, has long held a place of mystique and reverence in the annals of monstralogy and folklore.

Seeking falcons are indeed a species of grand proportions, commonly standing between three and four feet tall, a size that commands attention in the avian world. However, their most remarkable physical trait lies in their iridescent plumage. These birds are adorned with feathers that exhibit an astonishing play of colors, shifting from a deep, midnight blue to a lush, forest green depending on the angle of incident light. This iridescence contributes to their ethereal and almost otherworldly appearance, enhancing their mystique.

The seeking falcon derives its name from its extraordinary ability to locate individuals with uncanny precision. While the exact mechanisms behind this remarkable skill remain a subject of study and debate, it is widely acknowledged that seeking falcons possess an innate sense that enables them to track down specific individuals. Whether through scent, electromagnetic fields, or other sensory cues, these birds have proven themselves to be unparalleled in their quest to find their designated target.

The Hunter's Guild, an organization steeped in tradition and secrecy, has harnessed the unique abilities of seeking falcons to serve as messengers. These remarkable birds are entrusted with critical messages, bearing tidings across great distances with speed and reliability that no other avian species can match.

One of the most captivating aspects of the seeking falcon's search and locate prowess is the transformation that occurs upon finding their target. When a seeking falcon locates the person that it has been seeking, its eyes begin to glow with a brilliant, almost unearthly, bright yellow hue. This phenomenon remains a subject of fascination and intrigue, with researchers eager to uncover the biological mechanisms responsible for this remarkable display.

While seeking falcons are generally known for their loyalty and service to the Hunter's Guild, they are not without their quirks and potential dangers. Legends abound regarding the fate of those who have attempted to pilfer or otherwise interfere with the falcon's mission. Many such tales end tragically, with the would-be transgressors succumbing to the talons and beak of the fiercely protective seeking falcon.

The domestication of seeking falcons by the Hunter's Guild has led to a decrease in the sightings of these magnificent birds in the wild. Their exact status in the wild remains a subject of concern, as their domesticated counterparts continue to fulfill critical roles within the Guild.

BATTERFLIES

The batterfly, typically the size of a small egg, has captured the imagination of monstralogists due to its distinct physical attributes and its vital role as a nocturnal pollinator.

The most conspicuous feature of the batterfly is its unorthodox wing structure. Instead of the membranous wings commonly found in bats, batterflies possess wings reminiscent of butterflies, characterized by their fragility and intricate patterning. These wings are primarily white and adorned with subtle shades of light gray, which, under the moonlight, emit an iridescent sheen comprising a mesmerizing array of colors. The presence of such dazzling hues on these creatures has led to their nomenclature, drawing parallels between their appearance and that of a hybrid creature, combining the grace of butterflies with the allure of bats

Batterflies play a crucial ecological role as nocturnal pollinators, a role that distinguishes them from their more well-known diurnal counterparts. As they flit from flower to flower under the cover of darkness, these creatures inadvertently aid in the transfer of pollen. Their fur, designed for insulation and warmth in cooler nighttime environments, has a unique characteristic: it readily captures pollen grains as they navigate through the blossoms. This attribute ensures that batterflies are unwittingly effective agents of cross-pollination, facilitating in the reproduction of a variety of plant species. Consequently, they contribute significantly to the maintenance of biodiversity and the overall health of ecosystems.

These diminutive creatures pose no threat whatsoever to humans, as they lack the carnivorous tendencies of some bat species. On the contrary, batterflies are entirely benign and non-aggressive. Their primary focus is on foraging for nectar and pollen, and they are known to avoid human contact whenever possible.

Furthermore, the batterflies' ecological significance extends to agriculture. Farmers have recognized their value as pollinators, particularly in regions where other pollinators may be less active during the night. By facilitating the pollination of crops, batterflies contribute to increased yields and agricultural productivity, making them invaluable allies to those who depend on farming for their livelihoods.

GIANTYTAS

The giantyta is an imposing and formidable creature native to the Serveni Mountains, spanning the rugged landscape from Oqira to Acantia in the continent of Phyrra. Resembling an enormous owl, the giantyta reaches a towering size, equivalent to two grizzly bears standing on top of one another. This immense size grants it dominance over its habitat, making it one of the most feared predators in these mountainous regions.

Primarily solitary in nature, giantytas are known to congregate only once every decade to mate. This infrequent mating cycle results in a relatively small population, as pairs of giantytas typically produce only one or two eggs per mating season. The offspring, nurtured with care until they can fend for themselves, maintain the population without causing an overabundance of these predators in the already harsh and competitive environment of the Serveni ranges. The spectacle of these gatherings, observed from a distance by the bravest of monstralogists, reveals a complex courtship dance— a haunting reminder of the power and beauty of the natural world in the high, cold peaks of Phyrra.

The Serveni Mountains offer a challenging ecosystem where giantytas play the role of apex predators. Their diet consists mainly of large mountain-dwelling mammals such as urynxes, deupins, cerlines, and direwolves. However, their opportunistic hunting behavior becomes most evident during the unforgiving winters. When prey becomes scarce, giantytas are known to descend from the higher altitudes, posing a grave threat to human settlements. Desperate for food, they have been documented besieging mountain towns, using their powerful talons and formidable strength to breach fortifications and raid livestock. This behavior has cemented the giantyta's reputation in folklore and local history as a creature to be both revered and feared.

THE TALE OF DRAL'GOTH THE DEVOURER

In the primordial days of the world, Odea, the Mother of All, was the weaver of life, a being of infinite compassion and creativity. From her breath, she shaped all manner of creatures and plants, filling the world with life and harmony. Her husband, Mortem, the God of Death, stood as the eternal balance to her creation, ensuring the cycle of life did not tip into chaos.

In her desire to explore the boundaries of life, Odea once crafted a creature like none other. She took the essence of the dark places of the world—caverns deep beneath the earth, where the sun never reached and the very air hummed with secrets. From that shadowy substance, she wove together the form of a single gargantula. Her many eyes gleamed with an unnatural intelligence; her sting dripping venom potent with powers untold.

Dral'goth was born, her very existence a symbol of Odea's boundless creativity. But in Dral'goth, Odea made a terrible mistake. Though the gargantula had the form akin to a spider, she was something far more malevolent. Unlike the animals Odea had previously made, Dral'goth did not find her place in the natural order. She was a creature of endless hunger, driven by a need to consume, not merely for sustenance, but out of a deep, primal need to destroy all that lived. Where she walked, the earth withered. Forests became desolate wastelands, and rivers turned to poisonous sludge. The creatures of the world fled before her, but none could escape her grasp.

At first, Odea watched, thinking her creation might find balance, as all living things do. But soon, Dral'goth's rampage grew unbearable. She slaughtered the great beasts of the land, feasting on their flesh and leaving their bones to rot in the sun. Entire ecosystems crumbled in her wake, her hunger knowing no end. Even Odea's most beloved creatures, the humans, found themselves hunted by the Devourer, as Dral'goth wandered farther and farther, leaving death wherever her monstrous legs carried her.

Odea, filled with regret, wept bitterly for what she had unleashed upon the world. But her sorrow was not enough to undo her mistake. Dral'goth grew stronger with each life she took, her power spreading like a blight. Odea knew that she had to act before the world she loved was consumed entirely.

In desperation, Odea turned to Mortem, her husband, the God of Death. She pleaded with him to intervene, to put an end to Dral'goth's destruction. Mortem, ever the silent observer of life's end, had seen the damage done and agreed, though he understood the weight of what was to come. His cold touch would bring balance to Odea's chaos, as it always had.

He descended to the earth with his hammer and clad in shadows. When he found Dral'goth, she was feasting upon the last remnants of a once-great dragon. Mortem's presence was enough to freeze the air, and for the first time, Dral'goth hesitated. She sensed the cold finality of Death, but even she, with all her hunger, could not resist the inevitable.

The battle was swift and terrible. Mortem's hammer cracked through Dral'goth's thick hide, spilling her foul blood across the land, burning the earth where it touched. With each strike, her body weakened, and though she fought with all her monstrous strength, it was no match for the God of Death. In the end, Mortem's hammer found its mark, cleaving Dral'goth's head from her body, ending her reign of terror.

But Mortem was too late. As he stood over Dral'goth's corpse, he could not have known the evidence of her final act. She had laid eggs, thousands of them, hidden deep in the earth. From these eggs, a new generation of gargantulas would be born, each as ravenous as their mother. Dral'goth's hunger would live on, and her children would continue her destructive legacy.

When Odea learned of this, her heart broke. Though Mortem had ended Dral'goth's rampage, the threat was far from over. Odea, in her sorrow and guilt, took Dral'goth's body and cast it into the sky, where it became a constellation, forever visible as a reminder of the destruction wrought by unchecked power. Dral'goth's form glimmers in the heavens, her legs stretched across the stars, a warning to all creatures below.

ABOUT THE AUTHOR

Lucille Anser grew up on a farm in rural Iowa. With nothing but time to kill, she spent many of her days of her adolescence and young adulthood out in the countryside, playing games of make-believe with her sisters.

Those tendencies to imagine worlds of magic and intrigue did not fade into adulthood. Now, Lucille writes down her imaginings to share with the rest of the world. For the Love of Beasts is the first full length book that Lucille has put to paper, and she has many more fantastical worlds that she can't wait to share with readers.

The characters and story from For the Love of Beasts will return in her second installment!